"The questions hovering in the background—Who owns a woman's image? Who benefits from a woman's beauty? What should a woman have to say about how her beauty is used?—are profound and treated gently enough to engage the reader without flights of annoyingly philosophical prose. The story itself leaves the reader with a vivid sense of the beauty in question, in both the painter's version, and the lady's herself."
—*San Francisco Chronicle*

"A compelling novel . . . Diliberto's writing brings Virginie to life in a way that Sargent's portrait does not. . . . The author uses evocative images and sharp descriptions of both people and places to create a word-picture of Parisian society at the turn of the century. . . . Highly recommended."
—*Library Journal*

"This fast scroll through history (the Civil War, the fall of the French Second Empire, the Belle Epoque, etc.) against a backdrop of parties, salons, operas, artists' studios, and sexual escapades is inviting for its wealth of well-researched period details."
—*Publishers Weekly*

"A credible fiction debut . . . Agreeable entertainment along the lines of *The Girl with a Pearl Earring* and *The Passion of Artemisia*."
—*Kirkus Reviews*

"An engrossing tale, *I Am Madame X* delves into a beloved work of art to create a stunning work of fiction."
—*BookPage*

"An intriguing novel, one that captures La Belle Epoque while telling the story of an American in Paris . . . Throughout, Diliberto explores the woman behind and beyond the painting."
—*New York Daily News*

"*I Am Madame X* is hard to put down. The characters are unique and well developed, the plot builds quickly, and the historical aspects are true but artistically rendered. . . . Diliberto has done a masterful job of both holding close to what facts are known about Gautreau and Sargent, and creating anew in a rich and satisfying literary way."
—*Rocky Mountain News*

"Diliberto expertly weaves art history into the story. . . . [She] excels at framing the atmosphere in which Sargent created the painting . . . engrossing." —*Providence Rhode Island Journal-Bulletin*

"A lively and delicious tale of 19th-century Parisian society."
—*The Washington Times*

"What's exciting about *I Am Madame X* is the liveliness and authenticity of the author's 19th-century backdrop." —*The Sunday Oregonian*

"John Singer Sargent's provocative portrait of Virginie Gautreau . . . has always intrigued me, enough that at one time I was considering writing about it myself, but wasn't quick enough. Now I'll luxuriate in what Diliberto has done with the story."
—Susan Vreeland, author of *Girl in Hyacinth Blue*
and *The Passion of Artemisia*

"Imagining her way into mesmerizing terrain, Gioia Diliberto has conjured a compelling memoir 'by' Virginie Gautreau, the Madame X of John Singer Sargent's notorious portrait. Diliberto's heroine is a startlingly contemporary woman who begins life in New Orleans and whose beauty and sexual courage take Paris by storm at the dawn of the Belle Epoque. *Madame X,* the masterpiece that nearly ended Sargent's career, reigns serenely now, a jewel in the collection of the Metropolitan Museum of Art—like Diliberto's beguiling novel, a cautionary reminder that an intelligent woman can turn scandal to her own ends."
—Honor Moore, author of *The White Blackbird*

"What a delicious book this is, half verifiable public history, half imagined private confession. Anyone who has ever stood before a painting trying to imagine its 'real story'—and better yet, a story about art, love, war, and beauty, gorgeously costumed, unfolding in fascinating times and settings—will find Gioia Diliberto's speculations both provocative and plausible, a very satisfying treat for their inner gossip!"
—Rosellen Brown, author of *Half a Heart*

ALSO BY GIOIA DILIBERTO

A Useful Woman: The Early Life of Jane Addams
Hadley
Debutante: The Story of Brenda Frazier

I Am Madame X

A NOVEL

Gioia Diliberto

A LISA DREW BOOK

SCRIBNER

NEW YORK LONDON TORONTO SYDNEY

A LISA DREW BOOK/SCRIBNER
1230 Avenue of the Americas
New York, NY 10020

This book is a work of fiction. Any reference to historical events, real people, or real locales is used fictitiously. Other names, characters, places, and incidents are products of the author's imagination, and any resemblance to actual events or locales or persons, living or dead, is entirely coincidental.

Copyright © 2003 by Gioia Diliberto

All rights reserved, including the right of reproduction in whole or in part in any form.

First Lisa Drew/Scribner trade paperback edition 2004

SCRIBNER and design are trademarks of Macmillan Library Reference USA, Inc., used under license by Simon & Schuster, the publisher of this work.
A LISA DREW BOOK is a trademark of Simon & Schuster, Inc.

For information about special discounts for bulk purchases, please contact
Simon & Schuster Special Sales:
1-800-456-6798 or business@simonandschuster.com

Set in American Garamond

Designed by Colin Joh

Manufactured in the United States of America

3 5 7 9 10 8 6 4 2

The Library of Congress has cataloged the Scribner edition as follows:
Diliberto, Gioia, 1950–
I am Madame X : a novel / Gioia Diliberto
p. cm.
"A Lisa Drew book."
1. Gautreau, Virginie Avegno, 1859–1915—Fiction. 2. Sargent, John Singer, 1856–1925—Fiction. 3. Americans—France—Fiction. 4. Portrait painting—Fiction. 5. Paris (France)—Fiction. 6. Socialites—Fiction. I. Title.

PS3604.I45 I12 2003

813'.54—dc21   2002026802

ISBN: 978-0-7434-5680-7

Illustration Credits

Page 1: Metropolitan Museum of Art, gift of Mrs. Francis Ormond, 1950; 7: Metropolitan Museum of Art, gift of Mrs. Francis Ormond and Miss Emily Sargent, 1931; 27: Private collection. Photograph provided by Richard Ormond; 49: Private collection. Photograph provided by Richard Ormond; 71: Fogg Art Museum, Harvard University Art Museums, bequest of Grenville L. Winthrop; 93: Metropolitan Museum of Art, gift of Mrs. Francis Ormond, 1950; 117: Fogg Art Museum, Harvard University Art Museums, bequest of Grenville L. Winthrop; 137: Collection of Lauren Rogers Museum of Art, Laurel, Mississippi; 167: Private collection. Photograph provided by Richard Ormond; 195: Metropolitan Museum of Art, Thomas J. Watson Library, gift of Mrs. Francis Ormond, 1950; 213: Jules Renard Draner, Le Charivari, 1884; 225: Isabella Stewart Gardner Museum.

Page 42: "Le Changement." by Michel St. Pierre, reprinted by permission of Louisiana State University from Our People and Our History, by Rodolphe Lucien Desdunes, translated and edited by Sister Dorothea Olga McCants. Translation copyright 1973 by Louisiana State University Press.

Material on nineteenth-century Creole culture is drawn from Creole Collage by Leonard Huber, reprinted by permission from the Center for Louisiana Studies, University of Louisiana at Lafayette.

For Joe Babcock

Foreword

Perhaps you've heard her name, Virginie Gautreau. You recall it like an old melody echoing yet from a long-ago party, or as a kind of epithet whispered harshly under the breath. Maybe you've even seen her picture—seen *the* picture. God knows, there are a few out there who truly have, though once all Paris claimed to have viewed it and recoiled at the insolence, the vulgarity, the unmuted sex. "Monstrous," one critic said. "A singular failure," sniffed another. John Singer Sargent's career nearly derailed, though he's famous now, living in England and making a fortune painting bored aristocrats.

He kept the picture in his studio for twenty years, exhibiting it only a handful of times, always in small shows in Europe. Until last year, I thought no one in America would ever see it. Then I heard that Sargent was sending the picture to San Francisco for the Panama-Pacific International Exhibition. I was in Paris on business, so I called Virginie with the news.

We had first met at a party in 1880, when I was a junior curator at the Metropolitan Museum of Art in New York and traveled frequently to Paris. For several years, we dined together whenever I was in town; then we lost touch. When I reached Virginie on the telephone, she seemed delighted to hear from me, and she invited me to tea the next day at 123, rue la Cour, where she was living alone in a grand eighteenth-century apartment.

I arrived at four, as a soft afternoon light filtered through the tops of the chestnut trees. A young maid answered the bell and showed me into a huge parlor with tall windows facing the street. Several groupings of settees and chairs were arranged on an immense Turkish carpet, and four sparkling crystal chandeliers illuminated the room.

Virginie kept me waiting, as she always used to. She appeared after twenty minutes, wearing a green silk dress that matched her eyes, and her auburn hair—the same exact shade of burnished copper it had always been—was twisted into a long roll at the back of her head, her signature style. Though her figure had become matronly, her finely lined face was still beautiful.

As she made her entrance, walking gracefully on high heels, whiffs of perfume preceding her, I was studying a picture on the wall—a sketch Sargent had made of her in the gorgeous black gown she had worn for her notorious portrait.

"Richard, my dear," she said. She embraced me with long white arms and kissed me quickly and chastely on both cheeks. She had noticed me staring at the sketch, and she tilted her head toward it. "I don't think I've seen you since—then."

I'm sure she was thinking back, as I was, to 1884 and the jeering crowds at the Palais de l'Industrie. It was the opening of the Paris Fine Arts Salon, an annual exhibition that was the premier social event of the era. To have a portrait championed at the Salon usually meant instant success for the artist and overnight fame for the sitter. Sargent, an American who had been raised abroad, had begun to establish a name for himself in Parisian art circles, and he had high hopes that his painting of Virginie would push him to the top.

At the time, she was one of the most famous women in Paris. A favorite ornament of the scandal sheets, Virginie flaunted her sexuality through exotic makeup, hennaed hair, and revealing clothes. She penciled her eyebrows, rouged her ears, and dusted her skin with *blanc de perle* powder. To whiten it further, people murmured, she ingested arsenic.

Sargent's portrait brilliantly captured her wanton sensuality. But it was too far in advance of its time. Instead of admiring the artist's achievement, the public was appalled by it. The portrait seemed to confirm French prejudices against Americans, proved that we were pushy, overeager, lacking any limits or refinement.

Like Sargent, Virginie was widely known to be American. She had been born in New Orleans to two of Louisiana's finest Creole families. During the Civil War, her mother had fled Louisiana, taking Virginie, who was a child, and her baby sister. The family settled in Paris in a Right Bank enclave of expatriate Southerners. Trading on their French ancestry and knowledge of French culture, they hoped to insinuate themselves into French society.

Virginie's looks and charm were her tickets into the haut monde. She was trained from the cradle to make a brilliant marriage. She preferred to make a brilliant show, and she never lost her ardor for dangerous liaisons. The day I had tea with her, she was expecting a new lover, a married lawyer named Henri Beauquesne, whom she had recently met on a train. He was handsome and rich, she told me, and nearly twenty years her junior.

I still think Sargent's portrait of Virginie was his best painting, and I told her so that day. "You know, I'd love to have it for the Metropolitan, Mimi," I said, using her nickname.

"Make Sargent a generous offer, and maybe you can," she said brightly as a maid wheeled in a cart holding a silver tea service and a plate of small fruit tarts. Virginie poured our tea into two gold-rimmed Limoges cups.

"Darling," I told her, "Edward Robinson, the head of the Met, has been after it for years, ever since he worked at the Boston Museum of Fine Arts. But so far, Sargent has refused to sell. He's hardly let it out of his house. When he does exhibit it, he never identifies you. He still calls it *Portrait of Madame ****, just as it was titled at the Salon, or simply, *Portrait*. And he always requests that your name not be communicated to the newspapers. Isn't that amusing?"

Virginie wasn't amused at all. In fact, she was furious. "Don't I have a name?" she cried, rising out of her chair. She strode across the room to a wall of windows and pivoted to face me. "If Sargent had any honor, he would call my picture *Portrait of Virginie Avegno Gautreau.* After all, it is *my* picture as much as his."

She stared fiercely at me. "This was *not* a commissioned work," she continued, more composed. "Sargent begged me to sit for him. He stalked me like a hunter does a deer, staring at me at parties and getting his friends to pester me—'Please, Madame Gautreau, let John pay this homage to your great beauty.' And so on. That so-called artist Ralph Curtis came to see me, then bombarded me with letters. I saved one."

She marched to an antique secretary, rummaged through a drawer, and pulled out a blue envelope. "My dear Madame Gautreau," she read from the letter inside. "We both know John is a genius. But the work he's done so far is somehow lacking in completeness and depth. He needs a great subject to unleash the full power of his brilliance. He needs you."

She folded the letter and returned it to the envelope. "I was the one who sat for hours on end, giving up an entire summer. I was the one who provided the magnificent profile, the willowy body, the white marble skin that 'unleashed his brilliance.' I was the inspiration for Sargent's masterpiece—the only one he's got." She tossed her head dismissively, provocatively, the way I had seen her do so many years ago. "Just compare my portrait with his stuffy pictures of horsey Englishwomen. Or that midget Mrs. Carl Meyer or that washed-out blonde, Mrs. George Swinton. I've seen their portraits and plenty of others over the years. I've kept my eye on Sargent's exhibits, and I want to ask you: Where are the bold lines in those pictures? Where is the mystery, the tension, the allure?" She dropped into a chair covered with cream damask and folded her arms across her chest. "Of course, I know exactly why Sargent won't attach my name to the portrait. He's a cowardly fussbudget, and he's still livid about the ruckus my mother made."

Obviously, the trauma of the Salon debacle still pained her. Seeing her now, her beauty turning brittle, her natural hauteur hardened into a lonely defensiveness, I could see how she had mourned the loss of her renown, and I felt shamed that I had stopped calling on her so many years before.

We chatted for several more hours, and the golden light outside the tall French windows fell to darkness. At eight, I rose to leave, but Virginie urged me to stay. "Please have dinner with Henri and me," she said, her eyes shining. I was curious to meet Beauquesne, her new young lover, but I had already made plans with friends.

"Mimi, it's been wonderful to see you again; now I must run," I said. She showed me to the door and kissed me again on both cheeks. "Good-bye, Richard, my dear. You've brought back so many memories."

I heard nothing from her for months. Then one day she sent me a package containing several hundred typed pages. Inspired by my visit, she had dictated a memoir to one of her maids. She wanted history to remember who Madame X was.

Two weeks later, before I had done more than glance at the manuscript, I got a transatlantic cable from Beauquesne. Virginie had died in her sleep. He hoped that I still had her memoir, as it was the only copy, and he wondered if I would help him find a publisher for it.

Thus, I make her story available here, in my own translation from the original French. As you read it, you will be lifted back to a time before this terrible war, a time when painting was a powerful indice of reality, and Virginie Gautreau was, as *Le Figaro* once put it, "a living work of art."

I can still see her as she looked then, on the night I first met her. She was tall and slim, her green eyes glittering in that porcelain face, and her silvery laughter floating across the table as she reached for a champagne flute with a long, shapely arm.

How could anyone forget?

Richard Merriweather
Curator of American Painting
The Metropolitan Museum of Art
New York, 1915

One

Recently, whenever I talk in my sleep—which has been quite often lately—I speak English. It's odd, since I've only spoken the language occasionally in half a century. But just last week, I woke Henri with some nocturnal gibberish. He roused me and repeated my mumblings as best he could, and I realized I was singing a few lines from "Oft in the Stilly Night," an old song Grandmère's servant Alzea had taught me before we fled Parlange, our sugar plantation in Louisiana. Fully awake, I can still recall a verse:

> *Oft in the stilly night,*
> *   Ere slumber's chain hath bound me,*
> *Fond memory brings the light*
> *   Of other days around me,*
> *The smiles, the tears, of girlhood's years,*
> *   The words of love then spoken,*
> *The eyes that shone, now dimmed and gone,*
> *   The cheerful hearts now broken!*
> *Thus, in the stilly night,*
> *   Ere slumber's chain hath bound me,*

*Sad memory brings the light
of other days around me.*

Dr. Freud is right. There really is an "unconscious" mind. Perhaps mine lives in the Old South.

I'd been dreaming of Tante Julie's wedding day, of watching her glide across the wide gallery at Parlange, her pale face streaked with sweat, the pink rosebuds braided through her hair turning limp and brown in the steaming heat. She was dressed in heavy cream satin—an old ball gown that Grandmère had dug out of a trunk the day before. Alzea had stayed up all night altering the sleeves and neckline, and I had sat beside her in the flickering candlelight of the kitchenhouse, sobbing like a baby.

I did not want Tante Julie to marry. Her fiancé, Lieutenant Lucas Rochilieu, was a short, fat toad of a man, with an ugly mole on the tip of his nose and a bloody patch over one eye from a wound he had received when he accidentally shot himself while cleaning his gun four months earlier. But I would have hated him even if he had been tall and handsome. He was stealing Tante Julie, the person I loved most in the world—more than my baby sister Valentine, more than Mama and Papa, I'm ashamed to say.

It was August 1861, the first summer of the war. I was six. Papa, a lawyer in New Orleans, had left to fight with the mostly Creole Louisiana Regiment, and Mama, Valentine, and I had joined Grandmère at Parlange, eighty-five miles west of New Orleans on False River.

Though the adults had strictly forbidden it, I slipped off to the fields after breakfast to cut myself an armload of sugarcane. For an hour, I sat on the front lawn in the gray shade of a magnolia, peeling and eating the sweet stalks as carriages rolled up the alley of oaks. A few guests had already gathered in the parlor, and I could see them through the tall French windows talking and sipping drinks under dark portraits of my ancestors.

Most of Grandmère's slaves had run off, and there was no time to make elaborate wedding preparations. Alzea had baked some cakes and hauled the last crates of wine and champagne up from the cellar. Mama and I fashioned bouquets from the few garden flowers that hadn't shriveled in the scalding sun, and we arranged them in vases in the parlor.

The air was heavy with smoke. Some of the neighbors had taken to burning their cotton to keep it out of enemy hands, and my head began to ache from the foul air and the heat. I decided to go to the gallery to cool off and talk to Julie.

The gallery was my favorite place at Parlange. The wide porch surrounded the entire green-shuttered house and provided enough space to accommodate a small orchestra and twenty dancing couples on Saturday evenings. The back portion looked out on the colorful garden and beyond, to endless fields of waving cane. At night, the twanging notes of banjos wafted through the treetops from the Negro quarters, which were screened by a tall fence. The front gallery held a collection of wicker tables and chairs. Julie and I spent hours there talking and reading.

Like all the women in our family, Julie was small and narrow-waisted. Her straight black hair hung like curtains from a center part and framed a gentle, oval face. At twenty-eight, she was two years younger than Mama, though she seemed closer to my age. It wasn't only her uncoiffed hair. There was something childlike about her flat chest and stick arms. She had a lovely singing voice, and she painted beautifully, in a distinctive style marked by insightful realism. Years later, many artists would ask me—beg me—to pose for them. But Julie was the first to notice my potential. "Mimi, you have exquisite lines, and your hair! I've never seen such a glorious copper color, like the kitchenhouse kettles," she told me. She did many studies of me— asleep on the brocade settee in the parlor, bathing in front of the fireplace in my room, on the swing in the garden—but she refused to display these pictures or any others that she did. She stashed her canvases under her bed, unsigned, and she scrawled on the back, "Not to be shown to anyone."

Julie grew up at Parlange and never left. She was content with her quiet life and once told me she had no desire to marry, the chief point of a Creole woman's existence.

"Men are bothersome beings. I don't want to spend my days worrying about one," she said.

"But don't you want babies?" I asked.

"*Chérie,* if I ever had a child, I'd want it to be exactly like you. In fact, I'd want it to come into the world exactly like you, a spirited little red-haired girl who reads and converses—and not a naked, screaming infant."

I don't remember any beaux calling on Julie. So I was surprised one evening when a portly Rebel soldier ambled up the alley of oaks, then mounted the steps. "Is Miss de Ternant, Miss Julie de Ternant, receiving this afternoon?" he asked. It was Rochilieu. He had taken the steamboat from New Orleans and he smelled of the cigars and brandy he had enjoyed on the trip.

That evening, I saw him sitting in the parlor with Grandmère and Julie. My aunt was perched stiffly on an armless "lady's" chair with billowing skirts draped around her, while Rochilieu and Grandmère talked on and on. The next morning, Grandmère announced that the marriage would take place in two days.

Now, as I approached the house, I saw that Julie was reciting her Rosary. She paced back and forth on the cypress floor of the second-floor gallery, twice stopping to lean against the railing, fifteen feet above the ground. She gazed off in the distance, over my head, as if expecting to see some far-off sail on False River. I'm certain she never noticed me. Suddenly she dropped her amber beads on the floor. Holding fistfuls of cream satin at her hips, she grabbed a white pillar and hoisted herself atop the railing. She posed there for a moment, like a ship's caryatid, her eyes closed and her chin to the sky. I thought she had resigned herself to her marriage, and this was her way of saying good-bye to maidenhood. But suddenly she let go of the pillar and slowly tumbled forward, swanning, then flipping once in the air, her dress ballooning out above her knees. By the time I jerked forward, instinctively moving to catch her with my childish arms, she had hit the ground with a dull thud.

A group of chattering adults rounding the corner of the house from the garden gasped to see the pile of satin on the lawn. Grandmère, her coffee-dyed brown hair tucked under a straw hat, ran to Julie, knocking over a butler's tray holding brown-sugar lemonade and a cornmeal pound cake. Others followed, hovering, crying. Someone called for Dr. Porter. The priest approached, but Grandmère pushed him away with her wiry arms. "Keep back!" she cried.

I stood frozen on the lawn, until a soft voice whispered in my ear, "Come with me." It was Charles, Julie and Mama's half brother. His eyes were red and filling with tears. Clasping my hand tightly, Charles led me past the murmuring circle of dark figures and up a back staircase to his room in the *garçonnière*. He removed a checkerboard and a box of checkers from a mahogany bookcase and arranged a game on a wicker table. "Let's play," he said.

Charles was a large boy, with a big head and a smooth, intelligent face. His blue eyes were fringed with curly black lashes the color of his straight hair—Julie's hair—and his mouth was a red bow. All his clothes came from Paris, and though I'm sure at times he wore homespun flannel like the other planters' sons, I recall him only in fancy breeches, broadcloth waistcoats, and stiff white linen collars. He was just six years older than I, but he had a sure sense of self and a serious manner that made him seem beyond his years. "You first," he said.

With a shaky index finger, I pushed a black checker forward. Charles responded with a red. For five minutes, we stared at the board and moved checkers silently. Finally I found the strength to ask, "Do you think Tante Julie is dead?"

"Probably," said Charles. He was trying to act manly, to speak flatly and show no emotion. But his voice came out in gulps. "The heat must have made her crazy. It's always horrible on the feast of Sainte Claire."

Charles was obsessed with the weather. He watched every change and spent hours studying the sky and the clouds. Several times a day, he consulted his *Almanach français*—the *American Almanac* was worthless, he said—which gave the saints' feast days and, he insisted, provided clues to weather patterns.

"Then we'll see her in heaven," I said hopefully. I knew from *The Gates Ajar,* an American book Papa read to me, that the gates of heaven were always open to welcome new arrivals. When I died, I would be reunited there with my lost loved ones. We would be happy angels, an unbroken circle of love, the book said, free from all trouble and harm.

Charles slid a red checker forward with two square fingers. "If only Julie had waited a few days, cooler weather would have come with the Feast of Chantal, and then she would have felt better," he said.

I placed my finger on a fat black checker, but this time I couldn't move it. The thought of waiting until my own death to see Julie—impossibly distant, I assumed—had stolen my resolve.

"Mimi, go on!" snapped Charles, fighting for his equilibrium.

My tears erupted in a single burst. I ran from the room, down to the end of the hallway, and hid in the large linen closet, intoxicating myself with the cool, soft linen sheets and the deep, sharp fragrance of vetiver sachets.

Parlange *was* Grandmère. She had won it, and she had willed it to survive. Even today, more than fifty years later, though it still stands and she is long gone, no one who lived through those times can think of the plantation without conjuring an image of her.

Grandmère's parents were Canadian immigrants who died in one of the many yellow-fever epidemics that raged through Louisiana with the summer heat. She was adopted by the plantation's original owner, Marquis Vincent de Ternant III, the descendant of a French nobleman, and his childless wife. Soon the wife died, and a few months later de Ternant married Grandmère. She was barely fourteen.

She quickly had four children—Mama was the first. But Grandmère was an indifferent mother and thought nothing of leaving her babies behind to go off to Paris for the social season. People still talk about the stir she caused boarding steamers in New Orleans, corseted nearly to suffocation in a brocaded gown and trailed by ten slaves dressed like African royalty in silk turbans and robes. In Paris, she kept an apartment at 30, rue Miromesnil and went to theaters and the opera, where her box was next to the box of Charles Parlange, one of Napoléon's colonels. After the marquis dropped dead of a heart attack one evening in the middle of dinner, his head falling into a plate of oysters, Grandmère married Colonel Parlange and brought him to Louisiana. She renamed the plantation in his honor.

The colonel didn't last long in the choking Louisiana heat. He died two years after the wedding, leaving Grandmère with another baby, Charles. After losing two husbands, Grandmère set out to run the plantation herself. During the next year, though two of her middle children—a boy and a girl—died, she didn't let grief stop her from learning everything there was to know: she pored over the plantation's ledgers and diaries at night, studied weather patterns, repaired the levees and irrigation canals, and organized the army of slaves for the fall harvest.

Grandmère considered herself French, but when it came to slavery, she was an American Southerner to the marrow of her bones. She did not believe slavery was evil, even though it had been outlawed in France. She thought Negroes were ignorant savages incapable of living on their own, and she took pleasure in the failures of those who had run away from Parlange or managed to buy their freedom.

She drove her slaves hard, though she was not gratuitously cruel. She wouldn't have dreamed of selling a mother away from her children, as some planters did, and she reserved beatings for serious offenses like stealing. She rewarded industry and once sent a slave who showed a talent for carpentry to New Orleans to apprentice with a famous *ébéniste*. He returned to make Grandmère's massive, intricately carved bed and most of the armoires in the house. Grandmère took care of her slaves when they were sick, fed and clothed them well, and gave them Saturday nights and Sundays off.

Grandmère and Mama were only fifteen years apart. They looked like sisters, both small and wiry, with pale skin, delicate features, and masses of dark hair. By the time I came along, Grandmère's hair had turned a dull, muddy brown, the result of rinsing it once a week in coffee, and there was a hardness around her mouth and eyes, as if her determination had finally etched itself on her face.

Mama and Julie were raised at Parlange and took lessons from a French tutor. They didn't learn to speak English until they were adolescents, and they never learned to read or write it well. Of the sisters, Mama was the more robust, but Julie was the one who enjoyed roaming the fields and playing with the dogs that were always lounging on the grounds. Mama disdained the slow, uneventful pace of plantation life. "Even as a child I was bored by it," she confessed to me once. "I was born sophisticated."

During frequent trips into New Orleans with Grandmère and Julie, Mama walked on the narrow banquettes of the French Quarter, past the rows of old houses with their lacy wrought-iron balconies. She was dazzled by the gaslights, the expensive trinkets behind the glass storefronts, and the elegant couples she glimpsed through carriage windows and hotel doorways.

When Mama was eighteen and Julie sixteen, Grandmère bought a house on Burgundy Street, a headquarters from which she launched her daughters into Creole society. She hosted teas and dinners and took the girls to the opera, where they sat sipping champagne in a loge lined with red velvet. Julie was indifferent to the social hurly-burly and often declined invitations to parties. But Mama never missed one.

At a dance at the St. Louis Hotel, she met Papa. She said they fell in love the moment their eyes locked across the ballroom. The orchestra was playing a waltz, and candlelight from two enormous crystal chandeliers flickered over the twirling couples.

Papa was perhaps the most eligible bachelor in town—tall and handsome, with flashing dark eyes and auburn hair that rippled from his forehead in glossy ridges. He was also brilliant, having studied the law and set up a practice on Camp Street by age twenty. And he was rich. His father, Philippe Avegno, had arrived in New Orleans from Italy in 1823, already wealthy from his Italian shipbuilding operation. After marrying the daughter of one of the city's most prominent Creole families, he amassed a new fortune in real estate and built a high-ceilinged mansion on Toulouse Street. The couple had ten children; Papa was the seventh.

He married Mama two months after they met, and took her to live in his father's house. "I felt like I was home for the first time in my life," Mama told me later.

It's hard to imagine what Papa saw in Mama, beyond her beauty. She *was* gorgeous—with large black eyes, flawless white skin, and a slender, graceful figure. But she was prickly and prone to imagining disasters. She also was a relentless complainer, always snapping and picking at Papa. Frequently, he lost his temper with her. I'd often awake in the morning to their loud, violent shouting. I remember the servants scurrying down the hall away from my parents' bedroom, the slammed doors, and my mother's pathetic crying when the storm was over.

Decades later, long after my parents' death, I was astounded to find a copy of divorce papers in Mama's desk. A few months after Valentine was born, she'd sought to end her marriage—an almost unthinkable act for a Catholic Creole. According to the court papers, during one of their arguments, Papa had socked Mama in the eye, drawing blood, and Mama had fled her father-in-law's home, taking Valentine and me to live in Grandmère's townhouse on Burgundy Street.

I vaguely recall moving there after Christmas one year, but I have no recollection of Papa not joining us. In fact, I have a distinct memory of him playing with me on the parlor carpet. He always was gentle and affectionate with his children. I don't believe he ever once spanked me.

Before anything could come of the divorce, the war broke out, and Papa left to fight. Grandmère thought we'd be safer at Parlange, so Mama agreed to join her.

But she didn't fit easily into the role of adult daughter living in her childhood home. Mama took no interest in helping Grandmère run the plantation, and she spent most of her time sitting on the back gallery, rocking Valentine's cradle with her foot and complaining loudly about the dearth of "congenial people" to call on or to pay calls on us. She had more grievances: the mosquitoes, the killing heat, the paucity of servants to help with the children.

Then Rochilieu arrived. With the excitement of the wedding, Mama perked up and helped eagerly with preparations, selecting the china and crystal to be used during the reception and dressing Julie's hair a few hours before the nuptials. I didn't understand why Mama was so happy about marrying Julie off to a fat, ugly old soldier. "Julie doesn't even like him!" I pointed out to Mama as I helped her collect plates from the cupboard in the dining room on the morning of the wedding. Mama looked at me sternly and said, "In the name of our family Julie must make a good match."

As it turned out, Julie did not die. She survived, though in very bad shape, with two broken legs, several cracked ribs, and a severely strained back. Each morning, Alzea picked her up and carried her from her bed to the parlor settee or to a wicker chaise on the front gallery, where Grandmère gave her the responsibility to watch for Yankee soldiers. At night, Alzea carried Julie back to bed. One day, one of the Negroes staked a pole with a white towel tacked to it on the road near our front gate, a signal to old Dr. Porter to come up to the house when he passed on his daily rounds. He fitted Julie with an elaborate steel brace that she wore under her clothes. The awful contraption chafed her skin, causing terrible sores that had to be washed twice a day.

I spent hours by her side, holding old copies of *La Vie Parisienne* up to her face so she could read it to me. Julie never complained about her infirmity, and seemed as cheerful and playful as ever. She composed a little English verse, which she recited to me every day:

> *A six-year-old child,*
> *A six-year-old child*
> *Is a wonderful thing to behold.*
> *I love you, Mimi,*
> *My six-year-old child.*
> *Please never, ever grow old!*

There was no more talk of marrying her off to Lucas Rochilieu, who had left grumpily the day after the aborted wedding.

Forever afterward, Grandmère and Mama spoke of Julie's leap from the gallery only as "a terrible accident." One day, Mama took me aside. "You must never say a word to anyone about Tante Julie's accident," she warned. "And you must never, ever ask Tante Julie about it."

Of course, I had already asked Julie why she did it. She looked at me ruefully and sighed. "Someday you'll understand, Mimi," she said. "There are things worse than death."

Though Julie's spirits stayed high, to the rest of the household her suicide attempt seemed a gloomy presage of future disaster. Even as a child, I knew that trouble was coming, that life was changing. Though the war hadn't yet stretched beyond New Orleans, Grandmère believed it was only a matter of time before Yankee soldiers marched through Parlange. Alzea made a French flag out of some old dresses and hung it from a cypress post on the front gallery as a signal of our neutrality. Still, Grandmère buried four metal chests full of cash in the garden and hid her best jewels in the hollow of an ornately carved bedpost. And she started carrying a large dagger in her belt.

Our tutor, a young man who lived in one of the *pigeonniers* on the front lawn, had enlisted in the Confederate Army when the war started, and no one bothered anymore with our lessons. Charles and I were left on our own most of the day to roam the woods and meadows. Sometimes we'd ride in the cane wagon out to the most distant fields and watch the workers, their backs bent against the sun as they sliced cane knives through the tall reeds. We'd go to the garden for picnics of peaches and smoked ham prepared by Alzea. Afterward we'd try to catch frogs in the stream by the side of the house. Or we'd spend hours playing with our pets at the barn. I had two chickens, which I had named Sanspareil and Papillon. Charles's pet was a brown bear cub he called Rossignol, who was chained to a thick post outside the barn. A slave had killed Rossignol's mother with a scythe after she wandered into the fields one day. Another Negro caught the cub and gave him to Charles.

The most tempting diversion of all, particularly on brutally hot days, was to sneak off to False River, a narrow ribbon-shaped lake that had formed from a bend in the vast Mississippi centuries ago. Mama had forbidden us to go near the water, even though we were good swimmers. She worried that we'd get eaten by alligators. But one day, when I was light-headed from the heat, I suggested to Charles that we go for a swim. Charles studied the sky, sniffed the air, and said, "There's no need to swim. I'm sure it's going to rain. Mama's corns were killing her this morning."

"If you won't go, I'll go by myself. You just don't want to swim because you know I'm a better swimmer than you."

"Mimi, you're a deluded child," he said in the formal, supercilious manner he used with everyone. "But if you want to be humiliated in a race, fine."

We ran down the straight driveway, across the main road, and up the bank to False River. "We'll see who's faster," I said. I pointed out a starting point near a large oak and indicated a spot about fifty yards down the bank as the finish line. We stripped down to our drawers and chemises, jumped in the water, and swam as fast as we could, furiously churning our arms.

Out of the corner of my eye, I saw a female figure striding toward us. Her stiff broadcloth skirt swung like a bell, and the wide ribbons of her bonnet flapped around her shoulders. At first I thought it was Mama, but as the figure drew closer I heard Grandmère's scratchy bark and saw the glistening dagger in her belt.

Charles had seen her, too, and now we stood in the muddy water up to our waists, shivering from fear under the burning white sky.

"Get out right now and put your clothes on!" Grandmère shouted. We scrambled into our things, and Grandmère pushed us up the levee, a bony, blue-veined hand on each of our backs.

When we got to the house, she took one of the long, thin keys that hung from a large ring on her belt and unlocked a door under the front stairwell. "Get in," she ordered. As soon as we were inside, she slammed the door shut and turned the key. The square enclosure was just big enough for the two of us. It smelled of damp wood. A shaft of sunlight slid under the door, providing enough light for us to see clusters of spiders and bugs.

"Mimi, you're always getting us in trouble," hissed Charles.

"And you're so perfect," I snapped.

For the next twenty minutes, we bickered and poked and nudged each other. Just when I thought I couldn't stand another second of it, I heard a rapping on the ceiling, followed by a loud *plink*. In the slice of sunlight at the door, I saw a key on the ground. Grandmère had left it on the table next to Julie's chaise, and Julie had pushed it off the gallery. By lying flat on my stomach, I could stretch my hand under the door and finger the cool metal key. Another scraping push, and I had it. As Charles and I freed ourselves and ran to the garden to hide, we heard Julie chirping above. "You're free, *chéris!* Free, free."

Our swimming adventure had put Grandmère in a particularly foul mood, and for the next week or so Charles and I stayed close to the house. One afternoon, we made a book for Julie, from a serialized novel in yellowed copies of *L'Abeille,* the Creole newspaper. We were cutting out the pages and sewing them together when a pale boy tore up to the house on horseback. He tied his mare to a cypress post and stomped up the steps. I went with Mama to answer the bell. The boy said nothing, but he handed her a white sheet of paper bordered in black. I couldn't read the words, but I saw the drawing of a tombstone and a weeping willow, and I knew immediately what it meant. Papa was dead.

Mama read the note with frightened eyes, then crushed the paper in her fist and fell to her knees. We both sobbed loudly, chokingly. Despite her broken relationship with Papa, or, perhaps, because of it, Mama was devastated. Grandmère, who was in the dining room helping Alzea set the table for lunch, heard us and ran in. "Papa! My papa is dead!" I cried. Grandmère crossed herself and knelt down to pray.

I ran out of the house and down the steps and the alley of oaks. I ran and ran—so hard that my lungs swallowed my sobs—along the banks of False River. It was a gray day, unusually cool for April, and the yellow anemones shivered along the river's edge. Eventually I came upon two farm boys fishing. Their bright blue calico shirts were the same color as their eyes, and they were dangling their feet in the sluggish water. "My papa is dead!" I cried and dropped to my knees, sobbing.

One of the boys laid down his fishing rod and rushed to my side. "There, there, little girl," he said, patting my shoulder with a hand reeking of fish. "My father is dead, too."

I later learned that Papa had been shot in the left leg on the second day of the Battle at Shiloh, and was put on a train bound for New Orleans. En route, his condition worsened and he was taken off at Camp Moore in Amite, Louisiana, where his leg was amputated above the knee. An hour later, he died.

That afternoon, Mama, Grandmère, Charles, Valentine, and I took the steamer for New Orleans. Julie stayed behind with Alzea. We arrived at Grandmère's house on Burgundy Street in late evening. Papa's coffin was in the high-ceilinged parlor, surrounded by dripping candles and white chrysanthemums. A prie-dieu stood before the casket. A line of mourners, some of them Papa's clients from his Camp Street law practice, surrounded the casket. When Mama and I entered, everyone dropped back to make room. Papa looked like he was asleep, his freckled white hands crossed over his chest and a gray blanket covering him to the waist to conceal his empty pant leg. Mama and I had been dry-eyed on the steamer, but now we both wailed uncontrollably. Grandmère pulled a nail scissors from her purse and clipped a tuft of Papa's hair, which she later had made into a bracelet for Mama.

I've tried all these years not to remember Papa as a corpse, to recall him as he looked when I saw him last. He was dressed in the uniform of the Louisiana Zouaves—brilliant red cap, dark-blue serge jacket with gold braid on the sleeves, and baggy silk trousers. Tears spilled from his eyes as he bent to kiss me on the New Orleans wharf before he marched up a gangplank and disappeared into a large transport ship with a thousand other soldiers. As the vessel pulled out, hundreds of handkerchiefs waved from the shore, and the violent shriek of the steam whistle drowned the shouts and cries of the loved ones left behind.

Mama and I held hands on the long carriage ride to St. Louis Cemetery, where Papa was interred in a large marble tomb next to his parents. For days afterward, Mama stayed up all night, pacing the galleries—I could hear her muffled sobs through the walls. In the morning, she had purple circles under her eyes and walked around like a ghost, clutching a torn linen handkerchief.

The next month passed in a blur of humid, rainy days. Grandmère convinced Mama she'd feel better if she got busy, so Mama began tending to Valentine and even helping Alzea a bit with the housework—something I had never seen her do before. Charles spent much of his time walking through the house, looking out the windows and watching the sky for climatic changes. Julie and I read and reread every book in the library. Sometimes neighbors called, sitting in the parlor on chairs pushed against the walls. Alzea would distribute palmetto fans, and people would fan themselves and chat over red wine and cornmeal cake.

Meanwhile, Grandmère worked nonstop. Though the war had caused land values to plummet, and the blockaded ports meant she couldn't sell her sugar, she was determined to keep Parlange going. She was up every morning before dawn and pacing the back gallery and reciting her Rosary, her thick heels clomping on the cypress floors. Sometimes she'd stop and curse loudly at one of the slaves who had stayed on the plantation; then she'd clasp her beads and start pacing again. Afterward she'd pin her skirt up to her knees, don a pair of men's cowhide boots, and tromp out to the fields to supervise the workers. In the evening, she balanced the ledgers by candlelight in her "office," a corner of the back gallery where she had set up an old table as her desk. She hired laborers—poor bedraggled white men—to replace the slaves who had left, and every Saturday morning they came to collect their wages. Grandmère would arrange several whiskey bottles and glasses on the table, and as each man approached, she would pour him a drink and place a few coins in his outstretched hand.

Doing a man's job had coarsened Grandmère and exacerbated her bad temper. She was always yelling at somebody about something, and I knew to stay out of her way.

Nothing infuriated her more than hearing a member of her household speak English. She had banned all use of *"les mots Yanquis"* at Parlange. In Grandmère's view, English was *"la langue des voleurs,"* the language of thieves, because all the words were stolen from other languages, chiefly, of course, from French.

She claimed that the few times she was forced to speak English she almost dislocated her jaw, which you'd understand if you heard her pronounce, say, "biscuit" or "potato." In Grandmère's mouth, they sounded like "bee-skeet" and "pah-taht."

Only Alzea, who had been raised on an American plantation before Grandmère bought her on a New Orleans auction block, was allowed to speak English. Papa had also known English, and, unbeknownst to Grandmère, he and Alzea had taught Charles and me some of the language. But we never dared breathe a word of it in front of Grandmère.

On her birthday, Charles and I prepared a little French poem to recite to her after dinner, before the cutting of the cake. We stood in front of her chair in the parlor while Mama played softly on the dainty Pleyel piano. I was waiting for Charles to nod, our agreed-upon signal to start reciting *"Oh, notre chère grandmère, oh, que nous sommes fiers."*

I looked at Julie crumpled under an old shawl on the settee. She looked so sad it broke my heart. I wanted to cheer her up, so I blurted out a fragment of an English verse:

> *Rats, they killed the dogs and chased the cats,*
> *And ate the cheese right out of the vats.*

Mama's playing halted, and I heard Julie laugh softly behind her shawl. Grandmère stared at me with bright blue eyes. She rose slowly from her chair, walked up to me, and slapped me across the face. I ran to my room and stayed there for the rest of the evening.

I dreaded facing Grandmère the next morning at breakfast, but when I entered the dining room, it was obvious she had more important matters on her mind. Julie's former fiancé, Lucas Rochilieu, was sitting at the table, dressed in frayed, grubby grays. He had grown desperately thin in the eight months since I had seen him last, and his brown hair hung over his collar in scraggly grayish strands.

He had fought at the Battle of Shiloh with Papa, I later learned, and then gone to Vera Cruz, Mexico, on orders from President Jefferson Davis, to buy guns. He was to rejoin his regiment in Richmond, but instead he deserted, bolting for Louisiana, traveling mostly by horseback through back roads and swamps. It took him two weeks to reach his plantation in Plaquemine, where he collected some money and valuables. Now he was on his way to the Gulf of Mexico. He hoped to flag down a foreign ship to take him to France. But he had heard that Yankee troops were in the area and decided to stop off at Parlange to warn us.

"Friends, you will be attacked for sure if you stay," he said heavily. "You don't know the danger! The Yankees have been shooting women and children in their beds." Rochilieu opened his square linen napkin and draped it dramatically across his lap. He tucked into the plate of beignets Alzea had placed in front of him. His mustache moved up and down as he chewed, and I considered the large mole on his nose. If Julie hadn't thrown herself over the gallery, she'd probably have to kiss that mole every day, I thought with a shudder.

From the opposite side of the table, Mama listened intently, with her long-fingered hands folded on the table. Her engagement ring, a diamond surrounded by six small rubies, sparkled in the sunlight streaming through the windows. I thought of Papa, and my chest tightened.

"Well, I'm in favor of going with you," Mama said.

Grandmère dropped her coffee cup onto its saucer, and a spray of tan liquid splashed onto her knobby hand. "You're not leaving Parlange!" she hissed.

"I'm not staying here and risking my daughters' deaths. Or worse, having them grow up to be country bumpkins like the Cabanel girls,"

Mama countered. Eulalie and Nanette Cabanel lived with their parents on a nearby plantation and were notorious for never wearing corsets, not even to pay calls or to attend church.

Ever since Papa's death, Mama had dreamed of Paris. She knew several women—Creole war widows like herself—who had moved to the City of Light and found, if not prosperity and happiness, at least a relative peace.

The argument that day was never resolved. But the next evening, while Charles and I were playing backgammon on the gallery, a shell whirled past the house. We looked up and saw a group of Yankee soldiers and a cannon in the middle of the road. The adults were in the parlor talking, and they ran outside when they heard the shell's high screech and, moments later, the explosion as it crashed in the garden, striking and killing one of the dogs. "My God, they're at our front door!" Grandmère cried. Mama wanted to leave at once. Instead we spent the night on mattresses in the basement. Rochilieu and Grandmère snored, and the rest of us didn't get much sleep.

The lone shell was apparently just a warning. Still, the next morning, Rochilieu said it was no longer safe for him at Parlange. If caught by the Federals, he'd be taken prisoner; if caught by the Rebels, he'd be shot as a deserter. "I'm leaving tonight, whether you come with me or not," he said.

He spent the day reading in the parlor, biding his time until night fell. No one said anything about our going with him, and I went to bed as usual at nine.

Grandmère awoke me at midnight. Holding a lighted candle, she led me through the darkened house, past the bedrooms where Charles and Julie were sleeping, and outside to the front gallery. Rochilieu and Mama, with Valentine swaddled against her chest, were inkblots on the lawn below. Beside them, the horses moved restlessly under a magnolia tree. "You're going with your mama and Lieutenant Rochilieu," Grandmère said. "Julie and Charles are staying with me." I ran to the barn to say good-bye to my chickens, Papillon and Sanspareil. Outside, Charles's bear, Rossignol, was tethered to his post, asleep. "Farewell, Rossignol," I sighed, feeling terrible that I had not had a chance to say good-bye to Charles himself.

Back at the house, Grandmère tied a gunnysack around my waist.

It was heavy and pulled at my abdomen whenever I took a step. "Mimi, this is very important," she said. "There are enough gold coins in here to provide for you and your mother and sister in Paris, and you must never let it out of your sight, ever. *Tu comprends?* If the soldiers stop you, they will not search a child."

She kissed me on the forehead, then embraced Mama. In all my days at Parlange, I had never seen them touch each other. In fact, if I didn't know they were mother and daughter, I would have assumed they disliked each other, so chilly and formal were their relations. Yet now they gripped each other with a fierceness that frightened me.

I started to cry. "What's this? What's this?" groused Rochilieu. "We can't have crying. You'll bring the armies down on us." Mama and Grandmère broke apart. Their faces were wet.

We mounted our horses and trotted along the path by the cane fields, away from the house. The moon looked like a pearl button above the roof, and the air was sweet with the perfume of magnolias and jasmine.

Under Rochilieu's plan, we would make our way to Port Hudson on the east side of the Mississippi, then follow the Old County Road to New Orleans. From there we would take the last leg of the river to the Gulf of Mexico and the open sea, where we would flag down a French or English ship.

As we rode through the forest, Valentine stayed as still as death. But Mama, who hated horseback riding, complained constantly about her mount, her saddle, her aching back. "Shut up!" grunted Rochilieu. "For all we know, the Yanks or the Rebels are behind the next grove of trees." He wiped the sweat from his brow with a handkerchief. Once, when a rabbit ran across the path, he clutched his chest and yelped. Mama was relying on God to see us through, and she mumbled prayers all night.

At daybreak, we reached the Mississippi, where a rickety skiff was waiting on the bank. We piled into the leaky boat and pushed off. Rochilieu did the rowing. Mama held Valentine, and I lay against Mama's legs with her shawl enfolding me. I fell asleep, and when I awoke, smoke from burning cotton on the levees rose against the pink sky. A pool of water from the boat's leaky bottom had risen and soaked my shoes.

After a while, the baby began to cry. "Will you hold her a moment?" Mama said. As I stood to take Valentine from her arms, a square of sunlight broke through the trees and blinded me momentarily. The boat rocked; I stumbled. The sack of gold slid from my waist, vanishing into the muddy water with a loud plop and narrowly missing the black, scaly head of an alligator lurking nearby.

Two

A half hour later, we came ashore at Port Hudson and plodded through the woods. I couldn't shake from my head the image of an alligator with huge open jaws. Cold terror, mingled with wretchedness over losing our gold, brought on a convulsion of sobs. I wailed loudly as we stepped over branches and brambles, wending our way to the Old County Road. Honeysuckle lined the shoulders, and the road was strewn with blue-clad bodies—Union men who had succumbed to illness and exhaustion on their march to battle. We didn't look at the corpses and sucked in our breath to avoid the stench.

It was a bright day and already boiling hot. Itchy red bumps had broken out on my neck where the tight collar of my dress met my skin, and I scraped them furiously with my fingers. "Stop that scratching. You're a girl, not a dog!" Mama cried. She was furious with me. As she walked with Rochilieu, a few yards behind me, I could hear her moaning refrain, "How will we live without our gold?"

A distant cannon shook the air, then another. "Right now, money should be the least of your worries," said Rochilieu.

We walked on, mile after mile, under the burning sun. A fine gray dust covered our clothes, and our shoes were cracked and coming apart. After a couple of hours, a rickety wagon driven by an old farmer rattled up beside us. "Don't tell him anything," Rochilieu warned. The farmer had a sunburned face, and when he smiled, two ragged teeth appeared in his black mouth. "Y'all look like you need a ride," he said. We clambered into the back of the wagon. I quickly fell asleep, and when I woke, we were in New Orleans, parked in front of a small, run-down hotel with laundry hung over the balcony. I jumped down to the pavement, and Rochilieu whispered to me, "Remember, if anyone asks, we're French refugees, and I'm your papa." Rochilieu gave the farmer a few coins, and the cart rolled away.

The hotel lobby teemed with people—mostly mulattoes and shabbily dressed whites. We ate a dinner of gumbo and rice in the stuffy, candlelit dining room and went to our room. Rochilieu slept on the floor, and Mama, Valentine, and I took the bed. In the middle of the night, Rochilieu woke us. "Hurry, ladies. Our boat is waiting," he said. We scrambled into our sour, dusty clothes, padded out of the hotel, and walked to the wharf. An oyster lugger bobbed against the dock.

The young sailor on deck extended his muscular arms and hoisted us aboard. The boat smelled terrible, and we had to stay in blackness down below as it pulled into the Gulf. By midday we were several miles out at sea and could climb to the deck. The wind whipped through a gray sky, and water churned around the boat. Mama pointed into the distance. "Look, a ship."

A frigate with a dark oak hull and huge squares of white sail swayed toward us in the surging water. A French flag flew from the mast. Rochilieu waved Mama's shawl and shouted, "Bonjour!"

As the ship drew up to the oyster lugger's side, a small man in a blue-and-red uniform threw Rochilieu a rope, and Rochilieu tied it to the lugger. He went aboard to talk to the captain and returned a few minutes later grinning broadly. "Ladies, we have a ride to France."

The ship, *La Belle de Jour,* had come from New York and was on its way home, carrying cotton and a few civilian families. From our state-room, I could hear the whoops and shouts of children on board. But I never saw them. I was violently seasick and spent all of the crossing in bed. I didn't start to feel better until we reached Calais and boarded a train for Paris.

We arrived in the city on a drab, chilly Tuesday. Mama, Valentine, and I settled into three furnished rooms in a hotel on Avenue Montaigne, a wide, leafy street not far from the Champs-Elysées. A servant brought us our meals from the hotel kitchen and did some paltry cleaning. But the apartment remained filthy. The draperies were ripped and stained; the backs of the sofa and chairs held grease marks left by the pomaded hair of the apartment's previous occupants. If the servant didn't come, Mama didn't bother to tidy up. Bureau drawers and armoire doors were left open. The bed was unmade. Corsets and stockings littered the floor.

Those first few weeks in Paris, Mama often seemed as indifferent to me as she was to the housekeeping. She didn't notice if I ate all the candy in the crystal jar on the sideboard, or if my stockings were dirty and my hair unbrushed. She had always been inattentive, but now she was worn down, I thought then, by mourning, though I see now she was tortured by guilt. Her grief over her ruined marriage was as raw as the day she learned of Papa's death, and her pale face and red-rimmed eyes testified to her anguished nights.

I spent most of my time playing with Valentine, who had grown from a quiet baby into a lively, chattering child. Each day, she looked more and more like Papa, with the same small mouth and round dark eyes. I loved reading to her and helping her assemble her blocks. Sometimes Mama left me in charge while she went out. I was alone with Valentine the day she took her first steps, toddling a few feet across the worn carpet and collapsing in my arms.

Because Valentine was small and thin, Mama worried constantly over her health. She fussed over the child's sleep schedule and diet, and every cough and sniffle was cause for grave concern. Such devotion, though, didn't prevent Mama from losing her temper with Valentine, or, indeed, from behaving cruelly toward her, as she did one evening when Lucas Rochilieu visited.

Rochilieu was living in a hotel around the corner and frequently came for dinner. That evening, he arrived at seven. Though he had spent the day doing nothing but reading the newspapers in his room and checking his balance at the bank, he was dressed as if for an audience at the Tuileries in pinstriped gray trousers, a starched white linen shirt, and a Prince Albert coat with a cameo stickpin in the lapel. He had regained much of the weight he had lost fighting for the Confederacy, and the wound over his right eye had healed into a thick purple scar.

"Good evening, my dear. You look lovely as usual," said Rochilieu as Mama opened the door. His face brightened when he saw her, and he straightened his body to appear taller.

"Thank you, Monsieur," she replied, bowing slightly.

I knew with the sensitive child's unfailing intuition in such matters that Rochilieu had fallen in love with Mama, just as I knew that she was repulsed by him. Still, he had brought us safely to Paris, and for that Mama had to be grateful.

We settled ourselves on the frayed furniture in the parlor. Then, as they did every time Rochilieu came to dinner, he and Mama replayed our escape from Louisiana. It was as if they were following a theater script, starting with the boat ride across the Mississippi, then the trek to New Orleans, and, finally, our rescue by *La Belle de Jour*.

"The captain of the French ship never would have taken us if I hadn't given him a few pieces from my sack of candy," said Rochilieu, patting Valentine, who nestled against him on the settee. Rochilieu pulled from his coat pocket, as he always did at exactly this point in the drama, a small chamois bag and turned it upside down on a table. Twenty uncut jewels of varying sizes tumbled out and scattered like glittering marbles.

"Ladies, what is your pleasure this evening? A cherry, perhaps?" said Rochilieu, holding a large ruby between his fingers.

Rather than embarrass Mama with cash handouts, Rochilieu made a little game of presenting her with a jewel every time he visited. Mama sold the gems at a shop on rue de Rivoli where all the expatriate Southerners took items to be pawned. The money paid our room and board.

As Mama reached for the ruby, Valentine grabbed a pearl on the table, popped it in her mouth, and gulped. "Valentine!" Mama screeched. She slapped the little girl across the face and then locked her in the bedroom. Valentine kicked the door and shrieked; then, after a while, she whimpered quietly. When Rochilieu had gone, I entered the bedroom to find Valentine lying on the rug sucking her thumb and clutching one of her dolls.

Each day, Mama's temper seemed to grow worse. Anything could set her off—an undelivered bonnet, say, or a rainy morning. She constantly bemoaned my losing our gold and said it was my fault if I never became educated. "How am I going to pay for your school?"

She must have mentioned something about it to Rochilieu, because on his next visit, he let Mama pick two jewels instead of one.

That's how I found myself on a cool September morning standing with Mama before a vine-covered archway on the rue des Fossés Saint-Victor, behind the Panthéon on the Montagne Sainte-Geneviève. A taxi had dropped us off, along with a small wicker trunk containing all my belongings. A chilly gust of wind blew leaves around my legs, and I shivered in my shapeless purple serge uniform. I did not want to attend the Couvent des Dames Anglaises. The thought of being cloistered with a group of strange girls and even stranger nuns filled me with misery. Streams of tears dripped off my chin and onto my uniform. Mama looked at me sternly through the black veil of her widow's bonnet. "Mimi, you must stop so we can go in. The mother superior is expecting us."

Taking my wrist with one hand and carrying my trunk with the other, Mama led me through the arched doorway. Before us was a small courtyard paved with flagstones and surrounded by crumbling buildings—on one side a church, on the other a cloister. The convent was one of several English Catholic communities established in Paris during the sixteenth century, and the only one still standing. For several centuries, Catholic women escaping persecution in England had been sheltered in the cloister, and female aristocrats were imprisoned here during the French Revolution. Mama claimed that an ancestor of Grandpère de Ternant had once been locked behind these walls. But the ancient family connection doesn't explain why she chose it for me. Mama was sending me here because it was the only school she could afford. For many years, the English convent had been a popular repository for the daughters of French nobles, who considered a knowledge of English a valuable social asset. But recently a rumor that Emperor Louis-Napoléon planned to raze the convent to make way for a new boulevard had driven enrollment down. To attract students, the English nuns had drastically reduced their fees. Now most of the girls were daughters not of the aristocracy, but of the petite bourgeoisie: tradesmen, doctors, professors, and minor government officials.

A porter unlocked a heavy wooden door and showed us into a spacious visiting parlor. A few moments later, two dark figures appeared in habits of deep purple serge—the same fabric as my uniform. One was Mother Superior Mary-Josephine, who lifted her veil to reveal a dry, pale face and watery brown eyes. The other nun was her secretary, Sister Emily-Jean, a young beauty with wide-set blue eyes and a fresh, pink complexion. The mother superior said something to Mama in French that was so poor, and in a voice so small and raspy, that I couldn't make out the words. Then she lumbered off and disappeared into her office, an old purple bear entering her den.

Mama kissed me good-bye, and I was alone in the parlor with Sister Emily-Jean. "Virginie, we're all so happy you're here, especially the junior girls," the nun said sweetly. "And the one who is happiest of all is Aurélie Grammont. She's also from Louisiana. Would you like to meet her?"

I nodded, too terrified to speak. Sister Emily-Jean led me through a maze of corridors and out a back door to a lovely garden shaded by chestnut trees. At one end stood a marble statue of the Virgin Mary and, at the other, a stone wishing well. On the old flagstones in between, the girls were playing prisoner's base, a tag game.

Sister Emily-Jean summoned a tall, thin girl who looked about two years older than I. I've always trusted my first impressions of people, and I knew immediately that I would like Aurélie Grammont. She had long, black corkscrew curls, a pleasant tawny face, and hazel eyes behind wire-rimmed spectacles, which I'd never seen before on a female under forty.

"Aurélie, this is Virginie Avegno from Louisiana. Will you take her to Madame Farnsworth's class, please?" said Sister Emily-Jean.

"Of course," answered Aurélie. Her manner was direct, and those deep hazel eyes radiated intelligence and kindness. It was impossible to imagine her ever saying anything stupid or mean.

The chapel bell clanged, announcing the end of recreation. I marched in line with Aurélie and the other girls, up a creaky flight of stairs to the juniors' classroom. As we entered, Aurélie pointed to a hat form on the windowsill holding a dingy muslin cap and warned, "Don't speak a word of French. If Farnsworth hears it, she'll make you wear that nightcap all day!"

A fat Englishwoman with a wiry mustache like a man's was standing next to an old wooden desk. The drafty room was painted a hideous yellow; the desks were wobbly and scarred. The only decorations were a torn, stained map of the world and a chipped plaster crucifix.

Madame Farnsworth looked at me indifferently and pointed to an empty desk in the second row in the middle of the room. "Grammar books!" she bellowed.

There was a scramble of rustled papers and slammed desktops. I found my book—its spine was broken and the pages were falling out—at the bottom of the well of my desk. Madame Farnsworth shuffled across the room. "Page forty-three," she announced. Then she turned to me. "Girls, we have a new student, Virginie Avegno from Louisiana in America, where, as you all know, English is the native tongue. Miss Avegno, please demonstrate how English is spoken in your country by reading the first two exercises."

A chill rippled through me. Though I understood English, I did not know how to read it. *"Excusez-moi, Madame. Je ne lis pas l'anglais,"* I stammered.

Farnsworth's face turned bright red, and her jowls twitched. It never occurred to her that an American wouldn't know English. She thought I was mocking her. "Miss Avegno, this is no way to start your career here. On your knees! Five times!"

Aurélie, sitting directly behind me, leaned forward and whispered, "Virginie, you have to kiss the floor."

I dropped below my desk. The worn wood floor was filthy with dustballs and tiny bugs. I bent forward and slipped my hand between my lips and the dreadful surface. But Farnsworth saw me and rushed over to push my face all the way down.

"Fetch the nightcap, Miss Boirsot!" she roared to another student, her palm still pressing the back of my head. Then she pulled me up by the collar, dragged me to the front of the classroom, and plopped the cap on my head. It smelled like moldy bread.

I stumbled back to my seat and sat with my face burning. For the rest of the day, whenever the nuns passed me in the hall, they made the sign of the cross and murmured, "Shame! Shame!"

The dark paneling of the dining hall was covered with portraits of English kings. At dinner, I sat squeezed between two five-year-olds. Throughout the meal, they stared at the nightcap and giggled behind chubby hands. No one began eating until the nun at the head of the table dipped her spoon into the food—a tasteless chicken ragout served on badly chipped green crockery. When we had finished eating, a servant passed a large bowl around the table, and each girl washed her silverware in it and then put the items away in a drawer underneath the table.

Bedtime came as a relief. The girls slept on cots crammed close together in a cold dormitory under the attic roof. As soon as I was in my cot, I began to sob, burrowing my face in my pillow to muffle the sound. A moment later, I felt soft arms around me and heard a gentle voice. "Shush, Virginie, it'll be all right." It was Aurélie. She stroked my hair and held me until I fell asleep.

The next morning at six, two servants entered the dormitory and woke us by slamming the windows shut. We washed our faces and hands in tubs of freezing water, dressed by candlelight, and marched off to chapel for Mass, followed by a meager breakfast of dry bread and weak tea. We spent all day in class, divided into two groups—the juniors, ages five to twelve, and the seniors, thirteen to seventeen. Our teachers were lay women, most of whom were badly educated peasants from the English countryside. The nuns spent virtually all their time either praying or working in the convent distillery, where they produced mint cordial, their main source of income.

After my first day, I tried to lay low in Farnsworth's class. But Aurélie, who didn't fear her as I did, regularly provoked her. One morning, as the old teacher turned her back to point out the location of Greece on the map, Aurélie whispered in my ear, "Look at Farnsworth's bottom. It's almost as wide as her desk."

Suddenly Farnsworth wheeled and marched toward us. Grabbing Aurélie and me by our ears, she dragged us out of the classroom. "Would you like to tell me what you girls were talking about?" she demanded. I felt faint, and my throat closed shut. Aurélie, though, remained calm. With perfect composure, she looked levelly at Farnsworth and explained, "Virginie was telling me about her grandfather who was a French marquis."

Madame Farnsworth's face softened. She was a snob in the most conventional sense—nothing impressed her like money and pedigree—and the thought that one of her students might have noble blood filled her with self-importance. She resisted the impulse to ask me for details and sent us back to the classroom with no further punishment.

Aurélie was the most clever girl in the class. She could memorize a poem after reading it twice, play a piano sonata after practicing it a few times. But what drew me to her was her warmth. I need to be cuddled. Mama and Grandmère were not demonstrative, but Papa had been. After he left for the war, I could always count on Tante Julie for hugs and kisses. Aurélie also was very affectionate. During my first homesick months at the convent, whenever I sobbed at night, she slipped into bed with me and held me until I fell asleep. In the morning, we brushed each other's hair and sat together in chapel, holding hands under the folds of our uniforms.

We never dared hold hands openly. The nuns strictly forbade it, just as they outlawed hugging and kissing. We could not even walk around in pairs—it had to be in threes—so fearful were the nuns that we would form "unhealthy attachments," as they put it. Once, in the garden, a nun slapped Aurélie and me for sitting too close on a swing.

But the nuns' vigilance was spotty. For long periods, particularly in the evenings between dinner and bedtime, we were left largely unsupervised. The lay teachers had retired to their rooms, and the nuns were in chapel. Aurélie and I often used these hours to lead expeditions of four or five girls in search of the convent ghost—a female prisoner who died during the Revolution and was said to haunt the catacombs.

Armed with candles, we wandered the convent, tapping walls and following narrow corridors in search of a secret door that would lead to the catacombs (we never found it). After a half hour or so, we'd give up, scale the stairs to our top-floor dormitory, and fall exhausted into bed.

Every other Sunday, when the girls were allowed to go home for a visit, Mama picked me up in a hack and took me to the Avenue Montaigne apartment. Usually, we passed the time sitting in the parlor reading or taking a walk with Rochilieu. Afterward he'd dine with us in our rooms. Sometimes Mama and I went to Confederate reunions, lavish parties hosted twice a month by John Slidell, a former Louisiana senator who was the Confederate ambassador to France. As a deserter, Rochilieu never showed his face at these parties.

Mama had known John Slidell and his plump black-haired wife, Mathilde, in New Orleans, and she looked them up as soon as we got to Paris. As leaders of the expatriate community, the Slidells were doing their best to keep up the spirits of the American Southerners. They helped new arrivals find apartments, schools, doctors, and dressmakers. They lent them money and introduced them to other Rebels and their sympathizers.

Invitations to their reunions, held at Rebel headquarters in a vast apartment at 75, rue de Marignan, were sought after not only by American Southerners, but also by the French—politicians, writers, newspaper editors, and society hostesses sympathetic to the Southern cause. Mama waited anxiously for her first invitation, and it came in October, two months after we had arrived in Paris.

Mama and I lifted the ornate brass knocker outside 75, rue de Marignan, and a maid in a black dress and a white organdy apron answered the door. Madame Slidell was standing nearby and rushed over to greet Mama. "Virginie Avegno! Just the person I was hoping to see. We need at least one beautiful woman in the room. Natalie has a cold and won't come." Natalie was Natalie Benjamin, the estranged wife of Judah P. Benjamin, the Confederate Secretary of State. She was a shapely, green-eyed blonde, famous for her many lovers.

Mrs. Slidell linked her arm through Mama's and led us into the parlor. The walls were covered in blue satin, and the room was softly illuminated by pink crystal chandeliers. Elegant women in flounced, high-necked dresses and well-fed men in dark frock coats were gathered in small groups on the enormous Aubusson carpet. A young man sat at the piano playing *"La Bannière bleue,"* which included the plea, *"Aides-nous, Ô France aimée,"* a song from the Creole Confederate songbook. A group of pretty girls stood around the pianist and sang. In one corner, two boys were bent over a chessboard. John Slidell himself—tall and thin, with long, straight gray hair and dark, hooded eyes—was leaning against the pocket doors that led to the dining room, deep in conversation with a fat gentleman who was smoking a pipe.

After about an hour, the singing and piano-playing stopped and Madame Slidell announced dinner. Twenty-five tables were set up in the cavernous dining room. I sat at the children's table next to a freckle-faced boy with coarse blond hair who introduced himself as Harry Beauvais from New Orleans. He fled to Paris with his mother after his father's death during the Yankee occupation of the city, and he was a student at the Lycée Condorcet.

The meal seemed to last all afternoon, with endless courses delivered on silver platters and carted away by servants wearing gray livery in honor of the Rebels at home. Finally, as the toothpicks and finger bowls were passed around, Mama came over to my table. "Virginie, we must leave," she said. "If you're not back by eight-thirty, you won't get into the convent."

Harry Beauvais escorted us to the street to wait for a cab. On the corner, a group of about twenty boys and young men stood bathed in the yellow light from a gas lamp. Several of them were carrying a banner emblazoned with the words "Down with Slidell the Slave-Driver!" The banner depicted a caricature of the ambassador dragging a black man in chains.

"I know some of those boys. They're students at my lycée," said Harry.

"French?" I asked.

"No, American. Yankees."

Just then, the massive double doors at Number 75 opened and Slidell appeared on the sidewalk with his wife and daughters. Loud booing rose from the swarm of boys. As the Slidells walked in the opposite direction, the swarm followed, hissing and singing "Hang Jeff Davis from a Sour Apple Tree." Several boys shot pea-shooters at the Slidells and wads of white paper bounced innocuously around the family. One boy, however, approached closely and aimed his shooter directly at Slidell's face. A hard wad struck the ambassador in the right eye. Slidell grabbed the boy by the collar. Just as he was about to strike him across the face, the boy slipped out of his jacket and ran away, leaving Slidell holding the blue garment. The band of boys dispersed, and we ran toward the Slidells.

"Are you all right, Monsieur?" asked Harry.

"Fine," answered the ambassador as he folded his arms around his wife. Slidell's daughters huddled behind them and cried into their handkerchiefs.

"I know some of those fellows. They're American Yankees. They go to school with me," said Harry.

"Well then, you can return this to them on Monday," snapped Slidell. He threw the jacket at Harry's chest.

When we got to the convent, Mama kissed me distractedly in the visitors' hall. The skirmish on rue de Marignan had frightened her, and I knew she wouldn't get much sleep.

The incident was one of the few times the war at home invaded my life in Paris. Mama and Rochilieu rarely talked about the war in front of me. At the convent, it was never mentioned. Letters from Parlange sparked floods of homesick tears, but Grandmère and Julie spared us the worst news of the war's devastation. They filled their letters mostly with cheery items—news about Julie's recovery (she was walking with canes) and Grandmère's efforts with the sugar crop.

I did receive one sad letter from Charles. His pet bear, Rossignol, who had grown huge and ferocious, one day broke his chain and lumbered into a worker's yard. Rossignol was about to attack an old Negro when the overseer shot the bear and killed him.

As the months passed and I settled into convent life, a surprising contentment enveloped me. My English became fluent through constant exposure (though I lost most of it after leaving the convent). I learned almost nothing of mathematics and history, but I discovered I had a talent for the piano. I had lessons twice a week with Madame Smithy, a thin, pale woman with a delicate face and silvery hair piled on her head. Madame Smithy was kind, but cats, not music, were her chief passion. Wherever she went, a trail of cats followed, and she always had a few with her during my lessons. It wasn't unusual for the cats to crawl all over the piano while I was trying to play scales. This didn't bother Madame Smithy. She laughed at their antics, called them "sweetheart" and "darling," and hardly noticed I existed.

Following piano, I joined the juniors for an hour of deportment and dancing. The ancient instructor, Monsieur Lermont, and the priest who heard our weekly confessions were the only two men allowed in the convent. Monsieur Lermont would have fit nicely in Marie-Antoinette's ballroom at Versailles. He dressed in blue silk breeches and waistcoat, buckled slippers, and an absurd curled and powdered wig that released clouds of white dust whenever he moved his decrepit head. We met with him in Mother Superior's office, where he taught us how to stifle a cough, carry a handkerchief, remove a glove, and open and close a fan. With elaborate formality, he also demonstrated how to bow on a sliding scale of deference to princes, dukes, marquesses, counts, viscounts, barons, knights, and mere heads of state.

His class became the scene of one of my few triumphs as a convent girl. One day during my second year with the English nuns, Monsieur Lermont instructed us in the waltz, demonstrating with his violin as a partner. "Like this, Mesdemoiselles," he said as he pranced stiffly in his buckled shoes on a square of wood floor in front of Mother Superior's desk. We tried to imitate his steps with our partners, tripping over each other's feet and giggling madly. "Silence, Mesdemoiselles!" Monsieur Lermont screeched.

The spectacle of this clumsy old man teaching dance struck me as high farce. Impulsively, I stepped forward. Raising my arms, I embraced an imaginary partner and began waltzing around the room, aping Monsieur Lermont's arthritic movements. The other girls looked on with wide eyes. Monsieur Lermont grimaced at me, and for a moment I thought he would strike me with the bow of his violin. Instead he smiled, his face wrinkling in all directions. "That's it, Mademoiselle Avegno. Beautiful! Beautiful!" he cackled through a row of small brown teeth. "Now the rest of you try it."

Aurélie and I practiced most of our fun during evening recreation. Over time, we grew tired of searching for the secret door to the catacombs and redirected our explorations. Often, in nice weather, we'd climb through a window of our attic dormitory and run around on the red-tiled roof. It always smelled of mint from the garden below, where the nuns cultivated the plants for their distillery.

From the roof we could see into the yard of the Scottish school next door. One evening, a group of boys were outside playing ball, and we decided to sit on the tiles and watch. One of the older boys, a brown-haired, muscular youth, was the first to notice us. He pointed out to his friends the spot where we were huddled on the sloping gable. For a few moments, their eyes flickered over us, and then they returned to their game. But the muscular boy continued to stand still, gazing upward, and I realized that he was fixated on my face. "Why is that boy staring at me?" I asked Aurélie.

"Don't you know, Mimi?" she said with sparkling eyes. "You're beautiful. People will always stare at you."

At ten, I was skinny and flat-chested. I thought I was unattractive, especially compared to Aurélie, who was two years older than me and already had graceful hips and round breasts. But if Aurélie thought I was beautiful, it must be true.

Aurélie and I were never caught prowling the roof, nor engaging in any of our other pranks—scattering melon rinds on the stairs, for example, or filling the pianos with chicken bones. Amazingly, considering how she taunted Farnsworth, Aurélie never had to wear the nightcap. I was punished with it only one more time. One day in my third year, during a particularly boring history lesson, I yawned vigorously, and Madame Farnsworth took the large cork from the ink bottle on her desk and thrust it into my mouth. I coughed and gagged, spurting blue ink over my books and desk, which further enraged the horrid teacher. "Nightcap!" Farnsworth thundered. She snatched the foul hat from the windowsill and slapped it on my head.

Fortunately I had Sister Emily-Jean to comfort me. We were forbidden to disturb the nuns in their cells; most of them wanted nothing to do with us. But Sister Emily-Jean loved the girls, especially me, and often invited me to boil taffy on a small stove she hid under her bed, or to accept a piece of chocolate from the tin on her dresser. Many years later, giving in to her yearning for motherhood, she left the convent, married a tradesman from Bristol, where she had been raised, and at forty-two gave birth to a baby boy.

Whenever I knocked on her door, Sister Emily-Jean greeted me warmly. Her tiny cell was furnished with a narrow cot, an old oak chair, and a little chest of drawers where she kept her few possessions, including a thick braid of silky, dark hair that she had cut from her own head shortly before taking her final vows. She showed it to me one day after I told her that I might like to become a nun.

"It's not a decision to be taken lightly. It's not something you can dabble in," she said. "In the first place, could you stand snipping off all your beautiful copper hair?"

I told her I wouldn't mind a bit. Then Sister Emily-Jean removed her veil and whimple. She was bald, except for a few coarse tufts on the top of her head. "Well, Mimi," she said with a sigh, "if you want to be a nun, even for a few hours, you can't have any hair at all." With that, I gave up all thoughts of devoting myself to God.

For several years I begged Mama to let me bring Aurélie home, but she always refused—she was embarrassed by our shabby apartment. Nor did Aurélie ever invite me to her house. Aurélie explained that her mother was an invalid and never entertained. Then one day, at the beginning of my third year at the convent, Mama said I could bring Aurélie to a Confederate reunion.

On the appointed day, Aurélie and I woke early, ransacked our trunks for our prettiest frocks, and were dressed and waiting in the visitors' hall long before Mama arrived at eleven that morning.

When we entered Rebel headquarters, a lively party was in progress. We made our way into the sunny parlor, where a thatch of straw-colored hair rose above the chattering crowd. It was Harry Beauvais, at thirteen as tall as a man, standing in a corner, drinking red wine.

"Bonjour, Virginie," he called out, lifting his glass in the air. I saw Harry at every reunion I attended, and he seemed to grow an inch each month. His feet and hands were huge. But the rest of him had not caught up. He still had a child's skinny arms and legs, and his chest was concave.

"Harry, this is my friend Aurélie from the convent," I said. "She was born in Louisiana, like us."

"Hello, Harry," said Aurélie.

Harry studied her for a moment, then turned to me. "It's boring here," he grumbled. "Do you want to go to the park?"

"Sure," Aurélie and I answered at the same time.

In the hallway, we donned our hats and coats and wrapped fringed shawls around our shoulders. As soon as the front door slammed behind us, we flew down the stairs and outside to the Champs-Elysées. Running past the wooden booths where vendors sold toys and candy, we arrived at a wide lawn. Harry watched Aurélie as she skipped toward a large marble fountain at the lawn's center, her black curls springing around her shoulders. Without saying anything to me, he chased after her.

When we were seated around the fountain, Harry asked Aurélie, "How long have you worn spectacles?"

"Forever!" she answered. Aurélie scissored her legs under her blue taffeta dress and threw her head back, laughing. Harry stared into the distance and began reciting a poem in French:

> *In a sweet indifference*
> *I lived, peaceful and content;*
> *To me love seemed without strength:*
> *Therefore, I often affronted it;*
> *But, the sweet pleasures of my life,*
> *Alas, they couldn't last always,*
> *Since your beautiful eyes, Aurélie,*
> *Have interrupted the course.*

I recognized the poem (though in the original version the girl's name is Amélie) as one by Michel St. Pierre, a Creole poet who was the most famous free man of color in New Orleans. The poem was contained in an anthology that Tante Julie used to read from.

"Did you like that?" Harry asked Aurélie.

"It's lovely," she answered, her eyes wide.

"You've never heard it before?"

"No."

Harry had never recited a poem to me, and I felt a twitch of jealousy. But it disappeared quickly as we set about playing in the park, laughing and running around. After several hours, just as the sky fell to black, we headed toward the rue de Marignan. Mama was waiting at the corner in a cab. "Au revoir, Harry!" Aurélie and I called out as the cab lurched forward toward the Seine. When we got to the convent, Mama kissed each of Aurélie's cheeks and said she hoped to see her soon. "Thank you, so much, Madame Avegno," Aurélie said. "I had a lovely time."

Two weeks later, on my next visit home, I went directly with Mama and Valentine to rue de Marignan for another Rebel reunion. When we arrived, Harry Beauvais was reading in the parlor. As soon as he saw me, he jumped up, throwing his book on a settee, and dashed into the foyer to help me with my coat.

"No Aurélie this week?" he asked.

"She's home with her family. I miss her, though. She's my best friend."

Harry handed my coat to a white-aproned maid and looked at me severely, his face hard and very white, his eyebrows a blond furry line above blue eyes. "Mimi, she's a Negro."

"No!" I stared at him, astonished.

Harry had been looking forward to this moment, and now his news tumbled out in a torrent. "My father knew Aurélie's father, a white planter named Sébastian Grammont. He owned Laurence Plantation near Monroe, where his wife and children lived. Grammont also kept a cottage in New Orleans for his colored mistress and children, a boy and a girl—your Aurélie. When he died, Grammont left his colored family some money, and they moved to France. My mother met Aurélie's mother once and says she looks African. I don't know how she gets by here—probably never leaves the house unveiled. Obviously Aurélie passes for white."

"You're wrong. Aurélie would have told me."

"Mimi, how can you be so stupid?"

I knew from listening to the adults that free American blacks had been emigrating to France for several decades, and, if they were light-skinned enough, slipping quietly into the white race. But Aurélie? A Negro? I felt angry and confused. Among the slaves at Parlange, there were several mulatto children. One of my uncles had a black mistress, and I played with the couple's children in New Orleans. I was fond of these Negro "cousins," but I knew that an impenetrable wall divided us. I knew, too, that theirs were doomed lives.

"Did you tell my mother?" I asked.

"I'm sure *someone* did."

But Mama said nothing about it. That evening, we rode silently to the convent. Mama said good night to me in the visitors' hall and kissed me perfunctorily.

In the dormitory, Aurélie's bed sat empty. It was still empty when I awoke the next morning. Aurélie did not appear for breakfast, nor Mass, nor for Madame Farnsworth's class. I asked the other girls where she was. No one knew. "She never came back from her visit home," one told me.

By the end of the evening recreation period, I was frantic. As the girls marched inside, I slipped out of the line and hid in an alcove until they had passed. Then I crept to the stairway that led to the cloister cells. The nuns were walking slowly down the hall, chanting their prayers in Latin, as they did every night before retiring at eight-thirty. When they reached the plaster Madonna at the end—the one Aurélie and I thought looked exactly like Empress Eugénie—they crossed themselves, muttered one final prayer, and then disappeared to enter their cells for the night.

I ran to Sister Emily-Jean's door and knocked gently. When the lovely nun saw me, she put her fingers to her lips, pulled me into the room, and closed the door behind us. The tiny space was dark except for a shaft of moonlight slipping through a thin curtain. Sister Emily-Jean lit a small candle.

"I know why you're here," she said.

"Aurélie."

"Mimi, she's been sent home."

In the silence, I could hear a nightingale's song wafting up from the garden. "Why?"

"Mother Superior thought it was the right thing to do."

I started to cry. I was certain I knew what had happened. Without saying anything to me, indeed, while pretending to like Aurélie, Mama had written Mother Superior to denounce Aurélie as a Negro. Sister Emily-Jean hugged me to her slender body, and my tears dampened the front of her habit.

The next afternoon, she took me to Mother Superior's office. The old nun was sitting behind her chunky walnut desk, a stack of letters in front of her. "Mademoiselle Avegno would like Aurélie Grammont's address so she can write to her," Sister Emily-Jean said, clasping my hand tightly.

Mother Superior looked at me with her gluey brown eyes and spread her square hands on the desktop. "I don't think your mother would like that," she said. She leafed through her pile of letters and removed a blue envelope. She pulled the letter from inside and handed it to me. I recognized Mama's round, spidery handwriting. But the words were English. Mama must have had someone—perhaps Rochilieu—dictate a translation. I began to read:

> It has come to my attention that a student in your junior class, Aurélie Grammont, is a Negro. I understand that she and her family are passing for white. I have asked around among my associates from Louisiana, where the girl was born, and I have it on good authority not only that her mother is fully African, but also that she is a woman of the loosest morals. Knowing the Negro's reputation for mendacity and immorality, I'm sure you will share my concern for my daughter Virginie Amélie Avegno, as indeed for all your students. If Aurélie Grammont is not immediately sent home, I will have no choice but to withdraw Virginie from your school.
>
> Sincerely,
> Virginie de Ternant Avegno

Too ashamed to say anything, I handed the letter to Mother Superior, who replaced it in its envelope and returned it to the pile on her desk. Sister Emily-Jean put her arm around my shoulder and led me out of the office.

Two weeks later, when Mama showed up at the convent to take me home for the day, I refused to see her. "Your mother is in the visitors' hall and she is screaming at the nuns to let her upstairs," one of the junior girls reported. Then an old nun with a rubbery face appeared at the dormitory door. "It's a sin to keep your mother waiting," she snarled.

"I won't go down," I said, firmly planted on my cot, my feet crossed, and my arms folded across my chest. The nun grabbed my ear, but she couldn't budge me and soon tottered off, mumbling that I was a "rotten, God-forsaken brat."

A few minutes later, she returned with Farnsworth.

"I knew you were trouble the moment I saw you," the old teacher lamented. "Girls like you go straight to hell." She clasped my leg and tried to pull me from the bed. I broke loose, knocking her off balance, and dashed across the room and out the door. I tried to shut the door behind me, but it slammed flat into Farnsworth's face. "Eeeow!" she screamed, clutching her nose. Then I ran to the end of the hall to a small window that opened onto the roof. With one leap, I was outside. I scrambled from gable to gable, chased by two of Madame Smithy's cats, and found a place to hide behind a chimney. As I huddled against the cold brick, I began to feel like a martyr. I told myself I would never live with my mother again. Maybe I would become a nun like Sister Emily-Jean, a beautiful sufferer for Christ and the Holy Virgin.

I stayed there for several hours. Eventually I fell asleep. When I awoke, it was dark. Frightened and hungry, I stumbled back to the window and crawled in. "It's Virginie!" squealed the other girls, who were getting ready for bed when I appeared in the dormitory. Their shrieks brought Mother Superior. She doused me with Holy Water to drown the evil spirits lurking within me. "You broke Madame Farnsworth's nose," she groused, though I thought I detected a trace of satisfaction in her voice. Perhaps the girls weren't the only members of the convent who were terrorized by the vile teacher. Mother Superior left me standing there, water streaming from my head in rivulets and puddling on the floor. "I'll deal with you tomorrow," she said.

But the next morning, I woke up with pleurisy and spent three weeks in the infirmary. God had punished me, relieving Mother Superior of the chore.

When I saw my mother again, she was standing in the visitors' hall, waiting to take me home for a Sunday visit. Her eyes blazed through her black veil, and she spoke to me with chilly disdain. "I hope there will be no more displays of madness from you, Mademoiselle."

In the months following Aurélie's departure, I couldn't sleep and grew so thin that my stockings wouldn't stay up past my calves. I sat listlessly through my classes and refused to go outside during recreation. Instead I attended evening services with the nuns. I always sat in the last row, where I had a good view of the back wall. Hanging there next to a window was a painting by Titian of Jesus dying in an angel's arms. The angel's black curly hair reminded me of Aurélie, and at the end of the service, as the organ music swelled during the Prayer for the Dead, I would weep bitterly for my lost friend.

One evening, as I approached the chapel entrance, Sister Emily-Jean was blocking the door. "Go play with the other girls," she insisted.

I walked into the garden. A silvery light slanted through the bare trees, and a cool wind churned the air. Most of the girls were playing prisoner's base, laughing and chasing each other around the courtyard. A tall, dark-haired girl had climbed the chestnut tree in the corner and, having pushed aside the branches, was spying on the Scottish boys next door. She, too, reminded me of Aurélie. My heart sank. I walked back into the convent, mounted the creaky stairway to the dormitory, and went to bed.

The next day, Sister Emily-Jean told me I'd been chosen for the starring role in the Christmas pageant. I was to play a silent and motionless Madonna in a tableau vivant of Jesus' birth. "You're a perfect choice!" she said brightly. Of course, I knew why I'd been given this honor—Sister Emily-Jean had pestered the teacher in charge to give me the role, hoping it would cheer me up.

A little before 2 P.M. on the second Saturday of December, the students' families—somberly dressed men and women with small children in tow—began filling the auditorium. I saw Mama, Valentine, and Rochilieu enter and take seats in the rear. Then the boys from the Scottish school trooped in, the younger ones in short pants, the older ones dressed in dark frock coats and starched white collars.

A priest led the audience in prayer, and the program began. The choir sang, followed by a piano soloist. Then a group of dancers performed a sequence choreographed by Monsieur Lermont, and two juniors, dressed like shepherds, read from the Gospels.

The curtain closed for a brief intermission. I took my place on the stage while a maid wrapped me in an emerald silk shawl. Several girls who were dressed as angels, in white choir robes, knelt nearby. The willowy senior who played Joseph stood behind me with her hair pulled under a wool cap and a yarn beard glued to her chin. Paresseux, Madame Smithy's most placid cat, lay swaddled in a blanket in a makeshift manger.

When at last we were assembled, Sister Emily-Jean called from the wings. "Poses, everyone!" I arranged my arms with palms pointing heavenward and tried to fix my face in an expression of deep religious ecstasy. Sister Emily-Jean pulled two thick ropes and the velvet curtain parted.

A loud "Ahh" arose from the audience. Suddenly a five-year-old named Isolde, who was always sick with a runny nose and whose nocturnal shrieks for her parents kept the convent up at night, bounded out of her seat in the third row and rushed the stage. Falling to her knees in front of me, she cried, "Mother Mary! Mother Mary!"

"*Formidable!*" a man in the second row exclaimed. "A Botticelli Madonna! Look at that wondrous hair!" cried a woman. But I didn't dare look up. I held my pose, gazing beatifically at Paresseux asleep in the manger and soaking up the crowd's adulation. I didn't want it ever to end.

Three

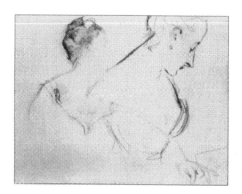

After she found out Aurélie was a Negro, Mama became obsessed with the color of *my* skin, as if Aurélie's hidden blackness had been contagious and I might have caught a touch of it. Whenever she saw me, she stared at me with furrowed brow and complained that I was losing my "bloom." To protect me from the sun, she gave me a parasol to carry when I went out with her, and a straw hat to wear in the convent garden. Still, she worried.

"I don't like the way you look," she said to me one Sunday in March. "You're turning brown." We were sitting in the parlor with Rochilieu, drinking tea and reading the papers while Valentine sat on the floor playing with her doll. The clatter of carriages floated up from the street through the open windows. Dusty sunlight formed stripes on the worn blue carpet.

"I'm not dark, Mama. I'm only a little bronze from playing outside," I said. It had been an early, warm spring and the nuns had let us spend more time than usual in the garden.

"Well, why haven't you been wearing your hat?" she huffed.

Rochilieu, who usually ignored our bickering, now folded his newspaper and looked hard at me. Then, scowling, he turned his gaze to Mama. "Really, Virginie, I don't see any change in Mimi at all," he said impatiently. "I wish you'd stop inventing troubles to worry over."

"I'm not imagining it! The child's color is changing." Sighing loudly, Mama sprang from her chair and strode off to the bedroom to sulk.

The next day, she made an appointment for me with Dr. Marcel Chomel, who had been recommended by Mathilde Slidell. Mama got special permission from Mother Superior to take me out of school on a Friday morning. We took a cab to the doctor's office at 42, rue de l'Echiquier, arriving just as Duchess Laure Castellian, a famous hostess and frequent focus of the society pages, was gliding through the front door under an enormous white hat. Mama stared directly at the blond duchess's creamy face, but Laure Castellian looked past us with large lilac eyes. "I wonder why *she* needs a doctor," Mama said.

A maid greeted us in the marble-floored vestibule and showed us into a large book-lined office. Dr. Chomel, slim and impeccably dressed in a gray morning coat and red silk tie with white dots, was standing behind a cluttered mahogany desk. He had a white mustache and wispy white hair that barely covered the large metal plate on the side of his head, a souvenir of a dueling wound. Dr. Chomel treated the most fashionable women of Paris in the early days of the Second Empire, when honor was paramount, when the tiniest insult was reason enough to pack one's pistols and take a morning carriage ride to the dueling oaks in the Bois de Boulogne.

The cemeteries were filled with tombstones inscribed, VICTIME DE SON HONNEUR and MORT POUR GARDER INTACT LE NOM DE LA FAMILLE. Dr. Chomel had been challenged by the grieving husband of a young woman who had died under his care. She had suffered from the starving disease and had simply wasted away. Her husband thought Dr. Chomel was to blame, and insisted he defend himself at the dueling oaks. They met on a damp September dawn. Dr. Chomel's shot missed its target and lodged in a tree; his opponent managed to graze the side of the doctor's head.

"What brings you here?" Dr. Chomel asked, after we introduced ourselves and settled into chairs in his office.

"My daughter's skin seems to be darkening," Mama said. "It turns duskier every time I see her, and she has more and more spots all the time." She pointed to the spray of apricot freckles across my cheekbones.

"Why would that be? Is she exposing herself to the sun?" Dr. Chomel asked. His voice was low and clotted—an old smoker's voice.

"Perhaps. A little." Mama shifted uncomfortably in her chair.

Dr. Chomel stepped from behind his desk. His legs were extremely short and did not match the normal proportion of the rest of his body. He strode up to me and took hold of my chin with a sturdy, thick-fingered hand. Narrowing his cool gray eyes, he lifted my face toward his and examined my skin. Then he released my face, ambled across the Turkish carpet, and leaned against his desk.

"Complexion changes are quite normal at this age," he said. "I don't see anything serious here. Is the child in good health?"

"Yes," Mama answered.

"Then I recommend my special compound, Chomel's Solution, to whiten the face and fade the freckles. I've had great success with it. Your daughter has some small eruptions on her forehead, and those will clear up, too."

I ran my hand across the cluster of tiny, hard bumps near my hairline. "What's Chomel's Solution?" I asked.

"It's arsenic-based, flavored slightly with oil of lavender and cinnamon."

"Arsenic! That's poison!" I cried.

"My dear girl, all medicine is poison. Now, enough questions. You come with me."

He led me into the hall, down a short corridor, and into an examining room. The white walls were lined with glass-front cabinets. A wooden table with a white sheet over it stood in the center. Dr. Chomel pointed to a footstool in front of the table. "Step up, please," he instructed.

He turned his back and fussed with some bottles in one of the cabinets. When he faced me again, he was holding a jar of cloudy blue liquid and a large silver spoon.

"I don't want any medicine," I said.

Dr. Chomel ignored me. Using the knobby middle fingers of his right hand, he pried my mouth open and poured in a spoonful of the cold, tangy liquid. I gulped and immediately felt sick to my stomach.

"That's it, Mademoiselle Avegno," he said. He placed the jar and spoon on a counter and looked deeply into my face, as if he'd just noticed me for the first time. "My, you are a little beauty, aren't you?" he said, smiling through his mustache, showing a row of tiny pointed teeth.

"That medicine tasted horrible," I said.

Dr. Chomel's smile disappeared. "Did you think I was giving you candy?" he grumbled. He led me back to his office, where he handed Mama a jar of Chomel's Solution and a small bottle with a label reading BLOOM OF YOUTH.

"Your daughter should take one teaspoonful of the Chomel's every night and apply two fingertips of the cream to her face. I'm sure the effect will be agreeable to you. Bring her back in a month," he ordered.

At the convent, Mama handed Mother Superior the bottles and told her I was to be given them every night before bed.

"What's this medicine for?" the old nun asked.

I started to explain, but Mama cut me off. "Virginie has some stomach trouble," she explained.

I took the medicine that evening and every evening afterward for three weeks. Almost overnight, I lost my tan and my freckles. My skin became smoother and more translucent, with a clear, bluish tinge from the veins showing through.

Then, almost as suddenly as the medicine had worked its magic to whiten me, it began to make me ill. I became overwhelmingly tired, I lost my appetite, and I suffered from an insistent, violent trembling on the right side of my face—typical symptoms I know now of the first stage of arsenic poisoning. What's more, my freckles reappeared. Soon, they had darkened and run together and suddenly my face was very brown indeed. I looked a lot like the red-haired slave girl in Grandpère Avegno's house, the one everyone gawked at because the black and white blood in her was so oddly mixed.

"My God, what's happened to you!" Mama cried when she picked me up at the convent on a warm April afternoon for my scheduled rendezvous with Dr. Chomel. She hustled me through the courtyard and into a cab. When we reached rue de l'Echiquier, she yanked me to the pavement in front of Dr. Chomel's building and scurried to pull the bell. We found the distinguished man in his office, standing on a ladder and searching for a book on a high shelf. "Look at my daughter!" Mama shrieked.

Dr. Chomel descended the ladder slowly and walked over to me. He leaned his face into mine and studied my skin. "This happens sometimes," he said, straightening abruptly. "A complete reversal of the expected effect." He shrugged his shoulders. "So we reduce the dose."

"I don't want any more medicine," I protested.

"Now, now, my dear, wise little girls listen to their doctors."

Dr. Chomel left his office and padded down the hall. A few minutes later he returned, carrying two jars, which he handed to Mama. "Let's see how she does with these," he said.

When we got to the convent, Rochilieu was waiting at the curb, glancing anxiously through a newspaper. He was pale and his forehead was slick with sweat.

"What's he doing here?" Mama whispered as the cab creaked to a halt under the skinny iron arm of a towering lamppost. Rochilieu ran over and opened the door.

"It's over!" he cried as Mama and I stepped to the pavement. "General Lee has surrendered!" Rochilieu embraced Mama, and they both wept.

Neither of them had expected the Confederates to lose. Living in Paris and cut off from the grimmest news about the war, they did not realize how hopeless the Rebel cause had become, nor the extent of the fighting's devastation to the South.

"The Negroes will own us now," Mama said bitterly. She pulled from her purse a black-bordered handkerchief—the one she'd carried since Papa's death—and lifted her veil to wipe the tears from her cheeks.

No one at the convent talked about the end of the war. Everyone continued to be much more interested in my face. Mostly, the nuns and the girls stared at me silently. But once Isolde, who at five was the convent's youngest student, ran up to me during recreation. "Are you turning into a Negro?" she asked. Sister Emily-Jean overheard her and rushed to defend me. "Isolde, Mimi is taking some medicine that makes her dark. When she stops using it, her skin will be white again," she said.

Later, though, Sister Emily-Jean whispered to me, "Mimi, I want to talk to you tonight about your skin treatments. Come see me after chapel."

That evening, while the girls were dressing for bed in the dormitory, I slipped downstairs to the nuns' corridor. The door of Sister Emily-Jean's cell was ajar, so I pushed it open and stepped inside. The lovely nun was sitting on her bed, weeping. A copy of *Le Figaro* lay on the cold stone floor.

"What's wrong?" I asked. I thought perhaps she was crying over my skin, and I planned to enlist her help in convincing Mama to take me off Chomel's Solution.

"Oh, Mimi, one of the greatest men in the world has died."

"Not Victor Hugo!"

"No, no. Your President. Mr. Lincoln."

He wasn't *my* President, but I didn't want to upset Sister Emily-Jean further by contradicting her.

"He was murdered," she continued, struggling to speak through her tears. "Shot by an actor as he and Mrs. Lincoln watched a play."

Lincoln had died ten days earlier, but the news of his assassination had reached France only that afternoon.

"Don't you want to talk to me about my skin?" I asked.

"Not now, dear. Maybe tomorrow."

I left Sister Emily-Jean's cell, tiptoed down the corridor, and mounted the stairs to the dormitory.

On my next visit home, Mama announced that we would be leaving Paris and returning to Louisiana with Rochilieu. He had booked passage to New Orleans on a French ship, the *Trésor*. But we would not be sailing for several months—Rochilieu needed time to get his affairs in order. Now that the war was over, he was eager to reclaim his plantation in Plaquemine and his townhouse in the French Quarter. Without his support, Mama, Valentine, and I could not afford to stay in France.

I was ambivalent about returning to Parlange. On the one hand, I couldn't wait to see Julie, Charles, and Grandmère again. But I had grown accustomed to the convent. The thought of leaving Sister Emily-Jean, in particular, filled me with sadness.

Mama wanted to leave Paris for only one reason: she expected to find riches awaiting her in America. Before the war started, Papa had told her that Grandpère Avegno had hidden several trunks of gold in the yard of one of the houses he owned in the Tremé district, an enclave of free blacks and mulattoes north of the Vieux Carré. This gold was all that was left of the once-magnificent Avegno fortune. Much of the dead patriarch's property had been confiscated by the Federals and his money lost, having been invested in the Bank of New Orleans, which sent its gold to the Confederacy in exchange for now-worthless Rebel notes. Mama planned to enlist help from her in-laws in tracking down the trunks, which she was convinced would turn up. Then, with our share of the gold, we would return to France—this time in style.

The next months at the convent passed uneventfully, until my last week. Six days before we were to leave Paris, I had a final skirmish with Farnsworth. I'm proud to say it was a battle I won triumphantly, and which, to my childish heart, compensated a bit for the tragic defeat of the Confederacy.

It started during a routine geography lesson. We were studying the American capital cities, and I had worked hard to learn every one. Indeed, I was applying myself in all my subjects, so determined was I to leave the convent with good marks.

"Mademoiselle Avegno, what is the capital of New York?" Farnsworth asked me at the start of class.

"Albany," I answered.

"And the capital of Maryland?"

"Annapolis."

Farnsworth looked furious. I was depriving her of the pleasure of punishing me.

"All right, Mademoiselle. What is the capital of Kentucky?"

"Frankfort." I felt a grin coming on and covered my mouth with my hand. Too late.

"You think you're so smart. Are you mocking me?" The old teacher's face turned red; a fiery blush spread to her ears and neck.

"No, Madame, I'm simply answering your questions."

"I'll teach you to be so impertinent."

Farnsworth slammed a ruler on her desk, sending a pile of papers fluttering to the floor. She strode toward me, grabbed me by the arm, and dragged me to the open window. Rage gave her astounding strength. Lifting me off the ground with her fat sausage arms, she pushed my head and torso out the window. Clasping my ankles, she lowered me all the way outside so that I was dangling in midair over one of the convent's low-slung annexes.

Directly below me was a skylight. If Farnsworth dropped me, I would fall twenty feet through the glass and into the room below it. My head felt like it would burst from the pressure, and cold terror snaked through my limbs, branching into every vein. I prayed to God to let me live.

"I'll teach you, Avegno, to put on airs. You think you're so smart. Americans! I spit on you!"

Suddenly I felt warm arms around my legs, as Farnsworth's grip on my ankles released. "We've got her! Bring her in!" cried one of the girls. Supple arms embraced me, and sweet voices rose excitedly as my classmates pulled me to safety. "Are you all right, Virginie?" several girls asked at once.

"I think so." My head was throbbing, and my limbs felt shaky.

Lying in front of me, with her huge flabby arms by her side and her right cheek squashed into the filthy floor—the floor she had forced so many of us to kiss—was Farnsworth. Suzanne, a tall, large-boned fourteen-year-old, had wrestled the hateful woman to the floor and was now sitting astride her fleshy back.

A minute later, Mother Superior stormed into the room, followed by a group of nuns. "All right, girls, we'll take her," Mother Superior said. Fury flashed across her face. The four nuns were as tall and strong as men, with big square hands and broad shoulders under their purple habits. They lifted Farnsworth off the floor and, grasping the groaning woman under her arms, led her away.

We never saw Farnsworth again. The next day, Madame Smithy, the piano teacher, took over our class. She was as indifferent to history and arithmetic as she was to scales and chords. During most of her class, we read silently at our desks. Meanwhile, Madame Smithy—her no-color hair hastily arranged on her head like a pile of sticks, an expression of dazed dottiness on her face—stared out the window, watching her cats as they ran and played on the tangle of gabled rooftops.

On my last day at the convent, Sister Emily-Jean gave me a rosary and a small statue of the Virgin. "Good-bye, dear. I promise I'll write to you, and you do the same," she said to me in the visitors' hall when Mama came to pick me up. A porter carried my wicker trunk across the ancient cobblestones of the courtyard, through the low vine-covered archway, and out to the street, where he helped Mama lift it into a cab.

At eight the following morning, I walked up the gangway of the *Trésor,* followed by Mama, Rochilieu, and Valentine. It was an ancient, hideous ship, but its name seemed a good omen. Madame Slidell and her daughters had come to the wharf to see us off. From the deck of the ship, I searched for their pretty faces in the crowd below. Before I could spot them, however, the old ship lurched from the harbor and rolled out into the gray sea.

We landed in New Orleans ten days later. I was asleep in our tiny cabin when the ship swung into its stall. The clanking engines snapped me awake. Mama, Valentine, Rochilieu, and I, our faces puffy with sleep, ambled up the gangway and down the wharf under a blanched sky. Rochilieu was staying on in the city for a few days, and we said good-bye to him on the wharf. He had tears in his eyes as he kissed us good-bye. Though I'm sure she didn't care if she ever saw him again, Mama urged the old soldier to visit us at Parlange, and he promised he would.

Mama, Valentine, and I boarded a steamer for the Waterloo landing on the Mississippi River, ten miles from Parlange. A gentle drizzle began to fall, and Mama and Valentine retired to our cabin. I stayed on deck, leaning against the railing and letting the soft wind lift my hair off my shoulders as the rain sprayed my face. The steamboat glided past the parishes of Saint James, Ascension, Iberville, West Baton Rouge, East Baton Rouge, and Pointe Coupée. Through the trees lining the shore, I glimpsed the burned-out shells of the once-grand plantation manors, and the fenceless fields where a few cows still grazed.

At five in the afternoon, the rain stopped and the steamer slipped into the Waterloo landing under a clearing sky. The wharf was lined with crumbling, empty warehouses. At a nearby shack serving as the sheriff's station and livery, Mama hired a wagon.

I climbed in back. Mama sat up front next to the driver and held Valentine on her lap. An hour went by, and the wagon swung around a wide bend, then creaked to a halt. Before us was Parlange. As Mama rummaged through her purse for a few coins to pay the driver, I scrambled to the ground.

The alley of oaks stood as it had for a century, massive, imperturbable, indifferent to fortune or war. I ran as fast as I could toward the house. Julie was reading in a wicker chair on the gallery. When she saw me, she grabbed two thin canes resting on either side of her chair and stood up. Slowly, awkwardly, she moved toward me. "Mimi, oh, Mimi!" she cried. I flung my arms around her neck. When we had last seen each other, I had barely reached Julie's chest; now I was as tall as she was. "Look at you," she said, tears spilling out of her eyes. "You've turned into a long, thin baguette!" Her face had grown leaner, and her body more womanly. A few threads of gray had sprouted in her black hair.

Mama and Valentine made their way up the alley and now stood on the front lawn. Grandmère, her skirts pinned up to her knees, clomped through the garden gate in heavy cowhide boots. The three ran toward each other, embraced, and then, with Valentine in Grandmère's arms, mounted the steps, laughing.

"Who is this lovely young lady?" said Grandmère, lowering Valentine to the gallery floor and rushing to hug me tightly. She had the fresh, lemony smell of cut grass, and I could feel her bony shoulders through her much-washed broadcloth dress.

We went into the parlor, where Alzea was placing a tray with a coffee service on the table. She wore a white kerchief around her neck, and her head was wrapped in a red calico tignon. "Thank God, you is all safe and sound!" she said, enfolding me in her black satin arms.

The parlor was astonishingly bare. Gone were the Aubusson carpet, the horsehair sofa, and the mahogany secretary. A ghostly-white rectangle marked the outline of the huge gilt mirror that had once hung above the mantel. All that remained of the room's former luxury were a few brocaded fauteuils, a marble-topped table, the piano, and, hanging in the four corners of the room, oval portraits of Grandmère, Grandpère de Ternant, Mama, and Julie, painted in Paris by the society artist Claude-Marie Dubufe.

"Where is the furniture?" Mama asked, flopping onto the round piano seat. She played a few tinny cords—the piano was badly out of tune—and dropped her hands in her lap.

"I sold it, along with most of our land," Grandmère said, her mouth tight. Sadness seeped from her eyes.

To pay her taxes and debts, Grandmère had had to spend all her cash and sell most of her land, about eight thousand of Parlange's ten thousand acres. Still, Grandmère was better off than most of her neighbors. The Yankees had destroyed many of the plantations and farms on False River. They stole livestock, furniture, clothes, food, and supplies, and dismantled barns and fences. They burned many sugar mills and houses to the ground.

One day in 1864, General Nathaniel Banks and several dozen Federal soldiers rode up on horseback to the front lawn. Banks gave Grandmère a choice: sign the Federal oath of allegiance or watch Parlange burn. She signed.

She gave General Banks her bedroom, and his troops set up tents in the fields. Every night, Grandmère served Banks and his officers dinner in the dining room, on her best china. General Banks was kind, and he doted on Charles. He spent hours in the evening talking to the boy about meteorology and was impressed by Charles's knowledge. Playing hostess to the Federals had not been as horrifying as it could have been, Grandmère said. But soon after they left, she discovered that the silver she had hidden in the garden was missing. The imbecile servant girl who'd been hired to help Alzea with the cooking had pointed the valuables out to the soldiers.

"You can't imagine the struggle we've had," said Grandmère.

At that moment, the tall pocket doors parted and Charles stepped into the room. He had come directly from the fields and was dressed in dirty cotton pants and a frayed blue-checked shirt. At sixteen, he was tall and muscular. The pampered softness was gone from his face, revealing a lean jaw and high cheekbones. But for his eyes, I would not have known him; those sensitive blue pools, fringed with long black lashes, were unchanged.

"Charles!" I cried, running to him and kissing him on both cheeks.

"Oh, it's so good to see you," he said. Charles hugged Mama and scooped up Valentine in his arms.

"Charles will tell you how it's been here," said Grandmère.

"Now, Mama, that can wait until tomorrow. Let these Paris belles enjoy their first night home." He sat in a wooden chair next to Grandmère and held Valentine on his knee.

"I'm afraid we need them in the sugarhouse this evening. I've got four workers down sick," said Grandmère.

It was September, a full month before roulaissant, the grinding season. But the unusually rainy fall had caused outbreaks of root rot and mosaic that killed a third of the crop. Grandmère was determined to get the rest of the cane cut, hauled to the mill, and ground into sugar before another blight struck. She and Charles had been working side by side in the fields from dawn to dusk and all night every third night in the sugarhouse.

"It's come to this, then. We're to work like darkies," Mama hissed.

"If we don't, we won't survive," said Grandmère. She took a lump of sugar from the china bowl, dipped it in her coffee with a spoon, and fed it to Valentine.

At dusk, Mama, Valentine, Julie, Grandmère, Charles, and I gathered on the front lawn, surrounded by the steady buzz of crickets. "Help Julie and your mother with their skirts," Grandmère ordered. She handed me a small box of straight pins. I pinned up Julie's pink gingham hem to reveal a pair of white lisle stockings sagging on her twig legs. Then I held out the box to Mama. She shook her head from side to side. "I'm not exposing my legs to the workers," she said.

"Virginie, please. Soap is a dollar and a half a pound," Grandmère pleaded.

"I won't do it."

A moment later, a cane wagon driven by an old black man rumbled down the road and parked under a magnolia at the side of the house. Starting with Valentine, Charles lifted each of us into the back and then hopped on next to the driver. We rode out to the fields, past a recently planted grove of fig trees and the small row of shacks that had once been slave quarters. A gaggle of barefoot black children played on a rickety porch.

"When I grow up, I'm going to build nice houses for poor people and a school for their children," Valentine announced. "And I'm going to buy them lots of shoes!"

"You're very kind, *chérie,*" said Julie. She nuzzled Valentine against her chest and composed an English verse to delight her: "Soon we'll be sugary lasses covered in molasses, as brown as berries and twice as merry!"

The two-story clapboard sugarhouse stood at the end of a desolate open field. Silver moonlight clung to the backs of four men who were unloading cane from a wagon and feeding it through a large chute at the side of the building.

Inside, in the largest room, giant rollers crushed the green stalks, releasing the sweet cane juice into barrels. In the room behind it, a dark line of men and women stood over a series of roiling kettles.

"Mimi, you go over there," said Grandmère, pointing to the middle of the line.

"Howdy, young missus," said an old black man. He wiped his wooden paddle on his apron and handed the paddle to me. "Now I'm gonna get me some sleep," he said.

I took the old man's place across from a skinny mulatto woman who stared impassively at me through the cane steam. Julie, Mama, and Valentine, perched atop a tall stool, replaced three workers at the kettle next to mine. Through the open doorway, I could see Grandmère standing at the crusher, clearing off debris and readying the rollers for a fresh batch of stalks.

Charles took his post at the last, smallest kettle. It was his job to judge when the reduced cane juice was ready to crystallize into sugar. Valentine and I loved to eat this grainy syrup on batter cakes and bread, and Charles planned to save a bit for us and carry it home tonight in a tin cup he tied to his belt.

Sweet, solid Charles. He had become indispensable to Parlange. His knowledge of weather patterns enabled him to anticipate droughts and freezing weather, and the long hours he spent poring over books on botany and farming helped him improve irrigation techniques.

Most important, however, he understood the new order. Grandmère still treated the workers like slaves. She forbade them to leave the plantation without her permission, and though she provided them with housing, clothing, and food, she had stopped paying them a year earlier, when her income had dwindled to nothing after the disastrous 1864 crop. The laborers complained to Charles, who devised a plan to pay them at the end of the year, after the cane had been harvested and sold. He let the workers vote on whether they wanted cash or a share of the crop. They voted unanimously to take the money.

"How y'all doing?" Charles said. Two hours had gone by, and he had interrupted his work to check on us.

"Just fine and dandy," said Julie as she rotated her paddle through the bubbling liquid.

Mama's face was white and glazed with sweat. She nodded to the back wall, where a group of Negro workers, former slaves, stood gaping at us, incredulous to see white females working in the sugarhouse. "Look at them, hanging back, not lifting a finger to help," she grumbled. "They've given us more trouble than their heads are worth!"

"Now, Virginie," said Charles. "We're all living here together. We must try to get along."

"The girls and I won't be here much longer. As soon as Anatole's father's money is found, we're going back to Paris."

"Oh, please," groaned Julie. "No one but you thinks that money is going to turn up."

I hoped Julie was right. Now that we were home, I wanted to stay at Parlange.

At midnight, Grandmère announced it was time to quit. We piled into the cane wagon. Mama carried Valentine, who had fallen asleep on the floor of the sugarhouse two hours earlier. We drove home in the cool, still air as the old Negro driver and Julie sang the Confederate tune "Dye My Petticoats."

The next day, a letter arrived in a pale blue envelope addressed in a small, cramped hand that Mama instantly recognized as that of Angeline Avegno Lapeyre, Papa's eldest sister. Mama disliked Angeline, an annoying blonde who bombarded Mama with inane accounts of the triumphs and miseries of her four dull sons. She tossed the letter unopened into the china bowl on the hall table.

When Mama finally got around to reading it several days later, I was sitting with her on the gallery. She had a pile of envelopes on her lap and was slicing through them with a bone-handled knife.

As she read Angeline's letter, her eyes grew wide. "My God!" she cried. She took a deep breath, then began to read out loud:

My dear Virginie,

A voodooienne I consulted last week about my money woes told me the answer to my troubles lay in the ground at 54 Conde Street. So I had Numa, my eldest, dig up the yard behind that green cottage Papa rented years ago to a quadroon and her brood of mulatto bastards. Well, he found all four trunks stacked up on top of one another like sardines! Imagine, they've been lying there practically under our noses through the entire war.

Oh, Virginie, I thought we were all going to end up at the Little Sisters of the Poor. Now there's enough to keep us all for the rest of our days.

I'm so happy to write you this wonderful news.

Your loving sister-in-law,
Angeline Avegno Lapeyre

The next morning, I had just opened my eyes when I heard Mama call, "Mimi, come say good-bye to us!" I tumbled out of bed and ran barefoot into the entrance hall, where Mama and Valentine were standing, identically dressed in pancake hats that were tied under their chins with black ribbons. Short wool capes covered their dark silk dresses, and they each carried a small carpetbag. Outside, Charles waited in the buggy to take them to the steamer landing in Waterloo. They were headed for New Orleans to collect our share of the Avegno gold. Mama had decided to take Valentine along for company. She was leaving me at home to help Grandmère and Charles.

I don't think I had ever seen Mama so happy. Her delicate face was luminous, and her beautiful eyes glistened as she kissed each of my cheeks. "Start packing your trunk, Mimi, we're going back to Paris!" she trilled.

"We just got here," I said, rubbing sleep from my eyes.

"I know, dear. But two weeks in the country seem like two years." She clasped Valentine's hand and floated out the door.

• • •

At a meeting with Papa's lawyers, Mama learned that her share of the Avegno gold amounted to seventy-five thousand dollars—more than enough to support us comfortably in Paris. "I'm rich!" she wired Grandmère. But her euphoria was short-lived.

I knew something was wrong the moment Mama stepped into the house on a cool, rainy afternoon a week later. Her pancake hat was askew on her head, and her skirts were muddy. Valentine lay inertly in her arms; the five-year-old child's pretty head was resting on Mama's shoulder.

"Is Valentine sick?" I asked, stroking my sister's back.

"She caught a chill on the steamer. I'm putting her to bed," Mama said.

The next morning, I awoke early and scurried to Valentine's room. The little girl was lying motionless in bed. "Valentine," I whispered, nudging her small, round arm. The skin burned under her cotton nightgown. "Mama!" I called. My mother ran into the room, followed by Alzea, who was carrying a pile of folded linen. Mama held her palm to Valentine's forehead. "Alzea, fetch Doctor Porter," she said, her voice edgy with fear.

When the bell rang an hour later, Mama was spooning broth into Valentine's mouth while I read to her from her favorite book, *La Belle histoire de Leuk-le-Lièvre,* a fable about a rabbit and his jungle friends. I heard a soft footfall on the hallway carpet, and then the short, squat figure of Dr. Porter appeared in the doorway. He greeted us cordially and set his satchel down next to Valentine's bed.

I hadn't seen him since Julie's suicide attempt, when he had come to the house to fit her with her steel back brace. He had grown stouter and balder, and the few hairs he had left on his head were now snowy white.

"How long has she been like this?" Dr. Porter asked. He hooked his thick spectacles over his ears and peered into Valentine's face. Mama recounted the morning's events and Dr. Porter took Valentine's temperature and felt her pulse. He moved his small hands, which had black tufts at the knuckles, over the glands in Valentine's neck and armpits, and he lifted her gown to examine her flesh, which was smooth but now had a sickly gray tinge. He pulled a syringe from his bag, filled it with silver nitrate, and jabbed it into Valentine's limp arm. She gasped and rose a bit as the needle went in, then sank back against the pillow, her tangled curls startlingly red against the white linen sheets embroidered with purple anemones.

"It's typhoid for certain. I saw four cases just this morning," Dr. Porter said. He unhinged his spectacles and slid them into his pocket. He snapped shut his black case and stood facing Mama.

"Will she be all right?" Mama asked. Her voice came out in a gulpy whisper.

"It'll be all right, Virginie," the doctor said. He squeezed Mama's shoulder. "I'll come back this afternoon to bleed her."

Dr. Porter returned at four carrying a strange metal contraption the size of a jewelry box. He placed it on the floor and sat at the edge of the bed. He tapped the length of Valentine's spine with his hands. I sat on the opposite side of the bed and held my sister's head as Dr. Porter placed the contraption on Valentine's back and pulled a lever to release a dozen tiny knives into the child's flesh. She yelped feebly, and I rubbed my cheek against hers in an effort to console her.

Dr. Porter removed the contraption and placed suction cups on Valentine's wounds. She cried out again as the blood was drawn out. Then she lay crumpled in the bed, moaning.

Dr. Porter returned every afternoon to reopen the gashes in Valentine's back and bleed her. The child's bed was soaked with blood, and I helped Alzea change and wash the sheets. Mama never left Valentine's side. She slept in a chair and said the Rosary over her every hour. But Valentine did not get better. Every day, she grew thinner and weaker.

One of my earliest memories is of the funeral of a little girl, a victim of scarlet fever, who lived on a neighboring plantation. I remember her small white face as she lay in her coffin, and how, when the pallbearers shut the lid, the child's sister, a much older girl, screamed and threw herself on the pine box. Her parents had to pull her away. It was my first experience of death, and it terrified me.

I couldn't bear to think of Valentine buried in the ground in a box. I tried to shake the image from my mind, but it kept sneaking in. It gave me nightmares. Ten days after Valentine first became ill, I awoke in the middle of the night to the sound of someone wailing. At first, I thought I was dreaming about the dead little girl. Then I realized the sound was real. Without lighting a candle, I ran down the black hallway to my sister's room. Mama, Grandmère, Julie, Alzea, and Charles were weeping around the small form in bed. Valentine was dead.

My knees buckled, and I collapsed on the floor. My sobs mingled with the others. "My baby sister! My baby sister!" I shrieked, over and over. I prayed to God to take me, too. I didn't care if I never grew up. Valentine and I would be happy children together for eternity in heaven.

Charles carried Mama out of the room. Then he returned and softly said to me, "Come, Mimi, Dr. Porter left something to help us sleep."

I took the medicine and awoke the following morning groggy and disoriented. I staggered to Valentine's room. Her bed was empty, stripped of all linens. Nearby, on three chairs pushed together and draped with white sheets, lay the body of my sister, dressed in a lace nightgown. While I wept at her side, Alzea slipped into the room and quietly tucked some greenery from the yard around the body.

The next day, Mama, Julie, and I took Valentine to New Orleans to be buried with Papa in the Avegno crypt at St. Louis Cemetery. Grandmère and Charles stayed behind to work in the sugarhouse. The weather was gray, rainy, and bleak, rare for a New Orleans fall. At the dock, men and women wore heavy wool clothes. The roses climbing the fences around the gates of Jackson Square and the leaves on the trees looked pathetic and limp.

Valentine was laid out for two days at the Maison du Mortuaire on Rampart Street. A stream of mourners, friends of my parents and grandparents, and my Avegno relatives filed past her tiny body, which was surrounded by white chrysanthemums. Rochilieu, who had come up from his plantation in Plaquemine, stood close to the casket with his arm around Mama. Once, a large glob of candle wax fell onto Valentine's forehead, and Rochilieu tenderly scraped it away with his fingers. Just before the mortician closed Valentine's casket, I placed the rosary Sister Emily-Jean had given me in my sister's cold, lifeless hands.

By the time we returned to Parlange two weeks later, the last cane stalks had been cut and ground, and the sugar had been packed into hogsheads. To save freight charges, Grandmère had arranged for a speculator from Cincinnati to buy the sugar directly from her. Still, the crop did not yield a sufficient price to cover the plantation's expenses. She had long ago sold her jewels and spent the money she had hidden in metal chests in the garden. After Grandmère paid the workers, there was little left. She had no choice but to ask Mama for a five-thousand-dollar loan, which Grandmère used to buy seed cane, repair the sugarhouse, and pay taxes.

No sooner was the last hogshead sold than Charles and Grandmère set to work repairing the ditches and fences, and laying the seed cane for next year's crop. I helped in the mornings, listlessly pushing myself through the motions of hammering and hoeing—all the while dreaming of a reunion with Valentine in heaven.

In the afternoons, I sat for Julie. She was painting a portrait of Valentine, working from a daguerreotype that had been taken in Paris. I posed for the coloring of flesh, hair, and clothes. Every day after lunch, we went to Julie's bedroom, which she had turned into a studio. Paints and brushes cluttered the dressing table; empty canvases leaned against the walls. Julie had removed the curtains so that light poured in, giving the mahogany furniture and gray walls a golden glow.

Julie posed me on a toile-covered fauteuil, wearing an old white chiffon dress of Mama's that Alzea had cut down to fit me. With a palette in one hand and a brush in the other, Julie perched at the end of her chair and painted briskly with long, vigorous sweeps. Sometimes she'd take up her crutches and hobble around the room to see how the light looked from different perspectives.

My limbs ached from holding them immobile for long stretches, but I tried not to complain. We took breaks every hour, and sometimes we talked as Julie painted. I told her about Farnsworth, about Aurélie's departure, about Mama's bizarre concern that my skin was darkening, about Dr. Chomel and his Solution. I had used up my last jars before we left Paris, and my face had returned to its former luster.

"Mimi, you have the most beautiful skin. The way the light catches it—sometimes casting a pink glow and at other times a blue shadow—is just extraordinary," said Julie. She held out a brushful of flesh-toned paint and squinted at me.

"Turn your head to the right, please. Ahh. Such a distinctive profile. You are a great beauty, *chérie*."

I knew I wasn't pretty like Mama and Valentine. My nose was too long, my chin too pointed, my forehead too high, my lips too thin. Yet, even at eleven, I was starting to sense I had something better than mere loveliness. By some strange alchemy, my features had combined into a face of extraordinary *interest*. That was why men stared at me, why Aurélie and Julie called me beautiful.

It took Julie two months to complete Valentine's portrait. When it was finished, Grandmère hung it over the parlor mantel—the first of Julie's pictures to be displayed. Valentine is frozen for all time in front of a window overlooking the garden. Dappled sunlight filters in, casting lavender and gray shadows in the folds of her frothy white dress. The blue ribbon around her neck echoes the color of the sky, and pink roses—Julie had painted them from memory—flash impression-istically in the background.

Mama loved the portrait. She created a little shrine on the mantel below it with flowers and candles, and moved the prie-dieu from her room in front of the fireplace. Every day, she prayed here for several hours, her head bent low over her rosary beads. Her tears fell silently, wetting the needlepoint hearth rug.

Mama had not mentioned Paris since Valentine's death, so I was surprised when she told me one morning in December that she had booked passage to France and we would be leaving in a week.

"I don't want to go," I protested.

"I can't stay at Parlange," she said. "Everything reminds me of Valentine."

Mama had no plans beyond using part of her inheritance to buy a house in a fashionable neighborhood and launching herself in society, which, she said, meant getting to know the best people and being invited to their parties. It seemed like a waste of time to me.

The thought of leaving Parlange filled me with distress. I had set-tled in so happily that now I couldn't imagine life off the plantation. What would I do without fields to roam in and a garden to play in? What would I do without Julie?

I'll never forget how quiet the house was on the cool, sunny Sunday morning when we left. Mama and I ate breakfast alone in the dining room while Julie, Grandmère, and Charles went to town for services at St. Joseph's Church. Our metal trunks, lying next to each other in the dim hall, looked like coffins. I thought of Papa and Valentine and gulped back a large sob.

From the dining room windows, I saw the buggy rattle up to the house. Charles helped Grandmère and Julie to the front gallery, where they settled themselves in wicker chairs. Then he loaded our trunks into the buggy and strode into the dining room.

"We better get going, ladies, if you want to make that one o'clock steamer."

We rose from the table and went to the gallery. Grandmère and Julie stood to embrace us. Julie was leaning on her canes. "Take care of Valentine's portrait for me," Mama said.

At the mention of Valentine's name, Grandmère began to sob. I had only seen her cry twice before. The first time was when we left Parlange, during the war, and the second time was at Valentine's deathbed. Then she had wept quietly, modestly. Now her tears came in a great, noisy torrent.

She had survived so much—the deaths of her husbands and two of her children, the war. Those tragedies had somehow hardened her will to endure. But she was an old woman now, with creaky joints and liver spots on her cheeks. She thought of Parlange as a refuge, a nest in which her family could gather for comfort and protection. Valentine's death had shattered her.

Mama and I climbed into the buggy next to Charles. He snapped the reins, and the two brown mares trotted off. Grandmère leaned against the railing, her chest heaving, her face contorted with sobs. Turning and waving, I watched Grandmère as the buggy rattled down the alley of oaks, until she disappeared into a blurry dark form between the gallery's tall white posts.

Four

Following an uneventful crossing to Le Havre, Mama and I boarded a train for Paris, arriving on a cold night at Gare Montparnasse. We took a cab to a small Right Bank hotel, the Albion, left our trunks with the concierge, and went to the dining room, where a fire crackled in an enormous stone hearth. Settling ourselves at a table by the window, we ordered the bouillabaise and ate silently.

Our room on the third floor was a cramped space just big enough for a chair and a small four-poster. That night, Mama and I slept side by side under a heavy, flowered cotton quilt. The next morning, we awoke refreshed, donned clean frocks and warm jackets, and set off for a walk along the boulevards.

It was a frigid day, though clear and sunny, and after a half hour our toes and fingers stung with numbness. At the Palais Royal, we ducked into a restaurant for coffee and croissants and visited several shops. Mama bought each of us a wool shawl and herself a fox-fur pelisse. Then we boarded an omnibus headed in the direction of the Couvent des Dames Anglaises.

We were on our way to talk to Mother Superior about my reen-rollment. At first, Mama had insisted I attend Sacré-Coeur, the most fashionable girls' school in Paris. She thought hobnobbing with the mothers of little nobles would make her more elegant. But I had put up such a storm of protest at the idea of a new school that she finally agreed to send me back to the English nuns.

The omnibus clattered along the new asphalt boulevards, past the old, crooked side streets with their small shops and high shuttered houses. Fifteen minutes later, we arrived at rue des Fossés-Saint-Victor. We stepped to the curb and walked a block north. My eyes darted up and down the street in search of the convent's entrance. Gone. In place of the dear old buildings was a vast triangular lot filled with rubble. Next to it, at the spot I gauged to have been the nuns' mint garden, was a circular pit—what I later learned was the ruins of an ancient arena, the Arènes de Lutèce. The site had been buried for twelve centuries; no one knew it existed until the convent was destroyed.

I ran toward a group of men who were bowed under heavy coats, their breath steaming in the cold. They stood in the rubble, consulting a long scroll.

"What happened to the convent?" I cried.

"It was razed last month on orders from Baron Haussmann," said one man. "We're putting a street through here."

"Where are the nuns?"

"I'm not sure," said the man through his ice-spangled mustache. "I heard they were relocated outside Paris."

The thought of never seeing Sister Emily-Jean again, of never playing in the lovely garden with the old wishing well and the statue of the Virgin, triggered a fresh sorrow, and tears sprang from my eyes. As I stumbled away, a shard of red glass flashed in the rubble beneath my feet—a piece of one of the chapel windows. I picked it up and put it in my jacket pocket.

Mama was standing on the corner with her small fists digging into her hips. "Well, I guess you're going to Sacré-Coeur after all," she said triumphantly.

"I'm not!" I shouted.

"You will do as I say, Mademoiselle."

"I will not. You can't force me."

I ran toward the tree-dotted place de la Contrescarpe, past the flower sellers and the dingy cafés. I ran and ran, down the steep pitch of the rue Mouffetard, dodging pedestrians and baby prams. Two stocky matrons who were walking with linked arms cried, *"Mon Dieu!"* as I sped toward them, and they swooped apart to let me pass.

"Mimi! Mimi!" Mama called after me. I turned and saw her about a block behind. She was running, holding her skirt up with one hand while she held on to her feathered hat with the other. I picked up my pace but tripped on my hem and stumbled in front of Plessy's tobacco shop. A second later, Mama caught up to me and grabbed my jacket sleeve. She slapped me hard across the face. I slapped her back.

A few passersby, appalled at the sight of a mother and daughter publicly fighting, stopped and whispered to one another behind gloved hands. A tear rolled down one of the red stripes that blotched Mama's left cheek. Her eyes burned into mine, and she spat her words: "I *used* to have a daughter."

Over the next few weeks, Mama and I saw little of each other. Most days, I would stay in our tiny room, reading and writing letters to the family at Parlange. Mama wandered Paris in search of a permanent home for us. Eventually she settled on a large, elegant three-story house—a *hôtel particulier*—at 44, rue de Luxembourg, in the heart of the faubourg Saint-Honoré, a gleaming neighborhood of freshly paved streets, new stone buildings, and trimmed trees, not far from the Madeleine.

The double parlor and dining room had trompe l'oeil ceilings painted with dancing cherubs, and elaborate paneling carved with garlands and birds. Mama filled the house with red-and-blue velvet upholstery, billowing taffeta draperies, gilt mirrors, crystal chandeliers, china, silver, and marble busts—a sumptuous decor that used up a great deal of her inheritance. Indeed, after buying and decorating the house—a fit setting, she believed, from which to launch herself into French society—we had left an income of thirty thousand francs a year, about what a bourgeois doctor earned.

Servants were cheap—a month's wages for a maid was equivalent to the price of a bottle of table wine—so Mama was able to hire a staff:

two footmen who boarded out, a driver who bunked in a room in the carriage house, and three maids who lived in cramped rooms under the eaves. But our budget for clothes, food, and entertaining would be tight.

After considering her finances, Mama decided I didn't need to go to Sacré-Coeur after all, or, in fact, any other school. At my age—eleven—she announced at breakfast one morning, "a girl has all the education she needs."

I was ecstatic at the thought of no more school. What child wouldn't be? I envisioned a life of sleeping late, reading romances, and wandering Paris whenever I wanted. The fact that not going to school would mean I'd have little chance to meet friends my own age, or that it would push me into adult activities before I was ready, didn't occur to me. When I did think of friends, of course, I thought of Aurélie, and always with deep regret. I wondered what had become of her, and I longed to see her again.

Since I had musical talent, Mama decided I should continue piano lessons, and she hired as my teacher a middle-aged man named Edward Vaury. He showed up for my first lesson on a Wednesday morning. I was waiting for him in the main parlor, and a minute after I heard the bell ring, the maid brought me his card. Monsieur Vaury turned out to be a short, round man dressed in an ill-fitting black suit that was shiny with age. "Bonjour, Mademoiselle, I'm very pleased to meet you," he said, bending stiffly at the waist.

"It's my pleasure, Monsieur."

As a little boy growing up in Vienna, Monsieur Vaury had been taught by a student of Beethoven's, and he resembled the great composer, at least superficially. The top of his long head was bald, while a semicircle of sparse gray hair sprouted from just above his ears and fell in a frizzle to his shoulders. He was the only man I knew in those days who didn't have a mustache—perhaps he was *trying* to look like Beethoven—and he wore thick, round spectacles that slid down his fleshy nose.

"Well, let's see what you can do. What would you like to play?" he asked, pushing his spectacles in place with a curled forefinger.

I volunteered to try Chopin and from memory played the Polonaise in A Major.

"Very good, my dear," said Monsieur Vaury, clapping his dry red hands. "I heard a few wrong notes. But never mind. Now let's see how your sight reading is."

He fumbled in his case and placed several yellowed sheets on the music stand. It was the difficult third movement of Beethoven's "Moonlight" Sonata. I struggled through the first measures—I had never played it before—striking many wrong notes, faltering, and finally giving up.

"Not bad for a first try," Monsieur Vaury encouraged. "You can work on it this week."

He put me on a rigorous schedule of scales and finger exercises. The grand piano in the parlor had a clear, beautiful tone, but I preferred to practice on the spinet in the privacy of my blue toile-walled sitting room. The piano stood between two windows fronting rue de Luxembourg. With the shutters open, I could hear the hooves of cab horses lightly clicking along the smooth asphalt, a pleasing metronome.

Here, at the piano in my room, I did not feel Papa's and Valentine's deaths as crushingly as I had everywhere else. The harmony and rhythm of music eased my sadness and pushed me back toward optimism, my natural temperament. I practiced as much as I could, sometimes for four or five hours a day.

Monsieur Vaury marveled at my progress. He rarely criticized me, though one morning after I had been studying with him for about two years—a period during which I had grown two inches and sprouted breasts—he complained about my fingering in Chopin's Etude in E Major. "Mademoiselle, you should not be using the one and the four in the right hand. Try the one and the two. Then you can reach up with the five to hit that G." He was sitting next to me on the padded piano bench, and now he swung his right arm across my back and placed his hand on top of mine. He arranged my fingers under his in the desired position and pressed my hand into the keys. A lovely inverted E chord splashed into the air.

"There. Much better," he said.

He released my hand but did not shift his weight, so that he was still leaning into me. I felt his stale breath on my neck. Then he moved his hand to my shoulder and stroked it slowly. I leaned as far as I could to the side while still keeping my fingers on the keys. But he moved even closer. A lock of his stiff gray hair fell across my cheek. I shuddered.

Later, after he left, I told Mama what had happened.

"I'm sure you're imagining it," she said.

"I'm not! He's a lecherous buffoon. I wouldn't be surprised if we saw him one night at Velfour's with a *fille publique* from La Farcy's brothel."

"Mimi!" Mama's eyes widened.

"Besides, he isn't a very good pianist. I don't care if he studied with Beethoven's student. He has no ear, no true feeling for music. I would like another teacher. Or no teacher. I can work on my own."

But Mama refused to dismiss Monsieur Vaury, because he also taught Princess Mathilde's nephew. I don't know how Mama hoped to benefit from this weak connection to Napoleonic royalty, but one of her chief ambitions was to secure an invitation to the Princess's salon at her palatial hotel on rue de Courcelles.

The following week, I began a campaign to drive Monsieur Vaury away. I refused to smile at him, ignored his compliments, and spoke to him as little as possible. No matter how coldly and unpleasantly I behaved, however, his ardor grew. He stared adoringly at me. Sometimes he was so moved by my playing that he would grab my hands and cover them with kisses. Other times, he stretched his long ape's arm across the back of the piano bench, which led inevitably to his touching my shoulder. Then one day, as I finished playing Schubert's Sonata in C Minor, he moved his hand to the back of my neck and stroked it lasciviously. I vowed to get rid of him.

For several days, I thought of little else, but by the time of my next scheduled lesson, I had not come up with a suitable solution. Then, as I waited for Monsieur Vaury in the parlor, my eyes wandered toward the Louis XVI secretary near the fireplace. Suddenly I had an idea. I grabbed the sheet music off the piano stand, unlocked the door of the secretary, and removed a pen and bottle of ink. Holding my right hand steady with my left hand, I drew in two flats in the third and eighth measures on the first page. Just as I finished, the bell rang, and I heard the maid's heels clacking across the floor. I dashed toward the piano, replaced the sheet music, and flopped into a settee. My heart was hammering in my chest.

Monsieur Vaury stepped into the room. His smile showed a jumble of large, knobby teeth. "Good afternoon, Mademoiselle. How is the Chopin coming?"

"You be the judge," I said sweetly.

I arranged myself on the piano bench and spread my skirt out so as to leave no room for the dry old man. But Monsieur Vaury pushed the folds of green faille aside with his forearm and slid onto the bench beside me.

I began to play. Monsieur Vaury stopped me in the fifth measure. "Excuse me, Mademoiselle. This is the key of E major, so that B is not flatted."

"But the composer *has* flatted it." I tried to sound innocent.

Monsieur Vaury blinked and squinted at the music as I continued to play. A minute later, he stopped me again.

"Mademoiselle, you have flatted another B."

"I know, Monsieur. It is flatted in the music."

"I've played this piece a thousand times, Mademoiselle. You are striking the wrong note."

"Look for yourself, Monsieur." I pointed to the music.

Monsieur Vaury pushed his spectacles over his head and leaned toward the music stand, scrunching his forehead and narrowing his eyes to study the altered notes. "What do we have here?"

He recoiled from the music stand and stiffened his back. "I knew it! These flats have been drawn in!" He stared at me severely.

"Are you accusing me?" I said, coquettishly moving my hand to the base of my throat. I was enjoying his discomfort.

"Who else? Do you see anyone else in the room?" Monsieur Vaury's jowls twitched, and he shook his gray strings of hair. "I won't have this type of thing, Mademoiselle Avegno. I'm a serious musician. I won't waste my time with foolishness."

He jumped to his feet and began gathering up his music, muttering that women were weak, vain creatures, that we were all deceitful wretches, and that he was glad he had never married.

Mama later wrote Monsieur Vaury an apologetic letter imploring him to come back. He refused. We were not only silly women, he explained to her, but also Americans—in his view, a hopeless combination.

At the time, an influx of nouveau-riche Americans had descended on Paris, and their loud, spendthrift ways had sparked waves of resentment among the French. Suddenly everyone from the United States was seen as pushy and vulgar, a prejudice that severely hindered Mama's social ambitions.

Above all, she aspired to the aristocratic society of old France. She wanted to be invited to dinner parties in the faubourg Saint-Germain, to have lunch with duchesses and vicomtesses, and to attend weekend parties at châteaux in the Loire Valley, where everyone's name was in *Almanach de Gotha.*

She had hoped that her grandfather's title of marquis and the noble particle in her maiden name would give her entrée to the best homes. But it had been generations since the de Ternant name had been attached to a landed estate, and Mama's ancestry no longer counted for anything in France.

Though the faubourg Saint-Germain was almost impossible for Americans to penetrate, Louis-Napoléon's court at the Tuileries was not. He had staged a coup d'état that made him Emperor in 1852, four years after he had been elected President of France, and his rule was marked by a love of pleasure and display that was far more extravagant than anything the original Napoléon had countenanced fifty years earlier. This was the era of spectacular imperial balls, glorious hunting parties, grand military reviews, and huge universal exhibitions. The Emperor was perfectly happy to include Americans in court festivities—as long as they were either fabulously rich or celebrities. Mama was neither.

Still, she aspired to be invited to Princess Mathilde's salon. A niece of Napoléon I and an intimate of the Emperor's, Mathilde was the chief link between the faubourg and Louis-Napoléon's court. At the Princess's *hôtel* on rue de Courcelles, the old aristocracy mingled with the most famous celebrities and the best minds of France. At Mathilde's salon, a guest might meet the composers Saint-Saëns and Gounod, the scientist Louis Pasteur, and the writers Emile Zola and Gustave

Flaubert. Sometimes the Emperor and Empress themselves showed up, as well as the brightest lights of the demimonde—actresses, actors, even occasionally a dazzling courtesan.

Once, while riding through the Bois de Boulogne, Mama and I saw Princess Mathilde. She drove past us in an open carriage, wearing a string of black pearls over her ample bosom. She wasn't as old as I had expected, but she was short and fat with the same imperious dark-eyed face as her famous uncle's.

That was the closest Mama would ever get to French nobility. Still, Mama's beauty made her a sought-after guest in the homes of the wealthier American expatriates and the newly rich bankers and manu-facturers who were our neighbors.

In this crowd, her social ascent had been swift. She had invitations to dinner and the theater several times a week, and her own receptions drew dozens of people. The first one was held on a warm Monday in June, three years after we moved into our *hôtel*. Carriages began lining up outside our door at four, and by five the street was clogged with landaus, victorias, fiacres, and coupés. Two wigged footmen in pink-and-black livery received Mama's guests in the marbled foyer, which was filled with potted palms, and led them upstairs.

A garden had grown from the packet of Louisiana seeds I had planted in the small plot at the back of the house, and the scent of camellias, parmelee violets, and magnolias—the scents of Parlange—drifted in through the open French doors. Candles flickered in silver sconces, and the soft pearly light of a Parisian summer afternoon slanted in through the windows, infusing the room with a rosy glow.

Mama held court in a chair covered in pink silk that matched the footmen's livery. I sat opposite her, in a gray satin dress trimmed with silver beads. A small fan of white feathers lay folded in my lap. I had put my hair up for the first time that day, twisting the heavy auburn mass into a roll and pinning it up at the back of my head. Mama had wanted me to add some fake curls at the temples, but I refused. I thought the simple twist looked elegant, and it set off the long white curve of my neck.

Soon our parlor was overflowing with bloated, blotched old men and their wrinkled wives, ugly in trailing dresses, their hair splashed with gold powder that unconvincingly covered the gray. Madame Slidell had brought two artists, minor painters who were skinny and badly dressed and who sat in the corner near the buffet table gobbling up Mama's caviar.

One member of the nobility, Baroness Micaela de Pontalba, showed up—though actually she was an American from New Orleans. Old and reeking of patchouli, she had a two-fingered stump for a left hand, the result of a wound she had received in 1834, when her father-in-law, enraged because she had withheld her inheritance from his son, had tried to shoot her to death. Still, Mama fussed over her because she had a title. "You're looking well, Baroness!" she enthused when the decrepit woman lumbered into the room, wearing a black crepe dress over an old-fashioned cage.

I was the accompanist for a pudgy brown-haired young tenor Mama had hired to perform. He sang William Tell's "Sombre Forêt" and Schubert's "Serenade" with one hand resting over his heart. Then I played two solos—a Chopin nocturne and a Mozart sonata.

Afterward I rose and took a bow with the singer. As I crossed the room to resume my perch near the fireplace, two puffy, perfumed dowagers eyed me enviously. "Don't worry, she'll fade someday," I heard one whisper to her friend.

As I turned around to glare back at them, I bumped into a spindly table that held an expensive porcelain clock. The table shook, and the clock tumbled to the parquet and shattered. "Oh, no," I groaned as one of the maids rushed to gather the jagged shards.

"Never mind, dear. It was a Louis, and a particularly ugly one at that." I looked up to see a slender black-haired man tuning the right end of his enormous mustache. He was dressed immaculately in a gray topcoat and striped trousers, with a lavender cravat tied neatly against his white silk shirt.

"A what?"

"A Louis. An object inspired by the ancien régime. Never in the history of the world has there been such hideous taste."

I was so used to Mama's gilt mirrors, crystal chandeliers, and flounced poufs that it never occurred to me they might be hideous. But I sensed immediately that the man was right. Around the room, the curvy legs and clawed feet on the furniture, the tasseled taffeta draperies puddled on the floor, the bright textured upholstery, looked fatally fussy, like the parlor in my dollhouse at Parlange.

The man read my reaction and smiled. "I'm Pierre Gautreau," he said.

"I'm Virginie Avegno. Would you like to show me what else you hate about our decor?"

"I'd be delighted."

For the next half hour, I toured the house with Monsieur Gautreau. Occasionally he commented on a painting or a piece of furniture. But mostly he asked me about our life in Louisiana. And he told me about himself. He had been raised on a large estate in Paramé outside the ancient walled city of Saint-Malo on France's northern coast. His mother belonged to a wealthy ship-owning family, and one of his uncles ran a lucrative business exporting guano from the islands off the coast of Chile. As a teenager, Monsieur Gautreau moved to Chile and grew rich working in his uncle's export business. Recently he had returned to France and settled in Paris, where he established an investment firm. He lived in a small *hôtel* at 80, rue Jouffroy and presided over his family estate at Paramé, the Château des Chênes.

Over the next few months, Mama and I saw a great deal of the cooly elegant Pierre Gautreau. He came to all of our Mondays and was always the first to arrive, stepping from his carriage a few minutes before four, dressed exquisitely in a gray top hat and a cashmere coat, his ivory-topped walking cane cocked on his shoulder. Within no time, Mama was addressing him with the familiar "*tu,*" and we were both calling him Pierre.

At thirty-three, Pierre was a year younger than Mama, and they became instant friends. There was much to draw them together. Both had grown up in the country, yet loathed rural life. Both were materialistic and worldly. Both were ardent social climbers whose love of society was eclipsed only by their passion for house decoration.

Whereas Mama's taste ran to the fashionable and pretentious, Pierre's was sophisticated and well in advance of his time. He loved anything Oriental, an interest that perhaps was sparked by recent political events. A trove of Japanese furniture, china, fabric, and art showed up on the European market in 1868, after the Mikado, tired of being a mere figurehead emperor, seized power. The ensuing revolution ruined Japan's old feudal families, many of whom were forced to sell off their treasures. Pierre was among the first in France to collect them.

He never liked anything inspired by the French Louis. He thought their style silly and frivolous (and also politically problematic). He soon persuaded Mama to sell her Louis XIV fauteuils, Louis XV chandeliers, and Louis XVI *boiseries*. He allowed her to keep only one Louis in the public rooms, a high-backed chair inspired by the relatively benign era of Louis XIII. Mama insisted that our boudoirs remain conventionally French. "I can't go to sleep unless I see a bit of toile," she said.

Pierre convinced Mama to put her money into japonaiseries, and within a year our house was transformed. Now, in the foyer, parlors, and dining room, instead of gilt mirrors, elaborately painted ceilings, heavily carved furniture, and sumptuous upholstery—a *"tous les Louis"* decor, as Pierre put it—we had bare ceilings, silk-covered walls, and Japanese screens, prints, and china.

Each room was dominated by a few exquisite pieces carefully chosen by Pierre. The entrance hall held an ancient Japanese incense bowl atop a round fourteenth-century table from a Tokyo palace. The salon featured a large harp and a collection of Oriental urns arranged on a tapestry-covered chest. The dining room walls were covered in jade silk, and standing in the four corners were painted screens of Japanese scenes.

Most of Mama's friends, especially the old Creole expatriates, were shocked at the decor. But a few collectors with advanced taste who attended her salon praised the house extravagantly. Soon people clamored for invitations to Mama's Mondays, eager to get a look. Even a few curious reporters showed up.

One Monday, after I had performed several piano pieces for Mama's guests, a dark, birdlike woman, expensively clad in high-necked red satin, floated toward me carrying an open notebook and a gold pen that was encrusted with four fat diamonds. She had a long, bumpy nose and thin, colorless lips set in a narrow olive-skinned face. A nest of coarse black hair sat on her head over a thick fringe of bangs. Yet her eyes were beautiful, long-lashed and sparkly black, and they radiated intelligence and charm. I thought she was the most attractive ugly woman I had ever met.

Everyone called her Etincelle, and she wrote a popular column, "Carnet d'un Mondain," that ran every Thursday on the front page of *Le Figaro*. Etincelle was one of those celebrities whose personality was so strong and distinctive that she needed only one name.

She had been born Henrietta-Marie Biard d'Aurnet to an old aristocratic family that owned an enormous crenellated château with vast lands in Burgundy. At seventeen, she had been married to the Vicomte de Perrony, whose aristocratic lineage was even older and more illustrious than hers. The vicomte died soon after the wedding, however, and Madame de Perrony never again showed an interest in men. She stayed on in Perrony's grand *hôtel* on rue Beaujon and took up writing for the newspapers. In addition to her column for *Le Figaro,* she wrote for a gaggle of illustrated journals, under a variety of names—Marie Double, Bonne, Henriette d'Isle, and Georges de Letoière.

Now Etincelle was standing before me, holding her notebook opened, poised to write. "I enjoyed your playing very much, Mademoiselle. Who's your teacher?"

"I don't have one. I study on my own."

"Such discipline in one so young and pretty!"

"Well, I've always studied on my own. Even when I was at school, I practiced a couple of hours every day."

"What school was that, dear?"

"Le Couvent des Dames Anglaises, on the Montagne Sainte-Geneviève. It's been torn down."

"Oh, yes, another victim of Haussmannia. I lost half my garden to one of his boulevards. Such a shame."

Etincelle scribbled in her notebook, then closed it shut and extended a thin, red satin arm. "I'm sure we will meet again, dear."

The next morning at seven—four hours before I usually rose—Mama shook me awake. As I opened my eyes, she waved a folded copy of *Le Figaro* in front of me. "Look at this, Mimi," she said excitedly, pointing to the fourth column on the front page. "It's unbelievable. Etincelle never writes about Americans!"

"Yesterday at Madame Avegno's," the article said,

I met the charming American woman's daughter, Virginie Amélie. She is an Ingres portrait brought to life, tall and graceful with an undulating swan's neck, whiter than white skin and masses of lustrous red hair (why is it American women have so much hair?).

In addition to possessing otherworldly physical beauty, Mademoiselle Avegno is a pianist of extraordinary talent. Yesterday she played Mozart and Beethoven. One could dream while listening to her. Her long, thin fingers fluttered like wings as they made the ivories vibrate in tender song.

Etincelle returned to Mama's salon the following Monday and every Monday after that, and she rarely failed to write about me in her "Carnet d'un Mondain." It didn't take long for the other society reporters in town to discover me, too. Soon they started showing up at Mama's Mondays, and I became the ornament and focus of dozens of columns in the popular press. The stories were all about my unique, exquisite beauty. I can assure you, there were other girls in town far prettier than I. But once an influential reporter writes something about you, all the other reporters jump on the bandwagon. Etincelle anointed me *the* Parisian beauty, and suddenly everyone wanted to meet me. Invitations poured in, including a few from the old Faubourg families Mama wanted so desperately to know. She insisted I accept every one.

My mother saw me as her ticket to the top, and she pushed me relentlessly. It never occurred to me to resist. I became caught up in an endless round of teas, lunches, dinners, receptions, parties, and balls. I was too busy to notice that I had no friends my age. Most of the people I met were old and boring, but somehow it didn't matter, because I was the center of attention. At fourteen, it's a heady experience to be told constantly how beautiful you are, to have men fawning over you and women eying you jealously. I loved it, and I began to expect it.

Whenever I entered a room, heads would lift and turn in my direction. People would murmur as I walked past. Sometimes, at parties, they would actually stand on chairs to get a better look at me.

Every night during the high season—from November to May— my *carnet de bal* was filled with noble names. After I danced with the duc de Rivaulde three evenings in a row, Mama began to dream of being a mother-in-law to nobility. I was barely into my teens, and already she was scheming to marry me off to a title.

There was some grumbling in the press about the inappropriateness of a girl my age appearing at every reception and ball in town. But many people assumed I was older than I was. Dressed up and wearing makeup, I *looked* twenty-five. I had reached my full height of five feet six inches, and my face and form had taken on the contours of womanhood.

Mama insisted that I dress elegantly, and we had endless battles over my toilette. Also, she insisted I go back on Chomel's Solution. She had gone to the doctor for a fresh supply of jars, and one night she stood by my high canopied bed with a spoonful of the sticky blue liquid in her hand.

"Open your mouth, Mimi," she ordered.

"I won't. It makes me sick."

"Don't forget who the mother is here."

I threw off the cream silk sheets and jumped to my feet. "I won't take it!"

I grabbed the spoon from Mama's hand and flung it into a corner by the armoire. Mama slapped me across the face; I slapped her back. "Don't ever touch me again!" I shouted.

Fortunately, Mama gave up on the Chomel's. The following week, however, she brought me some *blanc d'herbe* powder from the pharmacy. It was composed of mashed carbonate of lead mixed with a pomade made from veal grease and beef marrow. Mama showed me how to apply it in layers by patting a sponge in the grains and then daubing several layers of it on my face and shoulders. It lightened the skin well enough, but it smelled horrendous. Next we tried *blanc de perle,* an odorless powder containing the metallic chemical bismuth and bicarbonate of soda. That combination gave a bright whiteness to my skin. I use *blanc de perle* to this day.

At that time in Paris, the fashionable women who could afford it were dressed by the couturier Charles Frederick Worth. Mama longed to have him make my clothes as well. The problem was, Monsieur Worth was so busy, and so snobbish, one needed an introduction to enter his atelier. Etincelle was more than happy to provide it, and one morning Mama and I joined the long line of carriages outside 7, rue de la Paix, headquarters for Maison Worth.

We left the carriage with our driver, mounted the red-carpeted stairs, and entered a large foyer. Beyond, a series of salons opened off a long hall. Large glass cabinets in the first salon displayed black-and-white silks; in the second, colored silks; in the third, velvets; and in the fourth, woolens.

In the fifth salon, the tall windows were shuttered against the daylight. Soft candlelight flickered from crystal wall sconces so that customers could try on ball gowns in the same lighting they would find at parties.

Dozens of salesmen wandered throughout. Most were handsome young Englishmen with curled hair and pearl tiepins. A few beautiful models slid by in bursts of glittery tulle and jewel-colored satin.

In the waiting room, a dozen women sat on divans sipping Madeira and listening to a young man play Verdi on a grand piano. A thin middle-aged woman who was dressed like a schoolmistress, in a simple black skirt and white blouse, handed us a ticket, and we sat down.

An hour later, she returned and called our names. "Come with me," the woman said.

We followed her down the hall to a large room that was plainly decorated but well lit. Women were standing in front of tall mirrors against the walls while fitters pulled, tucked, and pinned their dresses.

Posed at the center was a short, stout man with droopy-lidded eyes like Emperor Napoléon's, and a wheat-colored brush mustache. His face seemed to have collapsed. His nose lay squished between his eyes, and his jowls disappeared into the fleshy folds of his neck. He was dressed like the portrait of Rembrandt at the Louvre—velvet beret, floppy silk scarf tied at the neck, and flowing cape, which he swept aside with his arms as he screamed at the beautiful woman who stood before him.

"Why do you wear those ugly gloves? Never let me see you in gloves that color again," he shrieked.

Hanging her head, the woman yanked the offensive brown items from her hands and stuffed them into her pocket. I thought she was going to cry.

Monsieur Worth turned to Mama. "By whom are you presented to me?"

"I have a letter from Madame la Vicomtesse de Perrony." Hands trembling slightly, Mama removed the letter from her purse and passed it to Worth.

He held the beige paper at arm's length and scanned it quickly. Then he looked Mama over, moving his eyes from the top of her head to her black buckled shoes. "Ah, yes, Madame. I know exactly what will look well on you. It will be easy to dress such a lovely woman."

Mama blushed and smiled softly. "It would be an honor to be dressed by you, Monsieur. But first, I had hoped you'd create something for my daughter."

Mama stepped back so Monsieur Worth could get a better look at me. His sleepy lizard eyes opened a bit, and a sigh escaped through his mustache. "Beautiful. Beautiful. Walk across the room please, Mademoiselle."

I obeyed, enjoying the admiration of this important man.

"Turn. Now the other way."

As I paraded and twirled, Monsieur Worth studied me, squinting and stroking the wrinkled folds of flesh where his chin should have been. "Come back in eight days," he announced abruptly. "Your dress will be ready."

Pierre Gautreau had offered to buy the dress for me as a present. On a cold, rainy evening, he took me in his carriage to pick it up, after treating me to dinner at Tortoni's. The low scudding clouds disappeared into blackness as we arrived at 7, rue de la Paix. It was nine o'clock, an hour before Worth closed his shop. A few salesmen scurried about, locking cabinets and stacking bolts of cloth on shelves. Through the parted curtains of the brocade salon, I glimpsed an army of seamstresses—gray-faced girls, some far younger than I, slouched over rows of sewing machines.

Worth was in the fitting room, talking to a short brunette in a pink gown trimmed in black fringe. When he saw Pierre and me, he waddled over on stocky legs to greet us.

"Bonsoir. Mademoiselle Avegno, your dress is waiting." He cocked his head toward a folding screen in the corner. I stepped behind it. A prune velvet gown, overlaid with tinseled tulle and dotted with pearls and gold beads, lay across a settee. I studied the garment as I undid the buttons on my jacket. It was too flounced and bedecked, and though the color might have looked fine on a blonde, it was wrong for a redhead. Morosely, I fastened the bodice and dropped the skirt, which had WORTH 7, RUE DE LA PAIX stamped in gold ink on the waistband, over my head.

Then I stepped from behind the screen. *"Un rêve!"* cried Worth.

"How much for this masterpiece?" asked Pierre.

"Two thousand francs," said Worth.

Pierre looked stunned. "That's quite a sum." He dropped into a chair and removed his checkbook from a pocket inside his coat.

"I am an artist, Monsieur. I have Delacroix's sense of color and form."

Pierre stopped writing and looked up. "For the price of this dress, I could buy her a Delacroix instead."

When I got home, I showed Mama the gown. She looked disappointed, too. "I never would have picked that color for you," she said.

"I know. It's ugly."

"Well, Monsieur Worth knows what he's doing. Let's see how you look in it."

I put the dress on and modeled it for Mama.

"I like it much better now," she said, as if to convince herself.

The following Saturday evening, I wore the prune velvet gown to a reception at the Ministry of Public Instruction. I thought it made my skin look chalky and my hair a dull brown, but that didn't stop the Paris correspondent for the *London Truth* from writing about me in his column the next day. Pierre picked up a copy of the paper at his club and brought it to our house after lunch. Under the headline, "La Belle Américaine: A New Star of Occidental Loveliness Swims into the Ken of Parisian Society," the paper's Paris correspondent wrote:

I am not going to chat with you about the crowned virago, Queen Elizabeth. The western star on whom I am about to descant has just risen from above the horizon. Of all the beauties I have ever seen, she is in face, form, hair, and complexion the most beautiful. My western star is Venus rising from the waves . . . in the country of George Washington.

Her head is classical, and she wears her natural wavy hair in Grecian bandeaux. If her nose were an atom shorter, one might admire it more, still I cannot say it is too long to be out of proportion with the other features, which her dress sets off.

At first sight, one is literally stunned by her beauty. Mademoiselle Virginie Amélie Avegno is a Canova statue transmitted into flesh and blood and bone and muscle. All her contours are harmonious. . . . A murmur of admiration greeted her wherever she went. The crowd opened, as if awe-struck with her beauty, to let her pass.

"The nerve! 'If her nose were an atom shorter.' Who does he think he is, passing judgment on my face!" I complained.

"You're lucky he noticed you," said Mama. "He could have written about the duchesse de Noailles instead. I saw her dancing with the prince de Ligne, and she was wearing the most beautiful white dress."

"Your mother's right. It's a huge compliment that he chose to write about you," said Pierre.

"Well, if I see him again, I'm going to cross my eyes and stick my tongue out at him. Then we'll see if he notices my nose and my lips."

The *London Truth* correspondent was a friend of the Minister of the Marine, and perhaps that's why I was asked to participate in the Marine Ministry's "Four Continents" ball in March. There were to be four corteges, representing Africa, America, Asia, and Europe, each featuring a celebrated beauty. I would star as America.

On the appointed evening, while a thousand guests enjoyed an eight-course banquet in the cavernous ballroom, a long procession of corteges threaded through a dim maze of corridors. At midnight, two butlers threw open the ballroom doors, and the thunder of voices stilled, as the gas lights from dozens of chandeliers rose.

Africa, played by the Minister of the Marine's young brunette wife, entered first. She rode in on a camel borrowed from the Jardin des Plantes. Following her were dozens of male "natives" wearing enormous black wool wigs and brightly colored sarongs.

Europe was next. The beautiful Duchess Laure Castellian was carried in on a throne covered in pink and purple flowers. She was dressed in a brocade gown covered with gold beading, and a diamond-and-gold tiara rested in her yellow curls. Trailing her were a gaggle of "peasants," Germans in leather vests and feathered caps, Italians in Roman togas, and Dutchmen in wooden clogs.

Then it was Asia's turn. An actress from La Comédie Française stood on a wheeled platform pulled by eight men hunched under animal skins. Dressed in ballerina tights and a leopard-skin tunic, she balanced a slippered foot on the back of a live tiger, while holding on to a fake tree.

Finally I was brought in, reclining on a hammock that was fastened to a wood platform. I was dressed as Pocahontas in a white leather sheath, a black wig with two long braids draped over my breasts, and a warrior's headdress of brightly colored cascading feathers. Following me was a parade of "Americans"—Puritans in wide white collars and large-brimmed black hats; plantation tyrants cracking whips; Mexican banderilleros with huge slouched hats and pistols bulging from their belts.

I struggled to keep my headdress in place while balancing in the swaying hammock. Sweat beaded my face and chest, and my stomach churned from the hammock's rocking. I looked into the crowd and recognized many people I had met at Mama's Mondays and seen in society. Wasn't that Dr. Tom Evans, the Empress's dentist, sitting with Mama and Pierre?

Now I had lost my concentration, and the hammock was swinging in a wide arc. Suddenly it pitched me to the floor of the platform and over the side, six feet to the ground. I landed on my shoulder with a shock of pain.

Several couples at nearby tables rushed to help, and within seconds a small crowd had gathered around me.

"Please, I'm a doctor." A bearded young man pushed his way through the perfumed group and knelt by my side.

"Don't move, Mademoiselle." He cupped my forehead with one slim, cool hand and held my right wrist with the other. A band of heat gripped my arm under the shoulder. "Yeeow," I cried.

"Don't move." The man looked directly into my face with dark eyes so shining they seemed to beam light.

Then another male voice: "Should I call an ambulance, Doctor Pozzi?"

"I don't think that will be necessary."

Now Dr. Pozzi was moving my legs and arms, first the right ones, then the left ones. "Good. Nothing's broken. Can you sit up?"

I rose slowly, feeling the weight of my upper body. My shoulder throbbed. Just then, Mama pushed through the circle of people who were surrounding me. "Mimi, are you all right?" she cried. Dr. Pozzi scooped me into his arms and, with Mama scurrying behind, carried me through the crowded ballroom, through the maze of corridors, and out a back door to the street.

"Let's see if you can stand up," he said, gently lowering my legs to the pavement. "Good." He smiled quickly. The contours of his handsome face were cleanly defined in the long white ribbons of light from the street lamps. I saw that he was tall and young—no more than twenty-five or -six—and though not at all effeminate, he was prettier than most women.

"Now, my lovely Indian maid, let's get you home." He tweaked my right braid, and a shiver of excitement shot through me. Mama glared at him, her jaw clenched.

It was one in the morning, and the streets were deserted except for a few cabs. Dr. Pozzi hailed one and directed the driver to rue de Luxembourg. When we arrived at Number 44, he walked Mama and me to the door and pulled the bell. One of the maids always waited up for us, and I heard her padding down the hall.

"If you have any problems, any stiffness or severe pain in the morning, come see me." He handed me his card: DR. SAMUEL-JEAN POZZI, HÔPITAL NECKER. His face looked pale, his dark eyelashes almost blond in the transom's harsh lantern light.

The door creaked open, and the maid appeared in the entry, wearing her black uniform, her face a smear of weariness.

"Thank you for seeing us home," Mama said icily, extending her hand to the handsome doctor.

"*Bonne nuit.* Sleep well," Dr. Pozzi said. He kissed Mama's hand and bowed slightly to me. Then he bounded to the pavement with two leaps on his long, elegant legs, and stepped into the night.

Five

The following afternoon at three, Mama and I met in our large square foyer with our hats and coats on. Mama had just come in from a lunch date, and her cheeks and nose were red with cold. I was on my way out.

"Where are you going, dear?" she said, yanking off her gloves finger by finger.

"Dr. Pozzi's office." I rubbed my shoulder and winced for Mama's benefit. I was a bit sore, but hardly in need of medical attention.

"I don't want you to have anything to do with Sam Pozzi!" Mama shrieked. "He has a heart like an artichoke—a leaf for everyone, as the old Creoles used to say."

"I'm not going to marry him, Mama. I'm only going to see him about my shoulder."

Mama blocked the door, planting her tiny frame in front of the huge wood panels.

"I won't allow it, Mimi. He's been notorious ever since his student days. I've seen how he operates at the theater and the opera, preying on girls younger than you and women older than me." She stuffed her gloves into her purse. "Anyway, I don't think you want to go out today. I'm sure you want to be here to greet Julie."

"Julie? Today?"

The corners of Mama's lips turned up in a gentle smile. "You were asleep this morning when I got a *petit bleu* from her. She landed at Le Havre yesterday and was getting on a train at ten. She should be here by evening."

This delightful news was not totally unexpected. Though Julie hadn't told us the exact dates of her departure and arrival, she had written us of her plans to come to Paris to paint. In the years since we had left Louisiana, Julie had become a professional artist. I don't think she ever would have considered selling her work had not a sugar broker who was visiting Parlange one day admired her portrait of Valentine and asked her to paint his family. That led to other commissions, including one from the archbishop of New Orleans, who hired Julie to copy two Titians at the Louvre for the St. Louis Cathedral. The archbishop paid Julie's passage to France and promised her three hundred dollars for each picture—enough to buy Grandmère a new plow.

In my excitement to see Julie, I forgot about Dr. Pozzi. For the rest of the afternoon, I read a little and tried to practice the piano, but I couldn't concentrate and ended up staring out the window, my heart pounding every time a cab rolled up the street. Finally, at a quarter to seven, I heard the doorbell ring and tore downstairs.

Julie was standing in the foyer next to Mama, her small figure dwarfed by two huge steamer trunks. A faded brown pelisse of Grandmère's hung on her childlike frame. Her black, gray-streaked hair was pinned up under a hat decorated with a stuffed pigeon.

"*Chérie!*" she cried as I ran into her arms. "Together, we're together, forever and ever!"

"Forever? Really?"

Julie hugged me tightly. "Well, for a long time, at least."

Those first days after Julie arrived in Paris were the happiest I had known since Valentine's death. I loved my aunt more than anyone in the world and felt consoled and protected by her presence. I think Mama did, too. With Julie around, she seemed less nervous, less irritable. You could see Mama's limbs relaxing and her face softening, losing its brittle mask of tension. The three of us spent days together, shopping, playing cards, and wandering Paris.

Though she still limped, Julie could manage now with a single cane. Her energy and boldness stunned me. One evening with Mama and me she climbed the steep, narrow stairway to the top of Notre-Dame to watch the sunset and inspect the cathedral's massive steel bells. Another night, at her suggestion, we walked through the city morgue, a popular tourist attraction that had opened to the public a few years earlier. As soon as Mama and I saw the gray, bloated cadavers laid out on marble tables—naked except for the strips of leather covering their sex—we fled outside to the Quai Napoléon. Julie, however, remained inside for a half hour, long enough to make a sketch of a female drowning victim.

A week after she arrived, Julie began work on the archbishop's Titians. She left the house every morning at nine-thirty, accompanied by one of the maids, who carried her easel, floor mat, and paint box. Usually she didn't return until after the Louvre closed at five. In two months, the pictures were completed. No sooner had they been crated and sent off to New Orleans than Julie announced she would remain in Paris indefinitely. She could make good money copying masterpieces at the Louvre and painting portraits of the expatriate community. She would continue to live with us, but for work she would share the Montparnasse atelier of two women artists she had met at the Louvre—Filomena Seguette and Sophie Tranchevent. Both were highly regarded painters who regularly exhibited at the Fine Arts Salon, the annual bazaar of new art that opened every May in the Palais de l'Industrie, the immense exhibition hall in the Champs-Elysées, and through which the careers of many artists were made or broken.

Early one spring morning, I helped Julie move her equipment to the atelier. The sky was black, and the streets were empty except for several blue-jacketed workers sweeping the pavement. Two sleepy horses pulled our carriage along, and by the time we arrived at the carrefour Vavin a half hour later, the blackness had receded and the sky was streaked a soft blue and pink, like stripes on a baby's blanket. The carriage swung around the carrefour, past the ghostly terrace of the Closerie des Lilas, and stopped on the boulevard Montparnasse in front of a run-down apartment building with a plain facade and dirty, unshuttered windows.

"This is it," said Julie.

The top-floor studio was reached by entering a small vestibule at the side of the building and climbing three flights of dark, narrow stairs. We found the door to the garret open and walked in. The large high-ceilinged space was flooded with light from tall windows on one wall and a huge skylight. Rickety easels were scattered about, canvases leaned against the walls, and in the center was a dais for a model. Casts of Apollo and Venus de Milo stood on pedestals. One corner of the room was arranged like a parlor, with an upright piano, a divan covered in red Turkish cloth, a screen for changing, and a spirit stove with a dented copper tea kettle on top.

A pretty, tiny-waisted woman with fine honey-colored hair sat on a wooden stool at an easel near the windows. As soon as we walked in, she rose and ran toward us.

"Julie!" she cried, embracing my aunt tightly. "I didn't expect to see you until after lunch."

"Oh, Sophie, I'm up with the birds. You're looking well for so early in the morning." Smiling, Julie turned to me. "I've brought my niece. Sophie Tranchevent, I'd like you to meet Virginie Avegno."

"Of course. The celebrity! I've been following your career in Etincelle's column." Sophie looked deeply into my face with bright blue eyes. "Why, you're just a child."

"Do you mind if Virginie stays while I get organized?" Julie asked.

"No, not at all. But she might have to pose for me. I can't depend on the model—that little seamstress Odette. I haven't seen her in two days." Sophie walked back to her easel, picked up a brush, and dipped it into a palette globbed with paint. She was working on a large portrait of the birth of Venus, which she planned to submit to the next Fine Arts Salon.

A moment later, I heard the sound of heavy boots clomping on the stairs. In walked a stocky woman dressed like a man in pants, a black jacket over a smock, and a worker's slouch hat. It was Filomena Seguette.

"Bonjour!" she shouted into the air.

"Mademoiselle Seguette removed her hat and jacket and hung them on a hook. Her wheat-colored hair sprouted from a center part in uneven chunks, as if it had been hacked off with a knife. Her jaw was heavy, her eyes a deep-set blue. Had it not been for the large round breasts swelling under her smock, I would have thought her a man.

Though it was illegal at the time for women to dress like men, Mademoiselle Seguette always wore male attire. The Paris police had issued her a special "permit to disguise oneself," signed by her doctor, for "professional reasons." The permit, which she was required to carry at all times, strictly forbade her from attending "spectacles, balls, and public meetings" while dressed in men's clothes. But it was a restriction the police ignored, and Mademoiselle Seguette stomped freely around Paris in trousers and boots. In the coming years, I would only once see her in a skirt—at a ball at the Finance Ministry. Even then, she was wearing a man's jacket with her art medals emblazoned across the pocket.

Mademoiselle Seguette got away with this behavior because she was the most famous woman painter in Paris, a master of technique and color who specialized in enormous canvases depicting the glorious history of France—imperial battle victories and sentimental moments in the lives of French heroes. In order to paint the dramatic backdrops of her work, she needed to climb mountains, cross rivers, and carry heavy easels, canvases, and paint boxes—activities that would be severely restricted if she was wearing a corset, dress, and women's shoes. That, anyway, was the explanation she gave the authorities.

"Philippe!" cried Julie, using Mademoiselle Seguette's nickname, as she grabbed me by the arm and hobbled over to greet her friend.

"Mademoiselle Filomena Seguette, I'd like you to meet my niece, Virginie Avegno."

"It's my pleasure," Filomena said, bowing slightly. Wasting no time, the artist shed her coat and prepared for work. Soon she was brushing paint onto her canvas, a huge portrait of Joan of Arc dressed in armor and kneeling in a battlefield. Filomena's Joan had a sturdy androgynous figure, but her blond hair and round-eyed oval face bore a striking resemblance to Sophie's Venus—the same model (the seamstress Odette, I assumed) had posed for both pictures.

I remained in the studio for the rest of the morning, playing the piano while the women painted. At eleven, we took a break for tea. Julie, Filomena, and I settled ourselves on the divan in the corner while Sophie prepared the tea and arranged cups and saucers on a little table.

"I heard Victor Hugo wants to buy my Homer," announced Filomena. She dropped three sugar cubes into a chipped white cup. "How much do you think I should ask?"

"Five hundred francs, no less," said Sophie. "Though Victor Hugo can certainly afford more."

"I guess that's about right," added Julie.

"I never thought it would sell," said Filomena. "Carolus wanted me to send it to the Salon last year. I refused. You've seen it. Hardly my best picture. He wants me to show my weakest work, so everyone will say, 'Oh, look, France's most talented woman painter is not as good as a mediocre man.'"

"Philippe, that's so unfair," said Julie. "Don't forget how much you've learned from Carolus."

Carolus was Carolus-Duran, a popular painter and teacher who had changed his name from Charles Durand to this more glamorous hyphenated version when he first exhibited his work. Carolus-Duran conducted a special class for women in his Montparnasse atelier on Thursdays. Julie, Filomena, and Sophie attended it regularly. Sometimes he dropped in on the women's garret, and he often stayed for several hours, carefully studying and criticizing the work of each woman. Occasionally he brought collectors, as he did one day when I happened to be posing for my aunt and her friends.

It was 1870, the end of the first summer after Julie arrived in Paris, and France was at war with Prussia. The fighting was along the Rhine, far from the city, and had yet to affect our lives directly. I had gone to the studio that morning, as I often did, to play the piano while the women painted. I enjoyed having an audience for my music, and I loved the atmosphere of the atelier—the lively talk about art, the sense of purpose that charged the air, the interesting collectors who dropped in to scrutinize the works in progress.

When I arrived that morning at ten, Sophie ran up to me, her blue eyes wide, her face pale with worry.

"Oh, Mimi, I'm so glad you came. The model didn't show up again. I think she's self-conscious because she's putting on weight. And only a week before the exhibition at the Cercle des Arts Libéraux. Would you mind posing?"

I said I'd be happy to. I hung up my shawl and stepped to the dais. Julie hobbled over to me. "Mimi, you have to take your clothes off," she whispered. "I mean, you don't have to. But if you're going to pose, you do. We need a *nude* model."

"Oh."

I slipped behind the screen, undressed, and donned the blue kimono that hung on a hook. Then I took my place on the dais. I loosened the kimono belt and let the blue silk fall from my shoulders. I did not mind being naked in front of these women. They were artists, after all, and were used to looking at bodies. I was flattered they judged me attractive enough to model. Freed from my corset, petticoats, and stockings, and warmed by the nearby stove, I felt as relaxed as I did in the moments before dropping off to sleep.

Two hours went by, and then I heard voices echoing in the hall, and the sound of stomping boots growing closer. A portly middle-aged man with a large head of graying black curls and a pointed, waxed beard pushed open the door and swaggered into the room. He was followed by a handsome, much younger man. I immediately recognized the younger man as Dr. Sam Pozzi, though I don't think he remembered me. In any case, he wasn't looking at my face. He was eying my body with a delighted expression, as if someone had just told him a witty story. He only got a few seconds to study me, though, because I quickly retrieved the kimono from the floor and wrapped it around me.

The older man was Carolus-Duran. He parked his bulk in front of Sophie's canvas. Scowling at the picture, he said loudly, "Sophie, Sophie, how many times must I tell you, paint what you see! What is all this light in the canvas—here and here and here? Look at the model!"

He glanced up at me and narrowed his eyes. "See?" he said. "There is only one broad light in her cheek." He picked up a brush and added a few daubs of paint to Sophie's picture.

"The snowy breast is good. But that left nipple has too many pinks. You've put in too many colorations, which I *know* you didn't see on the model's body."

Again he looked up at me, now with a blank expression. "Mademoiselle, drop your robe, please."

"I'm afraid that's not a model," Julie called out from behind her easel. "That's my niece, and she's about to get dressed." She limped over to the dais, took me by the arm, and hustled me behind the screen. She gathered my clothes into a bundle and handed them to me. "I knew this was a mistake," she said, her face stiff with embarrassment. "We won't mention any of it to your mother."

After I was dressed, I stepped from behind the screen and nearly bumped into Sam Pozzi. He had been hovering near the door, waiting to talk to me.

"I know where I've seen you," he said, his brown eyes glistening. "You're Pocahontas from the Marine Minister's ball."

"Yes, and you're the doctor who saved my life when I fell out of the hammock."

"I think you would have managed to live without me."

"I'm not so sure."

Dr. Pozzi looked deeply into my face. I was tired from the long posing session, and he sensed my weariness.

"Well, Miss Pocahontas. You look like you earned your feathers today. Can I take you home?"

"I suppose so."

At the other end of the atelier, Carolus-Duran and Julie were discussing her canvas while Sophie and Filomena were absorbed in their paintings. Without saying good-bye to them, Dr. Pozzi and I slipped out the door.

I felt light-headed with excitement as this handsome man led me down the stairs to the street. A cab was waiting at the curb. He helped me into the back and directed the driver, "Boulevard des Italiens."

"I live on rue de Luxembourg," I said.

"Wouldn't you like to have lunch with me?"

I should have gone home. I should have told Dr. Pozzi that my mother was expecting me. But I was a bored fifteen-year-old eager for adventure and quite confident in my ability to handle fawning men. "That would be lovely," I told Dr. Pozzi. "I'm famished."

The carriage creaked to a halt in front of the gray stone facade of Bignon's, one of the most popular restaurants in Paris. The maître d' led us upstairs to a private room with an iron balcony overlooking the street. It was decorated like a boudoir, with deeply cushioned settees, a Turkish carpet, and blue satin curtains pulled to the sides of the windows by the chubby hands of plaster cherubs.

The small lace-covered table in the center of the room was set with

gold-rimmed china, heavy silver, and crystal wineglasses. Dr. Pozzi
held a chair out for me, and I sat down. Then he took the place opposite mine and spread his linen napkin across his lap.

"Your aunt and her friends are very lucky to have such a beautiful
model," he said.

"Oh, I'm not their model. The regular girl didn't show up, so I
was helping out."

Two black-jacketed waiters in white tie appeared in the doorway.
The taller one carried an enormous silver tray containing a platter of
foie gras aux truffes, the shorter man a bottle of Château Lafitte. Dr.
Pozzi had ordered today's lunch the day before, as was the custom at
the time, when menus at the better establishments often ran thirty-six
pages. He thought he'd be dining alone; after we arrived, the maître d'
instructed a waiter to set Pozzi's table for two.

"You know, I love women painters," he said as a waiter poured
wine into his glass. He took a sip and nodded to the tall young man,
who moved to the other side of the table and filled my glass. "They're
an unknown power, and their position is really difficult. It's as hard for
them to get into the small private exhibitions as the big public ones.
That's why I visit the ateliers; otherwise one would rarely see their
work."

"You can go to the Musée du Luxembourg to see Philippe—I
mean Mademoiselle Seguette. Two of her paintings are there. And
she's always at the Salon. Mademoiselle Tranchevent is, too. And
they'll both be at the Cercle des Arts Libéraux next month," I said.

"Ah, but not your aunt. At least not yet. I really love her use of
color. I might buy that lovely nude she's working on."

"When I was growing up she never let anyone see her paintings. If
it hadn't been for the war and the desperate shape our plantation was
in, I don't think she ever would have painted for money."

One of the waiters laid plates of truffles in front of us. Dr. Pozzi
took a few bites, followed by a large sip of red wine. "Really? Well,
that would have been a shame."

I was too nervous to swallow a morsel. All possible motives Dr.
Pozzi might have for this lunch flashed through my head—from simple companionship to seduction. I pretended to eat, cutting up my

truffles and pushing them around the plate. By the time the salmon mayonnaise arrived, I had convinced myself he was in love with me. I held that feeling through the *boeuf flamand* and dessert—vanilla ice cream delivered in a single tall-stemmed bowl with two spoons planted in the soft mounds.

But by the time the meal was over and Dr. Pozzi had led me down the carpeted stairs—one hand on the polished wood railing, the other on the small of my back—I had lost all confidence in the love theory. He looked distracted; perhaps he was preoccupied by work. Worse, maybe he found me dull. We said little to each other during the cab ride home. I lied that I was meeting my mother at Bon Marché, so Dr. Pozzi dropped me off in front of the store and waved good-bye through the dirt-streaked window as the horses trotted off. I browsed in the glove compartment for thirty minutes, then took a cab home.

The next morning, the first post carried a letter from him. The maid brought it to my bedroom on my breakfast tray, and as soon as she closed the door behind her, I tore open the cream envelope. My heart was fluttering in my chest as I read:

Dear Mlle Avegno,

I enjoyed our lunch immensely. You have no idea how rare it is for me to talk of art and beauty, surrounded as I am all day by sick people. There is no one at the hospital who understands the true yearnings of my soul. Perhaps you would do me the honor of lunching with me at Bignon's next Sunday, September 4, at one. We can continue our discussion of women painters. I'd like to hear your views on Madame Alix Enhault. She's a particular favorite of mine.

Respectfully yours,
Samuel-Jean Pozzi

On the morning of September 4, I dressed carefully, donning my favorite day gown, a green silk dress with a scalloped hem. With Dr. Pozzi in mind, I sprayed my neck and the insides of my wrists with lilac scent. Though it was Sunday, Julie had gone to her atelier to work on a commissioned portrait she was struggling to complete. Mama expected me to go to church with her as usual. I told her I wanted to attend a concert at the Salle Pleyel, since two of my favorite Beethoven works were on the program.

She agreed to let me go, so I left the house at twelve-thirty and walked to the corner of rue Saint-Honoré to hail a cab. A crowd had gathered at the newspaper kiosk, and several men were running down the pavement waving their arms and shouting, "The empire has fallen!" I was thinking of my lunch with Dr. Pozzi and paid little heed to the troubling scene. A few moments later, a cab pulled to the corner and I directed the driver to rue des Italiens.

When I arrived at Bignon's, the maître d' rushed to greet me. His face was gray with distress. "Mademoiselle, haven't you heard? The worst has happened! The Prussians have captured Louis-Napoléon, and the Empire has collapsed! Dr. Pozzi has gone to join his unit with the Service de Santé Militaire. He asked me to give you his apologies."

I left the restaurant, dazed with disappointment. I was sorry for the Emperor, but felt worse for myself. All my life, I've needed to be in love and have someone in love with me. Even as a little girl, I had intense imaginary romances with characters in books—for years I was smitten with d'Artagnan in *The Three Musketeers*. But Dr. Pozzi was the first *real* man I had fancied myself in love with.

As I walked home, I wondered what he thought of me, or indeed if he thought of me at all. I was tormented by fears that he'd soon forget me, that our one rendezvous wasn't enough to spark his passion, that when he returned from the war, he'd have no interest in an adolescent girl.

So lost was I in this mournful vision that I barely noticed the chaos around me. Everywhere people were running and screaming. The street signs in the rue 10-Décembre had been smashed and replaced with boards on which RUE 4-SEPTEMBRE had been scrawled in black paint. I reached the Tuileries just as a scruffy mob was hoisting the tricolor above the Pavillon de l'Horloge, shouting "Long live the Republic!"

Our household, like most in Paris, had expected a quick victory over the Prussians. Louis-Napoléon's goal was to thwart Otto von Bismarck. War fever had been building for some time as Bismarck worked to unite the German states, thereby giving Prussia an edge over France in the European balance of power. After a dispute over the succession to the Spanish throne, France declared war. The Emperor, however, not only was ill and in agony from kidney stones, but also was badly prepared. He had half the number of soldiers he thought he had. What's more, the French troops were poorly trained compared to the Prussians. When Louis-Napoléon reached the battlefield at Sedan, he found his army hopelessly outnumbered. After several hours of fighting, he surrendered.

Soon afterward in Paris, a group of radical deputies of the Corps Législatif used the defeat as an incitement to overthrow the Emperor. Standing on the balcony of the Hôtel de Ville, where the revolutionary governments of 1789 and 1848 had been established, the radicals formally declared the death of the Empire and the birth of the Republic. A cabinet was hastily assembled, and a popular general, Louis Trochu, was pronounced president.

Over the next weeks, Parisian life as we had known it ground to a halt. The trains stopped running; the mail wasn't delivered; newspapers ceased publishing; shops and theaters closed. Though the Prussians had yet to invade the city, there was rioting in the streets, and our driver was afraid to take the carriage out. Cabs were impossible to find, so we ended up staying home all day, only venturing out for an occasional errand or walk.

The weeks and months wore on, and the days passed in a blur of boredom reminiscent of the languid summers at Parlange. Since Julie had no way of getting to her studio on the other side of the city, she set up her easel and paints in her bedroom, and I passed the time reading and playing the piano.

Our ennui was exacerbated by the freezing weather. Coal supplies across the city ran out, and for warmth we were forced to burn old books. Frost glazed the windows, and the walls felt like sheets of ice.

On January 5, the Prussians began to shell Paris from forts surrounding the city. During dinner, an explosion ripped the air and shook the house. Several wineglasses tumbled, spilling rivers of liquid across the white tablecloth. Mama burst into tears. "I can't go through another war," she cried.

"I know," said Julie. "All my courage is gone, too. We used it up in Louisiana."

I ran to the top floor, where the maids slept, and stuck my head out one of the dormer windows. A dozen shells flew past in the smoky, black sky. One struck a roof across the street and burned a large hole in it.

After that, the maids refused to sleep in the garret and moved into the basement. None of us got much sleep for the next few nights, as cannons boomed twenty-four hours a day. Eventually we grew accustomed to the noise. Other deprivations were harder to bear.

Food was scarce. The *boucheries* sold only horse meat and, for a while, the remains of the exotic animals in the Jardin des Plantes. Pollux, the adorable baby elephant who was the zoo's star attraction, was the last to be shot and butchered. After that, a few markets offered dead rats for a pittance. We ate no meat at all.

Most of the Prussian shells landed across the Seine on the Left Bank, too far to harm us. Still, we heard their thundering, and Mama's nerves were frayed. She couldn't sleep or eat and suffered from excruciating headaches.

A week before Christmas, the mail service resumed, and letters arrived that were dated months before. One, postmarked September 10 from Charles, contained the tragic news of Grandmère's death. She had suffered a heart attack in her sleep after spending the day balancing Parlange's books. Grandmère had always seemed indestructible; it was hard to imagine the world without her. Every day for the next two weeks, Mama, Julie, and I lit candles in her honor. We all cried a lot, but Mama was inconsolable to the point of madness, her grief exacerbated by guilt over her strained relationship with her mother. She took to her bed and refused to get up, even to wash.

After New Year's, Pierre Gautreau moved into the spare bedroom on the third floor to help Julie and me take care of Mama. We hadn't seen much of Pierre in the months before the Empire fell. He had been in South America on business and had returned to Paris only after learning of Louis-Napoléon's surrender. He said he came back because he was worried about us, though I'm sure he also was concerned about his house, his collection of japonaiseries, and his investments. But to be fair to Pierre, he *was* devoted to Mama. She seemed to brighten up with him around. They spent hours discussing plans to turn one of our parlors into a winter garden with Oriental trees and plants.

Soon after Pierre moved in, the provisional French government, the Third Republic, signed an armistice with the Prussians. Many Frenchmen regarded it as a humiliating peace. Claiming they wanted to save France from both the Prussians *and* the capitulators, a group of National Guard dissidents formed a rival government, calling themselves by an old name popularized during the Revolution of 1789, the Commune of Paris.

The loosely organized Communards—their ranks included songwriters, brothel owners, shopkeepers, journalists, carpenters, and soldiers—embarked on a reign of terror as devastating as the Prussian bombs. They set fire to government buildings, confiscated the property of aristocrats, looted abandoned homes, murdered suspected government sympathizers, and erected barricades to stop the legitimate army.

Many of the bourgeoisie had fled to their country homes at the start of the fighting. But by the time we thought of leaving, the city exits were blocked. The fighting escalated throughout the spring. Thousands of soldiers and Communards died, as well as innocent bystanders caught in the crossfire of Frenchmen fighting Frenchmen.

Thanks to a greenhouse garden and a chicken coop in our stable that provided a daily supply of eggs, we had more food than most of our friends. We had guests for dinner nearly every night. Sophie Tranchevent and Filomena Seguette came several times; and one night, Julie invited Carolus-Duran.

As the maids brought in steaming platters of omelettes and potatoes, our driver, an elderly man named Antoine, burst into the dining room with horrific news he had just heard from a neighbor's coachman: the Communards had set fire to the home of Duc de la Palletière on the boulevard Malesherbes. The duke, his wife, and their three children were found burned to death in their parlor.

"I wish we had left Paris when we had the chance," said Mama. Ever ready to cry or faint, she clutched a handkerchief in one hand and held a bottle of smelling salts to her nose with the other.

"I wouldn't worry, dear," said Pierre. "The Communards are only interested in destroying the property of French aristocrats. They will not touch the home of three lovely American women."

"Haven't you heard of accidents, Pierre? If they're aiming at the *hôtel* of the Vicomte Varlet across the street, they might just as well hit us!"

"I know, Madame. It's terrible," cried Carolus-Duran. "Our beautiful city and its treasures will be destroyed. The employees of the Louvre are extremely worried. They've taken some measures to save the greatest masterpieces, of course." He leaned his bulk against the edge of the table and lowered his voice. "The Venus de Milo is hidden under a trapdoor in the basement at the Prefecture of Police, beneath a pile of old dossiers. Some of the Ingreses, Rembrandts, and Titians have been taken out of their frames, rolled up, and stashed in vaults around the city. Sam Pozzi has Delacroix's *Women of Algiers* in the safe at Necker Hospital."

At the mention of Dr. Pozzi's name, my throat tightened. I hadn't heard from him since his letter inviting me to lunch.

"How is Dr. Pozzi?" I asked, trying to make my voice sound as flat as possible.

"Still with the Santé Militaire," answered Carolus-Duran. "For a while, he was following the army around. At Metz, he was knocked over by a horse that was lugging a wagonful of wounded men, and while he was on the ground, one of the wagon wheels rolled over his left leg. The wound was nothing serious, but he couldn't get around too well, so his unit commander sent him back to Paris. For a couple of weeks, he was at the Gare de l'Est treating the wounded and sick who were evacuated from the provinces. Now he's working at the ambulance in the Palais de l'Industrie."

"Oh, yes," said Julie. "Sophie Tranchevent and her sister have been going there every day."

I knew that temporary hospitals had been set up throughout the city, in theaters, restaurants, and private homes. But I did not know that the Palais de l'Industrie, the immense exhibition hall where the city's annual Fine Arts Salon was held, was being used for this purpose. The Palais was a fifteen-minute walk from our house.

I waited three days, sufficient time, I figured, for the dinner conversation to have faded in Mama's mind; then, before breakfast on the fourth morning, I knocked on Mama's door, praying that she wouldn't connect Sam Pozzi to what I was about to ask.

"Come in!" Mama called. She was dressed in her white morning gown, writing letters at her desk.

"I'm going out of my mind, being cooped up in the house," I said.

"I know. I am, too, dear. Go for a walk, if you must. Just stay in the neighborhood, please."

"I'd like to help at the ambulance in the Palais, like Sophie Tranchevent. It's only a short walk to the Champs-Elysées, and there's no fighting in the area now."

Mama rose from her chair and walked toward me. I expected a storm of protest. Instead, she put her arms around me and hugged me. "Oh, Mimi, I think it's a wonderful idea for you to do something useful. Just make sure you're back before dark." Her pleasure at my interest in good works outweighed her worries about my safety.

An hour later, I was ready to leave. As soon as I opened the door, I heard the distant spluttering of gunfire. I took a deep breath, checked my pocket to make sure I had my *billet de circulation,* a street pass signed by the American ambassador, and stepped outside.

As I turned the corner onto the boulevard Saint-Honoré, a loud pack of Communards marched by. The men had fastened leaves to their peaked caps, and some of the women, coarse-looking creatures in stained, ripped dresses, carried branches. A few of them waved red flags and shouted, "The Commune forever!"

I crossed the rue de Rivoli to the Tuileries. The large gilt "N's" on the towering wrought-iron gates had been covered in newspapers. The Napoleonic eagles had been ripped off; in their place hung two wreathes of *immortelles.*

At the place de la Concorde, the Communards had erected a huge barricade of barrels and cobblestones. Before it stood a line of cannon. I started to walk around the barricade, when a short, swarthy man in a threadbare National Guard uniform stepped in front of me. He held his rifle out to block my way. With one arm, he opened his coat, displaying a shiny badge. "I am an agent of the Commune's Public Safety Committee," he announced arrogantly. "Do you have a pass to be walking the streets?"

I fumbled in my pocket for my *billet de circulation* and held it out to him with a trembling hand.

The Communard glanced at it, then looked at me.

"Well, what do we have here? A pretty American redhead." He brought his leering face close to mine, and I could smell his burgundy wine breath. "Perhaps you'd like to help us build a barricade, Mademoiselle. Or maybe you don't approve of the Commune?"

"I have no feelings about the Commune," I said. "But I will ask the American ambassador, Mr. Washburne, how he feels, when I see him. I am on my way to his office now." I gave the Communard my fiercest look.

His unshaven, deeply-lined face slackened. "Americans!" he grumbled. "You want to live in our city, but you don't want to suffer with us." He spat on the pavement. "Fine! Walk on!"

Heart thumping, cold beads of sweat sprouting on my forehead, I ran across the Champs-Elysées to the Palais de l'Industrie and dashed through its lofty arcade. Inside the cavernous entrance hall, medical orderlies in white smocks with red crosses embroidered on their sleeves carried stretchers with groaning patients. Sophie Tranchevent and a group of women, all dressed in plain black bombazine, were standing in a corner folding sheets. Dirty laundry was piled on the grand marble staircase. Shirts and stockings hung to dry on the railings.

The first exhibition hall on the left had been turned into a hospital ward with rows of cots lining the walls. Dr. Pozzi was at the far end, bent over a small boy. He noticed me as soon as I entered, and he rushed to greet me.

"Mademoiselle Avegno!" he cried. "How wonderful of you to help us." His face looked leaner and his eyes darker than I had remembered them. He smelled of shaving soap and starched linen.

Though my heart was beating wildly against my chest, I tried to look nonchalant. "It's good to see you again," I said.

Dr. Pozzi's eyes wandered over me, lingering on the swell of bosom peaking from the décolleté neckline of my gray satin bodice. He looked pleased. His expression changed, however, as he took in my fur-trimmed skirt, gray suede gloves, and black high heels.

"My dear, that's a lovely costume," he said. "But I'm afraid it won't do for this kind of work. Ask one of the nurses to find an apron for you."

"What would you like me to do?"

"That boy over there needs some attention. He's from Belgium, a boarding student at the Lycée Condorcet. He was hit by a shell near the Parc Monceau this morning."

Dr. Pozzi pointed to the cot of the boy he had just been examining. The thin brown-haired child lay under several blankets, his chest and right arm wrapped in blood-stained bandages.

As I approached his cot, the boy's face brightened. "Hello. I'm Georges Bourdin," he said.

"I'm Virginie Avegno."

"Enchanted, Mademoiselle." He spoke with the odd formality children often adopt when speaking to their elders.

I pulled a chair to his bedside. "Is there anything I can do for you?"

"I'd be very grateful if you would take down a letter to my mother. I saw some paper and pens over there." He nodded toward a table across the room.

When I had retrieved the writing materials, Georges began dictating:

Dear Mama,

Please don't worry when you read this, but I wanted you to know before the headmaster told you that I got hit yesterday by a shell. I was walking to the park to play ball with my friends when it happened.

At first it hurt a lot, and I was very scared. But now I'm better, and they are taking good care of me. The doctor says I'll be well soon. Please give my love to Papa and all inquiring friends. And kiss Yoicks for me—a big kiss. I know you don't like to kiss dogs, but just this once, please, Mama, for me.

Love,
Your son Georges

When he had finished dictating, Georges dropped his head onto his pillow in exhaustion.

"Yoicks is my dog," he said feebly.

"So I assumed."

"He's an English spaniel. That's why we call him Yoicks. It's an English word. Well, it's not really a word. It's what hunters say when they spot birds in the sky. They go, 'Yoicks, yoicks,' and their dogs run after the birds. My Yoicks isn't a hunting dog, but I like the name."

"We had lots of dogs on the plantation where I grew up, in Louisiana."

"You're American?"

"I am."

"Do you know any Indians?"

"Never met one. Now, Georges, you must rest. We can talk more tomorrow."

I spent the rest of the day in a corner of the entry hall helping several women sort through the boxes of blankets and pajamas that had been donated to the ambulance. I think Dr. Pozzi was looking for excuses to talk to me, because he came by several times and asked us how we were getting on.

I returned to the ambulance the next day and every day for two weeks afterward. Though Georges continued to be weak and pale, his fever went down, and his brown eyes became clearer. One morning, I brought *La Belle histoire de Leuk-le-Lièvre,* and read a chapter of it to him every day. It had been Valentine's favorite book, one of several possessions of hers I had brought to Paris from Louisiana to remember her by.

Georges was nine, the age my sister would have been had she lived, and every time I saw him I thought of her. Like Valentine, he was sweet-tempered and bright, and when he looked at me I imagined I saw Valentine's spirit in his eyes. Ordinarily I'm not a superstitious person, or even very religious. Still, I became obsessed with the idea that Valentine was somehow alive in Georges. I began fantasizing that Mama, Julie, and I would adopt him. Of course, it was absurd. He had parents who adored him and would be horrified by the idea.

A few days after I met Georges, French troops marched into Paris and violent street fighting broke out between the Communards and the Republic's official army. At the same time, French troops continued shelling the Left Bank from the forts surrounding the city. The Prussians, meanwhile, waited on their side of the Rhine, ready to move in and support the Versailles troops if the need arose.

One evening, Mama, Julie, Pierre, and I watched through the windows of the maids' garret as a band of Communards dug up the cobbles on the rue des Capucines and carted them away in barrels to a barricade they were building at the corner of our street.

"Civil war in the streets of Paris. I never thought I'd see the day," said Pierre, shaking his head.

"What if they start fighting outside our door? We'll all be killed," Mama moaned.

"Now, Virginie, that's not going to happen." Pierre slid his arm around Mama's shoulder and patted it consolingly. Then Mama turned to me. "Virginie, you mustn't go to the Palais anymore. It's just too dangerous to go out."

As we made our way back down the narrow servants' stairs to the parlor, Julie whispered to me, "Promise me, *chérie*, you won't leave the house again. Your mother is right. It's too dangerous."

"I won't. I'll stay home," I said.

I went to bed that night fully intending to keep my promise. But before dawn, I was awakened by thundering cannons—so loud I felt the reverberations in my stomach—and couldn't go back to sleep. I got out of bed and dressed quickly, standing by the window in shards of light floating through the shutter slats from the street lamps outside. Then I wrote a note to Mama, telling her that I had gone to the ambulance at the Palais and not to worry.

Grasping the banister, I made my way down the steps to the hall. I left the note on the table, then crossed the parquet through the vestibule and went into the night.

Burned-out omnibuses and dead horses lay in the streets. The rue Saint-Honoré was a wall of flame, so I turned around and took the rue Duphot, past the Madeleine. I ducked under the ropes that had been stretched across the street to stop the French army, just as a shell whirred above my head. Had I been standing, I would have been hit.

Now I regretted having left the house. I thought of going back, but I was frightened by a group of men who were running up the street behind me, waving rifles. Just as I was crossing the rue de Rivoli, the stone facade of the Marine Ministry collapsed from a bomb, and huge chunks of its arcades crumbled and scattered into the street. I ran as fast as I could to the Palais and dashed under the immense archway and into the main exhibition hall.

Dr. Pozzi was examining a patient in the farthest row of cots. I saw that two screens had been drawn around Georges's bed. I knew what that meant. During the night, his fever had worsened, and his body had succumbed to infection. Georges was dead.

My knees buckled, and dropping to the floor, I began to sob. Dr. Pozzi saw me and ran to my side. Taking my elbows, he pulled me up and held me to his chest. Then he led me out to the hall and sat with me on a red velvet bench. I couldn't stop crying.

"Mimi, I'm going to get something to calm you down," he said. He walked back to the ward and returned a few minutes later with a syringe. A few tendrils of hair had escaped from the hastily arranged roll at the back of my head, and Dr. Pozzi tenderly brushed them away from my face. Pushing my ruffled sleeve to my shoulder, he jabbed the syringe into my arm and held it there for a moment. Then he removed it and wiped my skin with a cloth. "Now, you lie down, dear," he said.

I slept the entire day. When I awoke, it was dark outside, and Dr. Pozzi was standing over me. "Mimi, the Communards have burned down the Tuileries Palace, and the entire quarter is in flames. You can't possibly go home. You'll have to spend the night here."

"What time is it?" I said, sitting up. My head felt as heavy as a steel ball.

"Ten o'clock. You slept for fifteen hours."

Taking my hand, Dr. Pozzi led me through a tunnel of empty galleries as long and as wide as tracks in a train station, then up a service stairwell to a dark paneled room—an administrative office that had been turned into his bedroom. Dr. Pozzi's black medical bag sat on the floor next to a mahogany table stacked with books. A skeleton hung on a hook from the wardrobe. In an alcove by the window, a bed had been made up with pillows and blue satin sheets.

The skeleton intrigued me, and I started to walk toward it, but Dr. Pozzi placed his hands on my shoulders and turned me to face him. Looking at me with melting eyes, he kissed me. I felt the soft bristles of his mustache, and a current of excitement spread through my legs and arms. Wordlessly, confidently, he began unfastening the buttons of my bodice. When he had it unhooked, he yanked it off my shoulders and arms and threw it aside. Then he pulled my skirt over my head and started unlacing my corset. That came off, too, followed by petticoats, chemise, and drawers. I was naked except for my silk stockings. Kneeling on the floor, Dr. Pozzi took my right stocking in his hands and gently slid it over my leg as he kissed my inner thigh. Ripples of desire shot to my ears. When he had my left stocking off, he carried me to the bed and placed me on the satin sheets. In a moment, he had torn off his own clothes and was lying beside me.

The night was a thrilling discovery. I didn't think of Mama or Julie or poor Georges Bourdin. I thought only of this new intimacy. At dawn, Dr. Pozzi fell asleep, and I lay close to him, listening to the soft rattle of his breathing.

He awoke a few hours later, sat up, and swung his legs over the side of the bed. In the fan of sunlight slanting through the window, he looked white and luminous, like a painting of a medieval saint.

"Mimi, I think I should send you home," he said as he pulled on his trousers. "Your family must be very worried. And I have work to do."

"I want to stay here with you." I sat up, letting the sheets fall from my breasts, and placed my hand on Dr. Pozzi's sleeve. He leaned out of the light and, losing his ethereal glow, bent over to kiss my right nipple.

"You have to go, darling."

"Sam, please, let me stay."

His face tightened, and he looked at me severely. "You must never call me Sam," he said, his voice tinged with annoyance. "And you must never *tutoyer* me." During the night, I had addressed him with "*tu*," the familiar form of "you."

"But we're lovers. Lovers always *tutoyer*."

"Not always, darling. It's better to keep the *vous*."

"Even in bed?"

"Yes. That way you won't slip when we're around other people."

He walked to his armoire and retrieved a fresh white shirt.

"When will I see you again? Tomorrow?"

"I'm not sure about tomorrow. But soon."

After Dr. Pozzi left, I dressed and took a look at myself in the mirrored armoire. My cheeks were blotched and roughened, and tiny red bumps had erupted around my mouth—the result of Dr. Pozzi's bearded kisses. I splashed water on my face from the basin and arranged my hair. Then I made my way through the empty halls to the staircase and the first floor.

Pierre Gautreau, his face gray and drawn, his fine black jacket creased with wrinkles, stood talking to one of the nurses in the doorway of the main exhibition hall.

"Mimi!" he cried as I entered the gallery. His smile lifted the ends of his mustache and crinkled his tired eyes.

I ran to him and threw my arms around his neck.

"Are Mama and Julie all right?"

"They're fine, except they're frantic about you. But you did the right thing spending the night here. The quarter was an inferno." Pierre looked at me with concern glimmering across his brow.

"What happened to your face, dear?"

"I slept on a horsehair blanket in one of the offices upstairs," I lied. "It must have caused an irritation."

"Well, I'm just glad you're safe." Pierre cupped my elbow and led me toward the door. Looking back over my shoulder, I searched for Dr. Pozzi among the white-coated doctors milling about the cots. Finally I spotted him in a corner talking to a pretty blond woman who was sorting medicine bottles. Dr. Pozzi's arms were crossed against his chest, and he chuckled at something the pretty woman said. My body tensed with jealousy.

"Mimi, let's go," said Pierre softly.

I stopped in my tracks to watch Dr. Pozzi, and Pierre began exerting pressure on my elbow. I took a few steps, still looking over my shoulder until Pierre and I had walked through the door and Dr. Pozzi had dropped from sight.

Six

Outside, the air smelled of burning plaster, and smoke filled the cloudless blue sky. Pierre and I followed the yellow sanded pathways past the long row of plane trees and the place de la Concorde, to the Tuileries Palace, which was now a smoldering, blackened ruin. Dodging an army of rubber-coated workers who trained hose pipes on the immense roofless shell, we crossed the rue de Rivoli and turned onto rue de Luxembourg. A few houses opposite ours had been damaged by fire, but our *hôtel* was untouched. Pierre and I entered the courtyard through the iron gate and pulled the bell. From within, we heard feminine voices and rustling skirts. A moment later, Mama and Julie opened the door.

"Oh, Mimi, thank God you're safe!" Mama wailed. She clasped me in her arms and hugged me tightly.

"I'd have died if anything had happened to you, *chérie*," said Julie. She knuckled tears from the corners of her eyes and reached over to kiss me hard on the cheek.

Both women seemed to have aged overnight. The lines running from the sides of Mama's nose to the corners of her mouth looked deeper than I had remembered them, and dark circles rimmed her eyes. Julie's hair sprouted a trail of gray across the top of her head that I had never noticed before. Bent slightly over her horn-tipped cane, she looked stiff and arthritic.

With our arms encircling each other's waists, and with Pierre following, we moved to the main parlor. One of the maids had set a tea service on a table in front of the fireplace, and Mama and Julie sat on chairs facing each other across the table. Pierre stood by Mama, his right arm resting on the mantel, while I hung back at the front of the room near the piano. Mama poured tea into a rose-patterned china cup and held it out to me. "Come here, Mimi, this will do you good," she said.

I shook my head. "I'm exhausted. Would you mind if I went to bed?"

"Please, dear, have one cup."

"Let her go, Virginie," said Pierre. "The child had a long night."

"Very well," sighed Mama. She set the cup and saucer on the table. "Try to sleep."

Wearily, I climbed the curving staircase to my suite. Sitting at my writing table, I pulled a sheet of blue stationery from a lacquered box and wrote, "Dear Dr. Pozzi." I couldn't go further. I wanted to tell him that I loved him and hoped that he loved me, but I couldn't think of how to express myself without sounding hopelessly schoolgirlish. I chewed on my pen and stared out the window. Three starlings perched in the chestnut tree outside, their chirping drowned by the hissing hose pipes from the Tuileries. Suddenly a unit of *cuirassiers* charged down the street on horseback and turned into their barracks on the Place Vendôme. A moment later, a young couple strolled by, arm in arm. They stopped directly under my window, and as if to mock me, the man lifted his sweetheart's veil and kissed her lips. I crushed the paper in my hands, ran to the next room, and hurled myself on my bed. I lay there and slept fitfully for the rest of the day.

Over the next week, in a burst of brutal fighting, the French army won Paris back from the Communards. By June, the last of the insurgents had been struck down and either executed by the soldiers or imprisoned. The city began to recover.

My pain, however, had only begun. I wish I could say I forgot Dr. Pozzi, that my normal life resumed once I returned to the safe haven of home. But that did not happen. As the months wore on and I heard nothing from him, I grew listless, cried easily, and had trouble eating and sleeping. Mama and Julie misread my malaise as boredom and loneliness for friends my own age. Sometimes they invited young men and women—the children of their acquaintances—to dinner, but I had no interest in these strangers and never started friendships with them.

Music was my only solace. I spent most of my time shut up in my sitting room, practicing the piano. By now I had mastered most of Beethoven's and Mozart's sonatas, and usually I performed a few pieces at Mama's Mondays.

Her salon, like countless others across the city, resumed in June with the season's normal round of receptions, dinners, theater openings, and balls. It was amazing how quickly gaiety returned to Paris. Emperor Napoléon may have been gone, but the rich were still rich, and Parisians were as fond of pleasure as before the Prussian siege. Restaurants, shops, theaters, and designers' ateliers overflowed with patrons, and construction of a grand new opera house was underway. The city's devastation was even turned into a source for fresh amusement. A guidebook, *Ruines de Paris,* was rushed into print, and tourists flocked to the city to see the burnt-out shells of the Tuileries, the Palais de Justice, the Prefecture of Police, and the Hôtel de Ville.

The monarchy's demise had loosened social barriers, however, and Mama saw a golden chance for our advancement. She accepted every invitation that arrived at the house, and she insisted I join her in the social whirl. "You can't just sit around the house, Mimi," Mama said whenever I balked at attending some dull minister's reception or old dowager's dinner party. "You'll feel better if you start going out and meeting new people."

That summer, we were invited for the first time to the annual Fourth of July fête at the home of Dr. Thomas Evans, an American dentist who had been an intimate of the Emperor and Empress, both of whom had bad teeth and suffered from agonizing toothaches. After the Empire collapsed, Dr. Evans saved Eugénie from prison (and possibly the guillotine) by smuggling her out of the Tuileries and escorting her to safety in England, where she now lived with the ex-Emperor. Dr. Evans was the chief link between the expatriate community and what was left of Napoleonic royalty in France. Mama had met Dr. Evans at the Marine Ministry's "Four Continents" ball, and she had recently seen him again at the funeral of Mathilde Slidell, who had suffered a fatal heart attack while on vacation in Brighton. Mama was eager to become part of his coterie.

On July Fourth, Mama and I arrived in midafternoon at Bella Rosa, Dr. Evans's estate at the edge of the Bois de Boulogne. Named for its fragrant rose gardens, Bella Rosa sat in a lovely park with ponds, stables, a greenhouse, and an aviary for exotic birds. Carriages lined the circular drive in front of the lozenge-shaped stone mansion, the first home in Paris to have central heating, while a gaggle of drivers smoked under the hickory and walnut trees imported from Pennsylvania.

Mama and I entered the cavernous foyer with its bright paintings, mostly of American landscapes and heroes: a view of Niagara Falls; large, flag-bedecked portraits of George Washington, Ulysses S. Grant, and Lafayette. A butler directed us past the leather-walled library, the pastel salons, and the gilt-mirrored ballroom to French doors opening onto a clipped green lawn. At the center stood a huge white tent with an American flag waving from a pole on top.

We ducked under the flaps and entered. The air was close, oppressive with perfume and sweat. Dr. Evans, tall and middle-aged with copious brown side whiskers, stood on a chair, a champagne flute in his right hand lifted to the canvas ceiling, as he toasted the country of his birth: "And so I say to you, the flag of our fathers is never so beautiful or so glorious as when raised on foreign soil!" Polite clapping rippled through the tent.

I scanned the room. Most of the guests looked French, and I recognized a few, including Etincelle. Dressed in blue silk, notebook and pen in hand, she strode toward Mama and me, trailed by an emaciated young man with pocked, dough-colored skin and a nose like a purple gourd.

"Here comes Etincelle," Mama whispered. Crinkling her eyes, she studied the young man. "Why, that's the duc de Cheverny!"

"Who's he?"

"Only the scion of one of the oldest and richest families in France!"

A moment later, Etincelle and the young man were standing in front of us.

"Madame Avegno! Mademoiselle Avegno!" Etincelle cried. "Please let me present you to Monsieur le duc de Cheverny."

The gangly duke, his heavily oiled brown hair combed over his narrow skull, bowed dramatically. He took Mama's hand in his and touched it with his thin lips. Then he turned to me.

"Why, it's Pauline Bonaparte, back from the dead!" he cried, referring to Napoléon's favorite sister, who was revered as the most beautiful woman of the First Empire.

"Mademoiselle Avegno is much more beautiful than any of the Bonapartes," Etincelle said brightly. "Look at these lines." The well-dressed columnist reached out and took me by the chin, turning my head to present the duke with my profile. "Pauline's ears were so ugly they confounded Canova. Mademoiselle Avegno's ears are perfect."

"Indeed, they are," enthused the duke. "And so is her skin. So smooth, like a rose petal."

Why were they discussing me as if I were a statue, as if I weren't there? And what made this ugly man an authority on beauty? I felt my face grow hot.

The orchestra burst into a Strauss waltz, and a few couples twirled onto the dance floor.

"Would you care to dance, Mademoiselle Avegno?" the duke said.

"Thank you, sir. But I'm not feeling too well. I was on my way outside for some fresh air."

His narrow countenance registered a slight hardening. "Perhaps another time, then." The duke bowed, even more dramatically now. He took Etincelle by the arm and led her away.

When they were out of earshot, Mama hissed, "Why wouldn't you dance with him? He's worth thirty million francs!"

"What good are thirty million francs if you look like a corpse?"

"He doesn't look like a corpse. He's young. Well, maybe not young, but no older than Pierre Gautreau."

"Do you really want me to start a friendship with the duc de Cheverny?"

"I just want you to know the best people."

"If the duc de Cheverny is the best people, I hate to see what the worst people look like."

Mama scowled into her champagne. I fled the tent and took one of the gravel paths that meandered past the rose gardens to a little pond full of gliding swans. Faint strains of Strauss's waltz wafted through the trees. Regarding my wobbly reflection in the gray pools of water, I imagined myself dancing with Dr. Pozzi. He held my waist and stared into my eyes with an expression of dazed adoration.

"Mimi!" Mama's voice broke my reverie. I couldn't see her, but I heard her leather shoes scrunching the gravel. She appeared from behind the hedges at the edge of the pond.

"I just ran into Fanny Reed," she said, fluttering her white lace fan. "You remember her. She's from Boston and operates a boarding school for American girls."

"I've never met her, Mama."

"Well, anyway, she's just charming. She's having a young people's luncheon tomorrow to introduce her girls to some Frenchmen. She's invited you. Isn't that nice?"

"What Frenchmen? The duc de Cheverny, I suppose."

"Probably. But other young men will be there, too."

"I don't know. I'll think about it."

"Well, at least you could try to enjoy *this* party." Mama turned irritably and headed up the path to the house. A buffet supper of fried chicken and corn on the cob was set out on the terrace. Mama and I sat at a white iron table with Etincelle and the duc de Cheverny. The horrid aristocrat stared at me throughout the meal. Etincelle, meanwhile, nattered on about a new category of English women called PB's, or "professional beauties." "The *Whitehall Review* has been writing about them. These are the women who are received in the best society but have no other occupation, no other ambition than to be beautiful," she said, holding a corncob in her long fingers. She looked at me with glittering eyes. "Now, Mimi," she said. "You keep up your music, so you don't end up a dull, dumb PB."

Etincelle placed her corncob on her plate and shifted her gaze beyond the terrace. "Maybe I should do a story on PB's. I've got to write *something* for tomorrow's column."

She reached in her purse, pulled out her pen and notebook, and started scribbling. Mama and I excused ourselves, called for our carriage, and returned home.

The next morning, Etincelle's column appeared on the front page of *Le Figaro*. The last line read, "Mademoiselle Virginie Amélie Avegno, the young American dazzler who lives with her charming mother near the Madeleine, is more beautiful than any PB I've seen here or abroad."

I imagined Dr. Pozzi reading Etincelle's words and, being reminded of my beauty and charm, realizing he needed to see me. That fantasy put me in a sociable mood, so I decided to go to Fanny Reed's luncheon after all.

It was a beautiful day, clear and sunny but not too warm. I walked to the rue de Rivoli and hailed a cab. We followed a route to Miss Reed's house on the rue de Nancy that took us past the place du Châtelet and the boulevard Sébastopol, the wide, straight east-west axis of the Grande Croisée that stretches to the Gare de l'Est through a bustling business district.

At the corner of the rue Réaumur, the street was blocked to traffic, and a crowd of hatless men and parasol-toting women lined the pavement. All eyes watched a strange cavalcade moving up the boulevard.

At first, I thought it was a military parade. Then I noticed the men were not soldiers; they were medical orderlies in white coats with red armbands and caps emblazoned with red crosses. They were carrying stretchers full of medical instruments—knives, bottles, scalpels, and steel clamps. Two men at the end carried a wood operating table with four leather straps for immobilizing a patient's arms and legs.

"What's going on here?" I asked the driver.

"One of the surgeons of the Central Bureau of Consultations is on his way to a hospital in the First Arrondissement to perform an operation. This happens several times a week."

Suddenly, in the third row, I saw the erect form of Dr. Pozzi. Marching with a loose-jointed athleticism between two short orderlies with jutting paunches, he held his head high and stared straight ahead.

Quickly, I paid the driver and stepped to the street. As the procession passed, I followed it up the pavement. The men walked slowly, and it was easy to keep up with them despite the layers of petticoats I wore in those days. Forty minutes later, the curious parade reached its destination, the Lariboisière Hospital, where they stopped outside the iron gate to speak to a guard.

I walked toward them, as if on my way to an appointment, as if just by coincidence I was on the street at the same moment as these medical men. My heart beat faster as I passed the white-coated group. I shot a glance at Dr. Pozzi. He was talking to his colleagues, his hands thrust in his pockets. I had gone halfway up the block when I heard my name.

"Mademoiselle Avegno!" Dr. Pozzi jogged toward me.

"Dr. Pozzi!" I tried to sound surprised.

"What are you doing all the way up here?" He stood with his hands folded across his chest, smiling broadly.

"I'm paying a call on a friend of Mama's."

I worried that he'd ask me who, and I planned to invent a name. Instead he said, "I've been meaning to write to you. But I've been terribly busy. And I've moved." He pulled a silver case from his coat pocket, removed a card, and handed it to me. He looked over his shoulder at the hospital entrance. His colleagues had gone inside.

"Listen, I must dash. Can you meet me in two hours at my apartment for a late lunch? I don't have time to go to restaurants anymore. My housekeeper is a wonderful cook."

"Well . . ."

"Please. You must give me a chance to explain why I haven't been in touch."

"All right. But I can't stay long."

"Wonderful!" Dr. Pozzi bowed slightly, then ran toward the hospital entrance.

I looked at his card: DR. SAMUEL-JEAN POZZI. 131, BOULEVARD SAINT-GERMAIN. FIFTH FLOOR. I took a cab to the carrefour de Buci, bought copies of *L'Illustration* and *La Mode illustrée* at a newspaper kiosk, and settled into a wicker chair on the terrace of a café. I flipped through the magazines but couldn't concentrate on any of the articles or pictures. I fantasized that Dr. Pozzi would beg my forgiveness and declare his love for me. I would treat him with icy contempt, wounding him as he had wounded me.

At two o'clock, I paid the bill and walked toward the exit. *"Un sou pour le garçon!"* the waiter shouted after me. In my self-absorption, I had forgotten to leave a tip. Flushed with embarrassment, I went back and left a few coins on the table. Then I exited the restaurant and headed north. As I reached the rue de Seine, thunderclaps pierced the air, and a moment later a hard rain showered the neighborhood.

I'm insane to visit him in his rooms, I thought as I covered my head with *La Mode illustrée* and ran past the stone facades and iron balconies of the tall new buildings. *I'm only going to talk to him for a few minutes and then be on my way.*

By the time I reached Number 131, I was dripping wet. I was about to ring the bell, when Dr. Pozzi appeared at my side under an enormous black umbrella.

"Hello, Mademoiselle," he said softly. "Don't you believe in umbrellas?" His smile looked slightly sinister. But he was so beautiful, I felt my heart soften.

"This is a bad idea," I said. "I should leave."

"Don't be a little fool. At least come up until it stops raining."

Dr. Pozzi took a key from his pocket and opened the door. We entered a small dark foyer. "I'm afraid it's a long way to the top," he said, nodding toward a narrow staircase.

We said nothing to each other as we climbed the creaking stairs. On the fifth floor, Dr. Pozzi pulled another key from his pocket and opened the door.

I stepped into a small salon. The burgundy brocaded walls were hung with colorful paintings in beautiful gilt frames. Sophie Tranchevent's portrait of a young woman bathing had pride of place over the mantel. A small landscape by Filomena Seguette hung on the opposite wall over a table displaying a collection of Greek coins.

My bodice was soaked through to the skin, and I shuddered from chill and nervousness.

"I'll get you a wrap," Dr. Pozzi said. He disappeared into the bedroom and returned a minute later with a black wool shawl. "I want to explain why I haven't written to you," he said, draping the shawl across my shoulders. My heart quickened at his touch.

He took me by the hand and pulled me toward the settee. "You can't imagine how busy I've been. I'm a slave to the Central Bureau. All the young surgeons are. We must wait until someone dies or retires before we can get regular posts at one of the hospitals. Until then, we're on call to go wherever and whenever someone needs an operation. And for some reason I get the most difficult cases. Today I removed a fibroid tumor the size of a pumpkin from a woman's uterus." He searched my eyes for a reaction.

I was filled with longing for him but tried to fix my face in a blank mask. I've always been good at hiding my emotions—my daughter, Louise, would later call me *le visage impassible,* the poker face, and I was succeeding now with Dr. Pozzi.

He leaned over and stared deeply into my eyes. "My God, you are beautiful," he whispered. "The most beautiful girl I've ever seen." The next thing I knew, his mouth was crushing mine. He undid the buttons of my bodice and his hands moved over my breasts. Lifting my skirts over my hips, he lay me on my back and moved on top of me.

After we had made love, Dr. Pozzi stepped out to the balcony to smoke a cigar. I sat up on the settee and began buttoning my bodice. I considered removing it completely and retying my corset—one of the stays was pinching my skin—but just then I heard a key in the lock. The door creaked open, and a stout middle-aged woman walked in carrying several parcels—the maid.

"Good afternoon, Mademoiselle," she said. If she was surprised to see me, she didn't show it.

"Good day," I answered. I smoothed my skirts, and when the maid passed to the kitchen, I ran to the balcony. The rain had stopped, and a shimmering rainbow rose in the sky. Dr. Pozzi puffed on his cigar and looked out over the carrefour de Buci with its bustling arcaded shops beneath eighteenth-century apartments.

"Your maid is here," I said.

"Oh, good. Did she bring lunch?" He turned and, leaning against the rain-slicked iron railing, smiled at me. His calm manner was infuriating.

"If she'd arrived five minutes earlier, she'd have walked in on us!"

"But she didn't, darling." Dr. Pozzi blew a ring of blue smoke into the clean air. "Now, my love, let's have something to eat."

"I really should go." I wanted to stay, but I was too embarrassed to face the maid.

"Will you come back on Thursday, same time?"

"Perhaps." I ran through the apartment, not giving the maid a chance to speak to me, and out the door.

I did return the following Thursday, and every Tuesday and Thursday after that, for ten months. Soon I was no longer self-conscious around Dr. Pozzi's maid, a kind, sturdy Breton woman who always behaved toward me with motherly concern. Indeed, she sometimes helped me lace my corset, and once she mended a skirt I had torn getting out of a cab in front of Dr. Pozzi's building.

Dr. Pozzi always treated me tenderly, but looking back on that time, I see he wasn't very interested in me when we weren't making love. He chattered as much as an old peasant woman—I rarely got a chance to say anything—but the talk was all about himself.

He told me a great deal about his childhood. The eldest of two sons of a minister and his fragile wife, Dr. Pozzi had grown up in bourgeois comfort in a large house in Bordeaux. He lost his mother at ten, a tragedy which was one of the few things he didn't want to talk about. He had three sisters, but Dr. Pozzi was the beauty of the family, tall and slender with creamy olive skin, delicate, even features, and masses of wavy dark hair. His friends called him *la Sirène*.

He was as brilliant as he was gorgeous, and at eighteen he moved to Paris to begin medical studies at the Hôpital de la Pitié. For a while, he lived with his wealthy cousin, a doctor who treated many of the Napoleonic royalty. The cousin introduced Dr. Pozzi to Princess Mathilde, his prize patient. She was charmed by the handsome young man, and he quickly became part of her inner circle.

When I met Dr. Pozzi in 1870, he was only twenty-five but was already known for his surgical prowess. He specialized in treating female maladies, and if you thought that his ardor for women would be squelched by looking all day at female private parts, you'd be wrong. Dr. Pozzi was as famous for romance as he was for his looks and brilliance. Among his rumored conquests were several married noblewomen and Sarah Bernhardt, who called him Doctor Dieu.

Dr. Pozzi never mentioned his other women, and though it's hard to believe I was once so naive, I assumed he had given up everyone else for me. I actually believed that we'd be married when I was older and he had received his surgeon's title. He gave me a gold ring with six small diamonds, which I didn't dare wear, fearing the questions it would raise with Mama and Julie. During the day, I kept it under my pillows. I wore it only while I slept. Though Dr. Pozzi didn't speak of marriage, I regarded the ring as a sign of his honorable intentions. In return, I gave him a copy of Baudelaire's poems bound in embroidered blue silk from a chemise of mine he had once ripped in a moment of passion.

Mama and Julie were never home when I left for Dr. Pozzi's apartment at midday, or when I returned in late afternoon. Julie went to her studio every morning before eight. Mama usually left the house at nine, carrying a large case of calling cards. After paying a few visits, she'd have lunch at Bignon's or Tortoni's, followed by a little browsing in the shops. Typically, she returned at five. I always beat her home by at least an hour. Julie never returned before six.

That spring, my aunt had a painting accepted for the first time at the annual Salon. Her portrait of a young woman brushing her hair in front of a light-filled window was a superb example of Julie's talent for color and composition, and she had high hopes it would win a first-, second-, or third-class medal—the top prize, the Salon Medal of Honor, was reserved for French artists.

On varnishing day, Julie left the house early to join her friends for breakfast in the restaurant adjoining the Palais de l'Industrie. Mama and I followed two hours later. It was a beautiful spring day, fresh and clear. A warm breeze swirled the air, and white puffs of clouds drifted in the sky. We arrived at the Champs-Elysées as hundreds of men and women streamed under the Palais's massive arcade. The cavernous entrance hall was mobbed, and a great symphony of footsteps echoed on the cold flagstone floor. Mama and I pushed our way through the crowd to the fourth gallery on the left, where the program told us we'd find the "T's"—the artists' pictures were grouped alphabetically. Thousands of paintings, stacked row upon row, reached up twenty feet to the ceiling. White cotton had been stretched under the skylights to block the sun's glare, and a diffused light filtered in, bathing the canvases in a soft, dusty glow.

We found Julie in the fourth gallery with Sophie Tranchevent, Filomena Seguette, Carolus-Duran, and several men I had never seen before. Dressed in a new pink silk gown with a green moiré sash, her fine hair piled on her head and held in place with two shell combs, Julie stood without her cane as Sophie and Filomena supported her elbows.

Directly to Julie's left hung her painting. It had been placed "on line"—that is, at eye level—where the Salon committee hung those works it judged to be of the highest quality.

"Virginie! Mimi!" Julie cried as we approached.

"There's been a crowd around her painting all morning," said Filomena, beaming. Her own picture, a large canvas depicting a battle scene from the 1848 Revolution, was in a special gallery for previous medal winners.

"I guess I'm the failure of the group," moaned Sophie. "I've been skyed." She pointed toward the ceiling, where her picture of a reclining nude was barely visible, lost in a sea of similar nudes.

"The committee was in a bad temper when they looked at your picture," consoled Julie. "We all think it's striking. The best thing you've done."

"It's so exciting," Julie said, turning to Mama and me. "I've been standing next to the picture so I can hear people's comments. One man was complaining that Carolus must have worked on it. 'No woman is that good,' he bellowed."

Soon I was aware of someone standing behind me. I turned to see a willowy dark-haired woman expensively dressed in peach satin. She glared at me with black almond-shaped eyes. I stared back and scowled until she walked away. Then I forgot about her.

Julie had given Mama and me a list of ten paintings to see, and, armed with a program, we made our way through the galleries. There were pictures in every imaginable style—classical scenes, landscapes, history paintings, portraits. But the galleries were so packed with people—in some it was impossible to move from one end to the other—that we managed to find only four of the works on Julie's list.

"Mama, I'm exhausted. Can we go?" I asked after we had looked around for two hours.

"Yes! My head is spinning. I was only staying because I thought you wanted to," Mama said. "Let's have lunch at Magny's."

We left the galleries and walked through the entrance hall toward the exit. Standing at the ticket gate was the black-haired woman who had glared at me earlier.

"Do you know who *she* is?" I asked Mama, nodding toward the woman.

"The one in peach satin?" Mama narrowed her eyes to focus better. "Why, that's Marguerite Orléans!"

"Who's she?"

"One of the great whores of the Second Empire," Mama snickered. "A favorite of the Emperor's. Pierre pointed her out to me one night at the Bal Mabille."

Mademoiselle Orléans couldn't have been more than twenty-five, but her narrow face looked hard and worn. I don't think she had ever been beautiful. Over the years, I've met many of the grand *horizontales,* and few of them were even pretty, despite their reputation for glamour. Most of them had good figures, of course, and they disguised their ordinary faces with makeup and well-dressed hair. Mean and often stupid, they were old by forty, dead by fifty.

Marguerite looked up from the program she had been studying, noticed me watching her, and stared back.

"Let's go," I said and grabbed Mama's arm. I led her through the Palais's arcade and down the avenue des Champs-Elysées, past the long row of plane trees, the jetting fountains, and the statues of the mythical figures Prometheus, Venus, Diana, and Flora.

We got into a cab at the place de la Concorde and set off up the rue Royale. As we passed the Madeleine, a landau pulled next to us. Our cab speeded up, but the landau kept pace. We turned onto the boulevard des Capucines. The landau followed, then drew beside us, its white horses riding neck and neck with the cab's drays.

Through the landau's open windows I saw a flash of peach satin and raven hair. Marguerite Orléans was following us.

Our cab creaked to a stop in front of Magny's. Marguerite Orléans's landau stopped behind ours. Before we could enter the restaurant, she ran up to us.

"Mademoiselle, I demand an interview." Her almond eyes blazed fiercely.

"What is the meaning of this?" said Mama.

"Mademoiselle Avegno knows exactly what I want to talk to her about."

"I'm afraid I don't." I was trembling, and my voice cracked with fear.

Marguerite turned to Mama. "Your daughter may be the age of a schoolgirl, but she is just as experienced as me," she sneered.

The color drained from Mama's face. She opened her mouth as if to speak, but no words came out.

"She's crazy," I said to Mama. Then I shouted to Marguerite, "Leave us alone!"

"I want to return your earring to you." Marguerite reached inside her purse and pulled out a dangling gold earring with a pearl drop on the end—one of a pair Grandmère had given me before we left Parlange.

Mama's eyes grew wide, her face even paler.

"Mimi, what's she doing with your earring?"

"I found it in the bed of my lover, Dr. Sam Pozzi."

Mama grabbed my arm and jerked me toward the taxi stand. She pulled me into a cab. "Forty-four, rue de Luxembourg," she said, her voice quivering.

"It's not my earring," I lied.

Mama stared straight ahead, her face a stiff white mask. "As soon as we get home, I want to see the pair of earrings Grandmère gave you."

The cab pulled to a halt in front of our house. Mama pushed me to the pavement and marched behind me through our front door and up the stairs to my room. She retrieved my onyx jewelry box from the dressing table and held it out to me. "The earrings, please," she demanded.

I grabbed the box from her hands and flung it across the room. A shower of glittery objects scattered across the parquet.

"I don't have it!" I shouted and dashed to my sitting room. Mama ran after me, but I got the door shut and locked before she reached it.

"Mimi! Come out!" Mama banged on the door with both fists. "Do you realize what this means? No one will marry you now. You're ruined. And don't think I'll put up with your whoring. I'll turn you out. You'll end up working in the refreshment room of the women's prison at Saint-Lazare!"

"Dr. Pozzi will marry me. We love each other!"

"You love each other!" she snorted. "I've raised a fool!"

A moment later, I heard Mama's heels clicking down the hall. I fell to the floor, sobbing, and cried until I had no more tears left. I was still whimpering on the floor two hours later, when there was knocking on my door.

"Mimi, it's me, Julie. Open up."

"Is Mama with you?" I cried.

"No. She came to the Palais to get me, and I left her there with Sophie and Filomena. Let me in."

My head was throbbing, and I felt an icy sinking in my stomach. I was so ashamed for spoiling Julie's Salon debut. I opened the door and fell into my aunt's arms.

"Oh, Mimi," she said.

"I'm so sorry. I'm so sorry," I cried, my voice breaking with sobs.

"Today doesn't matter. It's you I'm worried about." Holding each other, we collapsed on the settee. "I blame myself for not paying enough attention to you. And I blame *him*." She frowned. "But this is not the end of the world. You can write to him tomorrow morning. You'll break with him and move on."

"But I love him!"

"I'm afraid he's deceived you, Mimi. You have no future with Dr. Pozzi."

"That woman Marguerite Orléans was lying. I'm sure of it."

"I doubt that very much, *chérie.*"

Julie stayed with me for the rest of the afternoon and evening. One of the maids brought us supper on a tray, though neither of us ate anything. I played the piano a bit; we talked; and eventually we both fell asleep in my big four-poster.

That night I dreamed of Valentine. She was running up the alley of oaks at Parlange, while I sat in a wicker chair on the gallery, knitting a child's sweater. She wore a blue cotton dress that reached just below her knees, white stockings, and black leather shoes. Her thin legs loped gracefully in the slow motion of my dream, her silky red hair undulated out from her shoulders. As she drew close to the house, she stumbled on a stone and began to fall forward. I rose from my chair, dropping my knitting, and leaned over the gallery railing. Then I, too, started to tumble head first, over and over. Before I hit the ground, I snapped awake.

I felt sick to my stomach. I got out of bed, staggered toward the basin, and vomited. It was the first time I had thrown up since I began to suspect I was pregnant, about a month before. The idea was too horrible to face, so I had pushed it to the back of my mind.

Julie rushed to my side, leaned over me, and wiped my forehead with a damp cloth.

"I think I'm *enceinte*," I said.

"Oh, God," Julie moaned. "When are you supposed to see him again?" She spat the word "him."

"Today, at one."

"I'll go with you."

"Mama will never let me out of the house."

"I'll take care of your mother."

Julie went to her room to dress. A half hour later, I heard her and Mama screaming in the hall outside my door. Mama was threatening to send me back to Louisiana, shrieking that I could "rot in the country" for all she cared.

"She's just a child, Virginie," Julie shouted back. "It's not her fault. That man is a horror. You know his reputation. I want to talk to her. I'm taking her out for some fresh air."

I heard Mama scurry down the hall, then a door slammed. A moment later, Julie entered my room. "The coast is clear," she said. "Let's go."

Outside, filmy white clouds scudded across the blue sky, and golden light filtered through the trees. We took a cab to Dr. Pozzi's building, arriving just as the maid waddled out the front entrance.

I followed Julie up the stairs to the fifth floor. At the top, she rang the bell.

Dr. Pozzi opened the door dressed as he usually was for our trysts, in a floor-length red dressing gown tied with gold cord. On his feet were red embroidered slippers. "Mimi, you've brought your aunt," he said, actually sounding pleased to see Julie.

In the parlor, Dr. Pozzi took our shawls and hung them on a coat-rack. Ignoring me, he said to Julie, "Congratulations, Mademoiselle de Ternant, on your success at the Salon. I hear you're likely to get a bronze medal." He smiled broadly.

Julie dug her cane into the Turkish carpet and glared at him. She was about to speak when I blurted out, "I'm pregnant."

Dr. Pozzi's smile evaporated, and his eyes hardened. "I rather doubt it," he said. He looked quickly at Julie, then at me. "Is that why you're both here? Well, let's have a look." He put his arm around my shoulder and began to lead me to the bedroom.

Julie took a step toward him. He put out his hand to stop her. "Don't forget, I'm a doctor. If you want to know for certain, you must let me examine her."

In the bedroom, Dr. Pozzi closed the door behind us. "Lie down," he ordered.

"Have you been sleeping with a whore named Marguerite Orléans?" I asked, trying to keep my voice level.

"Oh, God." Dr. Pozzi flopped into a leather chair near the window, pulled a handkerchief from his pocket, and wiped his brow.

"You've deceived me!" I cried.

"I haven't deceived you. I've supplemented you. We're not married, may I remind you, and I've never promised you anything."

"Well, you must marry me now!"

"Let's see if you *are* pregnant."

I lay across the green satin comforter. Dr. Pozzi lifted my skirts above my waist, fumbled under my petticoats, and pulled my drawers off over my shoes and stockings. He parted my legs, and placing his left hand on my belly, he reached deep inside me with his right hand. I felt a sharp pinching. Then he pulled his hand out and walked to the wash-basin. Along the way, he kicked the chest where he kept his French Letters, the sheepskin contraceptives that were popular at the time.

"The uterus *is* enlarged. It's true. You're pregnant," he said as he washed his hands.

"We'll get married, won't we?"

Dr. Pozzi looked up to the ceiling, then walked over to the bed and sat down next to me. "Darling, I can't marry you or anyone else right now."

"Why?"

"It's just out of the question—my work."

"What's going on in there?" Julie shouted through the door. Dr. Pozzi opened it, and my aunt hobbled into the room.

"She's pregnant," he said.

"You will marry her, then?" said Julie.

"I was just explaining to Mademoiselle Avegno that marriage is impossible."

"May I remind you of your honor, sir."

"I don't consider it honorable to ruin both our lives in a hasty marriage. Mademoiselle Avegno is not compelled to have this baby. I can cut it out. I've done it dozens of times. It's a safe, simple procedure if performed by an expert surgeon, which I am." Dr. Pozzi spoke flatly, his face a blank, dispassionate mask.

"Will it hurt?" I asked.

"I'll give you ether to put you to sleep," Dr. Pozzi answered.

"And it really is safe?"

"Absolutely—if I do it."

"It is *not* safe, no matter who does it," Julie cried. Her eyes looked frightened. "In fact, it is extremely dangerous. Why do you think so many prostitutes die?"

She shifted her gaze to Dr. Pozzi. "Abortions are for whores," she snapped. "I won't let you risk my niece's life. We will make other arrangements."

Julie grabbed my arm and dragged me out of the bedroom. She snatched our shawls off the coatrack and pulled me through the door and down the five flights of stairs.

On the boulevard Saint-Germain, the sun glinted on the cold expanse of new buildings, illuminating their carved cornices. The air smelled fresh, floral.

"What other arrangements were you talking about?" I said as we waited for a cab. My head throbbed with pain, and I felt a sob rising in my throat. Julie stared into the cloudless blue sky.

"Tell me! What other arrangements!" I screamed.

"I have no idea, *chérie,* no idea at all."

Seven

On a rainy evening two weeks later, I arrived by train at the gnarled stone depot in Saint-Malo on the northern coast of Brittany. The little station was deserted except for a lone carriage parked by the side of the road and a coachman in leather breeches standing next to it. As I stepped to the wet platform, the coachman ran toward me.

"Mademoiselle Avegno?" he asked.

"Yes," I said. I drew my thin shawl across my chest. Though it was August, the air was raw, and I was shivering.

"Come with me."

He took my carpetbag and led me to his carriage. No sooner was I settled inside than the reins snapped and the old broughham lurched toward the dark, dripping woods.

We were headed for Paramé, site of Château des Chênes, the estate where Pierre Gautreau had grown up and where his widowed mother still lived with her unmarried, half-witted niece. As the carriage clattered through the muddy roads, past the marshlands and forests where pirates once roamed, water slapped the windows, and the wind bellowed.

It took a half hour to reach the château. We entered through high stone gates and drove along a gravel road past an intricate pattern of gardens. As the rain beat down, water overflowed the fountains and streamed off the statues of Greek gods and goddesses. At the end of the road was a circular drive and, silhouetted against the sky, a four-story *malouinière* dominated by row upon row of white shuttered windows. The carriage halted; the driver jumped from his seat and opened the door. He helped me to the ground, then removed my carpetbag and placed it on the doorstep. "There you are, Mademoiselle. Good night," he said, tipping his hat as he ran back to the carriage.

I pulled a thick gold rope that hung on an iron hook, and heard chimes within. A minute later, a maid opened the door and led me through a marble-floored foyer to the salon. It was a high-ceilinged circular room, opening out to a terrace and a garden beyond. The room was decorated conventionally—Pierre's Oriental aesthetic was nowhere in sight—with red plush sofas and chairs, and mustard damask covering the walls. A porcelain clock ticked loudly on the mantel; the gas lamps hissed. Playing cards at a table at the far end of the room were two somberly dressed old women—Pierre's mother and aunt.

I hated them on sight. Madame Gautreau was short and wide-hipped, with hooded, watery brown eyes and a wrinkled, liver-spotted face. Her wiry gray hair was arranged in a bun at her neck, and she was dressed in a dark gown with a lace-bordered collar. The ivory-knobbed cane she used to rap on the floor to summon the servants rested across her pillowy lap.

The aunt, Millicent La Chambre, was the ugliest woman I had ever seen. She had a long, bumpy nose dotted with hairy, purple moles, and red-veined, bulging eyes. She was wearing a shapeless black gown with a traditional Breton collar of pleated white muslin. Her vacant expression suggested, as Pierre had warned me, that she was "not right in the head."

Though Millicent was Madame Gautreau's niece, they were exactly the same age. Madame Gautreau's mother had become pregnant at fifty, in the same month that her eighteen-year-old daughter conceived Millicent. The fact that the old mother gave birth to a beautiful child, while the adolescent's offspring was hideous, seemed a cruel irony. Madame Gautreau's mother had offered to switch children—"Everyone will expect an old lady to have an ugly baby," she had said—but her daughter had refused. She remained devoted to Millicent until her own death in middle age, at which time the poor creature moved in with Pierre's mother and father. Millicent had tried to be useful, helping with the light housework and sometimes, when the governess was ill, looking after Pierre. Her idea of amusing the little boy was to teach him to smoke cigarettes.

The old women interrupted their card game to stare wide-eyed at me. A moment later, Madame Gautreau spoke. "Good evening, Mademoiselle. I trust you had a pleasant journey." Her voice was raspy, heavy with round Breton tones.

Before I had a chance to answer, Millicent blurted out, "I've got cigarettes. Want one?" She reached into her pocket and started to rise from her chair.

"Sit down!" barked Madame Gautreau.

Millicent dropped into her seat. Her mouth was twitching slightly, and a wounded look appeared on her face. Madame Gautreau turned toward me.

"Well, I'm sure you're tired. Angeline will bring you something to eat in your room." She waved her large knuckled hand at me and returned to her cards.

"Thank you," I said. The old lady's rudeness annoyed me, though I was happy to escape her company.

Carrying a tray containing a bowl of soup, bread, and a bottle of red wine, the maid Angeline led me upstairs and through a maze of dimly lit corridors. "Here's your room, Mademoiselle," she said, opening the door onto a square, oak-beamed boudoir. Above the mantel hung a painting of Christ's Crucifixion. Old brown calico curtains draped the bed; the same fabric covered the sofa and two chairs. Angeline left the tray on the table and mumbled, *"Bonne nuit."*

After she left, I explored the warren of rooms surrounding the bedchamber. Door opened upon door, revealing a cluster of closets, antechambers, and a wainscoted *cabinet de toilette.* There were two garderobes. One held a large armoire; the other contained a bidet, a washbasin, and a chamber pot. A panel behind the bidet hid a door to a secret staircase leading to the garden. I learned later that in pre-

Revolutionary times, the house had been owned by the grandfather of Chateaubriand's wife, Céleste Buisson. It was here, according to local lore, perhaps in this very room, that the famous writer kidnapped Céleste, whose family opposed their union, and fled with her into the forest.

Just as I finished the meager supper prepared by Angeline, there was a knock on the door. I opened it to find Millicent standing in the darkness, holding a lighted candle stub.

"Do you want to see my rabbits tomorrow?" she asked.

"Where are your rabbits?"

"In a cage near the stables. My niece won't allow them in the house." She held the candle stub in front of my face and stared at me with her mouth open.

"Millicent, why are you looking at me like that?"

"I want you to see my rabbits. I have white ones and brown ones."

"Fine. I'll visit the rabbits tomorrow. Now it's time to go to sleep." I closed the door, got undressed, and fell exhausted into bed.

The next morning, I was awakened by chapel bells tolling for an old peasant who had died during the night. The storm had broken, and a cool, fresh breeze floated in from the windows. I flung wide the bed curtains, dressed quickly, and took the secret staircase to the garden to explore the grounds.

Château des Chênes was its own little village, busy with a greenhouse, stables, a laundry, a meadow with grazing sheep and cows, plum orchards, a caretaker's cottage, workers' huts, gardens filled with statuary, and a small stone chapel where Pierre's mother and cousin said prayers every day and heard Mass on Sundays. Surrounding it all was the forest of oaks that gave the compound its name.

At the end of the garden, I took a path that led through the woods to a burbling stream. I removed my shoes and stockings and walked along the edge, letting the water roll over my feet. As I strolled, inhaling the cool, briny air, I brooded about the events that had brought me here.

The discovery of my pregnancy and Dr. Pozzi's abandonment of me had plunged Mama into paroxysms of rage and grief. Now she had no hope of fulfilling her chief ambition—to marry me off to a French aristocrat. I wasn't in the room when Julie broke the news to her, but for days afterward Mama stormed around the house, threatening to pack me off to a home in Lyon for incorrigible girls or across the ocean to Parlange. I begged for the latter, but upon reflection Mama decided to keep me in France. "I don't want everyone at home to see what you've become," she hissed.

"I'll say I was married and that my husband died," I pleaded.

"So you'd lie? They'd all see right through you," Mama snapped.

That evening, Mama went out to dinner with Pierre Gautreau. They returned to the house together at ten and sent the maid to my room to bring me downstairs. When I entered the salon, they were sitting next to each other on a settee, looking white and solemn. Mama rose to let me sit next to Pierre, then settled herself on a chair by the mantel.

Pierre took my hands in his and gazed deeply into my eyes. "Your mother told me what has happened," he said gravely. "I'm offering to marry you and give a name to your child."

I yanked my hands from his and slid to the far end of the settee. "Marry you!" An image of Pierre lying naked on top of me flashed through my head. I shuddered.

As if reading my mind, he said, "I'm proposing a *mariage blanc*. I will make no claims on my rights as a husband. You and your child will live in my house, but for the most part our lives will be separate."

"Why would you do this? Don't you want a *real* wife?"

"I was engaged once, to a girl in Brittany. A childhood friend. But she died of typhoid five years ago."

Mama jumped to her feet, twisting a linen handkerchief in her hands. "Tell her about Madame Jeuland," she said.

"Who is Madame Jeuland?"

"Madame Jeuland is Pierre's *petite amie*—" Mama began.

"She's married to a well-known Paris lawyer," Pierre interrupted. "He knows about us but will not separate from his wife, as it would ruin his career. My marriage to you would give Madame Jeuland and me a convenient cover. And it will get my mother off my back about remaining a bachelor." Pierre stroked his beard. His eyes looked large and sad.

This was the first I had heard of his having a lover. I had always assumed he was secretly in love with Mama.

"Do I have any other choice?"

"No." Pierre and Mama answered at the same time.

Over the next few weeks, Pierre came several times to rue de Lux-embourg for dinner. It was just the three of us in the dining room, Mama and Pierre sitting at either end of the long table with me on the side facing the marble fireplace. Neither of them mentioned the baby, or marriage. Mostly they talked about furniture and their various plans for redecoration. I had no interest in this subject, and I said nothing.

For a while, I'd listen resentfully. Then my mind would wander off. I'd be far away in a daydream, imagining Dr. Pozzi proposing to me on bended knee, then our romantic wedding at Saint-Sulpice. Once, when I was envisioning myself floating down the steps of the church on Pozzi's arm, the train of my white silk gown billowing out behind me like a sail, Mama's voice burst through the reverie. "You're not eating a thing," she scolded.

"I'm not hungry," I snapped. I had lost all interest in food. I was dropping weight when I should have been gaining. I was sleeping badly, too. Often I dreamed of Dr. Pozzi and woke up yearning for his embrace. These spasms of longing were followed by fits of rage, not only at the handsome doctor but also at myself for behaving so reck-lessly. I was profoundly confused. One moment I vowed to snub Pozzi if ever I ran into him again, and the next I plotted a meeting with him. In my mind's eye, I looked breathtakingly beautiful and Dr. Pozzi found me impossible to resist; realizing that he couldn't live without me, he begged my forgiveness.

Eventually boredom and wretchedness drove me to act foolishly. One evening, I told Mama I was going to Julie's atelier, and I took a taxi to Dr. Pozzi's apartment on boulevard Saint-Germain. I had the idea of confronting him when he arrived home from work. I stood in the shad-ows by a newspaper kiosk. My heart raced, and my face felt flushed, though it was a balmy evening, luminous with starlight. What would I say to him? What would he say to me? I began to panic. Suppose he spoke harshly to me? Suppose he was with another woman? That thought brought a sob to my throat. I choked back tears, and at that moment, Mama's carriage pulled to the curb. She had followed me.

"Mimi, come here," she called as she stepped to the pavement. I ran across the street, hailed a cab, and beat her home by two minutes. By the time she arrived, I had locked myself in my bedroom.

At breakfast, Mama announced that I would leave that afternoon for the Gautreau estate in Brittany. Pierre telegrammed his mother to inform her of our engagement, and to let her know that he was sending me to Château des Chênes for a few weeks so I could get to know his family. It was undecided how long I'd remain in the country, or when we'd be married.

The walk through the woods that first morning in Paramé refreshed me, and I returned to the house at ten. A formal table had been set with china, crystal, and silver, and a footman stood behind each chair. Madame Gautreau was perched at the head; Millicent and I sat opposite one another. Hardly a word was spoken as we ate baked ham and croissants and drank coffee from large white bowls. When the footmen had removed the dishes and departed for the kitchen, Madame Gautreau leaned across the table and said in her coarse rasp, "Mademoiselle Avegno, that dress is too décolleté for morning."

My yellow silk gown had a low, but hardly plunging, neckline.

"In Paris, this is a regulation daytime toilette," I replied, not trying to disguise my annoyance. I wasn't about to let Madame Gautreau dictate my appearance.

"That might be true. But you're not in the city now. I'll thank you to wear a shawl at table henceforth."

Suddenly a frightened look came over Millicent's face. A moment later, a brown rabbit darted from under the square white napkin on her lap, sprang across the table to the floor, and scurried across the room.

"Millicent!" screeched Madame Gautreau.

Millicent looked terror-stricken. "It was a p-p-present for Mademoiselle Avegno," she stammered. "For her baby."

"What baby?" Madame Gautreau snapped.

I felt my face turn scarlet. Pierre had not told his mother about my condition; indeed, he had urged me to try to hide it. Though the increase was barely discernible, I wasn't taking any chances. That morning I had laced my corset by throwing the strings over the bedpost and then pulling them as tight as I could until I was nearly suffocating. No one would suspect my pregnancy by looking at me.

"For Mademoiselle Avegno's baby," Millicent insisted, with the uncanny prescience of an idiot savant.

"Millicent, I'm sure I'll have a baby someday," I said, my cheeks burning. "But I'm not even married yet."

"Babies love rabbits," said Millicent.

"For the love of God, be quiet!" screamed Madame Gautreau.

The old woman signaled for a footman, who held an umbrella over her head as she hobbled out of the house to a little gazebo in the garden, where she and Millicent perched on stone benches knitting. I sat between them and read a book. At two, we returned to the house for lunch and then a card game. Millicent usually won. It turned out that buried in her simple mind she had a remarkable facility for numbers. After the game, we napped. Dinner was at eight, and we retired at ten.

This dismal routine was repeated every day except Sunday, when it was interrupted to hear Mass at the château chapel. At ten on Sunday morning, Madame Gautreau, Millicent and I made our way down a gravel path at the side of the garden to the little stone church. Earlier, the priest had read Mass for the peasants, and the air was redolent of their old musty clothes and unwashed flesh.

We took our places in the first pew, and the chapel quickly filled with the haute bourgeoisie from neighboring châteaux, all of whom were old friends of the Gautreaus. I despised these dull, somber *gentils-hommes,* and their smug, overfed wives. They led narrow, boring lives but were too closed-minded to see it. Coasting through life on money and pedigree, they lived out their days tending to their lands and houses, enjoying shooting parties and card games, large meals and early bedtimes, with no thought to the outside world. At least that's how it seemed to me.

I felt superior to them, as I did to Madame Gautreau and Millicent. Yet, I must admit, I also was a bit jealous of their stability and their firm place in the universe. If we had been at Parlange, not Château des Chênes, the tables would have been turned. Among the sophisticated, pleasure-loving Creoles, these dour rural Bretons would be nothing, their commonness evident to all. But we weren't in Louisiana. We were in Paramé.

After a while, Pierre's mother gave up pestering me about my clothes. She also began averting her eyes whenever she spoke to me, which was as little as possible. Millicent, however, was fascinated by my toilettes and studied me carefully when I came down for breakfast in the morning. Once, during a Sunday luncheon to which several neighbors had been invited, Millicent stared at me throughout the meal. Finally, as the coffee was brought in, she blurted out, "Mademoiselle Avegno is a swan in a pond of ugly ducklings."

That's my secret solace, I thought, though I ignored her, as did everyone else.

My only diversion from the boredom at Château des Chênes was the rare occasion when I joined Madame Gautreau and Millicent on a shopping trip to Saint-Malo. Originally a fortified island at the mouth of the River Rance, Saint-Malo began as a monastic settlement, walled and built with the same gray granite stone as Mont-Saint-Michel, the famous spired abbey forty-three kilometers to the east. Later, during the interminable wars of Louis XIV and Louis XV, Saint-Malo became home to a brutal breed of pirate-mariners who grew rich from ship-building and slave trading and erected a network of tall stone palaces within the city walls.

One morning, after I had been at Château des Chênes several weeks, we took the carriage into town and parked on the rue des Marins, in front of the Gautreau Banking House, Pierre's Brittany office. "Would you mind if I went for a walk on the beach?" I asked.

"Do what you like," snarled Madame Gautreau as the driver helped her out of the carriage.

I left the main gate at Port Vincent and strolled out onto the sand toward the promontory of an islet, the Grand Bé. A plain black cross rose from the jagged rocks, marking the grave of Chateaubriand, who had died in 1848. A lone ship with a monogrammed sail bobbed behind the grim tomb; a few gulls swooped about. As I gazed out into the endless sea, a longing for my own death came over me.

Looking back at that time, I realize I was in a state of shock. My affair with Dr. Pozzi had scarred my heart and left me profoundly confused. I saw no relief from this agony, only more torment ahead in a *mariage blanc* to Pierre.

Impulsively, I gathered stones from the beach and filled the pockets of my jacket. Then I walked toward the water. Images of Papa and Valentine flashed through my head. Soon the waves would swallow me, and I would be with them in heaven.

But at that moment, I thought of my unborn child, and a picture of a red-haired little girl appeared in my mind's eye. She looked just like Valentine. I put my hands on my abdomen. Yes, I was sure it was a girl. Tears filled my eyes. I was beginning to love the baby. How could I kill it? It would be like letting Valentine die again. I saw ahead several years to when the baby was walking and talking. She would keep me company when I was lonely and Julie was busy with work. I had not had a real friend since Aurélie at convent school. Now the baby would be my companion. I thought of the games Aurélie and I had played, the hours we had spent whispering and laughing, and I imagined repeating those pleasures with my little girl. I grabbed the stones from my pocket and hurled them into the waves.

Suddenly my heart felt light, almost buoyant. I ran along the sand to the Port Vincent Gate and made my way to rue des Marins. Madame Gautreau and Millicent were waiting in the carriage, poring over a letter written in the burgundy ink favored by Pierre.

"My son wants to be married next Saturday," Madame Gautreau said as I entered the carriage. "I'll have to see if the priest is available." She was not planning a big celebration. She disapproved of me because I was American, because I had no dowry, and because I was too young. She had decided she didn't like me before she met me, and meeting me had not changed her mind.

Just as quickly as it had appeared, my lighthearted mood vanished.

"Does Saturday suit you, Mademoiselle Avegno?" Madame Gautreau asked. Her eyes looked as cold as stones.

I wanted to tell her that I hated her, that I wouldn't stay in her house another night, and that I'd never, ever marry her son. Instead I said, "Next Saturday would be fine."

Five days later, a month into my stay at Château des Chênes, Mama, Julie, and Pierre arrived from Paris. The civil marriage ceremony took place at city hall in Saint-Malo that afternoon, and the religious wedding at the château the next day.

The morning of the religious ceremony was overcast and cool. An early frost had withered the garden flowers, but the breeze floating through my bedroom windows held a faint floral scent, reminiscent of magnolia, as if Charles and the spirit of Grandmère were calling me across the ocean from Parlange. I closed my eyes and saw the familiar alley of oaks and the green-shuttered house with its white pillars and wide gallery, where I had spent so many happy moments. I longed to be there.

Julie had slept on the little bed in my *cabinet de toilette,* and in the morning we ate breakfast in my boudoir. As I sipped coffee, I gazed at the muslin bag holding the white silk gown that Mama had brought from Paris. Hanging from the top of an armoire door, it looked like a shroud. I felt a wave of misery in the pit of my stomach. I'd be dead in a *mariage blanc* to Pierre.

All morning, I had fantasized that Julie would come up with a solution to save me. But she said nothing.

"I can't go through with it," I stammered, choking back a sob. "I want to live with you. We could raise the baby together."

Julie laid her coffee cup on the table and moved closer to me on the settee.

"What would you do for money?" she asked. "My painting hardly brings in enough to keep you and a child. Anyway, it wouldn't be fair to the baby to grow up a bohemian bastard."

I started to cry. Julie took hold of the cane leaning against her knees and stood, stiffening her back. "It's time to get dressed, *chérie,*" she said. She helped me into my camisole, corset, chemise, stockings, and petticoats. Then she removed the dress from its bag and held it out for me to step into. As Julie fastened the buttons and smoothed the train, I thought back to her aborted wedding to Lucas Rochilieu. I'm sure she was thinking of it, too. Before we left the room, she hugged me tightly. "Have courage," she said.

I draped the train over my right forearm, and Julie held my hand as we made our way down the hall. When we reached the staircase, loud arguing rose from the first floor. In the salon, Madame Gautreau sat in her chair by the mantel barking at Millicent, who stood in front of her, bowing her head like a naughty child. On the wall behind her hung a large blue *immortelle,* the type of beaded funeral wreath placed on the tombs of loved ones on their feast days.

"Take it down at once!" Madame Gautreau shouted.

"It's for Denise!" implored Millicent. Denise was Pierre's dead fiancée.

"Well, then bring it to the cemetery later and put it on her grave."

"I want Pierre to go with me."

"You imbecile! It's his wedding day!" Madame Gautreau's face was purple with rage. If she hadn't been so fat and lazy, I'm sure she would have jumped up and slapped Millicent. Instead she banged her cane on the floor so hard it could be heard on the terrace, where Mama, Pierre, and the priest were chatting. Thinking Madame Gautreau's banging was a signal to start the ceremony, they stepped into the salon.

"Shall we begin?" said the priest, a thin, bald man who lived in rooms behind the château chapel. He stood in front of the mantel facing Pierre and me. Mama, Julie, Madame Gautreau, and Millicent sat on chairs around us.

The ceremony was over in five minutes. When the priest pronounced us man and wife, Pierre took my shoulders in his hands and brushed my lips chastely. "Long live the bride and groom!" cried Millicent. Then we retired to the dining room for a lunch of *écrevisses à la bordelaise* and *suprême de volaille.*

Afterward I changed into traveling clothes, and at four, Mama, Julie, Pierre, and I took the carriage into Saint-Malo, where we boarded a train for Paris. Mama and Julie sat on one side of the square compartment facing Pierre and me. Usually I read on trains, or sleep. But I was too restless for either. What's more, I was beginning to feel ill. My whole body ached, and my head pounded. I thought I might be coming down with influenza. The train rolled through the countryside, purple with heather, past the rough pastures and dark little villages. I tried to get comfortable. I removed my shoes, folded my jacket into a pillow, and leaned the small of my back against it. Nothing helped. The light began to fade, and the sky outside the window turned pink, then deep blue. Before it fell to black, a peculiar procession of gray clouds passed overhead.

Mama and Julie dozed while Pierre snored beside me. Suddenly a sharp pain gripped my abdomen. It subsided, then returned a minute later with stronger force. I felt sick to my stomach, like I might throw up.

"Pierre, I'm sick." I tugged on my new husband's sleeve to awaken him.

"What? Mimi? What's wrong?" Slowly he roused and looked at me through half-closed eyes.

"I'm sick."

"I'll get you a glass of water, dear."

Pierre left the compartment, and when he returned with the water, the pain was worse. I lay against his lap as he stroked my forehead.

The attacks of pain grew stronger. I was crying now, afraid I'd start screaming, I was in such agony. I clasped Pierre's hands and bit down on my own wrist; nothing helped. My cries had awakened Mama and Julie.

"What's wrong, Mimi?" Mama asked when she saw me slumped across Pierre's lap.

"We don't know," answered Pierre. "She started feeling ill almost as soon as we left Saint-Malo."

"Poor child," said Julie. She moved across the compartment and sat next to me.

By the time the train pulled into the Gare Montparnasse and the brakeman had parted the steel doors, I was in too much pain to walk.

As Pierre lifted me, I felt a warm wetness between my legs.

"My God! Her dress!" Mama cried. I looked down; the back of my skirt was soaked with blood. Pierre removed his coat, and Julie helped him tie it around my waist. Then Pierre, with Mama and Julie holding our bags, carried me off the train, through the crowded station, and into a cab. "Forty-four, rue de Luxembourg," Pierre directed the driver.

At home, he carried me up to my room and then left to fetch the doctor.

I lost consciousness for several hours. When I awoke, I was staring at the glint of a diamond tiepin in the blue-white morning light slanting through the window. My gaze shifted from the tiepin to the face above it. Staring down at me through thick, round spectacles was Dr. Marcel Chomel, who had once treated my skin with his arsenic-based Chomel's Solution.

"How are you feeling, Madame?" he asked softly. It was the first time anyone had called me Madame. It sounded strange.

"My head is so heavy," I said as I started to sit up.

Dr. Chomel gently pushed me back against the pillows with a cool hand. Mama and Julie stood on either side of the bed with pale, weary faces.

"*Chérie,* you lost the baby," Julie said.

I glanced at Mama. All the anger and tension of the previous weeks had drained from her face. She looked relieved.

"It's true, Mimi," she said softly.

"Where's Pierre?"

"He's gone to his office. He'll be back this afternoon to see you."

At that moment, I was too weak and sick to feel sad. But over the following days, as I began to recover, I mourned the infant as if I had lost a living child whom I had nursed and loved. Even at my young age, I'd learned how sorrow builds upon sorrow; the heart can take just so much. My grief for the unborn baby renewed my grief for Papa and Valentine, which always hovered below my surface cheerfulness, waiting to bubble up and overwhelm me. Some days I cried so much I thought I'd never stop.

About the only good thing I can say of this time is that Dr. Pozzi was not part of my misery. I had stopped loving him. One day, I woke up and felt no pain or longing when I thought of him—only regret that I had ever met him.

Sadly, my heart had hardened, not only to Pozzi but to his entire sex. Though I'd have several lovers over the years, I could never give myself entirely to any of them, never rely on their assurances, never persuade myself that things would work out. The only man I trusted was Pierre, but I dreaded spending the rest of my life with him. I wasn't ready to be a wife, not even a faux wife in a *mariage blanc*.

Thankfully, I didn't have to live with Pierre right away. A week after our wedding, he left on a long trip to Chile, where he had once lived and where he still had substantial investments. I remained at Mama's house, and my old life of sleeping late and spending the afternoons at Julie's atelier resumed. I didn't think at all about Pierre. I knew it was only a matter of time before he came back into my life, but I hoped that time would be postponed as long as possible.

Three months went by. Then, one afternoon while Mama and Julie were out, Pierre showed up at the house with two professional packers. I greeted him in the salon, and one of the maids took the packers—two young women—upstairs to load my things into trunks that would be sent to Pierre's house. I tried to hide my disappointment that he had returned. I was glad enough to see Pierre, but I was not looking forward to moving in with him.

"Pierre! It's been ages," I said after we kissed perfunctorily.

"I was gone much longer than I thought I'd be," he answered. "But now I'm here to claim my beautiful bride." He took a long look at me and seemed pleased by what he saw. My brief pregnancy had subtly but inexorably altered my body. I was more womanly, with fuller breasts and shapelier arms and hips.

"I've brought you a present," said Pierre. He left the parlor and returned a moment later with a large square box he had placed on the hall table. "Open it."

I lifted the lid, pushed aside the tissue, and pulled out a beautiful black dress. It was much simpler and more revealing than anything I had ever worn or seen anyone else wear. The skirt was a slim black satin tube with the train gathered in back. The heart-shaped black velvet bodice was nothing but a camisole constructed on a wire frame that was sewn into the fabric and held up with two thin diamond-studded straps.

"Do you like it?" asked Pierre, smiling broadly. "The designer is a talented young man named Félix Poussineau. I think he's going to give Worth a run for his money."

"I love it!" I exclaimed. The theatrical daring of the dress immediately appealed to me. Poussineau had gotten his start designing costumes for the theater, and throughout his long career he never lost a sense of bold showiness. Yet there was nothing elaborate or fussy about his clothes. Indeed, their stark simplicity was far in advance of its time.

Pierre had first learned of Poussineau through an antique-dealer friend, and he had visited the designer's atelier a week before our marriage. "When I saw his clothes, I knew they'd be perfect for you," Pierre said.

My husband was right. After my introduction to Poussineau, I rarely wore other designers. I held Pierre's present up to my body and ran my hand over the soft satin and velvet. "I can't wait to wear it."

"You can wear it soon," said Pierre. "I'm taking you to the opening of the opera."

The new gilt-and-marble opera palace, off the boulevard des Capucines, was finally opening after thirty-six million francs and fourteen years of planning and construction. Conceived during the height of Louis-Napoléon's reign, it was the crowning glory of the Haussmanization of Paris and had been wildly anticipated by a public nostalgic for royal glamour. Tickets had been sold out months in advance. Pierre, who had a genius for befriending the right people and was not shy about asking for favors, managed to get a box at the last minute through the Prefect of Police, his neighbor on rue Jouffroy.

I spent the next three days preparing for the opera opening. I tried on my dress over and over again, enjoying it more each time. It was a gown meant for a stage star, and it made me feel theatrical to wear it. I loved how the inky fabrics heightened the marble whiteness of my skin. At the same time, though, the dress made my hair look dull and brownish. My red tresses had darkened over the past few years, and, along with their vivid color, they had lost much of their shine. I decided to ask my coiffeur, Emile, to come to the house and henna my hair.

He arrived after lunch, and a maid brought him to my boudoir. A vain black-haired man with a stiffly waxed mustache, Emile had put on weight recently, and his gray trousers and waistcoat were two sizes too small.

"This is a messy job, Madame. And a long one," said Emile as he unpacked his jars, combs, and brushes from a leather satchel and set them up on my dressing table. As he reached up to adjust one of the projecting bracket lights on the side of the table, the top button of his waistcoat popped off and flew into my powder box. *"Mon Dieu,"* he gasped. "I must do something about this stoutness." He fished out the button with two thick, hairy fingers and stashed it in his pocket.

As I sat on a bench at my dressing table, Emile positioned himself behind me and draped a heavy muslin cloth over my shoulders. He twisted a lid off a glass jar and scooped a large ladleful of bright-green henna into a mixing bow. He poured some water into it and began stirring furiously.

"Like baking a cake," he said into the mirror in front of me, smiling widely and showing a mouthful of yellow teeth. After a few minutes of stirring, he dipped a paintbrush into the henna and, lifting small sections of my hair one at a time, applied the green goo evenly. Afterward he wrapped my head in a Turkish towel and told me to sit in front of the fire. "The heat will absorb the henna into your follicles. You see, I'm a chemist as well as a pastry chef," he said, chuckling.

Emile told me to stay immobile until he returned. He left the house for two hours, and when he came back, smelling of garlic and port, the maid followed him into my room. "I need an assistant for this operation," he said. The maid pulled aside the curtain hiding my claw-footed tub and arranged the mat in front of it. Emile instructed me to lean over the tub, and he held my head as the maid poured water through my hair. The liquid running into the drain was brown, but when I looked in the mirror, I saw that my hair was carrot-red.

"This is horrible! I look like a clown," I shrieked.

Emile glared at me. "You should have said you wanted it darker. Now we must try again."

The coiffeur sent my maid to the cellar for a bottle of burgundy, which he mixed with a fresh batch of henna. Then he applied it to my hair and had me sit in front of the fire for another two hours. This time my hair turned a deep, rich mahogany. I was very pleased with it, and I've maintained it to this day.

My new hair color seemed to demand more dramatic makeup, so I mixed some mauve tint in my *blanc de perle* powder and daubed it on my face. It highlighted the bluish tinge of my natural skin tone and, I thought, looked interesting with the mahogany hair.

Then I got the idea of rouging my ears. A few years before, I had seen the actress Yvette Sicard play Cleopatra with brightly reddened ears. The effect was bizarre yet striking. I dipped my index finger in a pot of lip pomade and drew it over the tops of my ears to the lobes. Then I studied myself in the mirror. "Perfect," I said to my reflection.

On the night of the opera, two hours before Pierre was to pick me up, the maid came to my room to help me dress. I stood before her, naked from the waist up, wearing only silk stockings held up with satin garters and a pair of drawers trimmed in lace. The maid looked at my bodice and skirt draped over the settee and turned pale.

"Where are your chemise and camisole? Your corset?" she asked.

"I can't wear any undergarments with this," I said, picking up the velvet bodice and handing it to her. "Here, help me."

She slipped the diamond straps over my shoulders and fastened the buttons at the back. Then she spread a thin petticoat into a ring on the floor, and I stepped into it. Finally, I dropped the satin skirt over my head and slipped on a pair of black satin pumps with three-inch "Louis" heels shaped in a graceful reverse curve.

"My fan, please," I said. The maid was astonished at the bareness of my outfit and stared at me with her mouth open. She handed me the fan and a small beaded purse.

"Have a good evening, Madame," she stammered before I descended the stairs.

Pierre was waiting for me in the parlor. His face opened into a broad smile when he saw me. "You're gorgeous," he said. We drove to the Place de l'Opéra, arriving just as the purple-robed Lord Mayor of London strode toward the entrance, proceeded by blaring trumpets. A thousand lights from street lamps and houses beamed, illuminating the frenzied scene. The entire Chaussée d'Antin was blocked by carriages, and soldiers on horseback galloped in front of the teeming crowds lining the boulevards.

Pierre and I entered the vast marble vestibule, gave our wraps to Pierre's driver, and made our way up the grand staircase, through a sea of ballgowns and black tailcoats. We found our box in the second tier. All around us were the brightest lights of France, a mingling of royalty and Republican politics. On the right of the proscenium were the President of the Republic, Marshal MacMahon, and a coterie of ministers and influential politicians. On the left was a descendant of the royal family of Poland and King Alfonso XII of Spain. Sitting nearby were the Duc de Nemours, a prince of the blood royal of France, and, in front of him, the Comte de Paris, the rightful successor to Louis-Philippe, the legitimate heir to the French crown.

The lights in the gigantic chandelier at the center of the ceiling dimmed, then flickered out. The curtain rose on the first act of Jacques Halévy's *La Juive,* and the orchestra began to play. No one was listening. Everyone was too busy scrutinizing the crowd and talking to their neighbors. Indeed, the chatter in the vast theater was so loud it nearly drowned out the music. I trained my opera glass on the Lord Mayor's box and was surprised to see that his wife was obese and wearing an ugly pink gown. Then I tried to find President MacMahon. As I scanned the dim canyons of the vast theater, I became aware that a high percentage of heads and opera glasses were turned on *me.* I was used to drawing stares, but this scrutiny was more intense than usual. I quickly realized it was because of my dress. The other women wore bulky, elaborate gowns trimmed with ruching, sequins, fringe, feathers, and lace. Though some of these dresses were décolleté, none of them exposed anywhere near as much flesh as mine.

I felt a quickening in my chest, a mounting excitement that I was the center of attention. I dropped my glasses into my lap, straightened my back, and set my face in a serene countenance. Pierre looked pleased, proud to be with me. I was beginning to understand that he had married me for more reasons than kindness and a desire to provide a cover for himself and Madame Jeuland. He was proud of my looks, and he liked showing me off. I was an exotic prize, like his Japanese screens and urns.

At the interval, Pierre and I made our way through the long, wide corridors lined with gilt mirrors and busts of famous composers, to the Galerie des Glaces, where we ordered champagne. Women snickered at me behind their fans. "Why, she might as well have worn a night-gown," I overheard a wrinkled blonde hiss. "It's indecent. How could her husband let her go out like that?" whispered her companion.

The men, however, were enthralled. As I walked past one group of middle-aged gentlemen with foreign medals emblazoned across their jackets, their chatter died abruptly and they stared at me with slack jaws. Two young army officers actually climbed on the bar to get a better look, ignoring a guard who shouted, "Get down at once!"

When the interval was over and we had settled ourselves in our box, I began to feel that the entire house was staring at me. Several men had left their seats and were standing in the aisles, their opera glasses trained on me. A few people were brazenly pointing in my direction. I felt a warm pleasure at being the center of attention. Then I realized why everyone was looking: my right breast had popped out of my gown. I had no idea how long it had been on display. A rush of horror and embarrassment coursed through me. The next thing I knew, Pierre quickly grabbed it and pushed it back inside my bodice. Then he leaned over and whispered in my ear, "My hand loved that."

The comment defused my anxiety. I suspected, too, that it sig-naled Pierre's awakening desire for me. Though he was committed to Madame Jeuland, and though he had promised not to exercise his "rights as a husband," as he put it, it would be hard to refuse Pierre. After all, we were legally married.

I focused on these thoughts to get my mind off the crowd's stares.

Sleeping with Pierre wouldn't be so bad, I decided. I liked the sensation of his hand on my breast, and it pleased me that he had rescued me from public embarrassment. Throughout the rest of the performance, he held my hand tightly and from time to time whispered in my ear, "Are you all right, dear?"

At 1:30 A.M., the curtain fell on the last entertainment of the evening, ballet performances from *La Source* and *Terpsichore*. We left our box as the dancers took their final bows and found our way to the vestibule, where Pierre's valet was waiting with our wraps. He led us to our carriage, and we headed to Pierre's *hôtel* at 80, rue Jouffroy.

From the outside, the small three-story house, a few blocks from Parc Monceau, was indistinguishable from the street's other bourgeois *hôtels*. Inside, though, it looked like a Japanese home. In the foyer, a bronze Buddha greeted guests from its perch on a round monastery table that was identical to Mama's. On the first floor, the walls were lined with blue silk painted with pink peonies, and hung with Japanese prints. The bookshelves were bamboo, and the low divans were upholstered in fabrics from antique kimonos.

While Pierre was in Chile, his servants had given me a tour of the house and, according to my instructions, had overseen the decoration of my boudoir suite opposite Pierre's on the second floor. In defiance of my husband's taste for the Oriental, I chose to reproduce nearly exactly my conventionally French bedroom at rue de Luxembourg, with blue toile on the walls and upholstered furniture, a large, carved four-poster, and a Louis XIV secretary.

Julie had offered to provide the art, and she invited me to her atelier one December afternoon to select three paintings from a group of canvases she had completed the previous summer in Provence. I was shocked when I saw them, so different were they from her typical work. Dark brown, black, sienna, and ocher had vanished from her palette, replaced by brilliant color—blue, violet, green, yellow, and orange. The previous April, Julie had attended the first exhibition of the so-called Impressionists, and she had been greatly influenced by their light-filled paintings. At the opening, she met many of the painters themselves, including Manet, Monet, Renoir, Degas, Pissarro, and Morisot, and she had fallen in love not only with their work but also with their philosophy of art.

After viewing the Impressionist exhibition, with its relaxed brush-work and contemporary scenes, Julie began to chafe at painting still lifes and studio portraits. She wanted to render only what she saw and felt, *"en plein air,* like Monet," she told me.

The art establishment and the public remained largely hostile to the new art. So did Filomena and Sophie, who tended to follow Filomena's lead in all things artistic. I got a whiff of their disdain for Julie's new calling the day I selected my paintings. When I arrived at the atelier, the women were crowded around an easel in the middle of the room, arguing about Julie's painting of a young woman in a white dress, strolling through a garden. Julie wanted to send it to the next Salon, a move Filomena strongly opposed.

"You'll never get it past the jury," she barked. "It's exactly the kind of thing they hate."

"I think she's right," echoed Sophie. "The colors are too shrill."

"It's no good, no good at all," said Filomena, shaking her head. "It's lazy, sloppy. Look at that mouth." She pointed to the canvas. "You did those lips in two brush strokes."

Julie scowled. "Stand back a few feet," she ordered. "You can't see it properly with your noses in the canvas."

Filomena strode to the center of the room. "No better," she announced.

"Why don't you send that wonderful picture of Saint Claire kneel-ing before a cross?" offered Sophie.

"I can't bear that picture!" said Julie, her voice rising. "I'm never painting a saint again. Or a knight or a nymph or a king or an angel."

"I don't know what's gotten into you," Filomena called from across the room. "Why do you like the Impressionists so much? All they do is slap color on the canvas. It's child's play, not art. For art, you must have careful drawing, you must have control."

Filomena looked crushed. Like many seemingly cold, distant peo-ple, she occasionally exposed bursts of emotion. She took personally Julie's enthusiasm for the new art. In rejecting the old methods, she felt, Julie was rejecting her.

Unlike Filomena, I loved the luminous magic of Julie's new pic-tures. Looking at them was like stepping into a sunny summer day. Perhaps one could not get as deeply into this kind of work as in tradi-

157

tional "finished" pictures, those that had been completed slowly, laboriously, with every detail fully, photographically articulated. But to me, the buoyant impulsiveness of Impressionism was its chief charm.

I chose three pictures that day—the portrait of the girl in white, another of the same model drinking tea, and a landscape of Provence.

Now, as Pierre led me into the two large rooms overlooking a small garden, I was pleased to see that the paintings had been beautifully framed and hung away from the windows. The packers had thoughtfully arranged my clothes in armoires and bureaus. A piano had been moved into the sitting room, and my music was stored on a bamboo étagère. It was almost like home.

"I hope you'll be happy here," said Pierre. Then he left the boudoir and closed the door behind him. While I undressed, I heard a carriage pull up to the house and the gate slam. The front door opened, and someone scurried up the stairs. I cracked my door and looked down the hall just as a woman wrapped in a sable-trimmed cape dashed into Pierre's room. Madame Jeuland.

I went to bed that night feeling disappointed and vaguely jealous. The next morning, I woke up with a headache and felt a stab of melancholy when I realized I was not at rue de Luxembourg. I passed the next weeks in a stupor of lethargy. I did a little reading and shopping and visited Julie in her atelier. Mama called from time to time, but mostly I stayed alone in the house, feeling sorry for myself.

I hardly ever saw my husband, except occasionally at breakfast and at the regular Thursday dinners we hosted at rue Jouffroy for Pierre's business associates and their wives. Every Monday morning, Pierre gave me his schedule for the week and told me those evenings during which he required my presence to accompany him to a reception or a party. In any given month, we spent only a handful of evenings together. The rest of the time, I was free to do as I pleased.

One morning, the maid brought my breakfast tray with a plain beige envelope tucked under the coffee cup. I sliced open the envelope and was astonished to see that the letter was from Léon Gambetta, the fiery Republican leader who was one of the chief architects of France's new democracy. He had been in the crowd at the opening of the Nouvel Opéra the month before and learned my address from our neighbor, the Prefect of Police. In those days, it was not unusual for me to get notes from strange men. Often, at parties, valets slipped me messages from their masters, and sometimes, after a story about me appeared in the newspaper, I'd get a bundle of letters from admirers. But this was the first time I had received a letter from someone as important and distinguished as a national leader.

"Dear Madame Gautreau," Gambetta began. "I couldn't help noticing during the opening of the Nouvel Opéra that you were one of the few people in the theater who actually was listening to the music. The Prefect of Police, in whose box I had the pleasure of sitting, tells me that you are a musician yourself, an exquisite interpreter of Beethoven in particular. I am writing to invite you to the Pasdeloup concert next Sunday, where the orchestra will perform, among other works, Beethoven's 'Emperor' Concerto. Perhaps we could have dinner afterward. If you consent to grant me the honor of your company, I will pick you up in my carriage at three. Most sincerely, Léon Gambetta."

I'd never seen Gambetta before, but I had heard much about him. The son of a grocer in Cahors, Gambetta had come to Paris as a young man to study law, and he quickly became involved in radical politics. As a member of the Corps Législatif, to which he had been elected in 1869, he was a passionate opponent of Louis-Napoléon. His speeches calling for the demise of the monarchy were said to be so thunderously eloquent that they made the windows of the National Assembly tremble.

When the Empire fell, Gambetta was named Minister of the Interior of the new provisional government. He escaped Paris in a dramatic balloon flight and oversaw the war effort from the provinces. Since then, he had worked tirelessly to establish a democratic French Republic.

I never answered letters sent to me by strangers. Most of the men who wrote to me were old wealthy gentlemen who had little to do but read the papers at their clubs and chase younger women. But Gambetta was different. He was young—only thirty-seven in 1875— and a celebrity in his own right. There was talk in the press that he might actually be president one day. I wouldn't mind getting to know him, I thought. I was ready for a romantic adventure.

Gambetta must have heard about my arrangement with Pierre through the Prefect of Police. Otherwise I don't think he would have been so bold as to invite me to dine alone with him in his rooms. Looking back at that time from the distance of age, I'm amazed at my wantonness. I was hardly the only woman in Paris who went out with men other than her husband. But I must have been among the most indiscreet. Yet, at the time, I didn't care about anything but my own pleasure.

I sent Gambetta a *petit bleu* saying that I'd be delighted to join him. At exactly three o'clock on the appointed day, the bell rang, and a moment later the maid brought me Léon Gambetta's card. It took me twenty minutes to finish my toilette; then I descended the stairs to the salon.

Standing at the window, looking down into the street, was a short, badly dressed man with long brown hair flowing from his huge head. His truncated arms gave him the appearance of an overgrown dwarf. His right eye was glass—he had lost the eye in a childhood accident. The glass stared opaquely at me while his good eye glittered. Needless to say, I was disappointed by his appearance. But as soon as Gambetta opened his mouth, I was charmed.

"Ah, Madame Gautreau," he said, bowing slightly as I entered the room. "How lovely of you to join me this afternoon. You know, these concerts are my only diversion, for work is the cruel goddess who rules my destiny."

"You must take time for leisure, sir, or your health will suffer."

"My health *has* suffered. In the assembly, I'm fighting all sorts of monarchists who'd actually like to put the Bourbons back on the throne. They'll be the death of me." He tossed his hair with the back of his hand.

"I'm surprised you can bear to sit through a concerto named 'Emperor,' " I said.

Gambetta laughed softly. "Ah, Madame, you are as witty as you are beautiful. Seriously, I don't hold the concerto's title against the composer. Now, we must dash or we'll miss the beginning."

In the carriage on the way to the concert, Gambetta talked of his recent struggles to amend the French constitution so that presidents would be elected every seven years by a majority vote of the Senate and the Chamber of Deputies. A group of legislators who wanted to restore the monarchy were fiercely opposing him. "We must put a new shirt on France. Ever since September 4, 1870, people have obstinately allowed the country to wear its old linen, all spotted and stained with the blood and dirt of former governments!" he exclaimed.

We arrived at boulevard des Filles du Calvaire, and the carriage pulled to a stop in front of the Cirque d'Hiver, the five-thousand-seat arena that the conductor Jules Pasdeloup borrowed for his popular Sunday concert series. Gambetta continued talking as we took our seats in the third row. Sun filtered through the windows, sharply defining the black-coated musicians. As Pasdeloup took the podium, three clowns, who had been rehearsing in their dressing room, wandered in and sat solemnly in the back row.

Gambetta continued talking until the orchestra began to play. Soon he fell asleep. I poked him in the ribs several times and got him to open his eyes once or twice; otherwise he slept through the entire concert.

Afterward we drove to his apartment at 53, rue de la Chaussée d'Antin, in a modest eighteenth-century building that housed the offices of *La République Française,* the newspaper Gambetta had bought several years before to give him a daily forum for his opinions.

Gambetta unlocked a door at the side of the building and led me up two flights of stairs to a small apartment. The Republican leader's attention to decor had not advanced past his bohemian student days in the Latin Quarter. The rooms were furnished with scarred secondhand settees and chairs. Framed political cartoons that had been cut from newspapers hung on the discolored, cracked walls. As we ate the dinner brought in from the restaurant next door, the portly orator talked on and on about politics, his thundering voice drowning out the loud clanks and thuds drifting up through the pipes from the rotary press downstairs.

The food was superb—a steaming pot-au-feu accompanied by bread, *haricots verts,* and an expensive wine. Gambetta ate two servings of everything and consumed his dessert—a large slice of apple tart smothered in *crème fraîche*—in two bites. Then he pushed his bulk from the table and crossed to my side. He pulled me to my feet and kissed me on the mouth. "Shall we retire?" he said. He took my hand and led me to the bedroom.

Until that moment, I had been undecided about whether or not

I'd sleep with him. His appearance hardly made me swoon. Still, I found him extremely attractive. His eloquent voice, the deep intelligence radiating from his good eye, the childish way he tossed his hair—all delighted me. What finally swayed me, however, was his kiss—romantic and tender, with a hint of unleashed passion.

When we were inside his bedroom, Gambetta closed the door, enveloped me with his short arms, and pressed me against his massive chest. He covered my neck with kisses, then pushed his tongue into my mouth as he fumbled with my clothes. He managed to get my bodice undone, and moved his hands over my breasts. When he had removed my skirt and petticoats, he maneuvered me onto the bed. He finished undressing me, took off his trousers, and, gently parting my legs, slid his bulk on top of me.

Despite the promise of his kiss, Gambetta wasn't much of a lover. He seemed eager to get it over with so he could get back to his real passion—talking. He finished quickly, rolled off, and immediately started gabbing. "Madame, I feel inexpressibly comforted to have received your consoling tenderness," he said as he lay by my side, staring at the ceiling. "What delicious repose I'm enjoying now, what delightful peace! I feel carried away to dream and to enjoy. It is like drifting down a river and letting myself be guided by the current."

He turned on his side to face me. "This will help me bear the irritating obstacles I'm sure I'll face in the assembly tomorrow." He smiled contentedly, then launched into a long catalog of those obstacles. I dozed off, and when I awoke an hour later, Gambetta was still talking—practicing a speech he planned to give the next day. Finally, at ten, I told him I had to leave, and he sent me home in his carriage.

The following morning, the first post brought a letter from him. "You are the most incomparable little charmer that nature's hands ever fashioned," Gambetta wrote, "and I feel myself overwhelmed with gratitude to fate for choosing me to witness last night's dazzling fairy tale of grace and enchantment." This glorification of our brief, sweaty exertions made me laugh out loud.

"What's this sublime new world we suddenly visited yesterday?" the letter continued. "Is it the lost Atlantis of the ancients, where, as the Golden Legend tells us, sister souls meet and love for eternity? How can I tell? I feel as if I were swimming in pure, ethereal light.

Words seem too vulgar and clumsy to express the delicate and almost fluid sensations I feel in this upper world into which you have led me. On entering these hitherto unexplored regions, one ought to invent a new language that has never been used by human mouth."

What did he mean by "hitherto unexplored regions"? I had adventured a lot further in bed with Dr. Pozzi than I had with Gambetta, and I was sure he had explored the regions of many other women.

I knew (as did all of Paris) that Gambetta had a longtime lover, an army officer's daughter who called herself Madame Léonie Léon. At the time of my affair with Gambetta, they were on hiatus. Gambetta had wanted to marry her, but Léonie, a devout Catholic, refused unless the Republican leader agreed to a church wedding. Gambetta was an ardent atheist who couldn't bring himself to enter a church, and Léonie had broken with her paramour, though eventually they reconciled. Years later, long after both of them had died, Gambetta's letters to Léonie were published. Some of them were nearly identical to those he had written me.

I saw Gambetta one or two evenings a week. If Pierre knew about it, he never said anything. Usually I met the Republican leader in his rooms, though occasionally we'd have dinner in a restaurant or attend a concert. I was not in love with him, as I had been with Dr. Pozzi. Indeed, I never lost my heart in that way again. But I genuinely liked Gambetta, and I learned a great deal from him. His knowledge of history and literature was astounding. He could recite by heart long passages from Shakespeare and Victor Hugo. If he hadn't gone into politics, he might have been a stage actor. Appalled at my lack of education, he gave me books to read and spent hours discussing them with me. He told me I was the most beautiful woman he had ever seen, and he liked the idea that, on my father's side, I was descended from Italians, as was he. "Your face and figure are reminiscent of the glories of ancient Rome," he said.

The physical side of love has always been important to me, and Gambetta's deficiency in this area proved deeply frustrating. Part of the problem was his terrible health. He was already showing signs of the physical deterioration that would contribute to his early death. He suffered from chronic bronchitis and couldn't climb a flight of stairs without gasping for breath. He had gotten into a pattern of working himself to exhaustion and then escaping to a spa for a week of rest and exercise. After he returned to Paris, he'd feel better for a few days. Then the cycle of overwork and illness would begin again.

He frequently urged me to travel with him to take this or that cure, or simply to rest for a few days at a country inn. As I was hostess at Pierre's Thursday dinners, and I still regularly attended Mama's Mondays, it was difficult to get away.

In the summer of 1877, after we had been together for a year and a half, I arranged my schedule so I could take a balloon trip with Gambetta to Normandy. We had to reschedule the trip twice because of inclement weather. Finally, one warm, sunny Friday, we decided to fly. I arrived at the Jardin des Tuileries, the launch site, at ten. The balloon had already been inflated and was being held to the ground by thick ropes wound around iron stakes. Gambetta helped me climb into the basket, and a moment later the pilot cried, "Let go!"

The men standing by the stakes unraveled the ropes, and the balloon slowly rose to the northwest. I had been terror-stricken, but now I had the delicious feeling of being carried along like a feather in the breeze. I looked down. The earth receded, and as we rose higher, Paris looked more and more like a toy village.

Within minutes, Gambetta had unfurled a tricolor. *"Vive la France!"* he shouted into the clouds.

A half hour into the trip, it started to rain, and the air turned cold. The pilot had trouble adjusting to the changed temperature, and the balloon rose up and down like an elevator. Gambetta grew agitated. "The weather, like everything else, is going to the dogs," he grumbled. "I've never seen such a summer! One would think that words had changed their meanings and that summer was only another term for winter." His face was bright red, and sweat poured from his brow, despite the cold air.

In midafternoon, we approached an open field near a forest. The pilot released the pressure valve, and with the gas whistling, we began our descent. As we picked up speed, the pilot shouted, "To anchor," and the crewmen threw ropes, with anchors attached, overboard.

"Bend your knees and grab the side of the basket," Gambetta ordered.

I obeyed, and a moment later we hit the ground with a hard thud.

Gambetta and I set off by foot along a dusty road to a country inn where he had made reservations. Fifteen minutes later, we came upon a dilapidated building that looked like a barn. Chickens scratched in the yard, and flies buzzed around an old woman who was sitting on the stoop, shelling peas.

"I can't possibly stay in this hovel," I said.

"I'm afraid there isn't any other place around," answered Gambetta.

"Can't we go into Rouen?"

"I suppose we could. But I like it here. Don't you find the country beautiful?"

"No."

"Open your eyes, Mimi! Nature has dressed herself in all her finery in our honor."

"Well, she forgot to outfit this inn."

Scowling, Gambetta led me inside to the dining room, where we sat at a small wood table with a group of rough-looking workmen and their haggard wives. A sullen girl served us steaming bowls of beef stew and red table wine, which Gambetta consumed greedily. I was too angry to eat a morsel.

Our room was low-ceilinged and suffocatingly hot. One small window looked out into the brown yard. The bedding smelled as if it had been in the cellar for a year.

"You don't really expect me to sleep here?" I asked.

Gambetta looked embarrassed. "Let's take a walk. We'll talk about it."

We strolled through the village, where a festival was in full swing. Groups of men sat on benches, drinking beer and talking loudly. Under the stone roof of an ancient market, a few couples danced to a sentimental waltz played by a little band.

Soon Gambetta was recognized. People began clapping, and a few men raised their glasses in the air in toasts. Then the band struck up the "Marseillaise." Smiling broadly, Gambetta left my side and strode through the crowd, shaking hands.

Disgusted, I walked toward the edge of the village square, where a man in laborer's clothes leaned against a rickety carriage.

"How far is it to the train station?" I asked.

"About an hour."

"Do you know when the next train leaves for Paris?"

"The next and the last. At ten. If you leave now, you can make it."

"I'll give you thirty francs to take me."

"What about Monsieur Gambetta?"

"When you get back, you can tell him I've returned to Paris."

"It's none of my business, Madame, but won't he be awfully angry?"

"You're right, Monsieur. It's none of your business. Please, let's go."

Eight

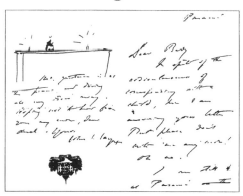

The carriage driver was right: Gambetta was furious. When he got back to Paris, he wrote me a letter ending our relationship. "I had been looking forward to one of those divine nights of ours, which seem to me like the memory of some supernatural happiness," he began. "Instead you gave me the slip. I will not be played for a fool, Madame. Good-bye."

If I had tried, I'm certain I could have won him back. But I had grown tired of his ill health, his shabby apartment, his endless monologues, his indifferent lovemaking. I never saw Gambetta again. Poor man, he died five years later from a massive infection after accidentally shooting himself in the hand with a loaded revolver. At least that was the official story. Madame Léonie Léon was with him at the time, and rumors flew around Paris that it was *she* who had shot him, in a jealous rage over another woman.

Mama suspected I had had an affair with the Republican leader—a friend of hers had seen us dining at a restaurant—and one day after Gambetta and I broke up, she confronted me. "Since when have you and Léon Gambetta become so close?" she asked. It was a Monday evening, following Mama's regular salon. The guests had left, and we were alone in the parlor, sipping tea.

"What do you mean?"

"Madame Hubert saw you with him at Bignon's, looking very cozy."

"How nice of her to tell you about it," I snapped. "Actually, Pierre and I met Monsieur Gambetta at a ball at the foreign ministry. He invited us to dinner. Pierre was busy, so I went alone." It was a lie, of course, and Mama saw through it.

"You expect me to believe that?"

"Why not?"

Mama put her teacup down and glared at me. "You're a foolish, foolish girl. You're going to end up in the street like a common whore."

"It's over with Gambetta, if you must know," I shouted. "But to tell you the truth, I hope someone else comes along. I'm too young to stay alone like a dried-up old lady." I almost added, "like you," but I stopped myself.

"If you had any sense, you'd try to win your husband's affection instead of falling into the arms of strangers. Pierre is a wonderful man." Mama stood up. She looked like she wanted to slap me. Instead she threw her handkerchief at me and stomped out of the room.

As it turned out, Pierre and I did begin spending more time together. Madame Jeuland unexpectedly moved to London with her husband, and suddenly Pierre was bored and looking for entertainment. We started going out to restaurants and parties several times a week. One evening on the way home from a dinner at the American Embassy, where we had both drunk too much champagne, Pierre kissed me passionately in our carriage. I expected him to invite me to sleep with him, and I decided to accept. I had enjoyed his kisses, and I was curious about what kind of lover he'd be. But when we entered our house and climbed the stairs to the second floor, Pierre said good night to me on the landing, as was his custom, and turned to walk down the hall to his bedroom.

I was annoyed. Why hadn't he followed up on what he'd started in the carriage? Didn't he want me? I went to my boudoir, undressed, and donned a peignoir. Then I walked down the hall to Pierre's room and knocked on the door.

"Yes?" he called from within.

"It's Mimi. I must see you."

I had disturbed him in the middle of undressing, and he answered the door in his shirt and stockings. "What's wrong, dear?" he said. He looked worried.

I stepped into the middle of the room and dropped my peignoir.

"What's this?" His eyes grew wide.

I walked toward him and began undoing the buttons on his shirt. "Are you sure this is what you want?" he said softly.

"Yes."

No sooner had I uttered the word than Pierre's hands and mouth were all over my body. We made love on the carpet and, a half hour later, on the bed. The next day, a Sunday, we hardly left his bedroom.

Pierre was a gentle, tender lover, far superior to Léon Gambetta, but he was hardly as exciting as Sam Pozzi. For one thing, he was rather old—well over forty. Also, he was far less handsome than Pozzi. Pierre wasn't unattractive, but he had a soft little paunch around his middle, skinny bow legs, and a flat, droopy backside that made me laugh every time I saw it.

Still, he knew how to please me, and for a month we had a grand affair. Then it ended as abruptly as it had begun. Perhaps living together as intimately as we had for so long without the ultimate intimacy prevented us from sustaining passion. Perhaps we simply ran out of it. One night, my husband stopped visiting me in my bedroom, and I soon discovered he was traveling to London regularly to see Madame Jeuland. We never slept together again, except once after a dinner at home after we had shared two bottles of Château Lafitte.

That's how we got our daughter, Louise. She was born on August 20, 1879, at Château des Chênes, where I had spent the last weeks of my confinement. Louise was a perfectly formed, beautiful little girl with black hair and a delicate little face. Pierre and I adored her with an intensity neither of us could have imagined before her birth. To celebrate Louise's arrival, Pierre gave me a diamond crescent for my hair, the symbol of Diana, the chaste Greek goddess of the hunt who, paradoxically, was worshiped in Roman religion as a symbol of fertility. A reporter once compared my "elegant litheness" to Diana's, and Pierre thought my body resembled the statues of Diana at the Louvre.

We had a nanny who slept with Louise in the nursery and took care of most of her needs, but Pierre and I spent more time with our baby than was typical of parents in our circle. Every morning after breakfast, we pushed her perambulator around Parc Monceau. We kept a cradle in the parlor so she could be with us after dinner, while Pierre read the papers and I played the piano.

Mama was thrilled to have a grandchild. Still, she worried that I had taken a new lover and that Louise wasn't really a Gautreau. She scrutinized the baby's face whenever she got a chance, and finally, on the day of Louise's christening, she exclaimed, "This infant looks nothing like Pierre!"

Mama and I were walking down the stone steps of Saint-Sulpice following the ceremony. Louise lay bundled in my arms in a white lace christening gown. Julie and Pierre followed behind us, out of earshot. It was a beautiful fall day, cool and sunny, and children romped around the huge jetting fountain in the square in front of us.

"Mama, Pierre is a middle-aged man with an enormous mustache," I said. "Louise is a tiny baby girl."

"You must tell me. Is this your husband's child?"

"Yes," I hissed. Mama didn't look convinced, so I added, "I swear it. On Louise's life."

My mother wasn't the only one who questioned Louise's paternity—speculation even turned up in the press. Most of it centered on Gambetta, with whom I had been seen in restaurants and at concerts. A reporter for *Frou Frou,* who claimed to have spotted Louise with her nanny in Parc Monceau, wrote that the baby looked just like the famous orator. *Gil Blas* ran a cartoon of Gambetta, Louise, and me leaving Paris in a balloon, and *La Vérité* claimed to have seen the three of us at Baden-Baden.

The reporters thought I was still sleeping with the hero of French Republicanism, and it infuriated them. Though Paris had adopted a cosmopolitan spirit after the Franco-Prussian War—foreign imports, from Russian novels to English aesthetic ideas, were suddenly celebrated—latent hostility toward foreigners bubbled up from time to time. Americans in particular were resented for their wealth, and the press loved to attack us for being vulgar, pushy, and overambitious. "Beware this people that grows ever larger," the society columnist for *L'Illustration* warned. "Uncle Sam threatens with his gnarled, industrious hands over our commerce, our agriculture, and our stables." I was sometimes singled out as the epitome of American crassness, and vilified in print for wearing makeup, dyeing my hair, and dressing provocatively.

The most outrageous stories about me had nothing to do with Gambetta. *La Vérité,* for example, claimed that I kept slaves at rue Jouffroy, and that I bathed in the nude at Paramé while a giant mulatto stood on the beach holding an armload of fluffy towels.

Pierre was too elegant and above it all to care what some reporter riffraff wrote about me in the scandal sheets. But Mama was hysterical over it. She actually visited the offices of the offending journals and demanded retractions. When none were printed, she urged me to sue for libel.

But the stories didn't really trouble me. No one in my circle paid attention to the scandal press. Many of the mainstream columnists still wrote glowing items about me. As I pointed out to Mama one day when she was nattering on about the negative publicity, "No scurrilous piece in *Gil Blas* is as bad as being ignored by Etincelle." That shut her up.

In those days, I took very seriously Théophile Gautier's dictum, "A woman's first duty is to be beautiful." I considered it my job to be stunning, and believe me, it took fortitude to endure the endless fittings, coiffeur appointments, the dieting and the costume changes of a professional beauty. I learned the art of making a grand entrance. At the theater and opera, I always arrived twenty minutes late. As soon as I reached my box, I'd drop my coat dramatically to give the audience a view of my shoulders, which were famous for their whiteness and exquisite shape. I never went anywhere—not even for a short walk—without full makeup and an impeccable toilette, without the maid spraying me with perfume as I twirled on a little stool, so the scent would be evenly distributed.

During the day, I paid calls, attended exhibitions, and visited shops and the dressmaker. Several evenings a week, I went out to a dinner, a reception, the theater, or a ball. I was part of *Tout-Paris* society, that chorus of bustled ladies and tailcoated gentlemen who went everywhere, knew everyone, and talked endlessly about art, politics, and literature. The crowd included faubourg aristocrats, celebrities, and the very, very rich (defined by one wag as anyone who could afford to pay a hundred louis d'or for a fan). I had entrée into this world because of my looks and notoriety, but I never was totally accepted by it. I remained an outsider, an American arriviste with a flimsy pedigree. Despite my frenetic socializing, I had only one true woman friend, Julie.

Though I had little time to spend with her, I visited Julie's atelier as often as I could. Sometimes I had lunch with her at Lavenue's, a restaurant opposite Gare Montparnasse that was popular with artists. One fall afternoon as Julie and I sat at a table near the window and were scanning the menu, I spotted a chestnut-haired man with a neatly trimmed beard, sitting across the room with a group of painters in baggy pants and loose smocks. I always manage to find the most attractive man in any room, and this fellow was obviously a cut above the rest of Lavenue's scruffy patrons. Dressed in brown worsted trousers, coat, waistcoat, and cravat, he looked like a banker or a lawyer.

"Who is that bearded fellow in the waistcoat?" I asked Julie. She put down her menu and turned around. Suddenly she straightened her back, and her face lit up. "That's John Sargent, the American artist! You've heard of him. His drawings are like Old Masters, and his painting is breathtaking."

John Singer Sargent had been the toast of the Paris Salon ever since he first exhibited his work there in 1877, when he was just twenty-one. With their dazzling brushwork, astonishing vitality, and showy, brilliant likenesses, his pictures blurred everything around them. The other painters, including his teacher, Carolus-Duran, were said to be deeply envious of him. Yet the young artist was so amiable and generous that they couldn't help liking him. No one begrudged Sargent his singular success.

"Do you know him?" I asked Julie.

"Yes, though not well. Carolus brought him to my studio a few times, and I visited Sargent's studio once with Sophie and Filomena."

The artist looked in our direction. He waved to Julie and, raising his chin and narrowing his eyes, appeared to study me. Then he rose from the table and walked toward us.

I liked John Singer Sargent the moment Julie introduced us. Tall, pale, and blue-eyed, with a soft body that already showed signs of future portliness, he had a pleasant, intelligent face and a charming, self-deprecating manner.

He pulled a chair up to our table and sat down.

"Julie tells me you're American," I said.

"My parents are. I'm an expatriate mongrel, born in Florence," he answered. Sargent's French was impeccable, with hardly a trace of an accent. "I didn't even visit America until I was twenty," the artist continued. He gazed through the window to the boulevard. Outside, a soft breeze swirled the leaves of the young plane trees, planted in 1873 to replace the ancient ones cut for firewood during the Prussian siege. "I must say, this delightful weather makes me homesick for the palm trees and fig orchards in Nice where I played as a child," he continued. "I'd fancy going to the country to sketch this afternoon. But don't you know, I'm chained to my studio."

"Who's sitting for you these days?" Julie asked.

"A very brilliant creature named Dr. Samuel-Jean Pozzi."

My face burned. I could never hear Pozzi's name without feeling waves of anxiety. Before Sargent could say anything else, a waitress stepped to the table with a steaming platter of *escalopes de veau*. Sargent eyed the food greedily. "That looks delicious," he said as he stood. "I had better get back to *my* lunch. It was lovely to meet you, Madame Gautreau." He nodded to me, then crossed the room to rejoin his friends.

Throughout the meal, I stole glances at Sargent. Once, I caught him staring at me, and I quickly turned away. Julie and I finished eating and paid the bill. As we walked out of the restaurant, I felt Sargent's eyes on me. When we were on the street, I asked Julie, "Is Monsieur Sargent married?"

"Oh, no. All he thinks about is work."

The temperature had dropped, and a cool wind blew debris across the wide boulevard. A handbill announcing a lingerie sale at Bon Marché clung to my skirt, and I peeled it off. "Doesn't he have a *petite amie*?" I asked.

Julie laughed. "You can't imagine how shy John Sargent is," she said. "Women embarrass him *to death*."

Two weeks later, Julie told me she had received a *petit bleu* from Sargent inviting her to an informal party. She asked if I'd like to go along. I was curious about both the artist and his work, and so I accepted.

Sargent's Montparnasse studio sat on the ground floor at 73 *bis,* rue Notre-Dame-des-Champs, a narrow, dusty street crammed with artists' ateliers and cheap cafés. We arrived at nine to find the party packed with fashionably dressed men and women. As we pushed through the elegant crowd, I noticed that the studio was sparsely furnished with a few chairs and Sargent's pictures, including his portraits of anonymous models and his copies of Velázquez and other Old Masters.

On an easel near the French doors stood Sargent's painting of Dr. Pozzi. It looked like a portrait of the devil. Virtually the entire canvas was red—the sumptuous curtains in the background, the carpeted floor. The doctor himself was dressed in the red slippers and the red wool dressing gown that I had seen him wear dozens of times. His pose was hypertheatrical; his face was caught in intense observance of an object outside the canvas, and his elongated fingers tugged nervously at his collar and the drawstring of his robe. His fingers were as sharp as pincers and seemed spotted with blood. Had Pozzi just performed a gynecological operation? Deflowered a virgin?

A small crowd had gathered around the portrait, and Pozzi himself was standing at the back of the room, surrounded by a group of friends. Seeing him now, I felt nothing but cold contempt. He was a hollow person. Sargent had captured him brilliantly—his beauty and his cruelty. Our eyes met for a moment, but Pozzi looked through me, as if I were invisible. Now that he was finished with me, I didn't exist.

"I had no idea this party was to celebrate Pozzi's portrait," Julie whispered to me, her brow knitted with concern. "Sargent just wrote that he was having a few people in. Let's go.

"She put her hand on my sleeve, but I pulled away. "We can't leave now. He's seen me. He'll think I've left because I'm upset that he's ignoring me."

"Did he snub you?"

"He looked right through me."

"He's a monster." Julie turned to the portrait. "My God, Sargent has a flair for the bizarre. This is the kind of painting designed to turn the subject into a celebrity."

"Pozzi's already famous," I said bitterly.

"Only in Paris. You watch. Sargent plans to send the picture to the Royal Academy in London. As soon as it's exhibited there, every Englishwoman who can afford it will scoot across the Channel to be treated by this vision in red."

And bedded by him, I thought.

The bright tones of a Spanish folk song filtered through the crowd's chatter. Sargent was sitting at a large upright piano near the windows.

"He plays as beautifully as he paints," I said.

Julie nodded. "As long as he plays, he doesn't have to talk to his guests. He loves society. But I don't know why he bothers entertaining. The poor man gets so tongue-tied in large groups."

Sargent's shy, awkward manner was totally at odds with the bold assurance of his art. His painting was mature; the artist himself seemed hopelessly boyish, cut off from the adult passions swirling around him. Julie told me he lived by himself in a small hotel near his studio, but dined with his parents nearly every night.

Julie and I stayed at the party an hour, chatting with Carolus-Duran and some of his friends. When we left, Pozzi was still holding court in front of his portrait while Sargent remained at the piano, lost in a Beethoven sonata.

Later, through Julie, I came to learn more of Sargent's background. He was born in Florence in 1856, descended from prominent Philadelphia families on both sides. His father, Fitzwilliam Sargent, was a doctor; his mother, Mary Singer, was a talented amateur musician and watercolorist who had a modest income from her family. After the death of their first child, the couple moved to Europe. Fitzwilliam gave up his medical practice, and the family lived a restless life, traveling back and forth between Europe's resorts and cultural capitals. They never had a permanent home. Sargent grew up extremely close to his sisters, Emily and Violet. Two other siblings, a boy and a girl, died young.

The artist once told me that his sister Emily was as talented as he was but that she wasn't disciplined enough to develop her gifts. Sargent, on the other hand, worked obsessively, starting at an early age. He said he could not remember a time when he hadn't thought of himself as a painter. His first memory was of a purple-red cobblestone in the gutter of a street near his house in Florence. Its color was so lovely that he dreamed of it constantly and begged his nurse to take him to see it on their daily walks.

In 1874, when John was eighteen, the Sargents moved to Paris to nurture the young man's ambitions. He joined the atelier of Carolus-Duran, one of the few artists who welcomed American students, and he quickly passed the rigorous exams to study drawing at the prestigious Ecole des Beaux Arts.

Sargent's rise was swift and dazzling. In 1877, the Salon accepted the first picture he submitted, a portrait of a family friend, Fanny Watts. Two years later, he won an honorable mention for his portrait of Carolus-Duran. In 1881, the year I met him, he won a second-class medal for his painting of Madame Subercaseaux, the dark-haired wife of a Chilean diplomat. Now his success enabled him to show *hors concours,* without approval of the Salon jury.

From the start, the critics applauded Sargent's work. He was endlessly and enviously talked about in artists' ateliers and drawing rooms across Paris, and reproductions of his work regularly appeared in the fashionable magazines.

Among the general public, however, the publicity had not translated into commissions. His Salon successes attracted a few clients, almost all Americans, but he could not earn a decent living, and he was shunned by the French *gratin*—the uppercrust—whom he most wanted to paint. Like me, Sargent was a victim of rising prejudice against Americans and a growing fear among the French that American dollars, talent, and boldness were overtaking native traditions. In June 1881, long before my famous collaboration with Sargent, Perdican, the society columnist for *L'Illustration,* condemned the artist and me as dangerous threats to French hegemony. "It is a stealthy war; but they come to hoist their victory flag over our land," Perdican wrote. "They have painters who seize our medals, such as Monsieur Sargent, and pretty women who eclipse ours, like Madame Gautreau."

On a frigid, snowy afternoon more than a year after Perdican's item appeared, I was reading in the parlor when the maid announced a visitor named Ralph Curtis. A moment later, a slender young man appeared in the doorway, brushing snowflakes from his lapels. He was dressed in a perfectly tailored waistcoat, coat, a blue cravat, and a white collar.

I had met Curtis a few times at parties. He had studied with Carolus-Duran and fancied himself a painter, though he had little talent. Curtis's real profession was as a bon vivant. He was part of a group of worldly American expatriates who dressed exquisitely and pursued social life as avidly as others practiced law and medicine. By day, they haunted the cafés and picture dealers. At night, they could be found strolling the boulevards and lingering over dinner at the better restaurants.

Curtis was devoted to John Sargent. Their fathers were cousins, and John and Ralph had spent time together as children.

"Hello, Madame Gautreau. I've something important to talk to you about," Curtis said. He settled himself across from me on a chair next to the fire. "John Sargent is wild to paint you. He's desperate to have something magnificent for the next Salon, a painting that will take Paris by storm. He feels you're the only woman in town who can give him a masterpiece."

"Can't he ask me himself?"

Curtis smiled. "You know how shy he is."

The maid wheeled in a cart with a tea service and left it in front of me. I poured two cups of tea and handed one to Curtis.

"My husband wants to commission Léon Bonnat to paint me," I said. Though Bonnat's work was rather dark and glum, he was very fashionable.

"Not *that* overrated mediocrity," Curtis exclaimed. "Bonnat can only paint men! And his talent is nil compared to Sargent's. Anyway, this wouldn't be a commissioned work. If you like the painting, you can buy it. If not, you're under no obligation."

"Tell Monsieur Sargent I'll think about it."

"Very well." Curtis drank his tea quickly and left.

If I could have been sure that Sargent's portrait would be as beautiful as the one he had painted of Madame Subercaseaux, I'd have agreed in a second to pose for him. But a portrait is, at best, an uncertain undertaking. My beauty was my claim to consequence, and though I loved the idea of being immortalized on canvas, I was leery of entrusting my image to an artist.

As it turned out, Curtis's visit was the first strike in an ardent campaign by Sargent to win my approval. Over the next year, his friends bombarded me with letters begging me to sit for him and help him "unleash" the full power of his brilliance, as Curtis once put it. Yet Sargent never approached me himself.

Oddly, when I'd occasionally see him at a party or a restaurant, he never tried to start a conversation. Sometimes, though, I'd catch him staring at me. Finally I confronted him.

The occasion was the opening of the 1882 Salon. I had wandered into the "S" room, the space dedicated to painters whose last name began with S. A large crowd had gathered in front of Sargent's *El Jaleo*. The painting was a monumental depiction of a frenzied Spanish cabaret scene, with the lower panel of the frame inverted to suggest footlights. Sargent stood to the right of the painting, accepting compliments from his friends.

I pushed my way through the crowd. "I see you've painted another masterpiece," I said, teasing.

Knowing his reputation for shyness, I expected a timid response, but he looked me in the face with shining eyes. "Ah, I'm still waiting for my masterpiece," he said. "I'm waiting for you."

His cool charm unnerved me, and for once it was I who stumbled for words. "And I'm still thinking about it," I said, more flippantly than I had intended.

He looked so disappointed that I thought he might cry. Immediately I was sorry. In a flush of embarrassment, I said good-bye, then scurried off to another gallery.

The next day, still brooding about our encounter, I decided to drop in on Sargent. He answered the door dressed immaculately in a waistcoat and a white collar, and puffing on a foul-smelling Egyptian ciga-rette. "Madame Gautreau! This *is* a pleasant surprise," he said. He looked ecstatic to see me.

In sharp contrast to Sargent's neat appearance, his studio was untidy. A film of dirt covered every surface. Old rags and abandoned sketches littered the floor. Jars of turpentine, brushes, and scrapers cluttered the tables. A tattered carpet covered the model's stand. I hadn't noticed the mess during the party for the unveiling of Pozzi's portrait the year before, but now I hesitated to touch anything.

Sargent removed a pile of newspapers from the divan and motioned me to sit. Then he settled himself beside me.

"Have you thought any more about sitting for me?" he asked.

"Tell me exactly what you have in mind."

He pulled fussily on his collar. "Something striking, something that will celebrate your beautiful lines and exotic color. I haven't worked out the setting or the pose. But I see you in a simple gown, something, er, décolleté. Your figure is perfect. Let's show it off."

"And jewelry?"

"No jewelry. The statues in the Louvre don't wear jewelry. Why should you?" Sargent looked deeply into my face and smiled kindly. Then he straightened himself and said, "If you have time, I'd like to make a few sketches."

"Now?" I asked.

"Why not?"

He retrieved some paper from a portfolio on the floor and posi-tioned himself in a chair, where he'd have a good view of my profile, the only angle of my face that interested him. He told me that my lines fascinated him—my sloping forehead, my distinctive nose (remi-niscent of portraits of Francis I, the sixteenth-century French king), my jutting chin. Working rapidly with thick pieces of black charcoal, he made three sketches in two hours. He had a fresh baguette on the floor by his side, and sometimes he'd break off a piece to use as an eraser. When he finished, he wiped the drawings with a rag dipped in turpentine and signed them in the bottom right corner, "John S. Sargent."

"Please take whichever of them you want," he offered.

I chose a simple sketch of my head and shoulders. Later I had it framed, and it hangs in my bedroom to this day. Before I left the studio, I told Sargent I still needed time to think about posing.

"I hope you'll say yes," he said as we shook hands at the door. "It will be an honor to paint you."

Over the next few days, I thought about the pictures I had seen in Sargent's studio, mostly copies of works by Velázquez and Frans Hals and a few portraits of female models. There was no doubt that Sargent was a master of technique and color. But one of his pictures, a head-and-shoulders view of a blond model, gave me pause. The young woman had a sad, plain face and a double chin. Did she really look like that? Or did the picture reflect Sargent's negative view of her character?

I began to worry that the artist might have a negative view of *my* character. Also, I was concerned that my beauty wouldn't translate well onto canvas. Certainly none of the photographs I had had taken over the years captured me accurately. At least that was my conclusion after flipping through our photograph albums. Perhaps, I thought as I studied the dull prints, I had never gone to a good photographer.

After mulling it over for a few days, I made an appointment to have my picture taken by Nadar, the most celebrated photographer in Paris. Nadar was said to be a brilliant interpreter of personality, and I was curious to see how his prints would compare to Sargent's sketches.

I arrived at Nadar's studio on rue d'Anjou at noon on a cold, sunny morning. A plump middle-aged woman showed me into a spacious waiting room. On one wall hung a collection of paintings by Manet, Monet, Sisley, and Degas—Nadar had been among the first to champion the Impressionists. The opposite wall held caricatures drawn by the photographer during his days working at the satirical *Journal Pour Rire*. This wall also featured framed photographs of some of the famous people Nadar had photographed: Baudelaire, Victor Hugo, Théophile Gautier, Sarah Bernhardt, Gustave Flaubert, Emile Zola.

In one corner, a man sat on a folding stool painting in oils over a blown-up photograph of a lovely young woman. This was Nadar's in-house artist. The studio charged four thousand francs to transform a print into an oil painting, a service that provided a large part of Nadar's income.

I had been waiting thirty minutes when the assistant called my

name and led me to the second floor and down a long corridor, past
the laboratories for developing negatives and the rooms for printing,
toning, and retouching.

At the end of the corridor, we entered a large rectangular room
that was lit from above by an enormous skylight. A tall young man
with reddish hair, Nadar's son, Paul, was adjusting muslin curtains on
a rolling screen used for backdrops. Nadar himself was buried under a
black hood behind a rosewood camera perched on a tripod.

"Madame Gautreau, how lovely to meet you," said Paul Nadar as
I entered the room. He looked to be in his early twenties.

A muffled cough emanated from under the black hood, and a
moment later a tall, gangly man dressed in a white cashmere coat and
blue silk cravat emerged. At sixty-two, Nadar's flaming-red hair had
turned gray, and his face was deeply lined. "Ah, Madame Gautreau,"
he said, taking my hand and kissing the knuckles lightly. "I hardly
spend any time here anymore. But when I saw your name in the
appointment book, I knew I wanted to photograph you myself."

Nadar had been born Félix Tournachon. As a teenager, his biting
wit prompted his friends to call him Tournadard (*dard* means sting),
which, over time, metamorphosed into Nadar. After a varied career as
a journalist, novelist, and illustrator, he took some photography
lessons, and by 1855 he had set himself up as a photographer, one of
the first in Paris. Now he was semiretired, and his son ran the business.

While Nadar fussed behind the camera, adjusting knobs and moving glass plates, Paul posed me sitting in a chair before the screen and
looking directly into the lens.

Nadar moved the tripod to about six feet in front of me and disappeared under the black hood. "You won't be sorry you've come to us,"
he said, his voice barely audible under the heavy cloth. "So many hacks
have set up shop on the boulevards. I'm sure you've seen their dreary,
cardboard work. For a likeness of the most intimate and happy kind, a
speaking likeness, you need Nadar!"

He slipped out from under the hood and smiled at me. "Yes, a
speaking likeness." Then he turned to his son and said, "That's what
we're after, isn't it, Paul?"

"You're right, as always, Papa," said Paul, nodding.

Nadar ducked under the hood again, removed the camera's lens cap, and slid open the back of the rosewood box. He raised his right arm and waved his long freckled fingers in the air. "Look at my hand, Madame," he ordered.

I obeyed. I heard a loud pop, then the fumbling of glass plates and lens caps. This went on for about an hour. Finally Nadar handed the plates to an assistant. "We're finished," he said. "We'll deliver the prints to you within ten days."

I left the studio feeling optimistic. The session seemed to have gone well. I liked Nadar, and his photographs had a kind of formal, timeless beauty—even his portrait of the jowly, mannish George Sand.

The following week, a box from rue d'Anjou arrived, and I opened it with great anticipation. Nadar had sent seven different prints, which I carefully took out and laid on the dining room table. They were hideous! Each full-faced view was uglier than the next. My nose looked huge, my eyes looked like dull coins, my mouth was nothing but a mean slit. I ripped up the prints and never again allowed anyone to photograph me.

I had thought photography could reflect the truth of a woman's beauty. But after seeing these horrible prints, I decided it was an imperfect art, impossible for the photographer and sitter to control. Painting, on the other hand, I began to believe, could reveal something greater than reality. In the right hands, with the right chemistry between artist and sitter, painting could illuminate a higher truth. More to the point, it had the power to immortalize. A beautiful woman captured on canvas is eternally youthful, eternally adored. I thought of Shakespeare's description of Cleopatra: "Age cannot wither her, nor custom stale her infinite variety."

Later in the week, I sent a *petit bleu* to Sargent, telling him that I'd sit for him. He wrote back asking if he could come to rue Jouffroy the following Monday, and requested that I choose a dress or two to show him.

I selected two new gowns, a dark-blue satin with a white sash and a silvery-green silk, both of which I modeled for Sargent when he came to the house. He liked the blue satin. After I had changed into it, the artist posed me in the parlor—where he had decided the light was best. I was draped languidly on a settee, my face in profile against a background of dark-green curtains. Perched stiffly on the settee, I watched Sargent out of the corner of my eye. As he worked, I felt a constant urge to question him, to ask him what he saw, what he was doing. But I restrained myself, as Julie had advised. "Leave him alone, *chérie*," she had told me. "Don't compete with him; don't try to control the portrait. You have one job and one job alone. to be quiet and look gorgeous."

I strove for indifference, but all I could think about was the painting. Sitting for hours on end, numbed, fatigued, and bored, I distracted myself with thoughts of a Salon triumph. I imagined the glowing articles that would be written about me, the exciting invitations that would pour in, the fascinating men who would pursue me. I dreamed about the pleasure of seeing my image reproduced in the popular journals and on calendars and chocolate tins, of Guerlain offering to invent a scent in my honor. The portrait would be my revenge on Dr. Pozzi and every other man who dared to reject me.

At first, most of the sittings were at my house, but as the spring wore on, we began working more and more at Sargent's studio, where there was more privacy.

"You are a wonderful subject," Sargent told me one morning. "I've had some very dull, unattractive clients recently, and it's almost impossible to turn them into interesting pictures. Women don't ask me outright to make them beautiful, but I can feel them wanting me to do so all the time."

"How do you manage it?" I asked.

Sargent nodded toward a battered wood screen near the piano. "If I can't stand my sitter, I go behind that screen and stick my tongue out at them. Then I feel better, and I can paint."

One morning when I arrived for my scheduled appointment, Sargent was working not on my picture but on a portrait of another woman, Margaret Stuyvesant Rutherford White, the wife of the American chargé d'affaires in Paris. Her picture was as conventional and light as mine was dark and exotic. Sargent had pictured Daisy White, as she was known, dressed for a fashionable evening out. Staring directly out of the canvas, she was swathed in billowy cream silk and pearls. In one hand she held a fan; in the other, opera glasses.

I had seen Daisy White at parties and receptions. She was pretty enough. But Sargent had transformed her, without sacrificing anything in the way of likeness, into the very image of dignified, modern beauty.

He had taken what was best about her looks and character, heightened and polished those qualities, and then preserved them in paint.

A shot of jealousy snaked through me. "So, you're planning to send *both* of us to the Salon?" I asked.

"Yes."

"I thought *I* was the only one."

"I never told you that."

"Well, your friends led me to believe it."

"I can't speak for my friends."

"You've been telling everyone in town how much you wanted me to sit for you, that you needed me to give you your masterpiece."

"That's true. Don't you know, Mrs. White is a *commissioned* work."

He spoke quietly and looked at me with gentle eyes. I felt a bit reassured. But the sitting didn't go well. I couldn't wipe the tension from my face, and Sargent's concentration was broken. After an hour, he said, "Maybe you should come back tomorrow." I gathered my things and left.

The next morning, when I rang the bell outside Sargent's studio, it took him longer than usual to answer. Finally I heard his heels clicking on the creaking floor, and he answered the door. "Good morning, Madame Gautreau," he said, his voice edged with despair. His eyes were bloodshot, his face pale.

I glanced at my portrait sitting on the easel next to the window and recoiled in horror. It had been slashed! A long gash ran from the upper right hand corner through the middle of my face, then cleaved my body in two and continued to the edge of the canvas.

"Who did this?" I could barely breathe. My voice came out in a whisper.

Sargent looked at me gravely. "I did."

"Are you crazy?"

"It wasn't right. It wasn't *alive.*" He shook his head from side to side.

"*I* thought it was alive."

"A woman can't judge her own portrait."

I was furious. I had devoted several months to the painting, posing for three hours every day. I felt like slapping him. "You had no right, no right," I shouted as I dashed for the door.

Sargent ran after me and grabbed my arm. "I know you so well now. I'm sure if you stick with me, I can paint something splendid and true."

I stared at him.

"Don't you know," he said, "that's Plato's definition of beauty: the 'splendor of the true.' " He smiled and looked so boyish and earnest that my anger melted away.

"But there's no time to start over and make this year's Salon," I protested. "You'll send Daisy White."

"Her picture isn't done either," Sargent said glumly.

"What will you do?"

"I have something else. The four daughters of a Boston expatriate named Edward Boit. But I'm counting on you for next year."

It seemed a long way off, especially since I was hoping to be this year's Salon Queen.

"I'm willing to continue," I said. "But I need to take a break. Next month, I'm going to the country with my daughter. You can join us there, if you like."

Sargent's face brightened, and he smiled broadly. "Wonderful!"

As I walked through the door, he called to me, "I'm not happy with the blue dress. Why don't you pack something black."

I spent several hours the next day trying on gowns in the room at the back of my boudoir suite, where I kept my clothes in four large armoires. Sargent had suggested I wear black, yet everything that had been made for me in the past year was jewel-toned—there were several emerald satins, a ruby velvet, a sapphire silk, and a pearly satin overlaid with tulle. I had several black afternoon dresses, but nothing stunning enough for a portrait.

By noon I had gone through my current wardrobe and started in on gowns from previous seasons. Usually I gave my outfits to the maids after wearing them once or twice, but I always kept a few pieces of which I was especially fond. At four, just when I was thinking I'd have to have something new made, I came upon a box on top of the walnut armoire. Inside was the Poussineau gown I had worn to the opening of the Nouvel Opéra in 1875. The maid buttoned me into the velvet bodice and helped me step into the satin skirt. I looked in the mirrored doors of one of the armoires. The dress still fit perfectly.

As I admired the white curves of my shoulders and arms against the black fabric, I remembered the stir the dress had caused at the opera—the men's admiring glances, the women's eyes hard with envy. That was exactly the response I wanted from Sargent's portrait.

On the first day of June, Louise and I boarded a train for Brittany, accompanied by the nanny and a maid. We arrived at Saint-Malo in early evening. Old Madame Gautreau showed little interest in her grandchild, but Millicent loved Louise and begged to take care of her. I allowed the nanny, a stout Scotswoman, to let Millicent dress and feed Louise, but only if the nanny was present. I made her swear she'd never leave the little girl alone with Pierre's dotty cousin.

The following morning, Sargent showed up at the château and was given a room on the top floor. After breakfast, I changed into my black gown while the artist waited with his sketch pad in the parlor.

Pierre had written his mother, extolling Sargent's talents and explaining that it was an honor for a member of our family to be painted by him. But the old lady was not happy about turning her parlor into an atelier littered with messy paints, brushes, palettes, and jars of turpentine. It didn't help that Sargent was American, a breed my mother-in-law loathed.

When I came downstairs in my black gown, I found her sitting in her favorite chair, glaring at Sargent as he awkwardly tried to make conversation. As soon as she saw me, she forgot about the artist.

"You can't wear that dress! It's indecent," she cried.

"I think it's gorgeous," Sargent said, addressing my mother-in-law. "It will look exquisite in the painting, I assure you."

"I doubt it," the old lady grumbled. She had seen enough. She signaled to one of the footmen, who escorted her out to the garden.

Sargent clapped his hands and did a little jig. "Your gown is just the thing!" he enthused. "I'd like to get started at once, the light is perfect this morning."

Sargent knew he wanted me in profile, but otherwise he couldn't decide how to pose me. He arranged my arms and my dress and ordered me to twist this way and that. Working in pencil, charcoal, and sometimes watercolor, he sketched me sitting, standing, and half reclining on a divan. Nothing satisfied him.

I had my own ideas of how I wanted to appear in the portrait, and our sessions often deteriorated into battles for control—exactly what Julie had warned me against. Sargent complained that I ignored his instructions about, say, not arching my back and raising my chin. We also argued about my toilette. One day I used a curling iron to twist my naturally wavy hair into ringlets, letting a few tendrils tumble around my face. I thought I looked like Madame Récamier as painted by Gérard. Sargent thought I looked "messy." He wouldn't continue until I had wetted my head down and redid my hair in its usual smooth roll.

As the days wore on, I began to despair that Sargent would ever settle on a pose. My patience wore thin. I was tired and distracted by the flurry of parties and dinners I was obliged to attend in nearby Dinard, where many of my Paris acquaintances had summer villas. It was hard to get up early to pose for Sargent when I had been out late the night before.

Then there was the heat. That summer of 1883 was unusually torrid for Brittany. During the middle of the day, with the sun pouring through the windows and tall French doors, the parlor was as hot as Parlange in August. Sweat dripped from my neck and armpits, and I had to take breaks to mop myself up.

The heat bothered Sargent, too. Though he started work every day wearing a waistcoat, by midmorning, he had removed it, folded it over a chair, and rolled up his shirtsleeves.

The boredom was unrelenting, and my body ached from trying to hold still for long periods of time. I began yawning through the sessions, and I'm sure Sargent thought I was hopelessly lazy. One day I actually nodded off, and the artist shook me awake. "Madame, sitting is a challenge to be met," he said. "Persevere. I know you can rise to the occasion."

He put a book on my lap and let me read while he sketched. But reading only made me more sleepy.

"I can't keep my eyes open," I said.

Sargent suggested I take a short break and catch some fresh air on the terrace. I got up, but before I stepped through the French doors, I heard Louise crying, her voice carrying from the second-floor nursery, down the staircase behind me. I turned quickly, pushing off with my hand from a round Empire table, and twisting and stretching my neck. One of my dress straps slid off my shoulder. I started for the staircase and Louise, but Sargent threw up his arms. "Hold that pose!" he shouted.

"What?"

"Don't move a muscle."

I heard footsteps scurrying across the floor upstairs—the nanny on her way to fetch Louise. A moment later, my daughter stopped crying. Louise was being tended to, so I obeyed the artist.

Sargent grabbed a sketch pad and some charcoal, carried his stool across the room, and sat directly in front of me. "Now let's have a whack at this!" he said as he began to draw.

He quickly completed two sketches, then placed them on the easel and studied them for a moment. "I think I've got it now," he said as I stood there, still twisted awkwardly.

Until then, Sargent had been determined to paint me in a languid, casual pose. Everyone who knows me well knows the sketches he did of me in this manner reflect my personality far better than the formal portrait. In the sketches, I'm sensual and a touch melancholy. But Sargent wasn't interested in that. He wanted something else, a cooler, more iconic image. I wanted my beauty reflected back to me. I wanted the painting to render me immortal—the eternally adored woman. Sargent wanted to personify elegance.

He did not know me, after all. He was a man who lived in a world of lines, forms, colors—a visual world, not an emotional one. He had expended his nerve force staring at me for hours, but he had never engaged me. I'll admit, he had a gift for finding a subject's personality in the physical elements. In countless casual sketches, he had approached that success with me. But he had never really paid enough attention to me—to what existed behind the lines and forms and colors—to understand what he was working with.

Perhaps, over the years, I've only come to fool myself, but I suspect that Sargent, in his shy, closed way, had accepted the common scandal-sheet characterizations of me as brazen and wanton. They weren't true—or, at best, they were true only at moments. I was a hopeless show-off in those days. But so was Sargent. His strutting, however, was confined to the canvas. He was intrigued by my self-display. Perhaps he even admired it because it was so far from his own reserved nature.

In any case, seeing me standing twisted before the door, he had been struck by the sinuous lines of my figure, the boldness of my gaze. In that accidental moment, his idea of me aligned with my pose. He had found his portrait.

After lunch, Sargent unwrapped the large canvas he had had delivered from Paris and put it on his easel. He moved the round table into the center of the parlor. Then he had me stand next to it and arranged my arms and torso in the exact pose I had struck earlier, complete with fallen shoulder strap. He ran to the back of the room and studied me for a minute.

"It needs . . . something," he said. His eyes darted around the room and settled on my black fan, which was lying on a chair. Sargent seized it and tucked it into my left hand. "Could you gather up a piece of your skirt, please?"

I obeyed.

"Perfect!"

Sargent wheeled his easel next to me so he could see both me and the canvas in exactly the same light. He leaned over his palette and dipped his brush in a hill of raw umber paint. With great sweeping movements, he outlined my figure. Then he wiped it down and started again. Over the next week, he changed the pose in the picture several times, adjusting my arms and the angle of my head until he had exactly what he wanted.

To achieve his dramatic effect, Sargent pushed reality to the brink. That was the genius of the painting's design. It was just realistic enough to be alive, and just bizarre enough to fascinate.

Over the following weeks, as I looked at the painting during our breaks, I saw that he had made one side of my body as curvy as he possibly could, and the other side nearly straight. He had pushed in my waist, turned my head as far as it would go, and elongated my left arm.

After Sargent had blocked in the general areas of light and dark, he spent several weeks on my right arm alone. One day he thought it was too close to my body, and he had me hold it farther out. But when he repainted it, it stuck out too far, so he scraped the paint down and started again.

That's how it went, day after day, week after week. Painting and scraping, painting and scraping. Sargent worked with amazing speed. He'd look at me a second, then dash a few brush strokes onto his canvas and glance at me again. From time to time, he'd dart to the back of the room so he could see how the light played on my figure from a distance. He'd squint at me for a few moments before running forward to apply more paint to the canvas.

For me, the ordeal was almost unbearable. My twisted right arm felt as if it would fall off. My back ached from standing for hours, and my eyes burned from staring out the windows into the full sunlight, which I had to do to keep my profile to Sargent.

On most days, I posed for three hours, from ten to one. In the afternoons, I took walks in the woods with Louise to collect wildflowers. Sargent usually used this time to paint the portrait's background. One day, as my daughter and I sat on a log by a stream, Sargent strolled by. In one hand, he carried a large butterfly net, and, in the other, a metal box, where he placed the creatures he caught after carefully asphyxiating them with the smoke from his cigar.

I often felt like one of those butterflies caught in Sargent's net. During my posing sessions, he let me take a break for only fifteen minutes every hour. Usually at this time I played the piano. Though Sargent himself was an accomplished musician, he told me I played better than he did, so he'd relax by letting me entertain him. Often I played Beethoven, sometimes Haydn and Chopin. Once, I made the mistake of playing a sonata by Mozart, a composer Sargent disliked.

"Really, Madame, you should learn some Wagner," he said.

"I don't care for Wagner."

"You should. Through its harmonic complexity, his music captures what is deepest about the human condition."

"And what is most unmellifluous."

Sargent looked annoyed. Richard Wagner was one of his musical gods. While I was socializing in Dinard that summer, the artist spent many evenings playing *Tristan, Die Walküre,* and *Parsifal* at the home of Judith Gautier, a writer and Wagner devotee who lived in a seaside house in Saint-Enogat, a short carriage ride away. Madame Gautier was the daughter of Théophile Gautier, and the estranged wife of Catulle Mendès, a writer and critic. I met Judith Gautier once at a Pasdeloup concert in Paris. Dressed in a huge caftan, she was overweight and shapeless, but her face was beautiful, as pale and shimmery as the moon. Her friends called her "the white elephant." In her thinner days, Madame Gautier was rumored to have been the lover of Victor Hugo and Wagner himself. I thought there was something sexless about her, as indeed there was about Sargent.

He was a priest of art, as celibate as a monk. Though the only nude drawings I saw in his studio were of men, I don't think he was an invert. I'm sure the idea of sleeping with a man would have been as horrifying to him as the idea of sleeping with a woman. Perhaps more so.

I never felt for a moment that Sargent desired me. He didn't see me as a human being, only as elements of his art. He was fascinated by my blue-white skin, the kind of skin Colette once described as milk in shadow. But he was having great difficulty capturing it.

"I'm painting paint!" he complained one day. "And the paint I'm painting keeps changing. One day you're the color of the blotting paper at Guiton's papeterie. The next, you're a chlorate-of-potash lozenge. If you're going to mix your own powder, I wish you'd keep it the same color."

"So when you look at me, you think of paying bills and gargling?"

He didn't answer. He was absorbed in studying me. "Maybe I'd have better luck if I could see your natural color. Could you try removing your makeup?" he asked.

I was reluctant. I wanted to decide the face I'd present in the portrait. Why should I let this artist see every vein and pore in my skin?

"I'll scrub it off, if you promise not to portray me without powder," I said.

"First, let me see your face," he insisted.

Grumpily, I retired to my room and wiped a wet cloth over my face, neck, chest, and arms.

When I returned, Sargent took a long look at me. "I've never seen such white skin," he said.

"When I was a girl, my mother took me to a doctor who gave me a concoction mixed with arsenic to make me even whiter."

"He gave you poison?"

"I know. It made me sick, so I refused to take it."

Sargent strolled to the table where he had set up his supplies and began mixing colors.

"You promised you wouldn't paint me without makeup," I protested.

"I know, Madame. I think I have a clearer idea what to do. You can reapply your powder now."

With my face redone, we began working again. But after twenty minutes, Sargent threw his brush down. He flopped into a chair and held his face in his hands. "Damn," he said, using the only swear word he allowed himself. "I can't do it. You're unpaintable."

Sargent decided he needed to get away, to take a vacation from my portrait. The next day, he left for Paris, then a brief trip to the Netherlands. But the excursion did little to settle him. When he returned, he was more agitated than ever. Studying portraits by Frans Hals in the Haarlem museum only made him despair of ever painting a masterpiece himself.

To add to his vexations, Mama had arrived for a visit, and she insisted on attending my sittings. She was full of complaints about the portrait. She didn't like the dark, plain background, the pose, the skin color. Above all, she objected to the fallen shoulder strap.

"You must paint it in place!" she insisted.

"Oh, Madame, a trifle like that you can do yourself when you get the canvas home." Sargent winked at me.

Mama glared at us. "And what makes you think I'd ever hang this picture in my house?" Her voice was shrill. "Look at the skin tone. She looks dead, two-dimensional. Can't you put some color in besides that sickly purple-white?"

"Mama, this isn't a commissioned portrait. Will you leave Monsieur Sargent alone?"

Sargent sighed heavily and put down his brush. "I'm working on the color," he wearily told her. "The picture is far from finished, Madame Avegno. You must wait to pass judgment until you see the completed work."

"I'll feel the same then," she snapped. With a great swish of her silk taffeta skirt, she strode out of the room.

Sargent dipped his brush into a hill of brown paint. "I'm beginning to regret you have a mother," he confessed.

"I regretted it a long time ago."

That evening, Sargent went to Saint-Enogat to visit Judith

Gautier. At nine, just as the sky was turning from orangy-pink to deep blue, the maids lit the paraffin lamps in the dining room and Mama, Madame Gautreau, Millicent, and I took our places around the long polished wood table. A moment later, the footmen brought in the first course, *soupe de cresson.*

"I like it when Monsieur Sargent isn't here, because then there's more food for the rest of us," Millicent chirped. It was true. Sargent had a gargantuan appetite. I've never seen anyone, even Gambetta, consume so much at one sitting, though at this point in his life he remained slim. At meals, Sargent looked lovingly at the food as it was brought in, and began to attack it as soon as it was placed in front of him.

Just as the maids cleared the second course, a delicious *suprême de volaille,* one of the footmen announced Sargent. The artist walked into the dining room carrying a small wood panel in one arm and a paint box in the other.

"I beg your pardon," he said, addressing Pierre's mother. "For some reason, I feel inspired tonight. Madame Gautier and I dined on the terrace; perhaps the sea breeze blew some fresh ideas through my head. Would you mind if I made an oil sketch of your daughter-in-law while you enjoy dessert?"

"If you must," growled the old lady.

Sargent moved his chair next to mine, and after setting up his palette, he began to paint. Night had fallen, and the room was bathed in warm, golden lamplight.

Millicent had been watching Sargent closely. Now she spoke up. "Monsieur Sargent, in honor of your absence tonight, I ate two servings of chicken, yours and mine."

"I'm so very glad it didn't go to waste," said Sargent without taking his eyes off me.

I picked up my champagne glass, raised it in Millicent's direction across the table, and said, "To Millicent, who has the great appetite of the great painter John Singer Sargent."

The poor woman rose from her chair and, nodding dramatically, bowed deeply to each person at the table. Mama stared down at her lap, and Madame Gautreau looked apoplectic with rage, though she said nothing.

An hour passed, and the three women went to bed. I continued to pose for Sargent until I couldn't keep my eyes open another moment.

"Please let me go to sleep," I begged.

"Very well. I can finish this tomorrow."

I slept through breakfast the next morning. When I came downstairs, Mama and Sargent were chatting in the parlor. They both looked happy and relaxed. My portrait sat on the floor, leaning against the wall. On the easel was the oil sketch that Sargent had done the night before.

He had caught me reaching across the table with a glass in my hand, my profile silhouetted against a velvety dark background. The painting was suffused with golden light; the pink roses on the table were rendered with a few bold, impressionistic strokes. My skin looked flushed and healthy under the organza wrap I had worn over a black silk dress. In the portrait's upper right corner, Sargent had inscribed, "To Madame Avegno, as a testimony of my affection, John S. Sargent."

Mama was thrilled. "Mimi, look, isn't it beautiful," she said as I entered the room. "I was just telling Monsieur Sargent, this is the picture he should send to the Salon."

Nine

The next afternoon, Sargent crated both pictures and made arrangements to have the oil on wood sent to Mama's *hôtel* and the canvas sent to his studio. Then he, Mama, and I took the carriage to Saint-Malo and boarded a train for Paris, arriving at Gare Montparnasse near midnight. Before bidding us *bonne nuit* on the station platform, the artist turned to me. "If you can stand it," he said, "I might ask you to sit once or twice more."

"That would be fine," I answered.

"I'll be in touch." Sargent tipped his hat and vanished into the crowd.

Months passed with no word from him. I had no idea what had become of the picture. Then one afternoon, while I was reading in the parlor, the doorbell rang, and a moment later Julie rushed in, her face bright and her eyes shining. "I've seen it!" she cried, throwing her gloves and cape onto a chair. I stopped reading and looked at her.

"You've seen what?" I asked.

"Your portrait. Carolus-Duran took me to Sargent's studio this morning. It's masterful, absolutely breathtakingly true. I have no doubt it'll be the hit of the Salon."

So Sargent had finished the portrait without my help. Why hadn't he told me? After Julie left, I wrote him a note, and he wrote back saying that actually the portrait wasn't yet complete. There were still a few improvements he wanted to make, and he'd let me know when he was ready to show it.

Finally, in February, he invited Pierre and me to his new studio to see it. We dropped by one evening on our way to the opera. Sargent had moved to an elegant house at 41, boulevard Berthier, not far from us. The artist lived in a small apartment on the ground floor and worked upstairs in a large studio, where Pierre and I found him. The walls were covered in William Morris prints and were hung with Sargent's paintings. Long dark-green draperies, against which Sargent planned to pose his elegant clientele—the clientele he expected to rush to his door following the success of my portrait—fell from the ceiling. A couch, a few tables and chairs, and an upright piano made up the furnishings. Sargent displayed his most prized possessions near the door—a suit of Japanese armor and, in a glass-fronted cabinet, his collection of mounted butterflies.

My portrait stood like royalty in the middle of the room, in an enormous gilt frame attached to the easel. It looked larger than I had remembered, more taut and stylized. Since I had last seen it, Sargent had slimmed the contours of the skirt by painting out part of the bustle, and he had removed swatches of the train that had flowed out from my left hand.

"My God, it's a masterpiece," said Pierre, his eyes glistening. "She's so alive. She looks like she's about to turn and step out of the canvas."

"Yes, it's beautiful," I echoed.

In fact, I couldn't tell how I felt about the picture. Even after all my anticipation, it was overwhelming—on a cheery Parisian night, when I was dressed in finery and occupied with thoughts of the opera we were about to hear—to come upon a dramatic life-size picture of myself. My gaze seemed to be galloping frantically over the canvas, tripping over details. The woman in the painting certainly cast a glorious figure, but I couldn't believe she looked much like me. Her visible eye was nothing but a black smudge, and her mouth a red blob. I kept coming back to the ear. It looked enflamed. My ears didn't look that red in real life. Or did they? I'd have to study them in the mirror when I got home. Perhaps I should stop rouging them.

As I stood there staring at the portrait, a flash of vertigo overcame me. I reached for Pierre's arm, and in that dizzying moment I did indeed see myself in the painting. For one confused instant, I wasn't sure whether I was on the canvas looking out or standing in Sargent's studio staring back.

The moment passed immediately. "Can I sit down?" I asked and plopped onto the couch without waiting for an answer. Sargent followed me to my perch. "I'm so pleased you like it," he said. "As you can see, I've made some changes. The background was too gloomy, so I dashed a tone of light rose over it."

"Maybe the ear is a little too red," I said quietly.

Sargent raised his thick chestnut eyebrows and, with mock annoyance, grumbled, "Women always find something wrong with their portraits." Then, in a serious tone, he added, "Maybe it isn't perfect yet."

He took a long look at me. I could see him thinking, trying to strike an idea. Then he began muttering to himself, "Something's missing, something's missing." I happened to be wearing the diamond tiara that Pierre had given me in honor of Louise's birth, and suddenly Sargent's eyes brightened. "That crescent is just the thing!" he cried. "Don't move, Madame Gautreau."

Pierre and I watched as the artist mixed some light-colored paints, picked up his brush, and dipped it into a white mound on his palette. With one quick, elegant stroke, he produced my diamond crescent on the canvas. Then he jogged to the other end of the room and studied the picture.

"There. That's it. A modern Diana," he said.

About then, I was surprised to notice, leaning against the piano, an unfinished replica of my portrait. The background and skirt were incomplete, and my right shoulder was bare; Sargent had yet to paint the fallen strap.

"What's this?" I asked.

"A copy," answered Sargent. "The surface of your portrait was so thick and overloaded from repainting it so many times, that I thought I'd start over. As you can see, I didn't get very far."

"What will you do with it?"

"I'm not sure. Perhaps your husband would like to buy it?"

"I've got my eye on the original," said Pierre. "We'll talk after the Salon opening."

He and Sargent shook hands, and Pierre and I went to the opera. Mozart's *Don Giovanni* was on the bill, but I couldn't get my mind off the portrait. Julie had raved about it, so I had expected to be thrilled, too. But I couldn't shed a vague feeling of disappointment and foreboding.

Most of my concerns were precise and even petty. If I had known my skin was going to turn out so bluish, I wouldn't have worn a dress that exposed so much of it. The picture was too stylized, I thought, like a heraldic figure on a coat of arms. I should have insisted on a more languid pose. And so on. Over the next few days, I regaled Pierre with my doubts and regrets. "Mimi! Stop it!" he finally shouted in exasperation. "Sargent is right. A woman can never judge the true worth of her portrait."

Behind my specific complaints lay a deeper feeling, born of that shuddering moment of confusion when I had studied the painting in Sargent's studio. He had caught me, and now in a small way he owned me. For one of the first times since my affair with Dr. Pozzi, I had the emptying sense of not being in control.

Still, I fought off those twitches of dread and didn't even mention them to Pierre. Meanwhile, though no reporters had seen the picture yet, there was great anticipation about it in the press. Rumors had flown around town about Sargent's mysterious *Portrait of Madame ***,* as the painting was listed in the Salon catalog. It was customary then not to identify the female subject of a painting in the title, but everyone knew it was I. As the opening of the Salon drew near, the society columnist for *L'Illustration* wrote, "Among the four thousand works soon to be unveiled, none are more eagerly awaited than the painting titled *Portrait of Madame **** by John Singer Sargent. An American painter of infinite talent, Monsieur Sargent has triumphed in previous Salons not only with his portraits of beautiful women but also with a picture of a wild Spanish dance and another of aristocratic little girls in an antechamber. The current portrait, which he worked on for two years, is said to be a brilliant likeness of the stunning Virginie Avegno Gautreau."

The advance notices enraptured Mama, who had suddenly decided that the portrait was brilliant after all. In her ear, the applause was already building for her splendid daughter. Having been deprived of giving me both a proper debut and a big society wedding, she intended to make up for it by throwing the most lavish pre-Salon party in the history of Paris.

Mama planned her fête for the night before *vernissage,* the grand social opening of the show. Historically, *vernissage,* or varnishing day, represented the moment when artists put the finishing touches on their pictures that already hung on the Salon's walls. But it had evolved in my time into the season's premier social event, when the *gratin* viewed the exhibit before the democratic hordes arrived for the official opening the next day.

Mama wanted her party to be perfect, and she began preparations months in advance. She spent lavishly and scrutinized every detail, making life miserable for the maids, the driver, the gardener, and the upholsterer. She hired the most expensive florist in town, Vaillant-Roseau, to erect trellises pinned with pink and red roses in the parlor. The carpets were rolled up, and the floor was strewn with petals. Mama had the glass removed from the floor-to-ceiling windows so guests could step directly from the faux garden into the real one, where she arranged to hide a small orchestra behind a wall of palm trees that were potted in gigantic ceramic tubs.

Bignon's prepared a buffet for 150 people. On the morning of the party, the restaurant's manager came to the house to set up two long tables that were soon laden with turkeys, roast beef, wheels of cheese, colorful fruit molds, and mounds of pastries. He brought with him an army of waiters, whom Mama outfitted in her pink-and-black livery.

The night before the party, I stayed at rue de Luxembourg and slept in my old room. Mama claimed she wanted me around to keep an eye on me, to make sure I'd be on time to her party. But I think she was so excited and eager that she really just wanted the company. That morning, while the staff worked downstairs, Mama and I got dressed in our white morning gowns and sat upstairs in her sitting room, sipping coffee and reading the papers. With the doors shut tight, we heard none of the commotion downstairs, only the occasional faint clomping of horse hooves wafting through the window from the street below.

Mama looked serene, happier than I had seen her in a long time. Tonight meant so much to her. I had vowed not to argue with her and to be charming to her friends at the party.

By now, I, too, was starting to feel more serene. I let myself imagine my portrait on a wall of the Salon, at the center of a large light-filled gallery, surrounded by admirers. I was in the middle of this pleasant reverie when Mama gasped.

"Is this some kind of a joke?" she whispered, clutching the newspaper.

"What?"

"Look at Etincelle's column."

I grabbed the paper and read out loud: "The party scheduled for this evening at Madame Virginie de Ternant Avegno's in celebration of John Singer Sargent's portrait of her daughter, Madame Virginie Gautreau, which will be exhibited at this season's Salon, has been canceled."

"Canceled? What is Etincelle talking about?"

"Get dressed. We're going to see her immediately."

Mama and I dressed hurriedly, roused the driver, and set off in the carriage. Fifteen minutes later, we arrived at rue Beaujon, where Etincelle's *hôtel* rose from the center of the street like a miniature medieval castle with crenellated towers and the Peronny coat of arms carved in stone above the front door.

A butler greeted us, and we crossed a vast foyer decorated with marble busts of Etincelle's husband's ancestors. We entered a rectangular salon. The room was decorated with spindly chairs that were covered in white plush threaded with gold; carved wood tables; and an enormous mantelpiece supported by two marble statues. Ancient tapestries hung on the bright-blue walls.

Soon Etincelle burst into the room, her intelligent dark eyes bright with curiosity. In her haste to complete her toilette, she had forgotten to secure two of the buttons on her bodice. A yellow satin ribbon had escaped her camisole and lay across her bosom.

"Bonjour, Mesdames. To what do I owe this pleasant surprise?"

Mama's face was flushed, her eyes blazing. She waved a folded copy of *Le Figaro* in the air. "Why did you cancel our party?"

Étincelle looked bewildered. She glanced at me, then at Mama, then at me again. "Because you asked me to."

"I did no such thing." Mama's voice jangled. "You know I've been preparing for this party for months. Why would I cancel it?"

"But you sent me a letter. It arrived yesterday."

"What letter?"

"I'll get it. Just a minute."

Étincelle flew out of the room, leaving a trace of violet scent. Moments later, she returned with a sheet of white stationery bordered in blue that I recognized as Mama's. "Here."

Mama snatched it from her and began reading out loud as I looked over her shoulder. Someone had gone to a great deal of trouble to imitate Mama's delicate handwriting.

"Dear Madame de Peronny," the letter began.

> The pressures and tensions of the season have put an enormous strain on my daughter, Virginie Gautreau, who, as you know, is the subject of John Singer Sargent's Salon entry this year. She came down with a high fever last night, and if she doesn't rest, I fear she will not make it out of bed for *vernissage*. Owing to her condition, I am forced to cancel my party tomorrow evening. I would be most grateful if you would announce it in your column.
>
> Very sincerely yours,
> Virginie de Ternant Avegno

"It's a forgery!" Mama screamed.

"Who would have done such a thing?" wondered Étincelle. She looked at me, scrunching her brow. "Do you have enemies, dear?"

"None that I know of."

I ransacked my memory to recall any disgruntled servants or others whom Mama and I might have offended. Of course, our lives were spiced with petty misunderstandings and disputes. But nothing I could think of came close to inviting a retaliation this large, this horrifying. Even the festering grumbles about the fact that I was an

American were just grumbles, as far as I could tell—not the kind of rage that would lead someone to strike back with cruelty like this.

Dozens of tradesmen had had access to Mama's house in recent months. Any of them could have stolen a sheet of her stationery. But why? Once again, I had the unsettling sense that I had lost control of what was happening to me.

"I'm so sorry, Madame Avegno," Etincelle said. I could tell she was genuinely chagrined.

Back at rue de Luxembourg, Mama and I set to work notifying the 150 guests that the newspaper column was a hoax and that the party was still on. Working at the dining room table with a box of stationery and several bottles of ink, we wrote furiously until five. Julie and Pierre joined us after lunch. Even with their help, we got through only half the guest list, and Mama's driver managed to deliver just a handful of those letters. Thanks to the mobs of tourists who had flooded the city to attend the Salon, the streets were virtually impassable.

The party was to begin at eight. At six, it was time to dress. I donned a new lilac silk gown and, an hour later, met Mama, Julie, and Pierre in the parlor. Mama was dressed in blue satin, Julie in gray taffeta. Pierre wore a black tailcoat with a lilac rose in his buttonhole, and a lilac tie in the same fabric as my dress.

An army of footmen stood behind the buffet and wandered around the house carrying trays of champagne and hors d'oeuvres. The small orchestra tuned up in the garden for an audience of two cats, while Madame Lebel, the pigeon-bosomed singer Mama had hired to perform, sat on a folding chair reading a magazine.

Two hours went by. Finally we heard a carriage clatter to a halt in front of the house, and a moment later the bell rang. A footman announced Etincelle.

Dressed in a black silk gown embroidered with silver roses, pearls threaded through the thick bun on top of her head, she greeted us with a wan smile and scanned the empty parlor. "I see everyone reads my column," she said.

"How nice for you," I snarled.

"Don't be rude, Mimi," scolded Pierre. "It's unbecoming."

"I don't blame her, the poor child," said Etincelle. She looked at me with pity as she took a glass of champagne that was offered to her by a waiter. "Tonight was to be her big night. Well, think of tomorrow, my dear. In a few short hours, you'll be the toast of Paris." She raised her glass to me and smiled.

Over the next few hours, perhaps twenty people showed up, including a few business associates of Pierre's and some women who frequented Mama's Monday salons. I was particularly disappointed that Sargent never appeared, though Mama's driver had managed to get word to him that the party was on. At midnight, after everyone had gone home, the manager of Bignon's packed up the uneaten food, and the orchestra members trooped out the front door, carrying their instruments in coffinlike black cases. The waiters followed.

Mama, Julie, Pierre, and I sat in the parlor, still struggling to figure out who might have canceled our party. I suspected Sam Pozzi's wife, Thérèse, or Léonie Léon, the former lover of Gambetta, but I felt too uncomfortable to mention their names in front of Pierre. Julie and my husband thought the culprit might be the xenophobic art critic Henri Houssaye, who had been feuding with Sargent.

Mama insisted it had to be a servant. "No one else would have had access to my stationery or a sample of my handwriting," she said. Yet the only worker she could think of who was disgruntled enough to seek revenge—a laundress whom she had fired a year ago—had moved to Toulouse.

"What about one of the guests at your Mondays?" I asked.

"That's impossible!" Mama gasped. "Those people love me."

We went to bed, no closer to solving the mystery than we had been that morning. As I undressed, I had a strong presentiment of escalating disaster, a sense that more terrible things were about to happen. Sleep was impossible. I lay in the blackness, tossing and turning, as the clock in the tower of a nearby church struck the hours.

At nine in the morning, one of the maids brought in my breakfast tray. I drank a cup of coffee and began to dress. Exhausted, wretched, I pushed myself through the rituals of my toilette. I washed, applied my makeup, and stepped into a new gown Félix Poussineau had designed for the occasion. As light and covered as the dress in my portrait was dark and décolletée, it had a high-necked white silk bodice with tight white sleeves and a slim white skirt overlaid with lace. I pinned on a jaunty felt hat with two ostrich plumes rising from the top, and pulled a pair of creamy kid gloves over my freshly manicured hands. The maid sprayed me with perfume and handed me a little gold purse. Then I descended the stairs, crossed the foyer, and stepped outside.

The weather was glorious, a perfect Paris spring day, mild and sunny with a cloudless blue sky. On the sidewalk, gentlemen tipped their straw boaters to the passing ladies, who twirled colorful silk parasols. The chestnut trees were in full bloom, and their large creamy blossoms filled the air with a fresh, sweet scent.

Mama and Julie waited in the carriage. Pierre stood on the pavement and held the door for me. As I stepped up from the curb, a nail in the carriage door caught the hem of my dress and caused a tiny rip—another bad omen, I thought.

At the Palais de l'Industrie on the Champs-Elysées, a ribbon of men and women filed under the massive entry arch. Inside, crowds of people mobbed the vast marble foyer and the grand staircase leading to the second-floor galleries. I recognized many celebrities, including the aristocrat-poet Robert de Montesquiou and Sarah Bernhardt, who was surrounded by a cabal of mincing, mustachioed courtiers. Princess Mathilde, now old and fat and swathed in black lace, stood near the entrance, looking like a waxen replica of herself.

The catalog told us that my portrait was number 2150 and that we would find it in Gallery 31. To get there, we had to walk a half mile, past hundreds of paintings displayed one on top of another on the walls. As always, bad art dominated. There were sentimental landscapes, hideous portraits, and the same stiff scenes from the Bible, history, and mythology that reappeared every year. Nudes and corpses figured prominently. Every wall seemed to display at least one bloody crucifixion or massacre and several naked women, whose bare bodies were somehow acceptable because they represented allegorical subjects like Spring and Dawn.

"Why is this stuff allowed in?" complained Pierre. "It's all so tedious. There's no fresh vision anywhere."

"If you want fresh vision, you have to go to an Impressionist exhibition," Julie told him. "That's where most of the talent is these days."

"Why hasn't Sargent exhibited with them?" asked Pierre.

"He could if he wanted to. But he'd rather be a success with the haut monde than starve with the avant-garde likes of Cézanne and Sisley."

"I don't blame him," said Pierre. "Life is too short to be poor."

As we approached the "S" gallery, my heart raced. The room was packed, and the air was moist with sweat. As I scanned the pictures closest to me, my eyes fell on what had to be some of the most insipid canvases in the entire Salon. One depicted a group of ships bobbing in a harbor. Another, called *The Convalescent,* showed a pallid, droopy-eyed young woman, head nestled in a fluffy pillow, looking out the window of her country bedroom. In another picture, a curly-haired little boy in a sailor suit relaxed with his hoop and stick on the seashore.

Then I saw my portrait. It had pride of place "on line" in the middle of the back wall, and a large crowd had gathered in front of it. At that instant, I saw the painting fresh, as if for the first time, saw its boldness and energy, an effect so powerful that it muted the pictures on either side (a view of the port at Boulogne and a portrait of Saint Jérôme). The color still bothered me, and the pose still seemed bizarre. But there was no question that it was much more alive than anything else in the room.

I was in the middle of this thought when suddenly, through the jumble of bobbing bonnets and top hats, I glimpsed the mocking grin on the face of a blond middle-aged woman who was studying the portrait carefully. *"Quelle horreur!"* the woman said. "She looks like a clown in a pantomime!" More ugly comments rose up from the men and women around her. "I recognize that harlot! It's Madame Gautreau!" "Oh, look. She forgot her chemise!"

My body tightened. My chest felt as if it were about to explode. Julie had heard the remarks, too; she leaned close to me and whispered in my ear, "Pay no attention to these philistines, *chérie.* They don't know what they're talking about. Trust me, it's a very grand work."

Pierre harrumphed but quickly recovered. "You'll see, Mimi, the critics will recognize its worth. We must wait for the reviews before we get upset," he said.

Mama, though, had turned white, her mouth a grim slit. I sensed at that moment that she would have given anything for a chance to cut the picture from the wall and tear it apart.

We were standing behind the crowd immediately around the

GIOIA DILIBERTO

painting. Someone recognized me, and people began to turn around and stare. I caught the eye of a man I had danced with the month before at a foreign ministers' ball, and his gaze seemed to fall somewhere between pity and contempt.

"Please, get me out of here," I whispered. Julie and Pierre each held one of my elbows, and we pushed our way through the crowd. In the doorway, I heard a woman with a catalog in her hand ask her husband, "Where is the portrait of Gautreau?" The man pointed to my picture with the end of his cane and hissed sarcastically, *"Ah, voilà! La belle!"*

We made our way to the morgue, a small, dim gallery where the works judged to be of the lowest quality were hung. It was empty and offered us a chance to catch our breath. I flopped onto a red banquette, and Julie and Pierre sat on either side of me. Mama paced before us.

"I knew it would be a disaster as soon as I saw the dress you posed in!" she raged. "And the color. Oh, this is terrible." She started to cry, her thin shoulders shaking. Pierre, with his brow furrowed, studied a sparrow that was flying near the skylight. Julie had removed her gloves and was examining the fingernails on her right hand. We knew it was useless to interrupt Mama's explosion.

"You're the laughingstock of Paris! I can't bear it. I won't be able to show my face again," moaned Mama.

"Be quiet!" I screamed, finally. Mama stopped pacing and glared at me. In a wounded tone, she said, "You have the nerve to yell at me? You're a disgrace to the entire family."

"All right, enough," said Pierre. "Let's get something to eat."

"How can you think of food at a time like this?" Mama hissed.

"He's French. He's always thinking about food," I snapped.

"Cheer up, Virginie," Pierre said to Mama. "You'll see. After lunch, the tide will turn."

We made our way through the galleries, down the stairs, and outside to Ledoyen's, a restaurant on the vast lawn next to the Palais. We found a table in the shade and sat on folding chairs. Soon Carolus-Duran came by with a group of friends.

"Your portrait is gorgeous, Madame Gautreau," he said.

"The crowd doesn't think so," I told him. "Didn't you hear the jeers?"

"It means nothing!" Carolus-Duran waved a hand in the air and

206

shook his graying curls. "The ordinary man always looks for a painting to hate. It's human nature. People need to vent negative emotions. The critics will appreciate Sargent's work, I'm sure of it."

He had a point. At nearly every Salon, the public singled out one or two pictures to revile. It was almost a sport. Some years, the outcry was fierce. In 1865, scorn poured down on *Olympia,* Edouard Manet's painting of the nude model Victorine Meurent. Now, nineteen years later, *Olympia* was considered a national treasure.

After lunch, we decided to take another look. The "S" gallery was even more crowded than before, and again the gawkers had bunched in front of my picture. The mood had not changed.

"It's a copy," I heard one man say.

"How is it a copy?" asked his companion.

"A painting made after *another* piece of painting is a copy," the man responded, setting off a chorus of cruel laughs.

"That's right! She's a painted American hussy," cried an old woman.

A portly, professorial-looking man with a round face and a monocle was holding an impromptu class to the side of the picture. "This is abominable color, just horrendous," he said, pointing his umbrella at the image of my chest. A group of bustled ladies hung on his words. Meanwhile, two adolescent boys posed in front of the canvas in exaggerated imitation of the portrait, waiting for the reactions of girls passing by.

I wanted desperately to be stoic, but by now my startled sense of horror had turned to despair. My tears overflowed. I abandoned Mama, Pierre, and Julie and dashed out of the gallery into the back halls, desperate to avoid running into anyone I knew. As I made my way toward the exit, I glimpsed a tall man who was half hidden behind a door at the far end of the corridor. I can't be certain, because through my tears he was a watery blur, but I think it was Sargent. The man saw me and took off sprinting down the hall.

I made my way to the ground floor, through the foyer, and outside. I took a cab home and hid in my bedroom for the rest of the afternoon.

Pierre returned at six, with Mama and Julie in tow, and sent one of the maids up to tell me to meet them downstairs.

As soon as I entered the parlor, Mama began berating me. "Why didn't you tell us you were leaving? We spent hours wandering through the galleries looking for you," she said.

"I couldn't stand it. I had to get out of there."

"You should have stayed," Julie offered. "I heard a lot of wonderful comments about your picture from some of the other painters."

"It's easy for them to be generous now that they know Sargent is a complete flop," I said.

Mama sat on a settee, nervously squeezing a handkerchief with one hand and holding a vial of smelling salts to her nose with the other. Her facial muscles twitched. "Sargent must withdraw the picture. It's the only solution," she pronounced.

"That's impossible," Julie told her. "You can't withdraw a picture after *vernissage*. It's against the rules."

"I won't have people laughing at me for two whole months," Mama insisted.

"They're not laughing at *you,* Mama," I pointed out grimly.

"Well, I'm going to talk to Sargent. He's a gentleman. I'm sure he'll listen to reason." She jumped to her feet and rang the little bell on the mantel that summoned a servant—Mama had no qualms about treating my staff as her own. After instructing the maid to call the driver, she went to the foyer to wait for my carriage.

I felt sorry for Sargent when I thought of the tongue-lashing he was about to get from Mama. He was so shy, so nervous around women. It wasn't his fault that the crowd hated my portrait. And perhaps Julie and Pierre were right. Perhaps the critics would appreciate it. A few favorable reviews from the right experts might turn public opinion. Yes, I told myself, it was too soon to talk about retiring the picture.

"Mama, I'm going with you," I said as she stepped out the front door.

In the landau, Mama started to cry. "I can't believe what a disaster this is," she wailed. "We'll never be asked anywhere again."

"Oh, stop being so melodramatic," I said.

She turned away, whimpering and sniffling the rest of the way there. When we reached 41, boulevard Berthier, I stepped out of the carriage and rang the bell. Sargent's friend Ralph Curtis answered the door. "Bonjour, Mesdames," he said. His voice was even, but his eyes looked anxious.

Mama fixed her tear-stained face on Curtis and handed him her card. "We'd like to see Monsieur Sargent," she said, working hard to modulate her voice.

"I'm afraid he's out." Curtis casually examined the gold embossed card. "He's dining at the home of some American friends."

"I don't believe it. You're hiding him," Mama insisted.

"Mama, please, let's go," I said, gently putting my arm around her waist.

She pulled away from me, pushed past Curtis, and ran upstairs to Sargent's large studio. I had never seen her move so quickly. She scooted around the room, looking behind the curtains and the canvases stacked against the walls. She even tried to pry open Sargent's suit of Japanese armor, with the crazed idea that the painter might be hiding inside.

"Madame Avegno, please," implored Curtis. He peeled Mama's arms away from the armor, and she collapsed against his chest. Her whole body was trembling. "My daughter is lost. All Paris mocks her. She'll die of chagrin," she sobbed. Mama was the one about to die of chagrin.

Curtis looked at me helplessly, his thin, pale face sinking in dismay.

"Mama, let's go," I pleaded.

I put my arm around her shoulder and led her out of the studio and down to the foyer. "I'm very sorry for this interruption," I told Curtis as I pushed Mama through the door.

"Think nothing of it," he said, by now somewhat recovered. "I'm sure you've had a very trying day."

My driver dropped Mama off at rue de Luxembourg, then took me home. I went to my sitting room and sat on a fauteuil, trying to understand why things had gone so wrong, why Sargent's meticulous calculations about style and design had backfired so spectacularly. The only explanation that made sense to me was that Sargent had offended the public morality of bourgeois Paris. The painting suggested what most people who read the scandal sheets thought about me, and gave them an excuse to jeer. It didn't help that everyone knew that Sargent and I were Americans; and the picture, in its boldness and ambition, seemed to spotlight what the French disliked about our countrymen.

I played a few scales on the piano. I hadn't practiced much recently, and my fingers were as stiff as an old woman's. I wanted to lose myself in the deep, affirming chords of Beethoven's "Pathétique" Sonata, I wanted the Cantabile to fill the air, redeeming me, making me forget my wretchedness. But I couldn't get the piano to do anything. The sonata sounded choppy and tinny. I gave up and lay down. Mercifully, I fell asleep quickly.

At ten, the bell rang, and the maid announced Mama. I splashed some cold water on my face and went downstairs. She paced in front of the mantel in the salon, her face creased with anxiety. She looked old and tired. "Monsieur Sargent won't do a thing, not a thing," she moaned.

"You saw him?"

"Yes. After you dropped me off, I went back to boulevard Berthier in my carriage and waited for him on his stoop."

"Mama, what's wrong with you?"

"He was very surprised to see me," she said, ignoring my distress. "But he invited me in. At first, he was sympathetic. He said there was no way the portrait could be removed, though he had petitioned Salon officials to repaint the strap onto your shoulder. He thought that would make it less objectionable. They have refused him. William Bouguereau, another Salon artist, told him he must learn the consequences of painting such inflammatory pictures."

"I'm the one who's learning the consequences," I pointed out.

"Exactly. And I told Sargent he wasn't doing enough to help. I guess I said some pretty unpleasant things, because he got very testy. He looked down his nose at me and insisted I had no right to complain. 'I chronicle. I don't judge,' he said in this snooty voice. 'I painted your daughter exactly as she looks.' "

"You've made things worse!" I cried.

"Me!" She held a white hand rippling with blue veins to her throat. "If you hadn't worn that dress. If you weren't so—"

"If I wasn't so what?" I interrupted.

"Oh, never mind. It's no use arguing. The fact remains, we're ruined. You, me, the entire Avegno line. I'll be amazed if this doesn't kill me."

I had had a slight headache since early afternoon. Now my temples throbbed. I put my fingers to the sides of my forehead and closed my eyes. "I'm going to bed, Mama, and you should, too."

"Good night," she huffed, slamming the front door on her way out.

Ten

The following morning, and every morning for the next few weeks, the maid left a stack of reviews on my breakfast tray. In an effort to be helpful, she went through the articles, underlining the sections about me without paying attention to what was being said.

The critic for *Art Amateur* wrote: "*Madame ***, by John Singer Sargent, is simply offensive in its insolent ugliness and defiance of every rule of art. The drawing is bad, the color atrocious, the artistic ideal low. It is impossible to believe that it ever would have been accepted by the jury of admission had the artist's previous successes not made him independent of their examination. It is depressing to look at this picture and to realize how Monsieur Sargent has abandoned true art to run after the Gods of notoriety and sensationalism."

The review in *Art Journal* was no better. Critic William Sharp noted the "almost willful perversion of the artist's knowledge of flesh painting. [It] has far too much blue in it [and] more resembles the flesh of a dead than a living body."

As the days and weeks wore on, the notices grew more scathing. "The profile is pointed, the eye microscopic, the mouth imperceptible, the color pallid, the neck sinewy, the right arm lacks articulation, the hand is deboned," wrote Henri Houssaye in *Revue des Deux Mondes.* "The décolletage of the bodice doesn't make contact with the bust, it seems to flee any contact with the flesh."

Then there were the caricatures. One by Jules Renard Draner in *Le Charivari* depicted me with a heavy jaw and a potato nose and the bodice of my Poussineau gown as a black heart. The caption read: "A new ace of heart model for playing cards."

Occasionally there were a couple of mildly positive reviews. One from Sargent's friend Judith Gautier in *Le Rappel* called the painting "the precise image of a modern woman scrupulously drawn by a painter who is the master of his art." And Etincelle, in a feature article in *Le Figaro,* concentrated on my dress, saying it was "prophetic of future chic," which I think was true.

I don't like to torture myself, but I read the reviews over and over, dozens of times, as though if I read them enough, I'd become immune to them, or at least they'd lose their sting. But each new reading was as hurtful as the first.

The insults to my looks were the hardest to bear. I had been hearing all my life that I was beautiful. Now the world was being told I was ugly. Could it be true? I stared at myself for hours in the mirror, studying my face from every angle. I decided my lips *were* too thin, my nose too long, my chin too pointy. That I had been considered gorgeous was a terrible mistake. I was a fraud, and I had finally been found out!

After a couple of weeks, still wounded and listless, I decided to force myself out of my misery with a change—a new hairstyle, something to better accommodate my new sense of my features. I sent for my coiffeur, Emile.

"What would you like to do?" he asked when the maid showed him into my boudoir after lunch one day. Emile seemed to grow fatter every time I saw him. Three thick rolls of flesh bulged under his narrow waistcoat. His sparse black hair was lacquered closely to his head and made his round, jowly cheeks look huge.

"I'm not sure. I only know I need a change," I told him.

As I sat at my dressing table, Emile removed the pins from my hair and brushed it out over my shoulders. Lifting sections of hair and pulling it through his wide manicured fingers, he said, "I have an idea."

He parted my hair in the middle and pulled it into a loose chignon at the base of my head. While he worked, he chatted nonstop about the weather, politics, and our mutual acquaintances, leaving no space for me to talk. He never mentioned my portrait, though of course he knew about it.

"This is a lovely change," said Emile as he sprayed my hair with a finishing lacquer. He seemed eager to leave and began packing up his supplies.

I studied myself closely in the dressing-table mirror. "You don't think it makes me look old?" I asked him.

"Madame, you are the picture of youth."

"My eyes don't look puffy?"

"Madame, *I'm* the one who's puffy." Emile stuffed the last comb into his leather case, bowed slightly, and darted out the door.

After he left, I experimented with makeup and tried on every necklace and pair of earrings in my jewelry box. Then I went through my wardrobe and tried on all my gowns to see how they looked with the new hairstyle. Finally I went back to my dressing table and worked a bit more on my face. Pierre found me there when he came home at six.

"Mimi, stop fussing with yourself," he said. He had invited some friends to the house for cocktails, and they were due to arrive at any moment.

"Nothing is right anymore," I told him. "I hate the way I look."

My husband stood behind me and studied my reflection in the glass. "I don't like your hair," he said. "It's more becoming the old way."

"I agree," I said, miserably. "I'll have Emile redo it tomorrow."

"Isn't there something you can do about it now?"

"Is it so awful that you don't want your friends to see me?" I felt my eyes well up, and I blinked back tears.

"Now, darling, please. It was just a suggestion."

The entire evening, I felt uncomfortable about my appearance. Pierre didn't say another word about it, though his mood was dark. In a way, he was more upset about the reaction to my portrait than I was. In the days following the first reviews, he stormed around the house and railed against the critics. When an unflattering article about me appeared in *Frou Frou,* Pierre bellowed that he ought to challenge the reporter to a duel.

I should have been warmed by such ardent support. Yet I couldn't shake the feeling that Pierre was less distraught over my feelings than he was over his own public humiliation. Though he'd never admit it, of course, he liked being married to an icon of beauty. He was enraged that my pedestal was toppling, just as he would have been enraged had someone destroyed his Japanese screens or expensive frock coats.

I had always felt in some deep, fundamental way that I could count on Pierre, but now I wasn't so sure. It dawned on me that he was more interested in my fame than my happiness, and that made me terribly sad.

For the first month after the Salon opened, I passed the time mostly by practicing the piano and playing with Louise. Mama called every afternoon, sometimes with a group of friends who sat in my parlor sipping tea and heaping abuse on Sargent. I suppose they meant to comfort me, but their clucking only made me more agitated and depressed.

They told me my portrait had become the talk of the town, the subject of heated argument in shops, restaurants, private clubs, and theater lobbies. Julie said the artistic community had taken up the case as well, and that the merits of the picture were passionately discussed in ateliers across Paris.

People couldn't decide whether the painting really looked like me, a question that generated more trouble. When I finally did venture outside, to go to the dressmaker, a group of gawkers ran beside my carriage, shouting, "Madame, over here! Look this way!" The next week, a young painter set up an easel on the pavement outside our gate and tried to create a portrait from the fleeting glimpses he got of me as I came and went.

One day I refused to leave the house because a small crowd of tourists had gathered outside our gate. "This will all stop when the Salon closes, and the painting is ours," said Pierre.

The Salon would be open for nearly two months, until June 20, but Pierre wasted no time offering Sargent six thousand francs for my portrait—twice the artist's typical fee. Pierre told me he was contemptuous of the public's taste, that he adored the painting and wanted to own it. I think he also hoped to spare it from further scrutiny. He couldn't bear the idea of my portrait in a museum or a fashionable home, where strangers would be constantly looking at it and mocking it.

Sargent, however, refused to sell. He told Pierre he feared that someone in my family (no doubt Mama) would destroy the painting. When Pierre asked him to name his price, Sargent held fast. "I wouldn't sell it to you if you offered me the moon," he said.

That must have taken incredible discipline, because Sargent was broke. At least that's what Julie had heard from Carolus-Duran. "He hasn't one commission," she told me. "The word in the ateliers is that no woman in Paris will dare let him paint her, lest he turn her into a curiosity, as he did you."

"What will he do?" I asked.

"Carolus says Sargent's about to flee to England. He's lined up some stuffy rich people who are willing to sit for him."

I appreciated Sargent's need to make a living. Still, I think he should have stayed in Paris and stood up for my picture. If he didn't believe in it and stay around to defend it, who would? Running away was cowardly.

But who am I to talk? I left town, too, traveling to Château des Chênes with Louise and her nanny, while Pierre stayed in Paris to work. Even in Brittany, far from the Parisian crowds, with summer in bloom and the workers bustling in the orchards, I was hopelessly sad. Living with Millicent and Madame Gautreau didn't help. At dinner the first night we arrived, my mother-in-law ignored me, and Millicent asked, "Is Pierre angry with you?"

"No. Why should he be?" I replied.

"Because you posed for that naughty portrait." Millicent smiled idiotically. I didn't know what Pierre had told his family about the Salon scandal, but they must have read about it in the Breton newspapers.

"It's a work of art," I said in a firm voice. "Everyone who knows anything about painting knows that."

At the far end of the table, my mother-in-law cleared her throat loudly. I wasn't sure whether she meant to express disdain for my comment or displeasure at the first course—an oversalted potato soup.

After dinner, Madame Gautreau went to bed. The maids lit the paraffin lamps in the parlor, and I sat reading in a chair by the French doors.

Millicent had fetched Louise from the nursery, and they entered the parlor, each carrying a box of paper dolls, which they spread out on the hearth rug.

"I'll be the painting, and you be the people," said Louise.

I snapped my head from my book and looked at my daughter. Millicent had given her an illustration of my portrait that had been clipped from a magazine. Louise held it up between her chubby hands while Pierre's crazy cousin picked through a pile of paper cutouts of elegantly dressed men and women.

I rose from my chair and hurried across the room. "What's wrong with you?" I shouted at Millicent. I grabbed the cutouts and crumpled them in my hands. Louise began to whimper.

"It's all right, darling," I said. "Nanny will make you some new ones tomorrow."

I gave Millicent my harshest look. The purple moles on her face seemed to have grown larger and hairier since I had seen her last, and her lower lip quivered under her enormous nose. "I won't let you play with Louise if you ever again mention my portrait to her," I said.

"I'm s-s-s-sorry," Millicent sputtered.

I left the poor woman slumped in front of the fireplace as I scooped up Louise in my arms and carried her to bed. Then I retired, too.

But I had trouble sleeping that night and the ones that followed. I kept replaying the Salon debacle in my mind, like an endless magic lantern show. The days were no better. I lost my appetite and grew so thin that my clothes hung loosely on my body. I had little energy to be a mother to Louise, and I left her mostly in the care of her nanny. The only time we spent together was on our daily trips to the beach to collect shells, Louise's favorite summer pastime. At five, she had already amassed a large collection of oyster and snail shells and small conches, which she discovered while picking through the fringes of receding tides.

Starting the first day after we arrived at Paramé, we took the carriage to the beach that was closest to the château, a stretch of sand called the Sillon, which linked the mainland to Saint-Malo. We halted the carriage by a dirt path that led to the sands, and Louise tumbled out, dressed in a blue sailor suit and a straw hat, followed by her nanny, who was carrying the child's bucket and shovel.

I walked toward the water, past a large dune called La Hoguette, on which stood four upright posts supporting a row of oak beams—an ancient hanging post for criminals. The stern ruin gave the beach a grim aspect, even on bright, sunny days.

To protect my skin from the sun and salt water, I wore what seems to me now a ridiculous costume—long white flannel pantaloons and, over them, a white, high-necked, long-sleeved tunic of the same fabric. White silk stockings and white buckskin shoes finished the outfit. My hair was gathered under a pearl-studded net, and I draped a hooded cashmere cape over my shoulders.

For the first week or so, I sat on a little folding chair on the sand under an enormous umbrella and watched Louise play. One day, however, when the weather turned unusually hot, I decided to swim. I strolled to the ocean's edge, dropped my cape, and threw myself into the water. The cold was a shock. I forced my arms to rotate through it as I swam farther and farther out. Soon the water felt as tepid as a bath. As I swam, I imagined I was a child again, paddling myself through a muddy Louisiana river. When I looked up, though, I saw not the cypress-lined riverbanks of my girlhood home, but gulls flapping away from the ancient hanging post, and, in the distance, the blue-gray horizon.

I swam for about twenty minutes, and for the first time since the Salon opening, I began to feel calm and peaceful. When I stepped from the sea, the nanny held my cape out for me, and I wrapped myself in it.

For the next week, Louise, her nanny, and I went to the beach every afternoon at three. Usually, we were the only people there, though sometimes there would be one or two other swimmers.

One afternoon, I was so soothed by the water that I lost track of distance and swam out too far. The sounds from the shore faded, and all I heard were waves crashing on reefs and gulls fluttering above.

Looking back, I could barely make out the figure of a woman—Louise's nanny, I surmised—standing at water's edge with a child, who must have been Louise, chasing an ebbing wave.

I stopped swimming and floated for a moment as I considered turning back. Then I became aware of a man furiously swimming toward me. Perhaps he was a peasant who had spotted me from the shore and thought I needed to be rescued.

But there was something about the man's frantic pace that unsettled me. My heart began to pound. I turned away from the shore and swam as fast as I could, farther and farther out. A wind stirred up, and the waves grew as tall as walls. Though I swam as hard as I could, I sensed the stranger gaining on me.

Suddenly a thick arm grabbed me around the waist. "I've caught a sea siren!" the man shouted. I couldn't see his face, but I could smell whiskey on his breath. His arm was bare and covered with black hair. "I want to see your marble shoulders!" he bellowed and pulled on my tunic with his free arm.

I flailed my arms and tried to push him away, but he grabbed both of my wrists in one hand while clasping my waist with the other. I began kicking. I aimed for his stomach and groin, but my legs thrashed uselessly. I lost my right shoe, then my left. The man ripped my tunic and was pulling it away from my body. I struggled for as long as I could. My head bobbed up and down in the water. I went under and came up again. I gasped for air and felt all the strength flow from my limbs. Then I blacked out.

When I awoke, I was lying under my white cape on top of a blanket in the sand. A policeman in a stiff cap and blue serge jacket hovered over me, while nearby several of his colleagues held a crowd of onlookers at bay. "Madame Gautreau, can you hear me?" he asked.

"What happened? Where's my daughter?" I tried to sit up but didn't have the strength to raise my head. My drenched clothes clung to me, and I felt chilled to the bone.

"We sent Mademoiselle Louise home with your driver and the nanny. She's fine," said the policeman. He carried me to his wagon. After placing me across the backseat, he climbed in himself. Then the wagon rolled across the sands to the road.

When we arrived at Château des Chênes, my mother-in-law, Millicent, and a gaggle of servants ran out. One of the maids took my arm and led me upstairs to my room. I sprawled across the bed and promptly fell asleep.

The next day, I learned what had happened from Louise's nanny, who'd had a long conversation with one of the officers on the scene. During my swim, a barefoot man in laborer's clothes suddenly appeared a few yards down the beach and began running toward the water, tearing off his jacket and shirt. He jumped in and swam furiously toward me. A peasant on the beach recognized him as a local fisherman and notorious drunkard who had been arrested many times for fighting in Saint-Malo taverns. The police were fetched from the gendarmerie at Paramé. Meanwhile, two youths who happened to stroll by dove in and rescued me.

As it turned out, my attacker had been drinking since morning at a tavern outside the ramparts. The bartender there had tacked up a picture of my portrait, torn from an illustrated magazine, and as the drunk fisherman stared at it, the other patrons began teasing him. "If you go down to the beach at La Hoguette, you can see the real woman," one man taunted. "If you catch her, I'll give you two louis," promised another. With that, the fisherman stumbled out of the tavern. At the beach, he saw a flash of red-gold hair bobbing in the sea, surmised it was me, and dove in to get a better look.

He ended up in the prison at Combourg for his gambit, but I never again went swimming that summer. The attack only confirmed my feeling that Sargent had stolen my life. Everything was changed since the world had seen my portrait. Even swimming, my one solace, had been taken from me.

Day after day, I lay listlessly in the hammock in the garden. After lunch, the nanny took Louise on walks in the woods to search for wildflowers under the gnarled oaks. Sometimes they went without me to the beach, though now Louise hunted for shells at a spot farther down the coast, out of sight of the hanging post of La Hoguette. The police kept curious onlookers away, and no one bothered them.

On Sundays, I usually roused myself to go to church, sometimes taking Louise to Mass in Saint-Malo at the Cathedral of Saint Vincent.

Holding candles to light our prayer books, we knelt side by side with aged peasants and sailors and their wives. Afterward we strolled along the ramparts, then through the old cobbled streets. Occasionally we'd make our way across the narrow causeway to the islet of Grand Bé to attend a fair. I'd give Louise a few coins to buy candy from the vendors who set up canvas stalls on the sands. Once we saw a puppet show and a performance by the famous fire-eater of Dieppe. In my weakened state, these excursions left me exhausted, and often I had to spend the next day in bed.

Just when I thought my world couldn't get blacker, on the first Wednesday of August, a gale hit the region and raged for several days. Torrents of rain lashed the countryside. The windows of the château rattled constantly from the roaring wind; the roads were impassable due to mud and fallen trees.

When it ended, many of our workers were left destitute, their homes damaged and their livestock killed. The priest suggested to Pierre's mother that she hold a *kermesse,* a charity fete for the victims on the grounds of the château. After grumbling for a few days about the expense and trouble of hosting such a gathering, she finally agreed.

On the day of the party, long tables were set up in the garden. The servants worked around the clock to prepare a feast of chickens, hams, potatoes, and bread. Jars of preserved fruit and bottles of wine, some of which had languished underground for generations and were coated with thick dust, were brought up from the cellar. The day was chilly and overcast, and the wind flapped about, blowing leaves and twigs onto the terrace. The peasant families began arriving at five, dressed in their best clothes. They came on foot or in simple horse-drawn wagons—old couples bent over walking sticks, parents with young children in tow, lanky youths, and pretty girls.

Millicent and I stood on either side of Pierre's mother as she presided from her chair. Since I did not know the laborers well, and since Madame Gautreau's manner was hopelessly ornery, the job of greeting chiefly fell to Millicent. Over the years, she had come to know all the families who lived on the château grounds, and she took the responsibilities of hostess with grave seriousness. She spoke to each person with exaggerated concern, parroting phrases she must have heard on the rare occasions when she herself ventured into society. "Hello, Madame Gaudel. How is your dear mother?" she asked a plump middle-aged woman who had brought her four young children. And to a couple with gray, wrinkled faces, "Monsieur and Madame Halou, have you heard from your daughter in Bordeaux?" A small boy with a round face and snub nose appeared in line, and Millicent knelt to his level. "Master Tanguy!" she said brightly. "If you like, I'll show you my rabbits later."

The peasants spoke respectfully to my mother-in-law. They seemed amused by Millicent, smiling kindly at her and shaking her hand warmly. They looked at me with awe. Many of them must have seen woodcut illustrations of my portrait in the newspapers and read about the Salon scandal.

After the last guests had passed through the receiving line, I strolled out to the garden. The wind had died down, though it still stirred the treetops, and the air was chilly. Men, women, and children lined up at the buffet, filled their plates, then sat down to eat. Louise played hoops with some of the peasant children under an old oak. The gardener strummed his guitar on the terrace, and a few couples danced.

When they had finished eating, the peasants drifted onto the lawn and chatted in small groups. The orchard overseer, a tall, muscular man in his thirties, climbed on a chair and raised a glass to the sky. "I would like to toast the women of Château des Chênes for their wonderful generosity," he said, and the peasants clapped politely. Just then, I heard loud scrunching on the gravel path at the side of the house. A moment later, two men appeared carting a heavy frame covered in muslin. They moved slowly and seemed to be shielding someone behind the frame. When they reached the garden, they stood the frame on the lawn in front of me. Then, with quick flicks of their wrists, they snapped off the fabric. There, on the damp grass, was my portrait come to life—a striking tableau vivant of Sargent's painting.

A lovely girl was dressed in a black gown similar to mine—though not as décolleté—with sparkly straps. She struck a profile pose with her right hand leaning on a round table (borrowed from the house, I learned later). Her virginal freshness, her bright face and supple body, reminded me of a young version of myself. She had gone to considerable trouble to look like me. Her hair was hennaed, and she was heavily powdered. She had even whited out her eyebrows and drawn new ones higher on her brow with mahogany pencil.

The peasants gasped. A few approached the tableau to get a better look. A small boy poked the model in the stomach. The young woman, who looked about sixteen, flinched momentarily but held her pose.

Since *vernissage,* thoughts of my Salon embarrassment had never been far from my mind. Now my memories of the jeering crowd were quickly drowned out by the pleasant murmurings around me. The peasants laughed and gushed compliments. None seemed to realize the pain the portrait had caused me.

For the next two hours, a stream of men and women congratulated me on the painting. "You are famous! The Breton Mona Lisa!" said one old man. "We are extremely proud to be living in the shadow of *your* château," added his wife.

As dusk fell, the first guests began to leave, and the model dropped her pose. The air was growing cooler, and the girl's father, a carpenter who had made the frame for the tableau, draped a shawl over her shoulders. As they walked to the gates, I raced to them and put a gold coin in her hands.

"Oh, Madame, thank you so much!" she cried. "This will get us through the fall."

Epilogue

One thing I've learned over the past thirty years is to not anticipate the future—life has a way of turning out quite differently than you've planned. Those who have a cool attitude to the world, an emotional remoteness from the twists and turns of fate, are lucky. Accepting life's unpredictability, I've observed, is the best antidote to despair.

My mood began to improve after the *kermesse* in Paramé. When I got back to Paris, I discovered that, far from causing me to become an outcast as Mama feared, Sargent's portrait had transformed me into an international celebrity. After 1884, I was more in demand than ever. Aristocrats across Europe, even a few royals who had viewed the picture, clamored to meet me. Over time, their memories of the painting faded, but their interest in me never did.

Once, the Bavarian king traveled to Paris just to see me in the flesh (as his secretary told the Prefect of Police, who told Pierre). On opening night at the opera, the king parked himself in a loge opposite mine and stared at me throughout the performance.

Soon afterward, at a ball at the Duchess d'Orly's, Empress Elizabeth of Austria asked to be introduced to me. When I curtsied to her, she took my hands in both of hers and said, "My dear, you have no idea how delighted I am to meet a living statue."

I took the compliment as an opportunity to invite her to tea. The Empress accepted and showed up at our house with her entourage at four the next day. I included Mama in the gathering and later teased her endlessly that she never would have met the Empress of Austria if I hadn't been painted by Sargent.

My portrait did not kill Mama, despite her predictions. She lives on in her rue de Luxembourg *hôtel,* entertaining on Monday afternoons as she always has, and often regaling her guests with tales of her final meeting with Sargent. Through the years, she has embellished the facts and concocted details to make the story more dramatic. I once heard her tell a friend that on the night of *vernissage,* she stood for hours in the pouring rain outside Sargent's door. Another time, she said that Sargent threw his shoe at her during their argument.

But her anger toward the artist had a happy effect closer to home: it took the edge off her resentment toward me, and our relationship improved. For the first time in my adult life, we could be together for more than a half hour without fighting.

The French are wildly chauvinistic about painting. They can never accept that an American artist is as talented as a French one. Perhaps that's why, over the years, practically every artist in Paris wanted to paint me: they all thought they could do a better job than Sargent. I agreed to sit for a few of them, including Lucie Chatillon, a friend of Julie's and one of the most popular woman painters in Paris. She posed me in profile, as everyone did, wearing a fur coat over a white gown and a five-strand pearl choker. In 1891, I sat for Gustave Courtois. In the three-quarter-length profile view, I'm wearing a frothy white chiffon dress, and one of my shoulder straps has fallen, just like in Sargent's picture.

People can't believe I allowed myself to be painted again in this manner after the brouhaha of 1884. But to tell you the truth, I really didn't care. Most of my evening dresses had shoulder straps, and they were always falling. I could never keep them up. What was more startling was how blatantly Courtois copied Sargent, though it's only a poor imitation, as conventional and boring as Sargent's picture is bold and striking. Yet Courtois's painting was a great success. It was shown at the Paris Salon of 1891, which by that time had moved to the Champ de Mars. Two years later, the portrait traveled to Chicago, where it was exhibited at the World Columbian Exposition. Now it hangs in the Musée du Luxembourg.

Courtois will probably sue me for writing this, but I don't think he has much talent. He's a good technician who has learned to paint in the highly finished—and lifeless—academic style that is so prized by the French art establishment. That's why Courtois's view of me is hanging in a major museum and Sargent's picture had been gathering dust in his studio.

A few years later, I sat for Antonio de la Gandara. A handsome man with flashing gray eyes and black hair rippling back from a broad forehead, La Gandara was a popular man about town and celebrated painter of fashionable women and historical subjects. He pursued me even more avidly than Sargent had, writing me notes, sending me flowers, calling on me nearly every afternoon to plead his case. Finally, in 1898, I agreed to pose for him. The completed portrait shows me dressed in a shimmering white satin gown, standing in strong light against a dark background, my face in profile, my back to the viewer. I'm holding an ostrich-plume fan, and my hair is twisted into a high, complicated knot. You can't see much of my face, and the figure is unremarkable. As a work of art, it doesn't amount to much. Yet it's stylish, and the creamy colors coordinated with our decor. Pierre liked the portrait enormously and had no trouble convincing La Gandara to sell it to him. My husband joked that it was "the white Madame X" and hung it over our parlor mantel.

To celebrate his completion of my portrait, La Gandara took me to dinner at Taudière's, which at the time was the most expensive and pretentious restaurant in town. Before dining on *canard à l'orange,* the waiter brought us a parchment document that listed the ancestors of the bird we were about to eat and the names of the luminaries who had consumed them.

Throughout the meal, La Gandara spoke passionately about his work. "Painting should appeal to the higher emotions, but beyond all else, it is the art of the senses," he said as he gazed deep into my face with those flashing gray eyes. "It should touch the eyes by a kinship with flesh and blood." Perhaps because I was moved by his words, or perhaps because I had consumed a duck that was descended from one eaten by Blanche d'Antigny, a famous courtesan, I agreed to go to a hotel with La Gandara after dinner. It was the start of an affair that lasted several months.

Though La Gandara was gentle and kind when we were together, he gossiped about our romance to his friends and acquaintances, which led to acute embarrassment for Pierre and a fresh batch of negative articles about me in the scandal sheets. One night after I had been seen dining out several nights consecutively with La Gandara, Pierre stormed into my boudoir and demanded an interview.

"People are gossiping about you. You must behave yourself," he fumed as I sat at my dressing table and brushed my hair.

"You're one to talk. You're out every night with Madame Jeuland," I shouted and threw my brush on the mirrored table. Since the death of her husband, Madame Jeuland had moved back to Paris, and she and Pierre had become inseparable.

"Not in public," Pierre snapped. "Anyway, that's different. Madame Jeuland and I have an enduring arrangement." He glared at me, then fled the room.

At the time, Pierre had just lost a bid for a seat representing Paramé in the lower house of Parliament. The office had been held for decades by the Gautreau family and was suddenly made available by the death of Pierre's uncle. Pierre's friends urged him to run. My husband quickly embraced the idea and spent all his spare time giving speeches and distributing pamphlets outlining his views on taxes and Breton agricultural issues. But from the start of his campaign, hardly a day went by that the Paris newspapers didn't mock him for being married to me. Even the Breton press chided him about it. On the day before the vote, *L'Evénément*, a paper that supported Pierre's opponent, ran this poem:

> *Dear citizens, I am not a genius.*
> *On this point we'll agree.*
> *Still, I deserve your votes,*
> *For in some areas I excel.*
> *My friends, run to the polling places.*
> Ah, ma femme est belle!

I AM MADAME X

So what if I've done nothing for France?
Absolutely nothing but escort my wife to balls?
Believe me, there's no job more tiring.
In fact, it's really hell.
Think of the gloves and shirts I've soiled.
Ah, ma femme est belle!

If women could run for office,
You'd elect my famous wife, I'm sure.
You've all seen her picture,
She's a society fixture.
Since you're French, my friends, be gallant:
Vote for me, ma femme est belle!

The opponent won 75 percent of the vote. Pierre never said anything, but I know he blamed me.

After La Gandara, I became more discreet about men. I took a string of lovers, including a couple of dukes and a few foreign dignitaries, but I was careful not to be seen with them in public. It wasn't only Pierre's feelings I was concerned about. Louise was growing up, and I wanted to protect her from my private life.

Dear, sweet Louise. Almost overnight, it seemed, she had become a young woman. At twenty, she looked much more like my side of the family than Pierre's, and much more like the Ternants than the Avegnos. Indeed, she closely resembled Julie, with her straight dark hair, her small figure, her large brown eyes, and her full, rosy mouth. She favored Julie in temperament, too. Louise was serious, intellectual. As a child, she had been tutored at home, and she had taken passionately to her studies, spending long hours reading. By age ten, she had gone through all the books in our library, so I began taking her to the bookstore every week to buy a new volume. She has never given me a moment of sadness, and we are as close as two people could be. With Louise, I broke the cycle of mother-daughter hostility that had plagued our family—my proudest accomplishment.

Throughout her adolescence, Louise and I often traveled together, and every summer we spent a week at Baden-Baden. One day, as we sat and sipped iced tea on the terrace of our hotel, we struck up a conversation with a handsome young man at the next table. He introduced himself as Olivier Jallu and said he was on vacation from his law practice in Dijon. Immediately, he was smitten with Louise, and she with him. They were inseparable for the rest of our stay, and as soon as we returned to Paris, Olivier began bombarding Louise with letters. Then he started showing up in person. For a while, he traveled to Paris every weekend. It was clear he and Louise were deeply in love, and it came as no surprise when they asked Pierre's permission to marry in the spring of 1900.

Their June wedding was at Saint-Sulpice, and the reception following at Mama's *hôtel* was a large, elegant affair. Finally my mother got to stage the grand society wedding of her dreams.

After a brief trip to Italy, Olivier took Louise to live in Dijon. I was thrilled that my daughter was happy, but I missed her terribly. The house seemed like a mausoleum without her. I was so lonely I could barely stand to be home. So I decided to embark on that favored antidote to melancholy—a trip abroad.

For years, Julie and I had dreamed of returning to America, particularly to see Parlange. This was the occasion. We booked passage on a new luxury liner, the *France,* sailed on July 10, 1900, and arrived in New Orleans ten days later.

As the ship pulled into the slip, the familiar screech of the steam whistle brought forth a flood of memories. A terrible sense of loss came over me, and I thought of Parlange with a stab of longing. I began to wish I had never left this country of magnolias and Spanish moss, of languid days and soft, warm nights. There's something to be said for staying where you were born and placed by God. I believe my life would have been easier if we hadn't moved to France.

On the dock, we pushed our way through the clusters of Negro fruit peddlers and stepped aside as wagons piled high with cotton bales clattered by. Church bells pealed, drowning the hoarse cries of the tallyman as he directed the wagonloads of cotton to the spots on the wharves where they'd rest until sold.

We hired a cab and directed the driver to 528 Esplanade, where Charles Parlange, my uncle and childhood companion, now lived with his wife and four children. The carriage stopped in front of a white house with an ornate Italianate cornice, tall windows, and an intricate cast-iron balcony. A tall, bald Negro answered the door. I handed him our cards, and we stepped into a large, sunny parlor. Two little boys hovered near the long, curving staircase in the adjacent hall and stared at us with wide eyes. I heard a commotion on the second floor, and a moment later two more children, both girls, bounded down the stairs, followed by a petite blond woman and a portly gray-haired man, Charles.

Had I met my uncle on the street, I doubt I could have discerned the slender black-haired youth I had known years earlier. It was only when he spoke, in his deep, major-key voice, that I recognized him. He smiled broadly, and taking Julie and me into his powerful arms, crushed us to his chest. "My God, it's good to see you," he cried.

After he introduced us to his wife, Lulu, and their children, we passed to the parlor and caught up on each other's lives. So much had happened in the long years since we had been together, and Charles had kept in touch only periodically through letters. After Grandmère's death in 1870, he had stayed on at Parlange and tried single-handedly to keep the sugar operation going, despite floods that destroyed the crop during several years and a steadily declining supply of laborers. For a while, he worked alone, plowing the fields himself. To make ends meet, he raised bees in the *pigeonniers* and sold honey. He made enough from that business to put himself through Centenary College in Jackson, Louisiana; then he read for the law and was admitted to the bar in 1873. His career had been a string of successes. In 1885, he was appointed U.S. attorney for New Orleans, and in 1890, he was elected to the state senate. Two years later, he became lieutenant governor of Louisiana and, the next year, a state supreme court judge.

Charles had married Lulu, the daughter of a planter in Pointe Coupée, in 1882. Like most New Orleanian Creoles, they clung ferociously to their French heritage and to the culture that was the last remaining tie to the prewar life they had once known. They spoke nothing but French at home and sent their children to schools where the lessons were in French. The boys also were learning English, and Charles was distraught that they had discovered the novels of James Fenimore Cooper. "Now all they want to read about are cowboys and Indians," he said with a great sigh. "They won't have anything to do with Hugo and Molière."

Soon the conversation turned to Parlange. "I know you want to see the old place," said Charles, a sudden sadness shadowing his face. "I'm afraid you'll find it much changed."

"We're very eager to see it," said Julie.

"The widow of one of the tenant farmers lives in the house now," Charles continued. "An old Negro woman. I pay her a bit to keep it clean. In summer, she changes the bed linens regularly, in case we show up. I've written her to expect a visit from you sometime this month. We try to go once or twice a summer. The children love it, don't they, darling?" Charles looked at his wife.

"Oh, yes," said Lulu. "They have the run of the place. But don't worry about your grandmère's valuables. I packed them up long ago and stored them in the attic. Feel free to take anything you like."

"We wouldn't dare take anything," I said. "Someday Parlange will be restored to its original splendor. Perhaps one of your children will live there."

"That would be lovely," said Lulu. "We *are* lucky to have it. So many of the old country places are gone. My family home was burned by the Yankees. Nothing is left, and we sold the land."

We talked until dinner, then retired early. The next day and for several days following, while Charles was in court, Julie and I passed the time getting to know Lulu and her children. The heat was sweltering, and we stayed indoors to escape it.

One afternoon, however, I ventured out on my own in the French Quarter. I bought some chocolate for Charles's children at a confectioner's shop and was headed home when I noticed a sign for Falconer's Books at the corner of Dauphine and St. Ann. I decided to pick up something to read.

The shop was empty except for a middle-aged woman who sat on a stool near the register, reading a book. When I walked in, she stood, laid her book on the stool, and stepped from behind the counter. I knew instantly she was Aurélie Grammont, my lost friend from convent school in Paris. When I had last seen her, she had been a slender, tawny-skinned, spectacle-wearing girl. Now her hair, arranged in two plaits pinned to the top of her head, was graying, and she was dressed in a simple blue linen gown instead of a purple serge school uniform.

But her bright hazel eyes, her tall, willowy figure, her intelligent expression, were just as I remembered them.

"Can I help you?" Aurélie said.

"I'm Virginie Gautreau. I mean Mimi Avegno." My heart was pounding as I waited for her reaction.

Aurélie studied me as if I were a rare volume. Then her eyes grew wide, and a gasp rose in her throat. "Mimi Avegno! My God!" She put her thin fingers together in front of her face and shook her head from side to side.

"My mother wrote the letter to Mother Superior behind my back. I had no idea," I stammered.

"I suspected that's what happened," she said coolly.

"It was that boy Harry Beauvais, who knew your father. He knew the story about   " I realized I was babbling and shut my mouth.

"That was a long time ago," Aurélie said with a deep sigh. "To tell you the truth, I haven't thought about it in years."

Aurélie took a long look at me. Her gaze traveled from the top of my little straw hat, with the wide satin ribbon tied under my chin, to the hem of my expensive cream silk dress.

"I knew you were going to be a great beauty. And I hear you're famous as well, always being painted by artists," Aurélie said. "At least that's what my mother writes me." She cocked her head to the side and looked at me over the top of her spectacles.

"Is your mother still in Paris?" I asked.

"Yes. We came back here after the war. That's when I met my husband, Henri Falconer. His family has owned this shop for years."

I wondered if Falconer knew Aurélie's background. As if reading my mind, she said, "He knows about me. But our sons don't. My mother moved back to Paris when the second one was born twenty-five years ago. She thought her presence was a threat to our status as a respectable white family."

"I would never dare say anything."

Aurélie looked at me with sad eyes. "My husband is in New York on a buying trip. We can go upstairs to talk."

An uneasy silence descended as Aurélie crossed to the front door and flipped the sign hanging from a chain so that the side reading

CLOSED faced the street. She led me through a dark corridor in the back and up a narrow flight of stairs. I sat in a wing chair by the window. Aurélie disappeared into the kitchen and emerged a few minutes later carrying a tray with a coffee service.

"I'm accepted as white by everyone I know here," she said as she handed me a cup of coffee. "I always have been."

"I won't say anything, I promise."

Aurélie sat in a chair opposite me and poured herself a cup of coffee. Outside, the summer day glistened. White light and long blue shadows poured through the cozy parlor. "I'm not worried about you," she said. "It's your mother."

"She's not here. She'll never know I saw you. I'm so ashamed for what my mother did. Can you forgive me?"

Aurélie removed her spectacles and pinched the bridge of her nose with her thumb and index finger. Then she put her spectacles back on, carefully hooking the arms behind each of her well-shaped ears.

"There's no need to ask my forgiveness," she said. "I have something to tell you, too." Aurélie looked at the floor and sighed heavily. Then, lifting her gaze to meet mine, she continued. "It was *my* mother who wrote the letter to the columnist, asking her to cancel your party in 1884. She was friendly with one of the upholsterers who was working in your mother's house."

I recoiled in shock. "I never dreamed—" The words died in my mouth.

"The upholsterer was a light-skinned Negro from New Orleans who was passing for white like me," Aurélie said. "When my mother told him the story about what had happened at the convent, he suggested she exact revenge by ruining your party."

"I guess we're even, then."

"I suppose so."

Aurélie and I talked for the rest of the afternoon, reminiscing about the convent and catching up on each other's lives. She showed me photographs of her sons, schoolteachers who had their mother's curly black hair and tawny skin. I told her about Pierre and Louise. When we parted, we hugged each other tightly and promised to stay in touch. In early evening, I returned to Charles's house, and went straight to bed after dinner, exhausted by the chance reunion with my girlhood friend.

It warmed me to see that Aurélie's life had turned out well, and to finally solve the mystery of our Salon party debacle. I rose the next morning feeling lighthearted. Julie and I boarded a steamboat for New Roads. Eight hours later, we stepped ashore at the Waterloo landing, hired a carriage with a pair of harnessed horses from the depot livery, and set off for Parlange.

We might as well have been in a foreign country, so changed was the landscape since I had last seen it. Nearly all the plantations I knew from my childhood were gone, the houses demolished, the gardens trampled, the fields overgrown with trees. Streets had been paved through some of the old farms, and the once-empty countryside was dotted with houses, churches, offices, even a department store, the Famous, a low-slung white frame building, which sold everything from coal and groceries to corsets, hats, furniture, and buggies.

The air was still, thick with humidity. I could hear the carriage driver's labored breathing, and from a stream near the side of the road, the croaking of frogs. By the time we reached Parlange an hour later, the weather had cooled a bit. Dusk had fallen, and the alley of oaks was softly lit by a golden-pink sunset.

The house was just as I had remembered it, with bright-green shutters and a collection of brown wicker chairs scattered on the gallery. As Julie and I mounted the steps, I noticed several buckets of water on the gallery floor. Then the door creaked open, and a fat black woman in a red calico dress and an old-fashioned tignon appeared on the threshold. She was carrying two more buckets, which she set down in front of her.

"You must be Miss Mimi and Miss Julie," the woman said. "I wasn't expecting you folks so soon." She spoke French in a lilting Creole patois. "Come on in. I'm sure I can find something to throw together for supper." She held the door for us, and we stepped into the foyer.

"I'm Cora Périne," she said. "My husband, Michel, and I used to farm that strip near the new mill. Michel's been dead now five years." Cora crossed herself with a pudgy, callused hand.

The light slanting through the windows was fading quickly. Cora reached into a pocket in her apron and pulled out a box of matches and two candle stubs, which she handed to Julie and me. She lit the candles and led us through the house. It was even barer than it had been when I had seen it last. Most of the chairs and tables were gone from the parlor, and of Grandmère's one hundred china plates in the dining room cupboards, only twelve were left.

Cora noticed my dismay and said, "There isn't much furniture here, but at least we've got some beds for you to sleep in. I've put you in the back corner room. Folks say it's the only place in the house where the she-ghost doesn't bother anyone."

"What she-ghost?" I asked.

Cora stood perfectly still and lowered her voice. "The lady that died here on her wedding day. She jumped from the gallery, they say, because she didn't want to leave her beautiful home. Now she comes back and wanders around. She doesn't hurt anybody, but she's scared a few folks, that's for sure."

"I know. I saw that ghost once," said Julie.

Cora's round eyes grew rounder. "Lord! Don't tell me such things!"

"Oh, it was long ago—before the war ended. It was in the middle of a very hot night. I couldn't sleep, so I went out to the gallery for some fresh air, and I saw the ghost flapping around."

"What did she look like?" asked Cora, almost in a whisper.

"I couldn't see her face well," said Julie. "Her head was covered in a veil."

I held my candle stub to Julie's face and stared at her in amused surprise. Then I turned to Cora.

"It's just a lot of nonsense," I said. "You shouldn't be scared."

"I'm not scared. As long as I've got the water buckets on the porch. That's what the voodoos do to get rid of restless spirits."

Cora opened the door to one of the back bedrooms and motioned for us to go inside. She followed us in and lit two candles on the table in the center of the room.

"Here you are, ladies. I'll have supper ready in no time."

After Cora had left and closed the door behind her with a loud click, I berated Julie, "Why did you do that to her? Don't you think we should tell Cora there's no ghost, that *you're* the bride who jumped off the gallery?"

"She'd never believe it," said Julie wearily. "Anyway, I suspect she likes dabbling in voodoo. It makes her feel important. Who knows what other gris-gris she's got stashed around."

Julie opened her carpetbag and began to remove a few items, then stopped and sighed deeply. "You know, *chérie,* the distance from the gallery to the ground wasn't high enough to kill me. I only realized it today when I was climbing the steps. I'm so stupid."

This was the first time Julie had mentioned her suicide attempt since the day I had asked her about it as a child.

"Perhaps, in a way, you knew that," I said. "You didn't really want to die."

"Perhaps. Of course, now I'm glad to be alive. But at the time, I did want to end it all. Can you see me married to Rochilieu?"

"I can't see you married to anyone."

"Neither can I." Julie hobbled over to the armoire, opened the door, and hung up a dress inside it. "I won't say I'm sorry I did it. But I'd sure like to be rid of this limp."

Julie and I stayed at Parlange a week. On several mornings, we took the carriage for a ride through the fields. The large wedge of land fanning out from the house was now divided into thirty tenant farms leased under contract with Charles. The farmers lived in the former slave cabins and sent their children to a school that had been erected on the site of the old sugarhouse. A new mill for processing cane had been built a mile away. Everything was changed.

It was only late on warm evenings, as I sat on the gallery, with the crickets buzzing in the grass, the scent of magnolia filling the air, and the pearly moon rising above False River, that I felt transported back to my childhood. Then it was easy for me to imagine Valentine romping in the garden and Charles feeding his pet bear outside the barn. I could see Grandmère stomping around in her men's boots, swearing at the workers, and Alzea bent over the kitchenhouse stove. Now Alzea, too, was long dead, buried, as she had requested, in one of Grandmère's dresses, under a cypress tree in the garden.

That weekend, Julie and I returned to New Orleans, and after a last, brief visit with Charles and his family, we sailed for France. The day after we arrived home, I went to the Galerie Demont to view a La Gandara exhibit. Pierre had lent the artist's portrait of me to the show.

When I walked in, the poet Robert de Montesquiou was holding court in front of my picture. He pointed to my image with a mauve-gloved hand and improvised:

> *To keep her figure, she is now obliged to force it*
> *Not to the mold of Canova, but a corset*

It was true. In middle age, I had begun putting on weight, as had my Avegno aunts. People who hadn't seen me in a long time were astonished by how matronly I had become.

I used to love showing myself off in public. I lived for being seen and admired. But it wasn't fun when I was no longer the most beautiful woman in the room. Even before my trip to America, I had started going out less. Now I hardly went anywhere. There were stories in the press that I had become a recluse, that I only ventured out swathed in opaque veils, with the windows of my carriage drawn; that I had all the mirrors in my house removed, for fear I'd catch a glimpse of my fading beauty. It was nonsense.

I had simply retired from the limelight. And, in fact, I enjoyed the quiet life. I returned to the piano, practicing all day sometimes. I played less Beethoven and more Debussy, modern music being one of the few things I admired about the twentieth century. Like many people my age, I felt I had little place in this new world of accelerating change. For one thing, I could never get used to the telephone and motorcars. To this day, I keep a carriage and horses, and though I had a telephone installed, I rarely use it, preferring instead to send *petits bleus*.

In the years after our visit to Parlange, I spent long hours playing the piano at Julie's atelier. She worked there alone now. Filomena Seguette had died years before, and Sophie Tranchevent had long ago given up art to marry and raise a family. In the still afternoons, especially in the stifling heat of summer, I imagined myself at the keys of the old Pleyel at Parlange, and a deep sense of contentment enveloped me.

I hardly ever saw Pierre, and we only spent time together when Louise and Olivier visited from Dijon. Still, it was a shock when the big brown envelope from my husband's lawyer's office arrived one day, containing papers for a legal separation.

Divorce became legal in France in 1884, the year of my portrait, and ever since, the number of families broken apart had been rising steadily. After Madame Jeuland's husband died, she began pressuring Pierre to leave me and marry her. Finally, years later, he agreed. As I write this, however, we are not yet divorced. Despite his advanced taste in art and design, Pierre was in many ways an old-fashioned man. He hasn't been able to bring himself to end our marriage.

For me, the saddest part of the separation was moving out of 80, rue Jouffroy, which had been my home for nearly thirty years. Pierre had offered me the house, but it had been his long before he met me, and it would have felt strange living there alone. Instead he bought me an apartment at 123, rue la Cour, on the second floor of an eighteenth-century building. It has elegant high ceilings and rooms large enough to waltz in. Pierre let me take as much of our furniture, china, and silver as I wanted. We divided up our art: Pierre kept La Gandara's portrait; I took the Sargent sketches and the oil painting the artist had inscribed to Mama. (She was so angry at Sargent after the 1884 Salon that she couldn't bear to look at it, and she gave it to me.)

A month after I moved in, I was astounded to receive a letter from Sam Pozzi. I had had no communication with him since that long-ago day when Julie and I had visited him in his apartment. Without alluding to our tortured history, he wrote that he wanted to talk to me about an upcoming exhibition of his private art collection at the Galerie Georges Petit. Pozzi explained that his cache of Egyptian and classical sculpture, textiles, and ceramics, and works by Tiepolo, Guardi, and Sargent was so impressive that "my friends convinced me it should see a wider audience." He added that he was including a few outside pieces to complement his own, and he very much wanted to borrow Sargent's painting of me offering a toast. "I understand from John that he gave it to your mother," Pozzi wrote. "I'm hoping you'll speak to her on my behalf, as I'd love to show it next to the portrait Sargent did of me. The two paintings, I believe, give an excellent sense of the artist's Paris period."

Pozzi's audacity stunned me. Did he actually believe I'd respond to his letter? He was so arrogant that he probably believed I was still in love with him and that I had been pining for him all these years. To be truthful, I never thought about him anymore. Too much time had passed for me to remain angry and hurt over what had happened between us. I was curious to see him, though, so I invited him to tea.

He arrived at four on a cool, sunny afternoon. Had the maid not announced him, I would not have recognized him. The handsome young doctor I had been so in love with was totally subsumed by a thick, coarse-featured, middle-aged man dressed in an ordinary wrinkled coat and trousers. His beard and mustache were white. His gray-speckled hair reeked of oil.

I later learned from Pierre, who sometimes saw Pozzi at his club, that my old paramour was the head of surgery at Hospital Broca, where he often invited his friends to witness his gynecological operations. The favorite physician of the Parisian *haute bourgeoisie,* Pozzi treated both men and women, but he was best known as an expert on female diseases. He lectured frequently on the topic and was widely published in medical journals. A pincer he invented for examining the uterus had been adopted by doctors throughout the world.

Apparently, age had not diminished his ardor for romantic escapades, though over time, if Pierre was to be believed, Pozzi's tastes had become exceedingly decadent. How my husband knew about it, I don't know, but Pierre claimed that Pozzi was the founder of a secret sex society, the League of the Rose, which met periodically in a private home, where couples acted out their fantasies on the parlor rug. Looking at Pozzi's round paunch and stiff legs, it was hard to imagine him frolicking on the floor with nubile beauties.

He took a seat opposite me in front of the fireplace. "It's good to see you, Mimi," he said, stealing a glance at himself in the mirror on the wall behind me.

"Congratulations on your success. I hear you're chief surgeon at Hospital Broca. Frankly, I wouldn't let you cut my toenails," I said. That was rude. I looked directly into Pozzi's still-beautiful brown eyes. But his face registered no emotion.

"I hope you'll never need a surgeon," he said quietly.

Averting my eyes from his, I changed the subject. "You want to borrow my Sargent."

"I'd be most grateful. Besides my own portrait, I have two other works by him. Ralph Curtis and a few others are lending me their pictures. I'll have a nice wall of Sargents for my little exhibition."

"Why should I do you a favor?" I asked.

"Because I introduced you to love." Pozzi smiled broadly, but his expression quickly changed to one of serious concern. "You know, I'm separated from my wife," he said, leaning his head against the high back of the settee.

"So I heard."

After tolerating his affairs for years, Thérèse Pozzi had finally thrown her husband out. Now he lived alone in a *hôtel* on avenue d'Iena.

"I heard you're separated, too," he said. Pozzi moved his weight forward and looked deeply into my face. I noticed with irritation that his hair oil had stained the upholstery.

"Neither of us is well suited for marriage," I said.

I like to flatter myself that Pozzi was flirting with me, perhaps even warming up for seduction. At the moment, I did not have a lover, and I felt a twitch of desire as I remembered our trysts in boulevard Saint-Germain. Quickly, though, I realized I did not want to sleep with this pompous white-bearded man.

I stood abruptly, back stiffened and hands folded primly in front of me. "Would you like to see the painting?" I asked.

"It's here? Sargent said your mother had it."

"She gave it to me."

I led Pozzi to the dining room, where the picture hung over the side-board. He studied it closely for several minutes. "It's stunning," he said.

"I'll make arrangements to have it crated and sent to you."

"Thank you." Dr. Pozzi bowed formally and brushed my hand with his mustache. A few minutes later, the maid handed him his hat and coat, and he left.

A month later, I received an invitation to Pozzi's exhibition. I declined. Several weeks passed, and the exhibition closed, but Pozzi failed to return my painting. I sent him a letter, and he wrote back that the picture had been slightly damaged as it was being removed from the gallery—a clumsy worker had inadvertently kicked it with his boot, and some of the paint in the lower right-hand corner was chipped. Pozzi claimed he was having it restored. That was several years ago, and he's yet to return it.

When I moved to rue la Cour, I urged Julie to join me. I had never lived alone before, and I thought the two of us could make a nice home. But Julie declined my invitation. She lived in her atelier now, and though it was far from luxurious, she enjoyed being surrounded by her work and being able to paint whenever she wanted. Still, we saw a great deal of each other. Julie often dined with me, and we frequently traveled together. Soon after my separation from Pierre, we took a trip to Berlin. On our first night in town, we went to the opera to hear Wagner, a composer whose genius I still struggled to appreciate.

During the interval, a courtier approached us in the corridor and announced that Kaiser Wilhelm II wished to see us. The courtier led us to the royal box, where a severe-looking man with a ferocious mustache and a withered left arm sat in a blue plush chair.

Julie and I curtsied deeply. "You are John Singer Sargent's Madame X," the Kaiser said, the words falling halfway between a statement and a question.

"I am." I was flattered. Someone had told him I was here.

"I remember seeing your portrait at the Paris Salon a long time ago and being absolutely swept away by it," the Kaiser continued. "It's the most fascinating woman's likeness I've ever seen. As a rule, I can't stand contemporary painting. But I do like Sargent's work."

"He's the master portrait artist of our time," Julie said.

"I'd like to organize a Sargent exhibition here," the Kaiser continued, addressing me. "But only, of course, if I can show your portrait. Do you have any influence with the artist?"

"I haven't spoken to him in more than twenty years," I confessed. "But I'd be happy to write to him."

"That would be wonderful!" The Kaiser nodded to Julie and me and dismissed us with a wave of his good hand.

The idea of a Sargent exhibit intrigued me. In fact, I was eager to see my portrait again, to test its power against my pained memories. I even had the confidence to put it before the public. Times had changed. Now, I was sure, people would appreciate it. Or perhaps my feelings had grown dull with age and experience, and I no longer cared what people thought. But I *did* care, I realized as I considered the matter further. And I suppose that a small piece of me hoped to remind the world of an earlier, glorious time, when I sat on the throne of Beauty.

I hadn't seen Sargent since the 1884 Salon, of course, and I hadn't talked to him since Pierre and I visited his studio the winter before. In all the years since, there had never been any communication between us—not even a letter. Julie and others had been happy to keep me apprised of his doings, however, even though he had virtually disappeared from the French art scene.

In 1886, Sargent moved permanently to London and quickly rose to become the city's premier portrait artist. Every day a steady stream of rich women and important men poured into his elegant studio at 33 Tite Street, where—I was told by some Parisian acquaintances who had been there—my portrait hung prominently on the wall. So valued was Sargent's work in his adopted home that King Edward offered him a knighthood. Sargent turned it down, as he did not want to give up his U.S. citizenship. In America, he was perhaps even more revered than in England. Many illustrious Americans, including writers and presidents, were painted by him on his occasional trips to his parents' native land. Other rich and celebrated Americans crossed the Channel to sit for him.

In France, however, his reputation has plummeted. Sargent never exhibits here anymore, and you can count on your left hand the paintings by him in French museums.

Still, I wrote to Sargent and told him about meeting the Kaiser, and of the Kaiser's desire to mount a Sargent exhibition in Berlin. "He's only interested," I added proudly, "if my portrait is included."

Weeks passed, and I heard nothing from the artist. I wrote to him again, and this time received a reply. "My dear Madame Gautreau," Sargent began:

> I am so sorry you felt crushed at my not responding to your first letter, but if you knew what a profoundly unsociable old crank I have become in the last twenty years, you would not take it as a personal matter. I am not proud of my epistolary tardiness, but neither am I proud of a bald head and other changes you will notice if we ever meet again.

As far as an exhibit of my paintings is concerned, I'm afraid I'm traveling abroad and so couldn't possibly manage at this moment to organize it. But to tell you the truth, I'm not keen to do it. It's a tremendous trouble for me to induce a lot of unwilling people to lend me their "pauthraits," as the London ladies would say.

In fact, the whole business of "pauthraits" has come to bore me to tears. At present, I'm thoroughly engaged in a set of commissioned murals for the Boston Public Library, and I'm thinking of shutting up shop altogether in the portrait line. I've come to hate doing them. Ask me to paint your gates, your fences, your barns, which I should gladly do, but please, not the human face.

Yours sincerely,
John S. Sargent

The idea of Sargent giving up portraiture was incredible but true. Julie started asking around and heard many stories about him turning down commissions. He was said to have lost interest in painting rich aristocrats, and to feel that it showed in his recent pictures of them, which he complained were common and lifeless. What's more, he was tired of pleasing his sitters, of satisfying their vanity at the expense of his artistic principles.

Around this time, *The Work of John S. Sargent, R.A.* (Royal Academician), a collection of sixty-two photogravures of the artist's paintings, was published in London. Julie got hold of a copy and brought it over one afternoon. My portrait was the third plate. It was the first image I had seen of it in two decades, and it stunned me. As I studied the picture, something struck me as different than I remembered. It took me a minute to realize what it was: Sargent had repainted the right strap of my dress so that now it was in place on my shoulder. In 1884, after the first blast of revulsion toward the picture, he had pleaded with Salon officials to allow him to retouch it in exactly this manner. They had refused, so he must have done it as soon as he got the canvas home.

The new strap, I thought, diluted not only the sensual impact of the painting, but also the brilliance of its design. Before, the viewer's eye was pulled to the left, beautifully counterbalancing the profile on the right of the canvas. Now the picture looked a little less interesting.

I wrote Sargent a letter gently suggesting that he repaint the strap in its former position. I pointed out that such a thing was no longer shocking. After all, Courtois's portrait of me with a fallen strap was in the Musée du Luxembourg. Someday, I noted, Sargent might decide to sell the picture to a museum. In that event, he'd want the painting to represent his original and, in my view, superior vision.

A week later, a plain beige envelope arrived here by balloon post from London. It smelled faintly of cigar tobacco, and my name and address were dashed across the center in a bold, confident hand. I sliced open the envelope and pulled out the letter inside. It was from Sargent. He wrote that he would consider my suggestion, though he didn't consider the strap's placement to be of grave importance. "No matter where it is," he wrote in a salute I was delighted to receive after all these years, "your portrait is still the best thing I have done."

Author's Note

I Am Madame X is a novel, though it is based on real people and events. The main character, Virginie Amélie Avegno Gautreau, was a gorgeous Parisian celebrity, notorious in the late nineteenth century for her bold dress, her passion for self-display, and her reputation for promiscuity. As the subject of John Singer Sargent's 1884 painting, *Madame X,* she also was at the center of a great fin-de-siècle art scandal.

I fell in love with the painting the moment I first saw it seventeen years ago. At the time, I was living in Manhattan, working on my first book, *Debutante,* the story of pre–World War II New York café society as told through the eyes of Brenda Frazier, a celebrated beauty much like Virginie Gautreau. I spent many days doing research at the New York Society Library on East Seventy-ninth Street, and on my way home to the West Side, I often stopped at the Metropolitan Museum of Art to look at *Madame X.* The woman in the painting seemed so alive, radiant with a mysterious, timeless beauty. Though Sargent had painted her in a previous century, she struck me as extraordinarily modern.

I decided to write a nonfiction book about the painting. But scant biographical material was available about Virginie Gautreau herself. I could find no letters, diaries, or memoirs that would enable me to re-create her personality, so I abandoned the idea.

Still, I remained fascinated by her image. After I moved to Chicago with my husband and son in 1991, I continued to visit the *Madame* on my trips to New York, and my interest in her never waned. Three years ago, after my third biography was published, I found myself thinking more intensely about the painting, and I decided to try my hand at a historical novel. *I Am Madame X* is the result.

In fashioning my story, I've used the sketchy facts of Virginie Gautreau's life as a blueprint. I've tried to stay faithful to the spirit of the truth—insofar as it can be determined—but I've taken a novelist's liberty in compressing time, altering dates, creating characters, conjuring scenes, and putting words into the mouths of historical figures.

Among the fictional characters inspired by real people are Filomena Seguette, who is loosely based on the artist Rosa Bonheur, and Etincelle, which was the pen name of a popular nineteenth-century Parisian journalist. The character of Julie de Ternant is based on Virginie Gautreau's maternal aunt. According to family legend, Mademoiselle de Ternant committed suicide on her wedding day rather than marry a man she didn't love. Actually, she died unmarried and insane.

What is known of Virginie Gautreau's life can be found in archives in Louisiana, Paris, and Paramé, France. She was born on January 29, 1859, in New Orleans, the daughter of a man and woman who belonged to prominent Creole families. In the novel, I made her four years older to enable her to comment on her childhood during the Civil War.

As a young girl, Virginie spent time at Parlange, her maternal grandmother's plantation in New Roads, Louisiana. Parlange, which looks today much as it did a hundred and fifty years ago, still grows cane and produces sugar, and the charming green-shuttered house built by Virginie's great-grandfather is still inhabited by her descendants.

The personalities of Virginie's grandmother and mother and the relationships between the women are invented. However, hints of severe family tensions can be found in the records of old Louisiana lawsuits.

Once, after Madame Parlange failed to repay $5,612 her daughter lent her to run the plantation, Madame Avegno filed suit in the 7th District Court in Pointe Coupée. Madame Parlange claimed that since the money was used to further the planting partnership of herself and her daughters, she should be allowed to keep the money. The court disagreed, ordering Virginie's grandmother to repay the loan, plus 8 percent interest for two years.

The family's most sensational court case involved Virginie's parents. In December 1860, Virginie's mother filed for divorce from her husband, Anatole, citing his mental cruelty and physical abuse. The divorce was never granted. Four months later, the Civil War broke out. Anatole joined the Confederacy and died in 1862 from wounds received at the Battle of Shiloh.

Playing the role of grieving widow, Madame Avegno fled with her daughters to Paris, where they joined a community of expatriate Southerners. In 1866, they returned to New Orleans, where Valentine died on March 11, at age five, probably from one of the many typhoid or cholera epidemics that periodically swept Louisiana.

At some point following Valentine's funeral, Virginie and her mother settled permanently in France in a house on rue de Luxembourg, which after 1879 was renamed rue Cambon. For the sake of clarity, I've referred to it throughout the novel as rue de Luxembourg. The family's descendants believe Virginie attended a convent school, though it could not have been the one I use in the book, the Couvent des Dames Anglaises, as that venerable convent was razed in 1860 to make way for a new street, the rue Monge. I placed Virginie there because, of all the nineteenth-century Parisian convent schools, it was the only one for which detailed information existed in English translation. For my account of the school, I've relied heavily on *The Story of My Life,* the autobiography of George Sand, who lived with the English nuns in the early 1800s.

Little is known of Madame Gautreau's personality, though there are references to her notoriety and regular appearances in the scandal sheets in a few extant journal and newspaper clippings, several of which I quote. She is barely mentioned in the memoirs of the time: the only one that discusses her in some depth, *Trente ans de dîners en ville,* by Gabriel-Louis Pringue, was published in France in 1948. Pringue, a friend of the Gautreaus' daughter, Louise Jallu, portrays Madame Gautreau (whose name he misspells) as a cold, stiff narcissist of great vanity and little conversation. I see in Sargent's painting a very different person—one who was vain, of course, but also sexy and high-spirited. It is this vision of the real woman that inspired the fictional character.

Nor does anyone know what the grown-up Virginie actually looked like from a straight-ahead view. The only artists' images of her are in profile. With the exception of one full-faced picture of her as a child in the Historic New Orleans Collection at the Williams Research Center in New Orleans and another of her adult profile in a private collection, there are no photographs of her.

Virginie Gautreau married Pierre Gautreau in 1878 and their daughter was born on August 20 of the following year. The marriage was widely rumored to have been unhappy, and Madame Gautreau was believed to have taken many lovers, including Léon Gambetta, the Republican leader, and Dr. Samuel-Jean Pozzi, a favorite surgeon of the *haute bourgeoisie*. Dr. Pozzi, an avid art collector, was friendly with many of the most colorful people of his day, including the poet Robert de Montesquiou, Sargent, and Marcel Proust, who immortalized Pozzi as Dr. Cottard in *Remembrance of Things Past*.

Aside from the rumors at the time, there is no hard evidence of these affairs. The best clue that Madame Gautreau and Dr. Pozzi were lovers lies in his ownership of Sargent's *Madame Gautreau Drinking a Toast*, the small oil painting that the artist inscribed to Virginie's mother. How Dr. Pozzi came to possess it is a mystery. It seems unlikely that Madame Avegno—who died in 1910, five years before her daughter—would have given the painting to her married daughter's married lover. Perhaps Madame Avegno gave it to her daughter, who gave it to Dr. Pozzi. In any case, Pozzi was murdered in 1918 by a deranged patient, and Isabella Stewart Gardner bought the painting from his estate. It hangs in the Boston museum bearing her name.

It is not certain how Madame Gautreau met Sargent. The artist painted Dr. Pozzi in 1881, and it's possible that Virginie attended one of the sittings. Or she might have met the artist through her cousin Ben del Castillo, who was a childhood friend of Sargent's. In 1882, Sargent wrote Castillo, "I have a great desire to paint [Madame Gautreau's] portrait and have reason to think that she would allow it and is waiting for someone to propose this homage to her beauty. If you are 'bien avec elle' and will see her in Paris you might tell her that I am a man of *prodigious talent*."

At the time, Madame Gautreau was twenty-three and the mother of a three-year-old child. Her exotic beauty, daring toilettes, and reputation for taking lovers had made her a favorite ornament and focus of the scandal sheets. Sargent was twenty-six and had been exhibiting his work at the Paris Salon since 1877, when he was just twenty-one. But there was prejudice against him as an American, and he was having trouble attracting business from members of the French *haut monde,* whom he was most eager to paint. He was searching for a subject who would give him a masterpiece, a portrait so wondrous that every woman in Paris would clamor to be painted by him. No doubt Madame Gautreau hoped the portrait would be her own apotheosis, the fulfillment of her (and her mother's) ardent social ambitions.

Sargent's struggle to capture Madame Gautreau in paint is well documented. On February 10, 1883, soon after Virginie began sitting for him, he wrote to his friend Vernon Lee, "In a few days I shall be back in Paris tackling my other 'envoi,' the portrait of a great beauty. Do you object to people who are *fardées* to the extent of being uniform lavender or blotting paper color all over? If so, you would not care for my sitter. But she has the most beautiful lines and if the lavender or chlorate-of-potash lozenge color be pretty in itself I shall be more than pleased."

That same year, Sargent also was working on a portrait of Margaret (Daisy) Stuyvesant Rutherford White, the lovely wife of the American diplomat Henry White, which the couple had commissioned. Apparently, Sargent initially had the idea of sending his portraits of both Madame Gautreau and Mrs. White to the Salon. But by March 15, 1883, the deadline for submissions, he wasn't satisfied with either painting. "This is the evening of the postal sending in day & I have sent nothing in," he wrote Mrs. White. "Neither you nor Mme Gautreau were finished. I have been brushing away at both of you for the last three weeks in a horrid state of anxiety. . . . Well, the question is settled, and I am beaten."

The following year, 1884, he sent in only his portrait of Madame Gautreau. As the May 1 opening approached, Sargent grew nervous. His teacher, Carolus-Duran, had visited Sargent's studio to view the painting and had told him, "You can send it to the Salon with confidence." But Sargent doubted Carolus-Duran's judgment and wrote to Ben del Castillo, "I've made up my mind to be refused."

As a previous medal winner, Sargent didn't have to go through the jury process. He could submit anything he wanted, and it had to be taken—unless the picture was judged obscene.

Sargent knew he had painted a masterpiece, but he also sensed that the picture was way ahead of its time. Though he had no trouble getting it past the Salon committee, he couldn't shake a strong presentiment of disaster.

The novel's depiction of the 1884 Salon *vernissage* closely follows the historical facts. No sooner had the doors of the Palais de l'Industrie opened than a jeering crowd gathered in front of Sargent's picture. In a letter to his parents, Sargent's close friend Ralph Curtis described the crowd's reaction to the artist's work:

In 15 minutes I saw no end of acquaintances and strangers, and heard everyone say, *"Où est le portrait Gautreau?" "Oh, allez voir ça"*—John covered with dust stopped with his trunks at the club the night before and took me on to his house where we dined. He was very nervous about what he feared, but his fears were far exceeded by the facts of yesterday. There was a *grand tapage* before it all day. In a few minutes I found him dodging behind doors to avoid friends who looked grave. By the corridors he took me to see it. I was disappointed in the color. She looks decomposed. All the women jeer. *"Ah voilà, la belle!" "Oh quelle horreur!"* etc. . . . Then the *blageur* club man—*"C'est une copie!" "Comment une copie?" "Mais oui—la peinture d'après un autre morceau de peinture s'appelle une copie."* I heard that. All the A.M. it was one series of bons mots, *mauvaises plaisanteries,* and fierce discussions. John, poor boy, was *navré.* We got out a big *déjeuner* at Ledoyen's of a dozen painters and ladies, and I took him there. In the P.M. the tide turned as I kept saying it would. It was discovered to be the knowing thing to say *"Etrangement épatant!"* I went home with him and remained there while he went to see the Boits. Mme Gautreau and *mère* came to his studio "bathed in tears." I stayed them off, but the mother returned and caught him and made a fearful scene saying *"Ma fille est perdue—tout Paris se moque d'elle. Mon {gendre} sera forcé de se battre. Elle mourira de chagrin,"* etc. John replied it was against all laws to retire a picture. He had painted her exactly as she was dressed, nothing could be said of the canvas worse than had been said in print of her appearance *dans le monde,* etc. Defending his cause made him feel much better. Still we talked it all over till 1 o'clock here last night and I fear he has never had such a blow. He says he wants to get out of Paris for a time.

The critics were no kinder. The next morning and in the following weeks, a storm of vitriol rained on Sargent and his painting. All the reviews quoted in the novel, except by the fictional Etincelle, are authentic.

There's been much speculation over the years as to the painting's impact on Sargent's career. Some art historians have argued that it was the reason he fled Paris and moved to London. Actually, he had planned to spend the summer of 1884 in England long before the debacle of *Madame X*. He did not settle permanently in London until 1886.

Far from ruining Madame Gautreau, as she and her mother feared, the scandal turned her into an international celebrity. Throughout the Belle Epoque, she continued to be sought after as an artist's model, and as the novel describes, she was painted by several successful artists: Gustave Courtois, Antonio de la Gandara, and Mademoiselle Lucie Chatillon. The Courtois portrait originally hung at the Musée du Luxembourg and was moved to the Louvre in 1933. It has hung at the Musée d'Orsay since 1981. The La Gandara and Chatillon portraits are in private collections.

At the time of her death on July 25, 1915, at age fifty-six, Virginie Gautreau was separated from her husband, though they were never officially divorced. In the municipal archives in Paramé, France, Virginie's name is crossed out of the ledger in a list of owners of Château des Chênes, though she is buried in the Gautreau family crypt. According to her will, which was filed in the Pointe Coupée Courthouse in New Roads, Louisiana, she left all her possessions and her share in Parlange to a married French tax collector named Henri Favalelli. The nature of their relationship is unknown.

Less than a year after Madame Gautreau died, Sargent offered his portrait of her to the Metropolitan Museum of Art: "I suppose it is the best thing I have done," he wrote to Edward Robinson, the museum's director, on January 8, 1916. The Met bought the picture for a thousand pounds. Sargent asked Robinson not to use Virginie Gautreau's name in the painting's title. "By the way," the artist wrote, "I should prefer, on account of the row I had with the lady years ago, that the picture should not be called by her name, at any rate for the present, and that her name not be communicated to the newspapers."

Robinson complied, and history remembers Virginie Gautreau as Madame X.

G.D.

Acknowledgments

In writing *I Am Madame X*, I have relied heavily on historical sources. I've borrowed atmospherics and anecdotes from some of the books I consulted (a selected bibliography follows). I've also used the actual texts of reviews of Sargent's painting and items about Madame Gautreau that appeared in *The New York Herald* and *L'Illustration*. The characters who are based on historical figures sometimes say what their counterparts in real life wrote, or what they were quoted saying in biographies and articles. When using the letters of John Singer Sargent and Léon Gambetta, I've often combined phrases and sentences from several letters, and, occasionally, taken sentences from the letters to use in dialogue.

I've also relied on the help of many people. First of all, I would like to thank Charles L. Crawford, a tireless researcher who is a descendant of Virginie Gautreau's paternal uncle Jean Bernard Avegno. Charlie has spent more than a decade researching the history of his family, and he generously shared his files with me. During the past two years, Charlie and I spoke on the phone frequently, trading information and theories about Madame X, our mutual obsession. Those conversations provided one of the many pleasures of working on this book.

The art historian Trevor Fairbrother, who has written brilliantly about Sargent in articles and books, patiently answered my queries, steered me to sources I would otherwise not have discovered, and corrected errors in the manuscript. Trevor was the first person to write about the real woman behind Sargent's *Madame X*, in a 1981 article in *Arts Magazine*, which also published for the first time since the nineteenth century a photograph of the painting in its original one-strap-off-the-shoulder state.

My debt to Richard Ormond, Sargent's great-nephew, is considerable. Richard is the author of several books about Sargent, including, with Elaine Kilmurray, the definitive catalogue raisonné of the artist's work. Richard told me about the existence of Sargent's *Landscape: A Dale in the Neighborhood of Château des Chênes*, graciously shared his insights about Sargent's art, answered my queries, and corrected errors in the manuscript.

My wonderful researchers—in Paris: Camille Goujon and Régine Cavallaro; in Paramé, France: Marie-Christine Ruellan—turned up a wealth of information I never could have found on my own. My son's French teacher, Fannie Clonch, corrected the spelling of French words and phrases in the manuscript.

I would also like to thank Christina Vella, for getting me started on my research in New Orleans; Lucy Parlange, for giving me a tour of her family's plantation; and the librarians at the Historic New Orleans Collection, Tulane University, the University of New Orleans, the New Orleans Public Library, and the New Orleans Notarial Archives Research Center, for guiding me through their collections.

My dear friend, the journalist and novelist Dinitia Smith, read the manuscript and offered invaluable suggestions. Another dear friend, Sara Stern, was my cheerleader on blue Mondays.

Everyone at Scribner has been a delight to work with. I am especially thankful to Lisa Drew for helping me make the transition from nonfiction to fiction, and for so carefully shepherding the manuscript through the publication process. Over the course of twenty years, my agent, Rhoda Weyr, has provided encouragement and unfailingly astute advice.

As always, my husband, Richard Babcock, was there at every stage of the project, spending long hours and days discussing the material with me, helping me shape it, and editing the manuscript during its various revisions. I am eternally grateful to him for his intelligence, his hard work, his skill with a red pencil, and, of course, his all-enabling love.

Selected Bibliography

BOOKS ABOUT SARGENT

Birnbaum, Martin. *John Singer Sargent*. New York: William E. Rudge's Sons, 1941.

Charteris, Evan. *John Sargent*. New York: Benjamin Blom, 1972.

Eshleman, Mettha Westfeldt. *Madame Gautreau*. Unpublished 1984 manuscript on file in the archives of the Metropolitan Museum of Art in New York.

Fairbrother, Trevor. *John Singer Sargent: The Sensualist*. New Haven and London: Yale University Press (published in conjunction with the exhibition "John Singer Sargent," organized by the Seattle Art Museum), 2001.

Hills, Patricia, editor. *John Singer Sargent*. New York: Whitney Museum of American Art in association with Harry N. Abrams, 1986.

Hoopes, Donelson F. *The Private World of John Singer Sargent*. Washington, D.C.: Shorewood Publishers, 1964.

Kilmurray, Elaine, and Richard Ormond. *John Singer Sargent: The Early Portraits*. New Haven and London: Yale University Press, 1998.

——, editors. *John Singer Sargent*. Princeton, N.J.: Princeton University Press, 1998.

Meynell, Alice. *The Work of John Singer Sargent, R.A.* New York: Scribner's, 1903.

Mount, Charles Merrill. *John Singer Sargent: A Biography*. New York: W. W. Norton & Company, 1955.

Olson, Stanley. *John Singer Sargent: His Portrait*. New York: St. Martin's Press, 1986.

Ormond, Richard. *John Singer Sargent: Paintings, Drawings, Watercolors*. London: Phaidon Press, 1970.

Ratcliff, Carter. *Sargent*. New York: Abbeville Press, 1982.

Simpson, Marc, with Richard Ormond and H. Barbara Weinberg. *Uncanny Spectacle: The Public Career of the Young John Singer Sargent*. New Haven and London: Yale University Press, 1997.

OTHER

Baldick, Robert, editor and translator. *Pages from the Goncourt Journal.* London: The Folio Society, 1980.

Bashkirtseff, Marie. Hall, A. D., and G. G. Heckel, translators. *Journal of Marie Bashkirtseff.* Chicago and New York: Rand, McNally, 1890.

Bierman, John. *Napoleon III and His Carnival Empire.* New York: St. Martin's Press, 1988.

Cable, George Washington. *The Grandissimes.* New York: Penguin, 1988.

————. *Strange, True Stores of Louisiana.* Gretna, La.: Pelican, 1994.

Carson, Gerald. *The Dentist and the Empress: The Adventures of Dr. Tom Evans in Gas-Lit Paris.* Boston: Houghton Mifflin, 1982.

Christiansen, Rupert. *Paris Babylon: The Story of the Paris Commune.* New York: Penguin, 1994.

Coleman, Elizabeth Ann. *The Opulent Era: Fashions of Worth, Doucet, and Pingat.* New York: Thames and Hudson, 1989.

Dumas, F. G. *Catalogue Illustré du Salon 1884.* Paris: Libraire d'Art L. Baschet, 1884.

Fink, Louis Marie. *American Art at the Nineteenth-Century Paris Salons.* Cambridge: Cambridge University Press, 1990.

Friedrich, Otto. *Olympia: Paris in the Time of Manet.* New York: HarperCollins, 1992.

Garb, Tamar. *Sisters of the Brush: Women's Artistic Culture in Late Nineteenth-Century Paris.* New Haven and London: Yale University Press, 1994.

Gheusi, P. B. *Gambetta: Life and Letters.* New York: D. Appelton & Co., 1910.

Girouard, Mark. *Life in the French Country House.* London: Cassell & Co., 2000.

Hambourg, Maria Morris, Françoise Heilbrun, and Philippe Neagu. *Nadar.* New York: Harry N. Abrams, 1995.

Hegerman-Lindencrone, Lillie de. *In the Courts of Memory.* Garden City, N.Y.: Garden City Publishing, 1911.

Huber, Leonard V. *Creole Collage: A Collection of Columns, Published in "Catholic Action of the South."* Lafayette: Center for Louisiana Studies, University of Southwestern Louisiana, 1980.

Jullian, Philippe. *Prince of Aesthetes: Count Robert de Montesquiou, 1855–1921*. New York: The Viking Press, 1965.

Laur, Francis. *The Heart of Gambetta*. New York and London: John Lane, 1908.

Marly, Diana de. *Worth: Father of Haute Couture*. New York and London: Holmes & Meier, 1990.

Marzials, Frank. *Life of Léon Gambetta*. London: W. H. Allen & Co., 1890.

Moore, George. *Modern Painting*. New York: Charles Scribner's Sons, 1898.

Morgan, Sarah. Charles East, editor. *The Civil War Diary of a Southern Woman*. New York: Touchstone, 1992.

Painter, George E. *Chateaubriand: The Longed-for Tempests (1768–93)*. New York: Knopf, 1977.

———. *Marcel Proust*. New York: Vintage Books, 1978.

Peiss, Kathy. *Hope in a Jar: The Making of America's Beauty Culture*. New York: Henry Holt, 1998.

Rice, Ann. *The Feast of All Saints*. New York: Ballantine Books, 1979.

Richardson, Joanna. *Princess Mathilde*. New York: Charles Scribner's Sons, 1969.

———. *Judith Gautier*. London: Quartet Books Limited, 1986.

Sand, George. Group translation edited by Thelma Jurgrau. *Story of My Life*. Albany: State University of New York Press, 1991.

Sitterson, J. Carlyle. *Sugar Country: The Cane Sugar Industry in the South (1753–1950)*. Lexington: University of Kentucky Press, 1953.

Stone, Kate. *Brokenburn: The Journal of Kate Stone (1861–1898)*. Baton Rouge: Louisiana State University Press, 1995.

Tinker, Edward Larocque. *Creole City: Its Past and Its People*. New York, London, and Toronto: Longman, Green & Co., 1953.

Vanderpooten, Claude. *Samuel Pozzi, Chirurgien et ami des femmes*. Paris: In Fine Editions, 1992.

Vella, Christina. *Intimate Enemies: The Two Worlds of the Baroness de Pontalba*. Baton Rouge and London: Louisiana State University Press, 1997.

Wade, Michael G. *Sugar Dynasty: M. A. Patout & Son, Ltd., 1791–1993*. Lafayette: Center for Louisiana Studies, University of Southwestern Louisiana, 1995.

Weinberg, H. Barbara. *The Lure of Paris: Nineteenth-Century American Painters and Their French Teachers.* New York: Abbeville Press, 1991.

Willson, Beckles. *John Slidell and the Confederates in Paris (1862–65).* New York: AMS Press, 1970.

Winters, John D. *The Civil War in Louisiana.* Baton Rouge and London: Louisiana State University Press, 1963.

Zola, Emile. *The Masterpiece.* Oxford: Oxford University Press, 1999.

ARTICLES

Audebrand, "Courrier de Paris," *L'Illustration,* February 15, 1879, p. 98.

Bouyer, Raymond, "A. de la Gandara et Son Oeuvre," special edition of *La Plume,* 1902.

Bowles, Hamish, "The Madame X Files," *Vogue,* January 1999, p. 174ff.

Fairbrother, Trevor, "The Shock of John Singer Sargent's Madame Gautreau," *Arts Magazine,* January 1981, pp. 90–97.

Fourcaud, L., "Le Salon de 1884 (Deuxième Article)," *Gazette des Beaux-Arts* 29, no. 6 (June 1884): 482–84.

Gautier, Judith, *Le Rappel,* May 1, 1884, p.1.

Houssaye, Henri, "Le Salon de 1884," *Revue des Deux Mondes* 63, no. 3 (June 1, 1884): 589.

Lacan, Ernest, "Photography in France," *The Philadelphia Photographer* 11 (1876): 44ff.

Minchin, Hamilton, "Some Early Recollections of Sargent," *Contemporary Review* 127 (June 1925): 736.

Olian, Joanne, "Charles Frederick Worth: The Founder of Haute Couture," *The Museum of the City of New York, Costume Collections,* July 24, 2000. Available on the Internet at http://www.mcny.org/worth.htm.

Perdican, "Courrier de Paris," *L'Illustration:* June 18, 1881, p. 412; February 11, 1882, p. 86; May 27, 1882, p. 342–43; June 16, 1883, p. 371; August 11, 1883, p. 83; March 22, 1884, p. 182.

Sharp, William, "The Paris Salon," *Art Journal* (1884): 179–80.

Sidlauskas, Susan, "Painting Skin: John Singer Sargent's Madame X," *American Art* (Fall 2001): 9–33.

L'Illustration, The Salon Issue, 1884

SELECTED BIBLIOGRAPHY

"In the Studio of Carolus-Duran," *The Art Interchange,* July 28, 1888; August 11, 1888; and August 25, 1888.

"La Belle Americaine," article by the Paris correspondent of *London Truth,* in *The New York Herald,* March 30, 1880.

"Eccentricities of French Art," *Art Amateur* 11, no. 30 (August 1884): 52.

About the Author

Gioia Diliberto grew up in Bethesda, Maryland, the daughter of a junior high school English and Latin teacher and a NASA engineer. She has worked as a newspaper reporter and a magazine journalist and is the author of three biographies. She lives in Chicago with her husband, the novelist and editor Richard Babcock, and the couple's teenage son, Joe.

A SCRIBNER
READING GROUP GUIDE

I Am Madame X

Discussion Points

1. In chapter 1, Virginie Amélie Avegno Gautreau (Madame X) surmises that her "unconscious mind" dwells in the Old South. Throughout the novel, Madame X is extremely nostalgic about the old days at Parlange. Why do you think she never returned permanently to New Orleans?

2. In the final chapter Virginie admits: "I believe my life would have been easier if we hadn't moved to France." Do you agree? If so, describe how life was harder for Virginie as an American in Paris. How would it have been easier in New Orleans?

3. Of the two settings, Paris and New Orleans, which do you find more appealing? More visceral?

4. Discuss the narrative voice of Madame X. What does her telling of the story reveal about her as a character? Do you find her narcissistic? Insecure? Does Virginie recognize her own beauty or is her self-esteem based on other people's commentary?

5. Describe Virginie's relationship with her mother. How did the mother-daughter dynamic affect Virginie's relationship with men? With other women? With her own daughter?

6. Do you think Virginie would have been as socially ambitious without her mother's influence? Do you feel she was prematurely thrust into the social scene? If so, what were the consequences?

7. The author, Gioia Diliberto, says that she found John Singer Sargent's 1884 portrait of Madame X to be "extraordinarily modern." Discuss how the painting affects you. Does the story of Madame X reveal a modern woman or a woman consistent with the era?

8. At the height of Virginie's popularity (or unpopularity, one might argue), she claims: "I considered it my job to be stunning . . ." (chapter 8). Comment on the "professional beauty" circuit in France at that time. Considering the lack of career opportunities for women, was sharing one's beauty with the public a valid profession?

9. John Singer Sargent spent a year trying to convince Virginie to pose for him. Why do you think it took her so long to decide? What was

the turning point in her decision? What were her feelings about the painting before the Salon premiere?

10. At one point (chapter 8), Virginie accuses Sargent of living in "a visual world, not an emotional one." Could she be accused of the same? Did everyone treat her with this sort of superficiality? Was there anyone with whom she maintained an emotional attachment?

11. Given Virginie's reputation for wanton dress and promiscuity, why do you suppose the Parisian community found *Madame X* offensive? Was the painting not an accurate portrayal of her personality? Were they lashing out against the subject of the painting rather than the painting itself? How did anti-American sentiments figure into the scandal?

12. Virginie's aunt Julie attempted suicide to avoid an unwanted marriage, but Virginie accepted the proposal from Pierre Gautreau for a *marriage blanc*. Why do you think she accepted? Did the marriage help or hurt her reputation?

13. Discuss the role of music in Virginie's life. Did her piano playing add dimension to her character? Did people take her more seriously after discovering she was an accomplished musician?

14. Is it ironic that the author chose to call the book *I Am Madame X*, when Virginie was so opposed to Sargent omitting her identity?

15. Why do you think the doctor, Samuel Pozzi, never returned the other painting that Sargent did of Virginie? Do you think it was a matter of possessing her beauty once and for all?

Look for more Simon & Schuster reading group guides
online and download them for free at www.bookclubreader.com.

Made in the USA
Middletown, DE
13 September 2021

48213727R00163